RAVEN CURSED

A Jane Yellowrock Novel

Faith Hunter

A ROC BOOK

ROC
Published by New American Library, a division of
Penguin Group (USA) Inc., 375 Hudson Street,
New York, New York 10014, USA
Penguin Group (Canada), 90 Eglinton Avenue East, Suite 700, Toronto,
Ontario M4P 2Y3, Canada (a division of Pearson Penguin Canada Inc.)
Penguin Books Ltd., 80 Strand, London WC2R 0RL, England
Penguin Ireland, 25 St. Stephen's Green, Dublin 2,
Ireland (a division of Penguin Books Ltd.)
Penguin Group (Australia), 250 Camberwell Road, Camberwell, Victoria 3124,
Australia (a division of Pearson Australia Group Pty. Ltd.)
Penguin Books India Pvt. Ltd., 11 Community Centre, Panchsheel Park,
New Delhi - 110 017, India
Penguin Group (NZ), 67 Apollo Drive, Rosedale, Auckland 0632,
New Zealand (a division of Pearson New Zealand Ltd.)
Penguin Books (South Africa) (Pty.) Ltd., 24 Sturdee Avenue,
Rosebank, Johannesburg 2196, South Africa

Penguin Books Ltd., Registered Offices:
80 Strand, London WC2R 0RL, England

First published by Roc, an imprint of New American Library,
a division of Penguin Group (USA) Inc.

First Printing, January 2012
10 9 8 7 6 5 4 3 2 1

Praise for the Novels
of Faith Hunter

Mercy Blade

"Fans of Faith Hunter's Jane Yellowrock novels will gobble down *Mercy Blade*, the third installment in this series, which has all the complexity, twists, and surprises readers have come to expect . . . a thrill ride from start to finish. . . . Hunter has an amazing talent for capturing mood." —SF Site

"There was something about the Jane Yellowrock series that drew me in from the very beginning. That hunch was solidified with each book I read into a feeling of utter confidence in the author. . . . *Mercy Blade* is top-notch, a five-star book!"
—Night Owl Reviews

"I was delighted to have the opportunity to read another Jane Yellowrock adventure. I was not disappointed, but was somewhat overwhelmed by the obvious growth in Faith Hunter's writing skill." —*San Francisco Book Review*

"A thrilling novel . . . Fans of suspenseful tales filled with vampires, weres, and more will enjoy this book. Jane is a strong heroine who knows how to take charge of a situation, and kick butt if necessary." —Romance Reviews Today

"Faith Hunter has created one of my favorite characters, ever. Jane Yellowrock is full of contradictions. . . . As with the other books in the series, good and evil are far from clear-cut, with sympathetic villains and many fascinating characters with shades of gray. Highly recommended." —Fresh Fiction

Blood Cross

"Mystery and action are at the forefront here, but the romance from the first book continues to build slowly. Readers eager for the next book in Patricia Briggs's Mercy Thompson series may want to give Faith Hunter a try." —*Library Journal*

"In a genre flooded with strong, sexy females, Jane Yellowrock is unique. . . . Her bold first-person narrative shows that she's one tough cookie, but with a likable vulnerability . . . a pulse-pounding, page-turning adventure." —*Romantic Times*

continued . . .

good and evil wage their eternal struggle in the world of flesh and blood. Strong characters and a compelling story."
—*Library Journal*

"This thrilling dark fantasy has elements of danger, adventure, and religious fanaticism, plus sexual overtones. Hunter's impressive narrative skills vividly describe a changed world, and she artfully weaves in social commentary . . . a well-written, exciting novel."   —*Romantic Times*

Bloodring

"A bold interpretation of the what-might-be. . . . With a delicate weaving of magic and scripture, Faith Hunter left me wondering: What's a woman to do when she falls in love with a seraph's child?"   —Kim Harrison

"Entertaining . . . outstanding supporting characters . . . the strong cliff-hanger of an ending bodes well for future adventures."   —*Publishers Weekly*

"The cast is incredible. . . . Fans of postapocalypse fantasies will appreciate this superb interpretation of the endless end of days."   —*Midwest Book Review*

"Hunter's distinctive future vision offers a fresh though dark glimpse into a newly made postapocalyptic world. Bold and imaginative in approach, with appealing characters and a suspense-filled story, this belongs in most fantasy collections."
—*Library Journal*

"It's a pleasure to read this engaging tale about characters connected by strong bonds of friendship and family. Mixes romance, high fantasy, apocalyptic and postapocalyptic adventure to good effect."   —*Kirkus Reviews*

"Hunter's very professionally executed, tasty blend of dark fantasy, mystery, and romance should please fans of all three genres."   —*Booklist*

"Entertaining . . . a promising new series. . . . Steady pacing, dashes of humor, and a strong story line coupled with a great ending neatly setting up the next adventure make this take on the apocalypse worth checking out."   —Monsters and Critics

"Enjoyable . . . a tale of magic and secrets in a world gone mad."   —*Romantic Times*

To my Renaissance Man,
who takes the Class IVs, lets me cry on his shoulder, and
brings me chocolate

ACKNOWLEDGMENTS

My deepest thanks (in no order whatsoever) to:

Mike Pruette, Web guru at www.faithhunter.net and fan.

The wonderful speakers at www.irishgaelictranslator.com for the spelling translations.

The Hubby, for the right word when my tired brain was stymied. And for the chocolate.

Joyce Wright, for reading everything I write, no matter how "weird."

Adonna at the authorpro.com for all the help with PR! Love you guys!

Dave Crawford of rapidexpeditions.com, Mike Kohlenberger at Wildwater, and Itty Bitty, for allowing me to use their names, monikers, and/or likenesses in the book. The realism you brought to the project was a huge help! Also to Mindy Mymudes for the biology realism.

Misty Massey, David B. Coe, A. J. Hartley, Edmund Schubert, Stuart Jaffe, C. E. Murphy, Lucienne Diver, and Kalayna Price of www.magicalwords.net, my dear pals, for making this journey so much easier than it used to be. It's wonderful to have you as my friends!

Kim Harrison (fan girl squeal)—thank you for the wonderful blurb.

My facebook fans at www.facebook.com/official.faith .hunter.

Jane's facebook fans at www.facebook.com/janeyellow rock.

Beast's facebook fans at www.facebook.com/pages/ Beast/135860763157310.

Lucienne Diver, for doing what an agent does best, with grace, kindness, wisdom, and forgiveness.

Rosanne Romanello and Brady McReynolds at Roc for excellent PR support (waves).

Last, but never least—my editorial team at Roc: Thanks to Jessica Wade, who loves the multisouled Beast in Jane, and who worked hard to bring the plot and conflict into a darker intensity. To copyeditor Karen Haywood, production editor Kathleen Cook, and Jesse Feldman (who came in at the end)—this book is far better for all of you.

Y'all ROCK!

AUTHOR'S NOTE

A lot of research went into this book, both to keep it factual, and to protect others. All mistakes herein are mine, and were not made by the kind people who helped me.

The factual parts I worked so hard on were the kayaking and the scenes set in the Appalachian Mountains. The scenes in Hartford, Tennessee, were as perfect as I could make them, and if you drop by, be sure to say hi to Dave Crawford and Jedi Mike Kohlenberger. Yeah, they are real people, the bigger-than-life kind who simply have to go into a book to keep it real too. Itty Bitty (not her real name) has moved away, or you could meet her too. While you are in Hartford, go rafting, or take a kayak lesson at Rapid Expeditions. Take a zip-line trip through the trees at Wildwater. It's a rush! Take a backcountry jeep tour. Hike up the mountain to the top. Go hungry, and eat in the Bean Trees Café. Have a day or three of fun! There is a lot to do for such a small place.

To protect others—for instance, law enforcement officials—I deliberately changed facts or left them out. A case in point—the law enforcement center in Asheville looks nothing like it is portrayed here, to help, in a small way, to keep our cops safe.

A scene involving a real search-and-rescue team, with K-9 and search dogs, was cut because the book was simply too long with it left in, but I'll post it someday on the Web site.

My thanks to all my fans, who are keeping this series in print. You have my everlasting gratitude.

Faith

CHAPTER ONE

Lots of Things That Go Boom and Kill Bad Guys

I rode into Asheville, North Carolina, for all the wrong reasons, from the wrong direction, on a borrowed bike, with no weapons, ready to work for the vamps again. It was stupid all around, but it was the gig I signed up for, and I was all about satisfying the client, keeping him safe, eliminating the danger, and finishing the job. Or staking the vamp, depending on the job description. "Finish the job" had become my second mantra, right behind "Have stakes, will travel."

I was not at all happy that I'd taken this gig, once again working for the Blood Master of the City of New Orleans, Leo Pellissier, though this time was different. Of course, that's what I always think—that there's a new and better reason to keep up a business relationship with the chief fanghead. Money counts, of course, and the MOC pays extremely well, but I've begun to think it's also because I'm a masochist and curious—as in, curiosity killed the cat.

At the thought, my Beast chuffed with amusement. *Not dead. Am good hunter. Smell cooked meat and running deer and mountains. Free flowing water. We are home.*

Yeah, we are. And that thought put a smile on my face, despite my misgivings. I'm Jane Yellowrock. I'm licensed and experienced in the security business but I made my street cred as a rogue-vamp hunter. I am, according to most, the best in the business. I am also a Cherokee skin-walker living with the soul of a mountain lion inside me, the one I call Beast. I may well be the last of my kind, since I killed the only other skinwalker I ever met when he went nutso and started killing and eating people. My occupation has a definite ick factor.

The job at hand was to set up and provide security for the vamp parley taking place in Asheville, and it wasn't likely that the location was accident or coincidence. Lincoln Shaddock, the most powerful fanghead in the Appalachian Mountains of North Carolina and Tennessee, had been applying to Leo for sixty years for the right to become a master of the city. Leo—who was a lot more powerful, territory-wise, than I ever guessed—had turned him down, until now. Leo always turned down vamps who thought they deserved to be the master of a city, because he was power hungry and had a god complex—that was nothing new. Now the chief bloodsucker of the South was willing to discuss a change in status for a vamp who wanted my hometown? No way was that a total fluke.

One factor that could have influenced the MOC was that a young vamp in Shaddock's scion-lair found her sanity in just two years. That was a record. That was huge. Vamps had been trying to find a way to shorten or defeat the devoveo for two thousand years. But was it huge enough for Leo to reverse course? I had my doubts. No, there was something else. I just didn't know what. Yet.

Leo never had just one motivation for anything, but layered motives, some focused on his political organization in the world of vamps—like the parley with the witches in New Orleans, which was not going so well, last I heard. Some focused on ancient history. And because the chief MOC of the South was intensely curious about me, maybe some focused on me. Vamps, politics, blood, and sex were all parts of a single whole, and since I was on retainer to Leo, I was now a part of that political maneuvering. Lucky me. My own curiosity was sending me right into the middle of it all, maybe because so many things from the last job seemed like untied ends blowing loose and frayed in hurricane winds. My life, once so uncomplicated, had become a storm that should have sent me running away. But I hadn't run. I had to finish the job.

The new bike took the hills of I-40 with a little wobble. It was a chopped Harley masterpiece named Fang, with a gleaming royal blue paint job and hand-painted sabertooth fangs on the gas tank between my legs. It was beautiful, comfortable, sexy as all get-out, and had saddlebags to hold my traveling gear, but it wasn't the best bike for mountain riding. I'd not be buying Fang, no matter how much the owner hoped I would.

My bastard Harley, Bitsa, had sustained damage in service to Leo and was in Charlotte for repairs at the shop of the Harley Zen-master who built her out of parts of old bikes. I liked to think of her being in a spa for some sustained TLC. I wish I was getting some TLC myself. Instead I was riding into my former hometown on a gig that all my instincts said was dangerous. But weren't they all? I'd feel better when I had my weapons back. Most of my guns, knives, and my wardrobe, were being shipped in on the flight from New Orleans that would bring the vamp assigned to this parley.

Roaring uphill around a big rig, I gave Fang some gas. Strands of loose black hair whipped in the truck's air-wave, pulled free by road wind. Most of my hair was well secured, braided down my back beneath my summer-weight leather riding jacket, but the shorter strands flew wild or stuck to me under the helmet's faceplate. The September sun beat down on me, parboiling me in my own sweat.

I was here a day early, meeting the security team, setting up protocols and methodology, and getting the lay of the land. I had a lot to do in very little time.

Near dawn, some thirty-six hours later, the helicopter landed. The vamp—or Mithran, as they liked to be called— had flown in to the Asheville airport from New Orleans in Leo's private jet and been transferred under heavy security to the helo, which had been sent ahead and kept under guard until needed. Now the artificial wind of the rotors whirled the hot, early-autumn air, mixing the stench of helo engine, the effluvia of the city, a mélange of restaurants, and the wood-scent of surrounding mountains. The helo settled with a skirling wind and a horrible whine that hurt Beast's ears. I touched my mouthpiece. "Report." If someone wanted to make a statement and send a message to the vamp community, now would be a good time.

"All quiet," Derek Lee said. He and two of his best were stationed in key spots on high ground, with low-light and infrared scanning devices, and all the high-tech toys that make former Marines happy. They also had lots of things that go boom and kill bad guys. They were in heaven. A sniper was scanning from the roof of the tallest building with acceptable line-of-sight, targeting the antivamp protesters who had set up in front of the hotel. Four other men had secured the path from the hotel's helicopter landing pad to the door. I'd brought Derek Lee on as my personal assistant, and he had already proven himself worth his weight in gold, not that I'd tell him. His expertise was costly enough, and he'd demanded at-risk pay for his crew, which meant they were all making a large piece of change on this gig.

Beast was close to the surface of my mind, adding her strength and speed to my body in case I needed it. My heart beat faster, breath drawing deep. I had done all I could to protect Katie, Leo's heir, and keep her safe throughout the parley. She was a blood-sucking killer, but I liked Katie.

Except it wasn't Katie who stepped to the ground. It was Grégoire, Leo's number two scion, the vamp Leo had been dangling at me for several weeks. Until now, it hadn't been anything obvious or overt, just seeing the slight, blond, prettier-than-a-girl vamp at every meeting, at every lecture teaching me how to deal with a high-class vamp parley, at three vamp-style tasting events to educate me on the practice, and at the security meetings. And now the big surprise. Of course, I could be reading it all wrong, but the signs pointed to the blood master of the vamps wanting me bound to him one way or the other, and since I hadn't fallen in a swoon at his feet or into bed with any of the other vamps who had offered, he was tossing his best bud my way. *Great. Just freaking great.* It wasn't like I could totally dis the guy—sock him or something. I was up to my neck in Mithran protocol, according to the Vampira Carta, and had to follow the rules of vamp etiquette. But that didn't stop me from glaring at him.

Grégoire, wearing a cloak that shimmered even in the predawn dark, tossed back the hood and found me in the shadows. He knew I wasn't human, they all did, because I smelled wrong, but none of them knew what I was, and I wasn't telling. His blond hair shifted and blew in the rotor breeze, the color of his scent a pale green, the honey gold of spring flowers, and luscious. He smiled, that slow smile they do when they're trying to charm, the one that starts in their eyes and melts to their mouths, transforming their faces into angelic beauty. Fallen angel beauty—deadly, but dang pretty. He was slight, at five feet seven, delicate, with dark blue eyes the color of the evening sky, and he carried himself with an elegance that put even the other vamps to shame. He started toward me, moving as slowly as a human, graceful as a dancer.

Beast huffed with amusement and stared back at him through my eyes. I could feel them start that weird gold glow they do when she's near the surface. Beast likes Grégoire, and she loves playing cat-games, but she wants to be in charge and not manipulated. Grégoire's slow stalk faltered, a slight, uneven hesitation. He recuperated quickly, but I saw it and so did Beast. Inside my mind, she showed some fang.

"Mon amie," Grégoire said. "You are lovely."

"Thanks, Blondie. Backatcha," I said, deliberately rude. I took his arm, pretending not to hear his chuckle. Apparently vamps think I'm funny. "Let's get you under cover before that loveliness gets you shot full of silver." It was a testament to his age and his courage that he didn't shiver at the thought. Or maybe it was all the wars he'd fought in over the centuries. Grégoire looked fragile, but his file suggested he liked a good war, battle, or barroom brawl as much as the next guy.

The four-star Regal Imperial Hotel in Asheville had suites suitable for visiting dignitaries, congregating heads of state, and vacationing vamps. Grégoire—whose standards are set a bit higher than most vamps, thanks to the century and the French royal court in which he lived prior to being turned—didn't turn up his nose as I led him through the secure employee entrance and the upscale restaurant, into the lobby. There was no fresh blood around to ogle him, which might have been a downer for some vamps, but he seemed okay with it. And when I opened the door to his suite on the third floor, he stood inside and nodded, hands on his hips, his dark silk brocade cloak thrown back like a young Batman, if Batman had weighed a hundred pounds, had fangs, and looked about fifteen. But gorgeous. Utterly gorgeous.

I quickly explained about the security and the bolt-hole/escape-hatch. The Mithran Suite was decorated all in gold—like the vamp—with gilded, armored steel shutters on the windows and an escape hatch in the floor at the foot of the bed, leading to a narrow passage down through the walls of the hotel and underground. The suite was secure up to RPGs—rocket propelled grenades. If an opponent was that determined, no one was safe.

"This is acceptable. I am not unpleased."

"You have no idea how happy that makes me." I couldn't keep the sarcasm out of my voice.

He laughed. "You may join me here. Your presence in my bed would please me."

And *theeeere* it was. The invitation I had been expecting. Fortunately, after all the vamp manners studies, I had my line all prepped and ready to go. "Grégoire, you are pretty beyond anything I've ever seen." He nodded as if I spoke only the truth. I resisted an eye-roll. "But I have a job to do, and climbing into your bed would surely turn my head and blind me to all proper responsibility." A strange look crossed his face, as if that one had never occurred to him. "So, I'll reluctantly decline and see to your daytime security placement."

I left, and Grégoire didn't try to stop me. I'd like to think he was flummoxed. Floored. Startled. But maybe he was tired. What did I know?

I worked like a fiend all day with my team and with Grégoire and Clan Arceneau's primo blood-servant twins, Brandon and Brian Robere, finalizing safety measures and arrangements, and reading them into my plans and protocols. Grégoire's finest were lean, narrow-waisted, broad-shouldered,

and former military. Though they looked young, the B-twins
were some of the oldest blood-servants I'd ever met. I liked
them and they had kept up with the changes in technology
and security protocols better than most old servants.

We also met with Shaddock's head of security, an Asian
guy named Chen, who had intense eyes and looked about
ten. He already knew the hotel layout and had little to offer
or request in terms of security changes. He was in and out
like a precise laser attack, and he set my predator instincts
buzzing. I wondered if we would both survive the parley, or
try to kill each other.

The big hoedown started just after midnight, with Lincoln
Shaddock, the vamp asking for MOC status, arriving in
Shaddock's limo and a group of three armored SUVs that
we had brought in to provide secure transportation during the parley. We hadn't announced the date and time of
the first meeting, and the antivamp protestors who had
assembled out front were caught off guard, as was the
media, so there was no big hoopla. Just a stately proces-
sion of vehicles pulling up out front and people emerging
faster-than-human.

The vamps were introduced in the lobby, which had
been cleared of guests and swept for explosives and video
and listening devices. Shaddock strode across the hardwood and silk oriental rugs like the beaked-nosed fron-
tiersman he had been as a human: tall, rawboned, and
rough around the edges despite his tuxedo. Grégoire stood
with his back to the massive central fireplace, resplendent
in gold brocade. I stood to the side, taking in Shaddock's
heir and spare, and his primo and secondo blood-servants.
I had studied their files extensively and, with a flick of a
finger, I repositioned two of Derek's men into better position to cover the vamps—not just to keep them alive, but to
make sure the newcomers didn't pull weapons and stake
Grégoire. Hey. It could happen.

"Lincoln Shaddock," said the vamp. His laconic tone was
marked by a strong Tennessee/Kentucky accent, and his
scent was unusual for a vamp, smelling like hickory bark,
wood shavings, and barbeque. The vamp owned a BBQ
joint in the middle of Asheville and he worked there most

nights, which explained the scent, though the idea of a job was odd for a vamp. But then, Shaddock wasn't as old as most master vamps. Maybe he had to work like the rest of us poor slobs. "I am blood-master of the Shaddock Blood Clan. Turned by Charles Dufresnee after the Battle of Monocacy, outside of Frederick, Maryland. Currently sworn to Clan Dufresnee, and with his permission, petitionin' the blood-master of the southeastern United States to acquire territory to include the city of Asheville, North Carolina, and to be granted hunting land and cattle and the rights to rule as Master of the City under his rule."

Hunting land meant territory where vamps would hunt humans to drink from. Cattle meant the humans they'd be hunting. Ticked me off, not that I had a say in the wording or the reality of the meaning. The phrasing had been established centuries ago as part of the Vampira Carta, the legal document vamps lived by. The Carta also established the laws that gave me the right to hunt rogue-vamps. That part of the law probably gave vamps the willies. I could only hope.

Lincoln Shaddock gestured to the tiny young woman standing behind him. "This here is Amy Lynn Brown, my youngest scion." The miracle-vamp, the reason that Leo had allowed the petition and the parley. The dark-haired, brown-eyed girl looked terrified, and no one did anything to alleviate her nerves. Grégoire stepped to the side and studied her like a piece of meat.

I hadn't known Leo was the blood-master of the entire southeastern U.S. until the first time I heard the introductions read during my parley training. He held the hunting license of every fanghead below the Mason-Dixon Line, from the eastern border of Texas at the Sabine River, east to the Atlantic and south to the Gulf, with the exception of Florida and Atlanta. The Atlanta MOC was an independent of sorts, and Florida was run by a vamp I hadn't studied yet.

Grégoire turned his attention back to Shaddock and bowed slightly, saying, "Grégoire, blood-master of Clan Arceneau, of the court of Charles the Wise, Fifth of his line, in the Valois Dynasty, turned by Charles—the well beloved, the mad—the son of the king. Here by decree of Leonard Eugène Zacharie Pellissier, turned by, and heir of, Amaury Pellissier, his human uncle and Mithran father, now true-dead, to negotiate the petition of Lincoln Shaddock for rights to claim Asheville and surrounding territory as Master of the City . . ."

Yada yada. I zoned out on the confab, seeing a flicker of shadow at the front entrance. The protestors were trying to get in, bodies pressed against the glass, voices raised, chanting, "Vamps go home. Vamps go home." Real original, and no threat unless they had guns or were willing to break in, which I had to consider. I touched my mouthpiece to com channel and said to Derek, "Moving to the front. Get the principals to the Black Bear Grill, out of sight."

"Copy," my second in command replied. He switched channels and relayed my orders.

We had two communication channels, a command channel between Derek and me, and a general channel that went to all the security staff. Moving to the front, I listened as the B-twins and Shaddock's Chen led the way to the hotel's restaurant, which we'd taken over for the first night of the parley. I felt immensely better as the doors to the restaurant closed with a firm snap. This initial meeting allowed the primary negotiators to chitchat and take one another's measure while their minions gave a final tweak to the rules the vamps would operate under, and shuffled and finalized the talk schedule.

I had never been a bodyguard, and I wasn't looking forward to the whims of vamps changing my security measures on the fly, but that was part of the job too—flying by the seat of my pants, moving my men here and there and hither and yon and trying to keep everyone out of trouble. Playing in the vamp sandbox was an exercise in creative use and placement of assets.

While they did what vamps and their blood meals do, I wandered around the hotel, making sure none of my men were mispositioned or left a blind spot where trouble might hide. I also triple-checked the communication gear and walked the entire external perimeter of the hotel, the nearby parking garage, and every hallway, stairwell, wine bar, nook and cranny of the joint. Again. It was obsessive but it also was keeping me awake.

Near dawn, the first *something unexpected* happened. I was checking out the men's rooms off the lobby when I was alerted over my com headgear. "Legs, something's up. The blood-servants are going ape-shit," Derek said.

Wrassler, my number two guy, and one of Leo's blood-servant security goons talked over the chatter. All I made out was, "—in here now . . . Leo . . ."

I hotfooted it out of the john, Beast-fast. "What?" I asked as I entered the Black Bear Grill. They were all watching a TV monitor, local cable news showing a scene of flashing emergency lights: police, ambulance, even an antiquated fire truck with Cocke County Rescue Squad painted on the side. In the background I could make out a bridge and the reflection of red and blue flashing lights on still water. On-screen was a wild-haired, heavily bearded man, maybe mid-twenties, with multiple piercings and lots of body art. "Dude, it was bad. I mean blood and guts and stuff. The deputy was saying it had to be fangheads, what with the injuries. Like one a' them rogues that goes psycho and eats people and shi—uh, stuff. Like, sorry, dude. I cuss a lot."

"Oh crap," I murmured. My cell phone rang. It was Leo. "Yellowrock."

"You will take any necessary personnel and deal with this. If it is a rogue, dispatch it. If it is something else, you will make this situation go away."

"Sure, Leo. But—" The line clicked off. I was just an underling, the paid help. Unlike the vamps, I didn't deserve good manners.

CHAPTER TWO

Vamp-Fang and Werewolf-Bite Scars

Eyes gritty from lack of sleep, I knelt on the bank, jeans absorbing the wet from the river-slick rock. Just upstream from me, two commercial rafts slid under the bridge where a couple had been attacked before dawn, the screaming voices of laughing children tearing the air. Someone slapped a paddle onto the water, the sound echoing. My Beast flinched deep inside, but I didn't react. I was too busy studying the scratches on the rock in the early morning light.

There were three parallel lines, the one in the center longer than the ones to either side. I put my fingers into the grooves, feeling the rough edges of the slashes. Using the excuse of a better view, I bent lower, getting my nose to the rock. I sniffed. The water smelled of iron and fish, sunscreen, treated sewage, chemicals, and age. The grooves smelled different. Still fishy, but with a particular, sour, dead-fish stench I recognized.

Grindylow, Beast thought at me. *Water smells of grindylow, not vampire, not pigeons.*

It took me a moment to understand. Beast was a literal creature, and the river was named the Pigeon. To her, it should either smell of the vampires who had been accused of attacking the boating couple just upstream of where I knelt, or of pigeons. Not a grindylow, a creature once thought to be mythical, from the U.K. by way of Africa and

New Orleans. A grindylow brought unexpected, puzzling possibilities into the equation. I stared up at Stirling Mountain, wondering just how much responsibility for this attack rested on me.

I rose to my feet and dusted the wet grit off my hands, watching rafts float toward me. They were filled with families, church teens out on a field trip, college kids lazing away a September Saturday, the river guides looking young and carefree. The water of the Upper Pigeon River rippled and frothed at the end of the run, spilling out into a wide placid pool beneath the bridge where the attack took place, dividing around islands and curling into smooth eddy pools where commercial rafts could launch or be pulled up the banks. Just downstream the river dropped again, becoming the Lower Pigeon, a slower, easy-paced river.

I scuffed a boot heel over the three cuts in the rock. I had an idea what supernat had mauled the two last night, and it wasn't a rogue-vamp. Proving that would make the local vamps and the parley safer. Despite the territory-marking sign and the grindy scent, the grindylow wasn't the assailant either. Leo had made this my problem, and it was, but not solely for the reason he thought. *Crap*. This was gonna be a booger. And if I could prove it, it was my fault. A sense of dread settled in my gut.

I held out my hand for the photographs of the couple who had been savaged. The poor-quality, grainy, low-pixel-count photos were clear enough to make my knees weak. Yeah. Provided I could find evidence to support it, I knew what had attacked the couple, unlikely as that might actually be.

According to witnesses, the young woman, who went by the moniker Itty Bitty, had been attacked first. Though in her twenties, she was tiny enough to look like a very young teen—hence the nickname. In the photos, she was swathed in bandages, except for a few superficial wounds on one calf, and those were familiar. I had a few fading scars that looked similar. The man, her boyfriend, was former military, and his wounds were more severe. He'd defended her and paid the price. In the dark of early evening, neither had been able to identify the creatures that attacked them and pulled them under the water, mauling and biting. Itty Bitty had seen nothing at all; her hero boyfriend had reported hairy men, dogs, and vampires.

Without looking up, I handed the photos back to the deputy. "Yeah. I know what attacked the couple." Holding in a resigned sigh, I pushed my sunglasses back over my eyes and tapped the scarred rock with my boot heel. "But it isn't what made this."

"So what did?" the cop asked. "Fanghead, right?"

I pulled my gaze from the water-washed rock to the river guides, the cop, whose name was Emmett Sontag, and my best friend, Molly—here for moral support and curiosity. "These three cuts were made by a grindylow." At the guides' blank reactions I said, "Grindys are like the enforcers of the were community. They kill weres who try to turn humans, and keep an eye out on the young weres to make sure they abide by were-law." When they still looked blank I spelled it out for them, keeping my own reactions inside, hidden. "I think werewolves attacked the couple last night."

"We got werewolves here?" a young guide said, his steel tongue stud catching the light. "Awesome." He turned and looked around, as if seeing his workplace in a new and exciting way.

Molly's eyes widened as she took in the implications of werewolves and a grindy in the Appalachian Mountains. From her mutating expressions, Molly was figuring out everything I just had, and most of that information was not something I was willing to share with the others. I caught her gaze, directed hers to the sheet of photos in the cop's hands, and let her read my concern. Her gaze slid up Stirling Mountain, as mine had, worried. She did an eyebrow shrug, raising and lowering them in sympathy, saying clearer than words, *This is gonna be a mess of trouble, Big-Cat.*

I managed a defeated grin at the sentiment.

"Werewolves. Damn." Emmett looked around, eyes narrowed, and rattled off a series of questions that suggested he was more than just gun, swagger, and belly. "Is this grindy thing dangerous? Can you prove it was werewolves? Do we need to pull the rafts?" He resettled his heavy utility belt, one hand on the butt of his 9 millimeter handgun. It was cop body language, looking for trouble and being ready for it. Not. A werewolf would eat his innards for dinner.

Pulling the rafts off the water would mean a financial hardship for the rafting businesses operating along the river. I started to say it was safe, but closed my mouth on the words. I had no idea what grindys ate, or whether they were primarily nocturnal. I was assuming that the grindy was here because of its life mission, but I'd drawn conclusions and made deductions before based on insufficient info, and humans got hurt. I didn't want that happening here.

Having weres in the hills wasn't gonna make the locals happy. Like the itchy deputy, local law enforcement types all over three counties were already agitated—passing out stakes, holy water, crosses, and garlic against vamps—and there was grumbling about taking down all the fangheads in an old-fashioned hunt. Now they'd be after weres too, and I had good reason to want them not to. I said, "Grindys don't eat people, and werewolves are mostly nocturnal. Keep everyone off the water after sunset, but you don't have to pull the rafts during daylight hours."

Emmett didn't like it. He wanted action, and he wanted it now, but he was also conscious of Cocke County's economic situation. He pursed his lips, thinking, fingers tapping his gun butt with little pats of sound. "Mike, Dave," he said, addressing two river guides, "you'll see word gets passed? I'll run patrol down here throughout the night, but I'd rather not have to arrest somebody or pull a dead stoner outta the water."

The two men nodded. Mike Kohlenberger, also known as Jedi Mike, or the Old Man of the River, had over thirty years of rafting experience, and Dave was a raft guide, a Class-V kayak paddler, and a Level Four instructor—meaning the two were the best of the best. I'd met them back when I was a midlevel investigator at a security company, before I went out on my own. Someone in the small paddling community had been breaking into local businesses protected by RJY Securities and I'd been sent to look around. They weren't friends, but, for business competitors, they had a good working relationship.

Mike squinted into the sun glare on the river, his lined

face drawing tight, one hand adjusting the red scarf he wore like a do-rag. Voice booming, he said, "We'll pass the word."

I started the climb back up the riverbank, still looking for evidence of the creature I believed had attacked Itty Bitty and her boyfriend. At the top of the short rise, I stopped, a fresh scent reaching me. My sense of smell is a lot better than most humans, likely because of the decades I spent in Beast-form, before I found my human shape again and reentered the human world. I flipped my hip-length braid out of the way and dropped to hands and knees in the brush.

The dead-fishy smell was here too, but this time it overlay another familiar scent, the scent I had expected to find after seeing the pics of the injured. With one hand, I pushed aside the sharp-edged grass, not touching the ground beneath or disturbing the roots, but exposing a partial paw print. I had found my evidence and I didn't know whether to be pleased with myself or even more worried. "Werewolf," I said, louder.

The cop jostled closer to get a better view.

I pressed more grass aside, revealing more paw prints. They were as large as my hand, the nonretractable claws leaving long indentations in the damp soil. One forepaw had been bloody, the smell of dried blood, rank and old. Not much of a leap to assume it was Itty Bitty's blood. I bent and sniffed. Witch blood. Itty Bitty was from a witch family. I motioned to Molly to take photos of the prints while I crawled forward, pressing the long, sharp grass to either side of the wolf tracks.

I bent lower, letting my nose tell me what my eyes couldn't, the musky scent rising to fill my head. And I shivered in the heat. I knew these wolves. I'd fought them. I put it together fast, dread leaping back onto me. I had helped to kill off all the members of the Lupus Pack of werewolves, except for two wolves who had been in jail during the raid. I had forgotten about them, until now. They had made bail, tracked me down, and that one forgetful mistake was coming back to bite me on the butt. I had gotten sloppy. Directly or indirectly, they were here because of me. "Two wolves, at least," I said, keeping my head low so they couldn't read my face, pretending that it was visual clues giving me the information. "I may know them. Contact Jodi Richoux at New Orleans PD for names and mug shots."

The cop cursed and reached for his cell phone. "I gotta tell the sheriff 'bout this, 'n secure the area. Get me some backup. Crime scene."

"Good idea," I said. Crime scene techs would have been a better idea this morning, before several hundred tourists had access to the area, and before the powerhouse released thousands of cubic feet of water, but who was I to point out someone else's mistake.

While Emmett pushed back the guides and gawkers and called the sheriff, I followed the tracks on my hands and knees across a gravel parking area to the small, two-lane road. The scent of shifter magic filled my nostrils where the wolves had changed back to human form. Yeah. I knew them. And I knew it was no coincidence that they were here. The attack, here, now, so close to Stirling Mountain, so close to the parley of vamps I was guarding, wasn't an accident. It was a personal challenge and a private threat, issued on the body of innocents.

A growl vibrated through me—Beast, angry, thinking of the photographs. *Yearling human. Not experienced kit.* Her claws milked into my mind, piercing and withdrawing. *Too young to fight off pack hunters. Hate pack hunters. Stealers of winter food. Thieves of meat.*

I stood and brushed off my hands again, looking from the street back to the river and the bridge, envisioning the wolves waiting in the tall brush just downstream of the bridge, slinking into the water in the dark, attacking the young woman, Itty Bitty. The wolves dragging her—bleeding profusely, terrified, screaming—to shore and deliberately infecting her with the were-taint. In my mind's eye, I saw her boyfriend leaping from his kayak, seeing indistinct shapes swarming in the night, hearing her cries, rushing in, swinging a sharp-bladed paddle, only to have the wolves turn on him, savaging him for interfering. Other predawn paddlers coming fast. The weres slipping away in the ruckus. Anger burned under my breastbone. This had happened because of me. The wolves were here because of my actions and decisions. My advice. My plans. *Crap.*

"The victims are both going to go furry at the next full moon, aren't they?" Mike said. After the decades of shouting to be heard over rushing whitewater, the guy had a voice with little volume control, but this time, his words were muted with worry.

"Maybe not," I said. "I have a few contacts with the vamps. They have some healers."

Emmett snorted, not impressed with vamp healers. He muttered under his breath something insulting about suckheads, weres, and witches in his county. I glanced at Molly, an earth witch, who ignored him, so I ignored the comment too, thinking instead about the logistics of getting a Mercy Blade here to heal the injured couple. I didn't know if there was a Mercy Blade in North Carolina or Tennessee, but I'd find one somewhere. I turned my attention to other logistics.

"How far"—I paused, uncertain, trying to recall the distance from a long-ago vacation—"is it from here to the Mississippi River?" The last time I saw a grindylow was on a bayou that emptied into the Mississippi, west of New Orleans. And New Orleans was the birthplace of everything that had happened to me for the last six months, most of it bad. I wanted to know how the green-skinned, semi-aquatic grindy got from *there* to *here*. Sure as heck not on a Harley.

"It's four hundred miles from Knoxville to Memphis," Dave said, his voice raspy and soft, in contrast to Mike's booming volume. Memphis was a Mississippi port city, and the most direct route overland to the river, but the water-loving grindy hadn't taken an overland route.

I indicated a group of playboat kayakers coasting in after a run on the Upper Pigeon. The small, human-teenager-sized grindy would likely need as much water as a playboat. "Is it possible to paddle from the Mississippi to here, if you only count water big enough to handle something that size, and you prefer cold water, rocks, and privacy?" I looked around at the numbers of boaters. "Usually."

The guides both looked northwest, downstream. Dave squinted, shading his blue eyes with a hand, and said, "If you can jump dams and paddle a lot of miles of waterway, all upstream," he paused to draw in air, and my eyes slid to the scars on his throat. They looked like the result of a down and dirty tracheotomy, though I'd never asked how he came by them. "Then yes. The Pigeon goes west to Knoxville, eventually joins into the French Broad and heads south into northern Alabama. It empties into the Tennessee River, which empties into the Miss."

Mike added, "I know people who've paddled the distance downstream, but it's a hell of a long paddle even moving with the current. I don't know *any*one who's paddled it *up*stream."

I didn't know what the grindy's speed was, or if it could handle long distances, or upstream currents. Which might mean that the grindy had hitched a ride on boats, making it a once-mythical supernat who was comfy with modern transportation. I smiled sourly. I didn't know much about grindys, and had been hoping to keep it that way. But the grindy wasn't my problem. The wolves were.

I looked up and out, seeing the gorge where the rafting businesses were nestled in the little town of Hartford, Tennessee. Just in visual distance, there were thousands of square acres where wolves could run and hunt and never be seen by a human. If I was wolf-hunting in Beast form, it would take a long time to cover this much territory. Wolves liked to run long distances. Beast wasn't fond of it, wasn't built for it, and even with humans in danger, she would fight me every step of the way. *Beast is not dog,* she murmured into my mind, sounding sleepy. *Do not hunt nose to ground.* I scowled and walked from the water, its tinkling quickly muted by the sound of nearby Interstate 40, back toward Fang.

The wind changed and I caught a scent of wolf away from the water. On the far side of the road, something gleamed in the bright sun. Silver-tipped wood. It was mine. I sometimes lost stakes in the heat of battle, easy for an enemy to take. I bent and picked up the sterling-silver-tipped ash-wood stake.

Deep inside, my Beast hissed with displeasure and showed killing teeth. The wolves had left me a personal message and challenge. I looked around. No one except Molly had seen me pick up the stake. She watched with a quizzical expression as I sniffed along its length, smelling wolf, sweat, and motor oil, something spicy like Mexican food, and cheap liquor. No help here. No scent-clue jumping out and saying, "The wolves stayed *there*, in that hotel, in that town, last night." Giving her a small shrug, I tucked the stake into a belt loop.

Boots crunching on gravel, I walked back to the parking lot of Rapid Expeditions, the mom-and-pop rafting and kayak business owned by Dave Crawford. Molly and I sat on the old church bench in front of the shop and accepted Cokes from Dave, pulled from an icy cooler. Molly sipped delicately, tucking a strand of bright red hair behind an ear. She'd always been a lady, contrasting to my motorcycle mama image. I popped the top and drank deeply before rolling the can over my forehead for the chill. It was hot for September. Global climate change and all that.

Dave lounged in the middle of the church bench, propping one bare foot on the old wood. He was lithe as a snake, solid muscle, and bare-chested in the heat, water-wicking pants hanging from hips to knees, exposing more surgical scars. His dog, Josie, leaped up and curled beside him, her eyes on me and her ears back. The mutt was gentle and sweet, but she didn't like the way I smelled and wanted to make sure I knew it.

Mike pulled hard on his Coke, standing in the sun with one fist on a hip, looking around as if expecting the wolves to reappear any moment. "You want to see the other sites?" he asked, gesturing to the river behind the shop. "I can take you down anything that'll take a two-man raft or ducky. If you paddle, Dave can get you into any tight areas in a hard boat." He pronounced it as if it were one word, *hard*boat.

I wasn't familiar with the lingo, but hard boats sounded like kayaks. And no way was I strapping myself into a kayak and bouncing down a mountain creek. Beast hacked softly, stressing her opposition to the activity. And then I actually heard the question. "*Other* sites?"

"Places where that thing made the three scratches."

I stopped, the Coke can still on my head, and let a smile form. If a grindylow was marking territory, then it was likely leaving scratches where it smelled weres, tracking them to take them down. Justice among weres was quick and final. The grindy could do my work for me. I lowered the can and drank, finishing it off. "To start, can you put out the word to the locals," I said. "I need a map of all the places where people have seen the grindy's scratch marks. Kayakers, rafters, hikers, park rangers, anybody who's seen anything. If we can get a decent count and locations, we can determine the perimeters of the grindy's territory, and maybe pinpoint the center of it. I can start my search for the werewolves there. I can pay you for your time."

Money talks. Dave and Mike met eyes and nodded. "Yeah, we can do that." Mike stuck out his hand and I took it for a firm shake. Shouting for the river guides he managed at the competing rafting business, Mike branched off toward the Bean Trees Café, demanding maps, GPS coordinates, beer, and PowerPoint displays, leaving Dave, Molly, and me sitting in the shade. I looked over at Emmett, who was waving in another deputy driving a marked car. This place was going to be a circus again tonight.

Dave turned his intense blue eyes to me and focused on my scars, the visible ones on my throat, and the ones on my left arm that hadn't yet disappeared. Mine were vamp-fang and werewolf-bite scars. "How dangerous are they?" he asked.

"The grindy? Not much, unless you're a were who hurt a human; then you get to die, as soon as he can catch you. The wolves?" I lifted my arm to display the scarring around my elbow. "You ever think about taking on a full-grown mountain lion? Bare-handed?" When he shook his head, an almost-grin on his lips, I said, "Well, two wolves will take on a big-cat. And sometimes win." Beast growled low in my mind, not disagreeing. "They have claws hard enough to rip skin and jaws that can crush a human skull or take out a human throat with one swipe. Werewolves are worse."

He pointed to my throat. "Is that where you got those scars?"

"No. Vamps did that."

His eyes widened and a small smile played on his lips. "And you still work for them?"

Molly snorted. "She never was too bright."

I shrugged. What could I say? It was true. I followed Mol to her newish van, and leaned in the open window. "Thanks for coming," I said. "I wasn't sure if we'd need your healing talents."

"I'm always happy to help," she said, arranging her belongings in the passenger seat. "It was interesting. I like watching you work when you're not staking vamps and trying to save people from them." Together, we had gone up against vamps before, and not everyone made it back alive, but I'd saved her children, Angie Baby and Little Evan, and her sister and baby the year before that, before I left the mountains for New Orleans. I gave her a wry half smile.

Molly patted my arms on the window. "I need to get home. Big Evan wasn't happy about me getting involved with this."

"Yeah. I know. I really appreciate it. Breakfast at the café soon?"

"Almost every morning. I'm always there after I drop Angie off to school. Which still feels strange. She's growing up so fast." She shook her head at the passage of time. "My sisters know you're back in town and ask after you every morning. They want to see you." I didn't make friends easily and knowing that Molly's family had all but adopted me after I helped to save the pregnant Carmen from a young rogue-vamp made me feel all sappy inside. Her eyes twinkled at me. "You could bring a boyfriend."

"I already said, I don't have a boyfriend."

"Hmmm. There's Rick LaFleur. He stands around with his tongue hanging out whenever you're around." I sighed and Molly shook her head, vexed, starting the van. "Take care, Big-Cat."

She was pulling away before I realized that she hadn't asked me to the house for dinner. No invitations to visit with her there had been forthcoming at all, and I didn't think it was because of my schedule. It was because her husband no longer trusted me to keep Molly safe. And he had good reason.

•

CHAPTER THREE

You Fight Dirty

I straddled the long seat, turned the key starting Fang, and waved to Molly taking off in her minivan. I eased the bike along the road in the opposite direction and stopped in the middle of the bridge where the wolves attacked Itty Bitty. The water was up, several feet higher than last night, the power company having opened the dam to make power and provide water for the businesses that depend on the releases. Evidence not collected overnight, or missed before the water release, had been washed away. A commercial raft rounded the bend in the river, the occupants wet and laughing. Kayakers played in eddies and small currents. Remembering Itty Bitty and her beau, I found my phone and texted Bruiser and Leo a request for someone to get up here pronto and heal the injured, before the were-taint turned them furry. That would go a long way to making the locals more vamp-friendly. Satisfied I had done all I could for the injured, I gunned the bike.

On the far side of the river, I followed my nose, tasting grindy on the breeze. The scent seemed to be part of the air currents falling from Stirling Mountain. No big surprise there, yet my heart started to pound. The grindy-scent worried me. Gunning the bike, I passed in front of the RV camp and up the mountain along back roads. Not long after, I headed sharply uphill, crossing the state line back into North Carolina.

The peak of Stirling Mountain is nearly six thousand feet high with a metal fire tower on top, but I wasn't planning on hiking all the way up. I would be stopping at the national park to check out a theory and talk to a guy I had been avoiding—pretty boy Rick LaFleur, the boyfriend-who-wasn't, that Molly had mentioned. This little side trip was why I had taken the bike instead of asking one of the twins to fly me in Grégoire's helicopter. Well, that and the fact that Beast had flatly refused to fly in the metal contraption.

The climbing ride to the park was beautiful; Big Creek—its massive boulders scored by grindy markings and rank with grindy scent—on one side of the road was dried to a trickle this time of year unless a heavy rain hit. Then the hair-head, adrenaline-junkie kayakers would be all over the place, taking the steep, highly dangerous creeking-run through its rocks, trees, and boulders. All around me on the climb were farmhouses on small farms, fallow land, horses, cattle, and harvested fields, some with big round hay bales on the peripheries. Wildflowers were everywhere. If I had been riding a quieter machine, I might have seen deer, turkey, even bear this time of year. But it wasn't likely, not riding Fang. Harleys weren't built for stealth.

I made the park entrance, taking the narrow gravel road that had been cut from the side of the mountain. It was steep on both sides, one side straight uphill, the other down, sharply, to the boulders of Big Creek. I passed through the horse area with its special camping sites and hitching posts, the distinct scent of horse and manure heavy on the cooling air.

The day-camp parking was full of cars, but I maneuvered on through, undergrowth and trees dense on both sides, to the campground. I left Fang in the bathhouse parking area. The air was twenty degrees cooler here, fresh and damp and rich with scent. I closed my eyes and breathed deeply. The weak bouquet of wild orchids that bloomed in August was faint on the breeze. Stronger were the odors of flowering bee balm, mountain mint, milkweed, and crushed jewelweed, the musky scent of rich soil and the smell of verdant green ferns and moss. Pungent and gamey were raccoon, squirrel, opossum, with dozens of bird varieties, and the horses. Faintly, from far off, came deer and bear scent. Overriding it all was the stench of man—the showers, park toilets, the tang of beer, food, charcoal, and seared meat from last night. It wasn't the smells of The People, the Cherokee of my distant memory, but it was reminiscent.

And over it all rode three of the scents I'd come looking for. One was the grindy, letting me know my theory had been right. *Crap. Why'd I have to be right this time?* The other scents didn't belong in these hills, not ever. They had the under-tang of foreign lands, of jungle, rushing violent rivers, and darkest, most remote Africa. Big-cat smell, feral, fierce, ferocious. Alien.

I opened my eyes and tracked that scent across the parking area and higher up the mountain. Moss-covered trees rose above me. Moss-covered ground muffled my boot steps. I hadn't been here recently, but I knew where I was going. The scents told me.

Despite the slight chill, I slipped out of my leather jacket and hung it by one finger over my shoulder, following the stink of big-cat. I wasn't armed, not during the day in a national park, no matter that I was licensed to carry concealed. Sometimes it wasn't smart to taunt law enforcement officials, especially when a mauling had taken place last night.

I followed the scent up a trail, cool and dark beneath the shade of trees, through the acreage set aside for rough, dry camping. Tents dotted the greenery like upside-down flowers in rainbow colors. I took the path higher still, my breath coming harder as the grade increased, to a tent far back from the others. It was close to a runnel of water that emptied into Big Creek, and the tent had been in place for several weeks, grass beginning to grow up at the tent sides. The smell of grindy was strong here. So was the smell of black were-leopard. Kemnebi.

Kem-cat's wife was dead at the claws of her pet grindy-low because she fell in love with Rick LaFleur and tried to turn him into a black were-leopard, like her. Spreading were-taint broke were-law, and killing Safia had fulfilled the grindy's primary function—protecting humans. Kem was taking it out on Safia's lover boy. My boyfriend. Ex. Whatever. Rick's scent still carried some of the wolf-taint too.

He'd suffered—been tortured by werewolves—because I hadn't figured out he was in trouble. I didn't know if I loved him, but I knew that I owed him.

"Hello the tent," I said softly.

"I heard when you bring that machine into the park," a cultured, accented voice said.

I followed the dulcet tones to the back of the tent where a woven, dark green hammock hung between two trees, a long, lean man lazing in it. One leg was draped over the side, bare foot and calf dangling. A matching arm, equally naked, held a bottle of beer. The body between the two was hidden by hammock, and hammock and beer were banned in the park, hence the positioning of them behind the tent. I grinned, skipping the niceties. "You are dressed, aren't you?"

He toasted me with the beer and wiggled his toes at me in a drunken wave, which didn't answer my question. The dark skin of both limbs was smooth and unscarred, the flesh of a shape-changer, forever untouched by damage, re-made with every shift. Given a few more hundred shifts, my own skin would be as perfect again, assuming I stayed out of mortal danger. For reasons I didn't know, scars from a lethal wound were hard to heal. "Jane Yellowrock, Rogue Hunter," he said. "My *alpha*." I had made Kem my beta, forced him to bring Rick here, and care for him until he shifted into his big-cat. Kem wanted me to understand that he didn't have to like it. "My alpha, who smells of cata-mount and Eurasian owl and *dog*."

The last was a slur and I let a hint of my grin out. "Kem-nebi, of the Party of African Weres, *my beta*, who smells of black leopard and sweat and very strongly of beer."

He lifted his hand, the bottle disappearing behind the hammock edge. I heard a slurping sound and the bottle re-appeared, now half empty. "Good beer. Samuel Adams makes the most acceptable beer I have yet discovered in America. I have been tasting all of them. Extensively." He sipped again. "There are more in the cooler."

"No thanks, I'm driving." I dropped my jacket, plopped into a folding sling chair, which was far less comfortable than it looked, and lifted the cooler lid anyway. "I'll take one of these, though." I opened another Coke and sipped, wondering how much beer it took to keep a shape-shifter drunk. Our metabolisms are fast, and it had to be a lot of beer. With a toe, I lifted the lid of a large, blue recycle pail. It was three-quarters full of broken beer bottles. Yeah. A *lot* of beer. After a companionable moment of silence I said, "How long ago did the grindy get here?"

"Safia's pet arrive two week ago." The words held no inflection, but were carefully, drunkenly enunciated. Interesting.

"It was a long swim, I take it."

The hammock moved with what may have been a shrug, noncommittal. "He was most unhappy with me at first. But *he forgave me*." There was a heavy dose of bitter irony in the words. I wasn't real sure about the symbiotic relationship between the two races, but it would seem difficult to maintain, when one was always in danger from the other. I didn't know what to say to that, but Kem was drunkenly loquacious and carried on the conversation without my contribution. "They are like pets until we err. *Affectionate . . .*" The words trailed off, then picked back up again. "He killed my mate. And then he came beneath my hand for caress. He . . . *licked my hand*." He spaced the last words widely, and they were full of venom. "I forced him to leave, yet I still smell him on the wind. He watches."

I wanted to say I was sorry, but that might have been offensive as well as disingenuous. I had a similar relationship with the vamps. I killed them when they got out of line, much like the grindy did the weres. Of course I didn't lick Leo's hand afterward. The thought's accompanying mental picture made me grin, which I hid behind the Coke as I drank. My sense of humor was gonna get me killed one day. "How is he?" I asked from behind the can, changing the subject.

Kem raised his head at that one, his black eyes wide, showing above the hammock edge, trying to focus in my direction. His face was darker in the shadows beneath the trees, but his eyes were vibrant. "He is *alive*. He is *unchanged*. He is *frightened* about the full moon, which comes again soon. He is *lonely*. As lonely as I am."

The *he is lonely* was directed at me for not coming to visit. Asheville is only sixty miles from Hartford. A nice ride. One I hadn't made, even though I'd brought Kem and Rick here in the first place. I'd hoped the black were-leopard could ease Rick through his first shift, teach him something about being a were-cat. The International Association of Weres had agreed, and insisted Kem help the newbie. For a lot of really good reasons, Kem had been less than enthusiastic. "Still no shift?"

"He will not try again until the full moon. His pain is too great."

That got me. I'd seen Rick try to shift on his first full moon. It had been agonizing. Like watching a man try to turn himself inside out. "So where is he?"

"He likes to fish."

I smiled at that one and stood. I rinsed the can and crushed it, tucking it in the sealed, bear-resistant recycle basket. "Tell him I said hi." I turned and stopped. Dead. As still as a vamp.

"Tell him yourself," Rick growled.

My breath caught. Kem chuckled. He'd seen Rick approach behind me, quiet as a cat. Rick was unshaven and shirtless, his jeans hanging low on his hips, chest hair sparse and straight and forming a line pointing into the top of the jeans. His black hair had grown, the ends curling at his nape and over his ears. His eyes were shadowed, black as night, steely, pinning me to the path. His torso and shoulders were a mass of scars from big-cats and werewolves, the scarring ripping through his tattoos, nearly obscuring the bobcat and the mountain lion. Except for the cats' golden-amber eyes and the blood on their claws. There was something about that naked chest and the scars that begged to be touched. I curled my fingers under. Rick's eyes dropped to them, then back up in a leisurely perusal that made me acutely aware of myself. My breath hitched slightly, and I tightened all over, warming from a lot more than the heat. *Boyfriend? Oh my.*

Rick LaFleur was a pretty-boy when wearing city clothes. Half-naked, in the wooded site, ungroomed and feral-looking, he was gorgeous. He smiled then, exposing white teeth, one bottom tooth slightly crooked, and I realized I'd said part of that aloud. *Crap.*

"I've missed you too," he said, amused. He moved past

me, and only then did I catch the smell of fresh fish. Even the breeze had been hiding the man. He carried a bait bucket, two rods, a tackle box, and a string of fish. They looked like smallmouth bass, about eleven to sixteen inches long. One still flapped. Rick stowed his gear away and carried a long curved knife and the fish to a board set up between two trees; there were traces of blood on the wood, and part of the dead-fish smell I had attributed to the grindy actually came from the fish-cleaning station.

Movements economical, almost graceful, Rick hung the fish chain from a nail and slid the hook from the gills of the top fish. It moved weakly when he sliced through below the gills and cut off its head. I wondered if Rick thought I'd run at the sight of the casual cruelty, but Beast sometimes ate her food still kicking. I figured she could outdo him in the gross-factor if I wanted. Of course, Rick didn't know about Beast. Rick didn't know a lot of things. I hadn't found a way to tell him most of them. Others were complicated.

Okay. I was lying. I was a coward, that's why Rick didn't know a lot of things.

The knife moving with swift, sure strokes, he scaled the fish, the iridescent scales flying everywhere. I thought fishermen scaled fish before they beheaded them, but I wasn't a fisherman trying to gross out an old girlfriend.

"Beer," Kem said from behind me. Rick stopped, wiped his hands on a towel hanging in the tree, and walked to the cooler. He took out a beer, opened the top and handed it to Kem without meeting his eyes. It was the action of a submissive animal to an aggressive alpha. Beast hissed quietly inside, the hair of her pelt rising, stiff, the phantom reaction tight inside my skin.

Wordless, Rick returned to the fish. I narrowed my eyes, putting things together. I walked to the hammock, placing my feet without care, so that Kem would know I was coming, if he wasn't too drunk to notice. I stood over the hammock, seeing his body, lithe and fit, wearing baggy shorts and a sheen of sweat. He smelled of bug spray and old beer. He was watching me with savage glee on his face. Expectant. Eager. "You want a fight, don't you. Fine."

Drawing on Beast-speed, faster than he could see, faster than he could react, I flipped the hammock. Rode him down to the ground. He landed on his stomach. Face in the dirt. My knee in his back, pressing him down. I grabbed his short hair and yanked back. Bowing his spine, arching his neck. Shoved the stake I had found under his chin. The hammock spun and settled. The sound of fish scales flying stopped. The beer bottle landed, spilling in a froth. Everything stopped.

"I am your alpha," I said. "Listen. Or I'll make you my dead beta." Kem growled softly, but after a long moment, relaxed into submission under my hands. "Two of the werewolves I fought in New Orleans got away because they were in jail when I helped kill the rest of the pack. A big guy and a little scrawny guy. They followed me here, looking for the same thing you want. A fight. To get my attention, they attacked and tried to turn a young woman and her boyfriend last night. They left this silver-tipped stake, *my* silver-tipped stake, for me to find.

"Your grindy knows about them and is hunting them. *I'm* hunting them. When I call you, you will get off your drunken ass, get sober, and hunt them too." I dropped his head. His face bounced on the ground. I stood and walked away. I caught a glimpse of Rick's face as I did. He was smiling slightly. His eyes were too warm to be remembering me making Kemnebi my beta, so maybe Rick was remembering the first time I took him down. It was our first date, walking along the Mississippi waterfront after a good meal—a great meal—in a New Orleans dive. Rick said something, I don't remember what, and it ticked me off. I dropped him, but he'd been face up for it. I tilted my head on the way past, letting a half smile touch my lips.

"You fight dirty," he murmured. "Like you do everything."

I stopped. He was talking about sex. My face heated. He leaned across the fish-cleaning board, blood and fish and fish heads between us, and breathed in, his nose only inches from my neck. Beast reared up and took me over, faster than I could think. She sniffed, pressing her face, my face, into the soft tissue of his throat. His scent filled my nose, my head, and reached right into the center of me. I/we rubbed my jaw along his, his bristles far softer than they looked.

Pelt, Beast thought. *Good mate. Mine.*

I wrenched away. Moments later I was down the path and keying on Fang. And *sooo* outta there. Tears would have made the narrow road hard to follow, but I wasn't crying. I was mad. And not sure why. Halfway down the park road, my cell vibrated in my pocket. I pulled onto the narrow shoulder and flipped it open, looked at the display. It was Rick's number, his picture in the small screen. I heaved a breath that hurt my throat. "Yeah?"

"The grindy smells weird," Rick said, "and he's not hanging around much."

"Maybe the grindylow is tired of Kemnebi's drunken anger."

Rick laughed softly. "The grindy and I would agree on that one."

I thought about how I might get the little green-golem-Yoda to partner with me. Beast rumbled, *Would taste like dead fish. Good eating. Big meal for winter food.* I pushed her away as Rick spoke again.

"Kem says he smelled wolf last night. He'll hunt with you when you call." His voice dropped an octave, soft as the pelt on a big-cat's stomach, "So will I." I laughed, the sound hoarse in my aching throat. "I've been given the rest of the day off," he said. "Wanna do lunch?"

"Yeah," I said. "Not raw fish."

"Wait for me at the crossroads. I'll be there in fifteen."

CHAPTER FOUR

If the Vamp-Poo Became Airborne

We stopped for a late lunch at a little mom-and-pop store that sold local produce, local honey, jellies and jams, chutney, molasses, homemade breads, used books, and local arts and crafts: leather belts, handbags, handmade quilts. They also had a lunch bar and sold the best egg salad sandwiches I'd ever tasted. Between us we ate six sandwiches, out under the shade tree, sitting silently at a heavy cement table on hard, cool benches. The view between the trees, straight down the mountain, into the gorge, was entertainment.

In the middle of a bite, I noticed Rick's new key chain and lifted it, letting one corner of my lips curl up as I swallowed. He mirrored the expression and added a little shrug, laughter in his eyes. The old key chain to his red crotch-rocket Kawasaki hadn't been seen since he was captured and tortured in a hotel room in New Orleans. The new one was a growling, enameled, black leopard on a silver base. Were-humor. Beast hacked with amusement. I pulled out my own and set them together, my Leo key chain with the female African lion and a stylized sun at one paw, next to his black leopard. I left them there, side by side, wondering if now was the time for the *Big Talk*.

I finished off a chocolate Yoo-Hoo with the last sandwich and ate a banana MoonPie for dessert. They were food I remembered from my youth and brought back memories I didn't have time to think about just now. Not with Rick suddenly turning his attention from the view to me.

"We gonna talk?" he asked. *Yep. Time.* His voice was smooth, calm, not at all accusatory. Even pleasant. There was no reason for me to cringe inside, but I did. "Talking's overrated," he added, searching my face, "but there're things between us that need to be said."

I crumpled up the papers and carried them to the garbage can, knowing I was dithering and not knowing how to stop.

"Jane."

I halted with my back to him. Not seeing the view. Not seeing anything. My eyes filling with unwanted, stupid tears. There was so much gentleness in the sound of my name on his lips.

"I cheated on you with the were-bitch."

My shoulders tensed. I raised a hand and brushed away the tears. I took a breath that shuddered through me. But I didn't turn around, keeping my back to him. *Coward.*

"You and me, we weren't . . . *going steady*, or whatever. And I didn't have any choice in the matter, once I was infected with the were-taint, but I cheated on you. I knew it even when I was sick. I was used to talking my way into women's good graces and beds for information. It was easy; always had been. And I paid the price for it. I lost my humanity—"

"Maybe," I interrupted.

"Maybe," he conceded. "Probably, if the pain of the last full moon was an indication. But I also lost you. And that's the part I can't stop thinking about. I cheated on you, and yet you came and got me out. You saved my life."

"Maybe," I said again.

He chuckled, the tone mocking, and I hitched a shoulder. The were-bitch's dead body had been crumpled at Rick's feet when I found him. If the werewolves had found her, they'd have killed him without a second thought, holding him responsible. I found her, and Rick, first.

"But you don't have the wolf-taint. You're infected with black were-leopard," I said. And that was the sticking point. The were-bitch had raped him. I knew that from the smell on the mattress in the hotel room where he had been tortured. But Safia had—

"I was infected, but not by sex. We didn't—" He stopped. "It never went that far. Safia bit me."

I blinked, letting my eyes go unfocused, putting the timeline together. It fit. It was possible. My mouth opened slightly. I inhaled, feeling the air move through me. Tension, anger, jealousy, and something even more primitive, lifted off me, as if a rotting, uncured pelt had been resting on my shoulders, and had then fallen away. Deep inside, my Beast began to purr. She smelled the truth of his words. "Rape isn't cheating," I whispered. "And were-taint makes humans crave sex." I turned and met his eyes. "Not your fault. Not your guilt."

He shrugged, clearly holding himself responsible still. "Your turn," he said.

I came back to the table, and sat on the edge of the hard, concrete seat. I was as far from him as I could get and still be at the table. "What do you want to know?" I hedged.

He laughed, the sound free and easy. He looked so good sitting there, the black T-shirt accenting his olive skin, the tips of the cat-claw tats and scars peeking beneath the sleeve of one bicep, the white and jagged scars marring the flesh on his other arm. He bent up a knee and clasped his hands around it. "I'll likely turn furry eventually, into a black were-leopard, maybe one with a wolf tail or wolf ears. I'm not human. Neither are you. What are you? Start there."

I opened my mouth. Closed it when nothing came out. Opened it again. Blinked slowly. *The Big Talk.* "Uhhh . . ." Rick chuckled again. I smiled and shook my head, looking away from him to the view. It wasn't often that I said the words aloud. I took a breath and said, experimentally, "What do I smell like?"

Rick shook his head. "I knew you weren't gonna be easy, not you." When I didn't reply, he said, "I haven't turned yet. My sense of smell is heightened but not what it will be. Maybe," he said, beating me to the equivocation. "But you smell like big-cat. Mostly. Like Kem, but not like him. Like a bird. And like a dog. Just a whiff. But mostly like big-cat. You're not a were."

"No," I said. My mouth went dry. "I need something to drink." Before he replied, I was up and inside, my head in the drink cooler. I stayed there too long, cooling off, but eventually, the sales lady called out to me. I made my purchases and came back out with two colas. I put his on the table and opened mine. Drank half of it and still felt dry-mouthed. I took a breath and blew it out. "I'm a"—the words were raspy, and I had to stop in the middle and take a breath—"a skinwalker."

Rick nodded, sitting there, looking calmly at me. "Did you try to turn me," he asked, "when we had sex?" There was no accusation in the words, just honest questioning.

I thought about being offended, but I had sex with him without telling him anything about me, which was a form of lying. I'd lied once so I might lie again, right? "I can't turn anyone. I was born this way."

"Okay. I'll buy that. Black magic practitioner?"

"No!" I stood fast. Inside, however, Beast hacked with derision. *Stole my body. Stole my soul. Jane is killer. Worked black magic.* I forced her down, and myself back to the seat. I put my hands on the table, fingers splayed, staring at them instead of the man I had lied to. And who had lied to me. Things were so screwed up.

"My kind were the protectors and the warrior leaders of the Cherokee for a thousand years, until the white man came. The word Cherokee once meant *people of the caves*, or *people who came from out of the ground*. Something like that. They were cave dwellers; skinwalkers kept them safe. Then the early Spanish came, and, I think, brought some contagion, maybe. My kind started to die out. Started to turn to the dark arts. But we don't have to do evil. I don't have to." Beast didn't respond to my claim this time; she was too tightly focused on Rick.

"Can you shift into any animal? Tiger, sparrow, catfish?" He hesitated. "Mountain lion?"

"I need bones or skin to change. I use DNA to adopt the shape I want. I can't change mass very well. It's dangerous. So I stay with animals of my mass most of the time." He wasn't looking at me like I was an escapee from a supernat zoo. That did happy weird things to my insides, and I clenched my hands into fists before relaxing them again. "I've never tried water animals. Only land mammals. Rarely birds. We were protectors so predators are easier."

I stopped. He'd asked about mountain lions. Though he'd been on the brink of death, Rick had seen me in my Beast-form once, the first time I'd saved his life; I'd made a habit of that lately, in between occasions of leaving him in danger. I knew what he was asking.

I drained the rest of my drink. "I usually choose mountain lion. And yes, that was me you saw when the sabertooth attacked you." I'd been at a larger mass than my own, thanks to a glitch in the shifting process. That was what I was calling it, a glitch. Not a Beast-took-control-and-forced-a-mass-change-to-the-top-of-the-genetic-range-situation, which was closer to the truth.

Rick nodded, which I saw in my peripheral vision. I risked a direct look at him. His eyes were steady, calm, non-reactionary. "Have you been in counseling or something?" I blurted.

He laughed and said, "No. Not unless you count Kemnebi's drunken ramblings. Not since I woke up sick, in pain, and bleeding, with the Mercy Blade. Gee DiMercy talks a lot, and I was too sick to push him out of the room, so I listened." He waved that away, wry, self-deprecating. "But I've had time to do a lot of thinking." He bent over the table and rested his weight on his elbows, chin in hand, holding my gaze. "Time to get over the anger. Time to remember. So that was you."

He was back at the memory we shared of Beast. Rick being attacked by a shape-changer in sabertooth lion form. Me saving him. Beast having forced the mass increase was the only reason I'd been big enough to fight the sabertooth lion off.

"Yeah. Me. I chased the sabertooth off you and got help."

He nodded. "Okay. So if I go furry, can you do the whole black leopard thing?"

Beast moved closer inside me, padding, shoulders hunched, belly tight against me, the way she would hunt unwary prey. I smiled slightly. "If I have the bones or skin or teeth of a female black leopard, yes. Probably."

Good mate. Strong, Beast thought.

"A real one?" he asked. "Not the bones or teeth of a were-female. Not Safia's bones?"

"No! That's black magic." And besides, I wasn't sure

how the DNA of a were differed from the DNA of a normal animal or mundane human or skinwalker. And I wasn't curious to find out. "I can become a real black leopard. If I want to. If I have the DNA material. Soooo. Are we . . . good?" I asked, not sure what I meant by that. Beast hacked in amusement. I ignored her.

Rick extended his hands across the table and I placed mine into them. "We're good. Or as good as we can be until we find out if I survive the next full moon, furry, or not. Till then, it's a good day to be outside and free." He lifted my hand to his mouth and kissed the back of my fingers. His lips were warmer than a human's and soft, and something melted inside me. Beast purred. This man was one of very few people on the face of the earth—to include Molly, her husband Evan, and Angie Baby—who knew I was a skinwalker. And he was okay with it. His scent warmed as if he knew my thoughts, and he pressed my Leo key chain into my palm. "Let's go for a ride."

We helmeted up and I followed Rick's red crotch-rocket Kawasaki out of the small parking lot and up and down switchback roads. We didn't talk. We roamed the hills, catching one another's eyes, much like mated big-cats might, pointing to prey and old barns and cabins covered in undergrowth. We followed the scent of grindy and once of werewolf until it faded.

At the first shadows of night, we were back at the campground. I keyed off Fang, set the kick, and straddled the bike while the engines cooled, studying Ricky Bo. While I watched, he secured his bike for the night, his movements more graceful than once upon a time. Though he hadn't gone furry, he was picking up the traits of a cat: stealth, grace, improved senses. He unstrapped his helmet and I pulled off mine. His hair swung forward, damp, matted by sweat.

I caught the scent of him, musky, salty, cat, all male. I stood and took a step toward him. He met my eyes for a single moment. Heat flared between us, and I was in his arms, his mouth on mine. The world tilted, my hands clawing under his shirt. I was slammed against something hard. Pinned. Bark gouging through my leather jacket. I curled a leg around his, pulling him close. Breath hot. Tongue and mouths and the rising scent of musk. One hand cupped my head. The other my butt. Pulling me close into him. Grinding.

"Get a room," someone said. Too close.

Rick jerked back, baring teeth. But the man was gone, the scent of sweat and irritation on the air, footsteps receding. Rick huffed a laugh and I made a sound perilously close to a giggle. He bent his forehead against mine, our hearts pounding together. "Holy Mary, Mother of Jesus," he whispered, catching his breath. "What the hell was that?"

"Cat scent?" I gasped. "Mating pheromones? It's just a guess."

"You never did it . . . I mean not with another skinwalker?"

My smile faded. So did my joy. I put my hands against his chest between us. Pressed until he let me to the ground and stepped back, though Rick refused to be pushed entirely away. His hand was still on my nape. I turned my head and rested my cheek in his palm.

"What?" he asked, and I could smell Rick's confusion, his worry. *His cat.*

"There are no other skinwalkers," I said. I tilted my head and searched his eyes. "I killed the last one when it went crazy and started eating people."

I could see him putting things together. "Leo Pellissier's son? Was a skinwalker?"

"Maybe. Probably. One who did black magic, took a vamp's DNA, and the two natures didn't mesh." When he didn't comment, I said, "It was a lot older, I think. Like weres, walkers live a long time. They don't get nutso until they get *very* old, or do something stupid like try to become vampire on top of being a walker. I've never met another one."

"Once Kem goes back to Africa, I'll be the only black were-leopard on this continent, and the only one on the face of the earth who might not be able to change at the full moon. Looks like we get to be singularities together." He gathered up my hands and pulled me away from the tree, back to Fang. "You've got a long ride back. Be careful, Jane Yellowrock."

I helmeted up, feeling curiously empty and full all at

once, drained and vacant and joyful. "You too, Rick La-Fleur. I'll be back."

"I'll be here," he said, "at least until the day after the full moon. If I'm alive then, my whole world will be different." I reached for Fang's key. "But I'll still want you, Jane."

I looked up at that, but Rick was gone, fading into the lengthening shadows.

Back in my suite in the Regal Imperial Hotel, I rushed through a shower, looking longingly at the whirlpool tub with its candleholders and plush towels. And at the bed I hadn't used in a day and a half. *Maybe at dawn.* Which seemed a long time away. I braided my black hair, which was windblown and needed a scrubbing it wasn't going to get anytime soon, and tucked it up into a tight, compact queue. It could still be used as a handle in a fight, but the bun was better than loose hair over three feet long. I wasn't vain, and I could be called beautiful only by the most generous or the most inebriated, but my long hair was gorgeous.

I was security on this gig, not chasing rogue-vamps, and the different job description had required a change in a lot of my possessions, from clothes to weapons. The clothes had been commissioned by Leo Pellissier to give me "elegance and utility," his phrase. And I liked the clothes, which was such a girly thought that I'd not said it aloud. Dodging the bust of some long-dead founding father on its tall stand, I tossed clothes from the closet—all black, which made wardrobe decisions so much easier—onto the bed and drew on Lycra undies, narrow-legged pants, silk tank, tight vest, tall, leather boots, and slung an elegant nubby silk jacket over my arm.

Rushing the clock, I strapped on the knife sheaths and silver-tipped stakes, and gathered three new handguns provided by Leo, which was one of the nicer aspects of being on vamp retainer—access to all the latest toys. Thanks to a big check signed by Ernestine, the financial secretary of the Louisiana Mithrans, I was fully accoutered with new .380s.

Muscle memory giving me speed, I sat on the couch in the sitting area, handguns on the low table, and checked them all, holstering the new weapons. The .380s offered less stopping power than my 9 mils, and significantly less than my Benelli M4 tactical 12-gauge shotgun, currently hidden in the closet, but were perfect for this job where the possibility of collateral damage was not acceptable, meaning accidentally shooting a tourist or bellboy. So I loaded varied kinds of ammo in the new magazines. The Walther PK380s, I loaded with standard rounds in the event of a human or blood-servant attack on the talks between vamps. One went under my arm, its twin at the small of my back. Matching guns. How cool is that? The semiautomatic handguns were lightweight, ambidextrous, with bloodred polymer grips, and reengineered so the safety block wouldn't break off, a serious flaw of the first ones in the series.

Into my boot holster went a six-round Kahr P380, a small semiautomatic with a matte black finish. It was loaded with silver in case of vamp attack. I had strict orders not to tell the other security or the vamps at the chats about the silver ammo, and not to fire it unless "extreme measures are called for, in the event of unforeseen violence." Leo's words. I translated them to mean, "if the vamp-poop hit the fan," because with vamps, violence was always foreseen.

I stood and checked myself in the long mirror. Of course, if the vamp-poop became airborne I wasn't well prepared, not even with all the weapons on me. I wasn't wearing my protective gear, my armored and silver-studded leathers. And I had yet to replace my sterling silver neck, throat, and décolletage collar that protected me from the most common vamp killing techniques. I had nothing defensive on me at all. I was logistical and overall security for the hotel, transportation, any protesters who decided to make a point and kill a vamp, and the talks themselves, so I wasn't supposed to need my vamp-hunting gear. Yeah. Right.

I threw on the jacket, straightened my gold nugget necklace, and paused. I spun to the closet and stretched up on tiptoe. Spotted the wooden box in the far corner. Even though I knew it was there, it was hard to see, Molly's spell sliding my eyes to the side, making my brain ignore it. My fetish necklaces were inside, and no human would ever notice the box unless they reached back and felt for something they didn't see. Satisfied, I raced through the connecting doorway into the common area of the twins' suite. They were waiting, dressed and armed to the teeth. Brian tossed me a tube of red lipstick, which I caught and smeared on as I passed a mirror. The shade matched the Walthers' grip, which had made me laugh when I bought it.

"The princess is finally ready," Brandon drawled, his Louisiana accent thicker than melted praline candy.

"It was worth the wait," Brian said. Or maybe it was the other way around. Without seeing the tiny mole at Brandon's hairline I can't tell them apart, and when they work personal security for their blood-master, they dress alike. Exactly alike. So there's no telling them apart at a distance. Clan Arceneau's security blood-servants were gorgeous, and all gussied up in matching tuxedoes tonight.

"You boys look pretty," I said, tucking the lipstick into a pocket. I put on the ear wire and one of the twins helped me attach the receiver unit beside the Walther holstered at my spine.

"*I* look pretty. The ugly brother," Brian said, tugging on the holster, and telling me which twin was which, "looks acceptable as long as he leaves his hair combed over his imperfection."

It was an old joke. I just wish they'd wear name tags. I flipped the switch on and dropped the coat, checking its drape in the long mirror at the door. In its reflection, I saw the TV, with two mug shots on it, bearded men, rough and angry. Not that the werewolves would look anything like that by now. If they shaved, they'd be hard to recognize. The mug shots became a shampoo ad. "Okay. What's on the schedule tonight?" I asked as I followed Brian into the hallway.

He knocked on the door at the end of the hall, speaking over his shoulder to me. "The Noir Wine Room."

I touched my mike to the command channel and said, "Update."

Derek said, "The locals are still chanting out front. Apparently the Cocke County sheriff released your name at a press conference this evening. Our protestors think you were lying to protect the suckheads when you said no vamps attacked the couple in Hartford."

"Mmmm," I said. "Numbers?"

"Fourteen. I have a guy watching and taking video. We've ID'd most of them."

"Okay. We're moving according to schedule. The Noir Wine Room. Everyone in place?"

"Affirmative, Injun Princess."

I pushed the mouth-wire to the side as the door to the suite dubbed the Mithran Suite opened and Grégoire stepped out with a burst of vamp-scent. His was the perfume of freshwater streams and summer gardens, and if his security looked good, the blood-master of Clan Arceneau was devastating. He had been turned young, back in a pre-Revolution French court, and had been chosen for his beauty, which said something less than savory about his maker. Yet, Grégoire had a look of perpetual innocence that was unusual among the vamps. I didn't know him well enough to say if the innocence was real or practiced, but I'd have put money on faked if asked. Hard to maintain innocence for over seven hundred years. Tonight Grégoire was elegant in black tuxedo pants, cummerbund, vest, and silky black shirt with ruffles at cuffs and neck. His coat with tails was a gold cloth slightly darker than the color of his hair. The fit and cut were modern, the color scheme wasn't. I figured it must be based on something from his own time.

He studied us, taking in every detail, nodded once and started down the hall, Brian leaped in front at point, Brandon falling in at our six. I was slightly ahead at Grégoire's left.

We drew all eyes as we exited the elevator into the Regal Imperial's lobby with its huge central stone fireplace supported by stone columns, its art, statues, burned velvet and leather upholstery, and eclectic decor. I took note of who stared too long or looked away too quickly, who moved and who didn't. The hotel staff had been briefed and given a rundown of possible security problems. They had only one thing to remember. Don't stare at the patrons or the security, and if I shouted, "Lockdown," they were to call 911, lock the entry doors, shut down the elevators, and position a bellboy on each floor to keep the clients in their rooms. Easy-peasy. If they remembered and didn't panic. In my experience, nonprofessionals always panicked.

I looked to the night-dark windows to see Derek, the compact, muscular, black man standing to the side in his charcoal suit. He nodded once to me before returning to his study of the lobby. The nod meant that no one stood out as a possible troublemaker, terrorist, or vamp-hater. I nodded back, knowing he'd see even though he wasn't looking at me. He tapped his mike and said over the general channel, "Clear?"

"Clear," another voice said. That would be Wrassler, already positioned in the Noir Wine Room, making sure no one was there but the appropriate staff and sanctioned menu—meaning the humans who would provide sustenance during the negotiations. Which set my teeth on edge, but since no one was there against his or her will, I wasn't making a fuss.

CHAPTER FIVE

Two Cups and You're Done

They started again with the intros, which were each shorter by about half now that the two vamps had met a few times, but there was still a lot of chatter about Leo. The blood-sucker I worked for was arguably the second most power-ful vamp in the U.S. I insulted him on a regular basis, which made me really stupid, or really lucky, or proved that I had something Leo wanted, a hypothesis that scared me silly when I let myself think about it.

Intros done, the men in parley were ready to toast their clans and lineage—the vamp version of a wine tasting. Two blood-servants stepped up beside the vamps, a gorgeous Asian woman named Anling, which meant Placid Jade in Mandarin, and an equally beautiful Korean man named Chin Ho, which meant Precious and Goodness. Each blood-master introduced his servant to the other; then Grégoire took Chin Ho's hand, turned it palm up, and sniffed Shaddock's blood-servant's wrist. He dropped his fangs forward with a little snick of sound and bit in. As soon as he was latched on, Shaddock bit into Anling, Gré-goire's blood-servant. This part of the negotiations had been established early on, as the Carta left the location of the sampling up to the vamps in parley. Carotid, brachial, and femoral (ick), had been ruled out, as had sex with the servants while tasting. Vamps were pretty blasé about in-tercourse, and sex and dinner were often one and the same thing. Not something I wanted to be in the same room with. Double ick.

After a suitable amount of time—or maybe it was a volume thing, like two cups and you're done. What did I know?—the men broke off, eased their fangs from their drinks, and started talking about the *vintages*.

"Anling tastes like moonlight and jasmine," Shaddock said. Which sounded all kinds of funny with his country boy/mountain man accent. "Well aged and mellow as a good bourbon."

"Your Chin Ho is reminiscent of hazelnut and fine wine," Grégoire said. "A delightful offering. And young?"

"Only fifty years, but he's agin' well, or so I'm told."

"Lovely boy," the French vamp said. And he placed a kiss on the blood-servant's wrist. The Korean *vintage* blushed and lowered his eyes.

It was way too much like foreplay for me, and I held in a grimace. Listening to it all made me wonder why no blood-meal ever tasted like bacon or shrimp or a really good beer. I managed not to laugh, which would have brought a fast response from Grégoire. Likely a painful one. To the vamps this stuff was deadly important. For me, it was comic relief, even though I'd made a study of the relevant parts of the Vampira Carta and its codicils for this job, and understood the penalties for vamp-misbehavior, which were not comic at all.

Since nothing important was on the docket until after dinner, I let my mind wander back over the kiss and conversation with Rick, careful not to react to the memory in any way. I wasn't interested in becoming part of the tasting ceremony, and a physical response in any of the observers would have reached the noses of the vamps instantly in such close quarters. Noir Wine Room held space for only twenty or so, and the intimate accommodations meant we shared each other's scent reactions.

Rick's last words, before he disappeared, silent as a stalking cat into the long shadows haunted me. "But I'll still want you, Jane." He had meant it, totally and completely. But we both knew that we didn't always get what we wanted in life.

Good mate, Beast thought sleepily at me. *Big-cat. Big*

claws. Good killing teeth. She rolled over, her claws scraping across my mind. *We could be black leopard, mate to Ricky Bo.*

That statement pulled me out of my own thoughts and back to the enervating, mind-numbing boredom of the parley. The vamps were discussing the length of time Shaddock's scions were chained while they cured, which was my smoked-meat term for the time it took newly turned vamps, who always rose insane, to remember their own minds. It took only five years for most of Shaddock's scions to go through the curing process, a speed that had been well documented for sixty years. Most vamps, when bitten, spend ten years nutso—lost in what they call the devoveo, the insanity that comes to all freshly risen vamps—chained in their maker's basement, before they recall who they had been and develop bloodlust control, allowing them into human society. Or into the feeding pool, as Grégoire phrased it. The speed with which Shaddock's scions recovered had made him a master vamp at a young age. And now there was the two-year-wonder, the vamp who cured in two years. A record.

Beast flicked an ear tab, returning my attention to a subject she thought more important than the parley. *We could go back to hot, flat, wet place,* she thought, talking about New Orleans, *and take Bruiser as mate.* Slyly she added, *And Leo.* She sent a mental picture of the three of us in a big bed, the sheets ripped, slashed, and bloody. Beast's idea of a good time. I exhaled—not quite a sigh. Beast was less interested in a long-term relationship than I was, and far more interested in taking the biggest predators as mates. *Big-cats do not mate for life,* she thought at me.

Yeah. So you told me. Humans do. Sometimes.

I/we are not human, she thought disdainfully.

She had me there. We weren't human. And then I realized I had missed something. Maybe something vital. The vamps were gathering up their blood-servants and belongings as if to leave. My heart shuddered and Grégoire looked up fast. He had heard my heart-thump of anxiety. *Crap! What did I miss?* As Leo's head of security it was my job to pay attention, not woolgather.

Was not chasing sheep, Beast thought, humor in her

words. She sniffed and added, *Vampire, who smells of man-spices and cooked meat, has asked pale vampire, who smells of flowers and fresh streams, to see the den where he keeps his chained scions.*

Relief washed through me. *Scion Lair. Got it.* And, *Crap!* The field trips were planned for next week. Grégoire had been invited to pay a surprise visit to a location I had never been given the address or GPS coordinates for, and had not reconnoitered. Though Shaddock had been agree-able about a lot of info, he'd been reticent about sharing the coordinates of his Clan Home and scion lair until the night before the visit, which would have meant Monday night. I wasn't happy at allowing the vamps to go to some-place I hadn't scouted and set up a perimeter. Not that I had a choice.

Chen, Shaddock's security chief, gave me a flat stare, showing me how ticked off he was. I narrowed my eyes at him and gave my head a tiny jerk, telling him I hadn't known. Chen looked at his boss, puzzled, but this was Lin-coln Shaddock's idea, not Grégoire's.

Shaddock bowed slightly from the waist, a curious ges-ture, vaguely antique military, and said, "My Mithrans are honored that you accept our invitation to visit our chained scions."

I tapped my mike for the command channel that went directly to Derek. This was for his ears only. "Exit strategy alpha four," I said, choosing one of several prearranged and practiced exit strategies. It was all probably overkill, but I was staking (pun intended) my reputation on this gig, and leaving nothing to chance. "Bring the cars around front. Increase personnel on the street and the drive."

"Destination?" Derek asked.

"Unknown," I said, moving to the door. I cracked it and looked out, seeing Derek motion his guys into position at the entrance. "Tuesday has come early," which told Derek why I didn't know where we were going. From a safety measures standpoint this unexpected trip was a huge prob-lem. "I want both vamps in one car with the blood-servants, just as planned for Tuesday."

Two other limos would leave at the same time heading in different directions to confuse any observers. Two SUVs would ride shotgun with each limo, one in front, one in back, and rendezvous with us once they shook any tail. Security 101. It was standard because it worked.

I was riding shotgun in the last car, staring out the back window, trying to discern any pattern that might indicate we were being followed, and got the directions, address, and GPS coordinates when the drivers did. It came up on my digital video screen the moment they plugged it into the system, and instantly flashed onto a county map. The location of Shaddock's chained scions was halfway up a mountain at the end of a nothing road. Literally nothing. The coordinates identified no access roads for miles, which meant it was both easier and harder to defend. *Oh goody*. It was also Shaddock's Clan Home, which was weird, as most vamps kept their uncured (as in cold meat) children in a separate location.

The security evaluation of the clan home was scheduled for later too, making this a twofer. Tension crawled up my shoulders on little spider feet. This was a dangerous proposition. The worst case scenario for protection detail was the unexpected.

The city fell away as we headed north on I-26 past the Pisgah National Forest and took 70 toward Hot Springs. The blackness of mountains rose up before us, secondary roads off to either side, careening up and down steep terrain. Mansion homesites and subdivisions dotted distant hillsides with security lights, bright in the dark. Mobile home and RV parks, barns, sheds, and abandoned houses replaced suburban life with rural as we traveled. No one followed us.

My directional sense said we were getting close when we slowed, and turned onto an unlit gravel road. A quarter mile in, trees had closed in on both sides and the shadows were dense. Even with my better-than-human night vision, one of the gifts of my Beast, I couldn't see much out the tinted windows, not enough to pierce the darkness under the trees. We stopped, and I craned for a view. "Status?"

Derek said into his mike, "Barrier. Chain across the road. Two cameras at the gate, one static, one roving. Blood-

servant guard. Another in a tree stand at four o'clock."
Derek's low-light headgear units with infrared scopes had
come in handy. Vamps showed on low-light as human, but
showed cooler body temp on infrared, an easy way to ID
the species. "Vamps on the ground in the trees at ten
o'clock," he said, "moving fast, maintaining a perimeter."
The direction of the vamps put them deeply into the wood,
scrub, and steep hills, which meant Shaddock had a well-
trained security detail, composed mostly of vamps instead
of human blood-servants. Like a vamp army. "That make
sense to you?" I asked.

"Not so much," he said on the command channel. Which
meant his spidey sense had been activated by so many unexpected blips. I tensed. We started forward again at a
steady, slow crawl, and I watched the blood-servant lock
the gate behind us. My Beast did not like to be caged in.
She prowled within me, ears down flat, lips pulled back in a
snarl, showing killing teeth.

The house at the end of the long drive was situated on a
small bald knoll of solid granite. The house was tiny, a brick
and stone dollhouse with arched windows, arched entry,
four chimneys, peaked roofline with lots of sharp angles.
Chen exited the limo and opened the heavy front door,
punched a sequence into the security panel, squelching the
squeal of the alarm.

Derek and Wrassler took over, going in for a fast reconnoiter. Derek held a compact, matte-black, semiautomatic
selective-firing shoulder weapon—a submachine gun—in
both hands, high on his chest. Wrassler stood at the door,
not trying to hide his weapon, an ACR—Adaptive Combat Rifle—an adjustable, two-position gas-piston-driven
system with an enhanced configuration, supported by a
strap around his massive shoulders. He was wearing the
night vision headgear and was watching out over the
trees that circled the place. Boys and their toys. Out here
in the boonies we didn't have to worry about collateral
damage.

I got out of the SUV and stood close to it, protected by
the engine block, studying the trees at the edges of the
property, the cool night air whispering. The moon was up,
and the shadows under the trees were intensely dark. No

hint of security lights anywhere up here; vamps' night vision is way better than any human's—it might be better than Beast's. My shoulders ached and I realized I was holding them tightly. I forced them down into a neutral position; a relaxed posture wasn't possible. Derek reappeared and waved us in. I went to the limo and opened the door. Grégoire followed Lincoln Shaddock and his blood-servant inside and I felt secure only when the door closed behind us with an airtight thump.

The inside of the Clan Home was far different from the outside, barely seeming to allow for the known laws of physics. Derek said, "On the entry floor we have an expanded foyer, library on left, guest suite on right, and a wet bar. Steps down. Checking the lower level now."

"Wait here, please," I said to the vamps and their blood-servants. The foyer held a black baby grand piano, which I stepped around, double-checking behind Derek, verifying his assessment and making sure nothing had changed since he did a sweep. Most of the entry level was a large deck overlooking the bottom floor. All the living space was on the lower level, with the ceiling opening up three stories overhead, and the public area of the living space laid out to view. It was also carved into the rock heart of the mountain.

The rear wall of the house was windowed, revealing an extraordinary panorama of a cleft in the hills, all faintly lit with dim lights. They showed a narrow stream, a waterfall, tall trees, and tumbled rocks the size of small cars. The view opened up and down, and it was spectacular. Shaddock had made the mountains his own, bringing them inside without damaging the environment or habitats. Too freaking cool. Not that I showed it. Through the windows, a lone owl was poised in the top of a dead tree, searching for dinner. "Niiiice," one of the security guys said softly into his mike. I moved through the foyer and down the stairs, my boots silent on the stone, one of the twin Walthers pointed down at my side, held in both hands. I didn't remember drawing it. Derek preceded me, a weapon in each hand. I followed slowly. Vamps like hidey holes and they move faster than a human can see, hence the search—always paired up.

The living room was on the lower level, and open to the upper foyer. Shaddock had decorated in shades of charcoal, taupe, forest green, black, cloud-gray, and moss, colors likely taken from the daylight view outside, with lots of natural stone, bronze, and wood that was obviously all very old. I remembered from his file that Lincoln owned an architectural salvage business, buying buildings that had fallen into ruin, tearing them down by hand, treating, and reselling the wood. Here, old barn boards had been worked into the design of his clan home, even the floors, which were an appealing mix of oak, hickory, pine, and stone tiles.

Moving human slow, two vamps walked into the room together, Shaddock's heir and spare, Dacy Mooney and Constantine Pickersgill. The two were crafty and dangerous. Dacy had been a Southern belle when alive, and after being turned, had been a U.S. spy in World Wars One and Two, under different names and different covers. Pickersgill had been the power behind six U.S. presidents. Both had lived in the world of humans without giving themselves away, which meant they were smart, coercive, and very cool under fire. They were dressed in casual clothes, not expecting us. And they each acknowledged me with a nod when my eyes flicked over them.

Shaddock's bedroom was to the right of the living area—his personal sleeping space, not his lair. None of us would ever see that. I took in the understated room. A king-sized bed with luxurious linens, the headboard crafted from found articles: two narrow columns, a peaked door frame from a church, a rusted iron gate, and a carving of a swan, its long neck reaching back to ruffle its feathers, wings outspread. Things that didn't go together except here. The floor was bare, finished wood. Shaddock, whom I had pegged as a hillbilly, had the soul of an artist.

A black leather recliner and a bronze antique swan-shaped lamp were the only other furniture. There was a huge walk-in closet and marble bathroom big enough to hold a party in. Back in the living room, I took two seconds to scan it. The floor was covered with a taupe, handmade silk rug of a black swan rising from gray water in a rush of froth in the sitting area. The back wall was the finished stone of the mountain. The side walls were faced with shelving, and one antique banker's desk. Computers and laptops were on several surfaces, making the living room a work space and Shaddock a very unusual vamp. Most of them had trouble adapting to a world filled with modern electronics. Four couches, half a dozen chairs, a fireplace big enough to roast an ox or two made up a seating area. Bronze statues of wild animals, birds, a fox. Even an eight-foot-long taxidermied mountain lion, which Beast found interesting and wanted to study. *Later*, I thought at her.

On the other side of the living space was a barrackslike bedroom—if barracks had silk sheets and feather pillows; six bunks, made up in moss, celery, and serpentine green. It was the blood-servants' sleeping quarters. Two utilitarian baths and a locker room, all neat and Spartan. Tucked away in the corners were small, elegant bedrooms, walls hung with tapestries and beds in silk. Windowless. Vamp guest rooms. I pushed aside tapestries to reveal rock walls. No way was sunlight getting in here. "Clear. Let 'em in," I said into the mike.

Back in the main area, I looked up at the huge, three-story windows just as Grégoire reached the bottom of the stairs. He looked nonplussed, which must be a difficult emotion for a master vamp his age to experience. He waved a small hand at the wall of glass. "Sunlight?" he asked, sounding pained.

Shaddock lifted a remote device from a table and pressed a series of buttons. Instantly motors started to whine, followed by a muted clanking. As I watched, folding metal blinds began to close in from the side walls, covering the windows. One of the security guys cursed softly into the miked system. I couldn't say I blamed him. Shaddock had built what looked from the driveway like a gnome's house, tiny, old-fashioned, and impossible to secure. Instead it was a fortress. It took a little over thirty seconds for all the metal panels to close fully, and another fifteen for the automatic latches to seal. Over them, black insulated shades dropped—a final seal.

Grégoire smiled slightly and waved limp fingers in a circle. "Air? Water? Fire?"

"Got me an air duct cut into the rock. Fan works on solar batteries. A cistern with a thousand gallons of water," Shaddock said. He pointed up. "Sprinkler system. Got stores enough to last the blood-servants for a year." Chen stood to the side, expressionless, but conveying irritation in his stance. His boss was giving away trade secrets.

"Escape? Security system?" Grégoire asked.

"Got them too." Shaddock didn't volunteer the location of other protective measures. I frankly was surprised we got to see all that we did. Vamps were private creatures, and the fact that he let us see all this only meant he had a lot more security stuff hidden. Stuff he wouldn't tell us about, and certainly wouldn't show us.

"Your scions?" Grégoire asked.

Shaddock led the vamps into his bedroom where he pressed some more buttons; a shelving unit hummed, sliding behind another, revealing a narrow door, steel, banded with more steel. One-handed, he turned four levers, unlatching four manual locks, and opened the door. The smell of stone, cool cave air, vamps, and old blood filled the room. He stepped through. Before I could stop him, before the twins checked the room, Grégoire followed. I flew through the doorway after them and was brought up short, standing with two weapons drawn, feeling stupid. Especially when Chen raced in after me, his own weapon aimed at my head. I gave him a weak smile and holstered the Walthers. He frowned and reluctantly holstered his own.

The only scion-lair I had ever seen had been run by crazy psycho-vamps in New Orleans for their long-chained scions—uncured vamps who had never found sanity and who should have been destroyed centuries earlier. I had no preconceptions except modern fiction and scuttlebutt, which said that nutso young vamps were kept chained to the walls until they cured. Not so. These vamps were in steel-barred cells, maybe eight-by-eight feet. Bare mattresses on stone floors. The uncured-scions-to-be were naked. Vamped out. *Rogue*. My hackles rose. *Cages*. I fought down Beast's growl. She hated cages, and rogues almost as much.

The caged vamps reacted to the sight of company in different ways. One attacked the bars of his cell, throwing himself against the iron, screaming incoherently. One laughed, a chilling, insane sound. One wept, curled on her mattress. Others, frenzied, reached toward the humans, eyes crazed, fangs deployed. Only one looked at me with reason in his eyes. He was wearing a shirt and pants. Shoes. His cell was larger than the others, containing a bed, desk, chair, table, and recliner. A flat screen TV was mounted across the bars and the desk was loaded down with books, a laptop, and various other electronic devices. I made a swift mental sketch: brown and brown, average height, slender, flat nose, as if broken, which was odd. I assumed he was a chained scion who had found himself and was ready to be released into the world. Until he met my eyes, held my gaze. And smiled. His small fangs flipped down and he ran his tongue over the sharp, inch-long tips, the gesture almost taunting. *All righty then.*

I could *feel* their hunger, ravenous, demented. It would have been kinder to just stake the pitiful things, but that wasn't my job. The security arrangements were, which meant I needed to prepare a report on the safety measures of Shaddock's Clan Home and his scion-lair. *Crap.* I hated reports. Not hiding my frown, not caring if I threw off anger pheromones, I took in the arrangement of the overhead lighting, each bulb protected by metal grates, the switch by the door, and moved through the room. Security cameras were in the four corners, the dynamic, mobile kind, operated by remote from a secure location. The bars were bolted into the rock floor, rock ceiling, and rock walls with no sign of rust or corrosion. I checked for adequate fire protection, drainage, and a safe manner to feed the caged. There was a large round drain in the sloping floor and sprinklers overhead. A hose to clean the vamps and their cages was curled on a hook. A stainless-steel sink big enough to swim in stood in one corner, and from it a stainless trough ran around the walls.

Shaddock said, "Blood-slaves—or the occasional pig if times get hard—can be bled at the sink, and the blood'll drain around the room, feeding the vamps who slurp out of the trough." He sounded proud and I smothered my anger. It was barbaric, not that the scions cared. They were too wacky to care. No one cared that they were kept like prisoners, either. They had signed all the legal documents giving the vamp master permission to control, keep, and care for them for as long as he chose, and then acceding permission to be put down like rabid dogs if they didn't come out of the devoveo.

Actually, Shaddock had done a good job creating his lair. The Vampira Carta didn't specify that rogue scions had to have mattresses or space. And all Leo cared was that they wouldn't starve or get free. I had no choice but to be satisfied. I left the room, the two vamps still talking about the various nutritive techniques and systems of restraint for the chained ones. I was just angry. Deeply, silently angry. Chen watched me leave with flat, cold eyes.

CHAPTER SIX

Leo Pellissier's Right-Hand Meal

By dawn, the envoy was protected and safe in his window-less suite in the four-star hotel, his blood-servants around to defend and serve him. And I was free to hunt. Almost as important, I was allowed time away from the vamps—who were all sicko killing fiends—and the blood-servants who allowed them to continue living like kings, despots, and feudal lords.

Though I hadn't slept in nearly forty-eight hours, I was too ticked off to rest. Bruiser, Leo Pellissier's right-hand meal, had left me a text during the night. "It is in Leo's best interests for you to hunt down the weres and prove the Mithrans innocent." Well duh. No kidding. What did it? The national news media filming the protestors out in front of the hotel? Or the report that more campers had been attacked during the night, by something fanged and clawed? A second text added, "Leo has cleared this hunt with the International Association of Weres, who have placed a bounty on their heads. Leo wonders why they were not dispatched when the rest of the pack was exterminated."

I texted back. "Wolves were in New Orleans lockup. Not gonna shoot dogs with human witnesses." Privately I added, "Idiot," but I didn't type that part.

I was free to chase the werewolves and the grindy and Leo and the IAW would pay me for it. My eyes on the news channels, watching while I changed, I flipped through from

Asheville's local channels to the national ones, learning that last night's campers had been deep in a wilderness site near a small creek, over forty crow-flying miles from the previous attack site, and because it happened in the dark instead of by day, the media was again attributing it to vamps. Dressed in jeans, hiking boots, and layers of shirts, I filled a backpack with supplies I might need. I'd be hunting with the local sheriff and his deputies, guys I knew—cops who had questioned me extensively following another hunt—and so I was carrying only two handguns. No need to worry the local law enforcement by showing up armed like a mercenary.

Once dressed, I brought six knives and my backpack into the twins' common room and finished weaponing up in front of their large, flat-screen TV. Brandon, his hair washed and combed back, was stretched out on the sofa, wearing a heavy white robe with the hotel's logo on it. There was an open bottle of wine and an empty glass on the tea table beside him, and two dainty wounds in his neck. He looked satiated, and happy. Which ticked me off.

The local early morning TV personality was a cute, energetic blonde with a perky voice. When Brandon flipped back she was saying, "—pires kill like that, don't they Mason? With fangs, and claws?" A grim smile on my face, I shoved my favorite vamp killer, eighteen inches of heavily silver-plated steel in a hand-carved elk-horn handle into its sheath.

Mason, on a split screen, was standing in front of trees, emergency vehicle lights blinking in the distance. "The older ones don't *usually* kill their blood supply, Marcy, but the young rogues do often kill their victims. These attacks appear to the law enforcement and park rangers very similar to the wounds suffered by the people killed a year or so ago."

"Those attacks were brought to an end by Jane Yellowrock, the local vampire hunter, and a coven of local witches, right?"

I felt myself flush and an electric shock shot through me. *Oh . . . crap.* Molly's husband was gonna kill me.

"Janie is famous," Brandon said, laughing.

"For our viewers, here's some footage shot by an amateur videographer, the morning when a local sheriff detective, Paul Braxton, was killed trying to take down the vampires in the cave system of the old Partman Place."

"I remember that, Marcy," Mason said. "The Partman Place was a nineteenth-century homestead until gemstones were discovered and the land was sold to a mining company."

Marcy said, "The mine closed down when the gems ran out. Last year, a blood-family of young rogue vampires took it over and local residents started to disappear." A poor quality feed ran. "When a camper saw two blood-covered females walk out of the mine he took a short video." On the television screen, his feed zoomed in on my face, my peculiar amber-colored eyes seeming to glow, an effect that had been blamed on the golden sunrise. What else could it be, right? But it was Beast. And people might not be so sanguine about Beast in my eyes now.

"According to some sources, Jane Yellowrock is back in the area. What does she say about these attacks?" Marcy asked.

"We have people tracking her down now. But in unconfirmed reports, she told one law enforcement officer that no vampire caused the wounds." Mason's voice sounded skeptical. "Of course, one source suggests that she went to New Orleans to work for the vampires. So that might have changed her perspective."

"Weird, to go to work for your enemy. But I guess money talks," Marcy said.

I frowned. On the screen, Molly and I were both covered in blood, the sunlight hitting us as we came out of the mine, into the dawn light, me carrying Brax, Detective Paul Braxton, over my shoulder. Or what was left of him. One of the young rogue-vamps had killed him. The scar on my throat was clear in the video, the angled sunlight of early dawn catching on the raised, ridged, raw, partially healed, red scar. Back then it was four inches wide, brand-new, left over from a near beheading by an enraged young rogue. I had survived by shifting into Beast. And Beast had saved us all by taking down the last rogue-vamp. Dang Internet.

Brandon looked at my neck, still scarred, if you looked closely. "You heal up good."

I grunted. Swung the backpack over my shoulder, and

left the room. On the other side of the hotel, I raised my hand to knock at a room door. Inside, I heard the same announcer, still talking about me, and the rumors surrounding me. She said, "Some sources think it's possible that Jane Yellowrock may not even be strictly human herself." *That's just hunky-dory.* Derek already had questions about who and what I was.

I knocked and Derek opened the door. Fast. As if he had been expecting me. He was still wearing his suit from the night's work and he held a handgun at his side. His gaze whipped over me and settled on my throat. In my peripheral vision, I saw him unlatch the safety, his finger moving smoothly. Not good. I tensed, knowing that even drawing on Beast-speed, I wasn't faster than a bullet fired at point-blank range by a trained killer. "What happened to the scar?" His voice was low, emotionless, an interrogator, who intended to scare the crap out of his witness.

A knot rose in my throat, but my voice, when I spoke, was steady. "I took six months off after that kill. It took me that long to heal." Which was the truth, as far as it went.

"Skin grafts?"

"Something like that." Actually shifting two or three times a week, letting my body heal from the wound that had nearly decapitated me, but I wasn't sharing that with him.

"And your eyes in the film? You got an explanation for that?"

"No."

Suddenly Derek chuckled. "Injun Princess, did I ever tell you I was Creek Indian on my mama's side?"

"No." I wondered if Creeks had a skinwalker mythos. I wondered if he guessed about me.

He laughed again, slanting his eyes at me as he reset the safety. I remembered to breathe. "Watchu want Injun Princess?"

"Keys to one of the SUVs. Preferably one fully trucked out." Meaning one full of com gear, an onboard computer system, GPS, some extra armor plating built in, weapons, and all the other bells and whistles that Leo had provided. Though he didn't ask, and as the titular head of security on this gig, I didn't have to volunteer, I added, "They don't know it yet, but I'm joining the cops and the SAR team this morning." When he raised his brows, I said, "SAR, park service and civilian-speak for Search and Rescue."

Derek holstered his weapon and walked across the room. I heard metal clink against glass. "I'll call for valet parking to bring it around. You need backup?" He tossed a set of keys to me. I caught them one-handed.

"No." I stepped from his room and closed his door, moving fast, down the hallway. I knew Derek wasn't exactly a friend, but the sliding safety-off move had caught me off guard. It showed what our relationship was. And wasn't. In front of the hotel, I slid into the driver's seat of a partially armored SUV and closed the door. On the way past, I studied the protestors from behind the heavily tinted, bullet-resistant windows. Their signs were not particularly innovative, but they communicated their desires well enough: STAKE ALL VAMPS. VAMPS DIE! CUT OFF THE FANGHEADS. GOD GAVE THE WORLD TO HUMANS. That kind of thing.

I initiated the GIS, merged that info with the GPS as I drove. Buncombe County used GIS, the Geographic Information System, which was part of NC OneMap, a sort of geospatial backbone, mapping, and information project of the state, used by law enforcement, park rangers, realtors, and others who wanted to pay the fee. It allowed info about GPS positions, addresses, parcels of land, individual mountain peaks, etc., to be downloaded onto a spreadsheet or printable map, and was especially helpful in the steep, mountainous land of the county. Leo had provided us access to the system, making my job a lot easier and finding the cops nearly effortless.

It was after eight a.m. when I arrived at the location shown on early morning TV. If this new attack site had been a media zoo so early, it was a circus now. There were seven vans with satellite dishes on top: national broadcast news, local cable, and national cable. A dozen cop cars from different agencies were parked haphazardly among them: Asheville PD, Buncombe County Rescue Squad, a truck with the logo RRT, which was the interagency Regional Response Team, as well as sheriff deputy vehicles. There were maybe forty privately owned vehicles, mostly trucks, and most with stickers on the windows proving them to be owned by trained rescue volunteers. I saw two rescue support trucks, emitting strong odors of burnt coffee and greasy fast food. There was one ambulance, the paramedics sitting in the shade of a tree, chatting. Three trucks had cages in back for canine search units. Which meant that the cops were having trouble finding either the camping/attack site, or had found it and were hunting whatever scent the dogs had discovered. People milled everywhere.

I exited the SUV away from the cameras, tossed my pre-packed backpack over a shoulder, and melted into the trees to find the sheriff standing in the shade, shielded by heavy foliage from the view of the cameras. He stood with three other men and a woman at a makeshift portable table, a series of aerial maps in front of him, a laptop open to the side. Sheriff Grizzard had been in office for several years, surviving into his second term, and was already running for a third. He was a hale-fellow-well-met politician, a savvy back-slapping elected official. He didn't exactly hate me and all I stood for, but at one time he had blamed me for Paul Braxton's death, and had done everything in his power to put me in jail. There was no evidence against me, but Grizzard's detective, and Molly's friend, had been killed on my watch. I had survived. I could understand his animosity.

I stood, half-hidden behind a tree, drawing on Beast's better hearing, listening to the murmured conversation. From it, I gathered that the search area had been divided into grids early on, the campsite discovered just after dawn. The injured had been hauled up the mountain in rescue baskets and medevaced out. The dead were still in place. Crime scene investigators were working the site, which was widely scattered. And the dogs were tracking the things that had attacked the campers. Things. Multiples.

"I say it's fangheads, maybe with some sorta spell to hide their footprints, or maybe like that weird thing that killed those people in Louisiana." The speaker was a short fellow with a full brown beard. He spat to the side, a spew of tobacco, and patted the wad of leaves deeper into his jaw with an index finger. He wiped it on his jeans and kept talking. "Part fanghead, part something else." He was talking about a liver-eater, and I'd only ever seen or heard of one, but it was a good guess. The damage made by meat-eating predators was often similar. "Vamp and magic and shit." He added, "Maybe it's that woman who come back from there."

"I don't think Jane Yellowrock mauled three people and left them to die, then killed three more and ate them," Grizzard said.

"Okay, then—that leaves fangheads," the shorter man said firmly. "Never trust something that wants to eat you or drink you dry." Which sounded like good advice to me.

"Put in a call to Yellowrock," Grizzard said. "Let's get her take on this. If it's the same kind of creature she killed in New Orleans, that makes her the resident expert." He didn't sound happy. And Deputy Sam Orson didn't look happy when he pulled a cell phone from his pocket.

I sighed. This was not gonna be fun. Before my phone could ring, I stepped from behind the tree and walked closer, deliberately stepping on branch when I was halfway there. Grizzard looked up. My cell rang. I answered as I entered the area. "Yellowrock."

The deputy looked at me, looked at his phone, and disconnected. I lifted a hand. Closed my phone. "Sheriff. Sam." I nodded to the woman, "Betty." I didn't know the others but included them in my general greeting, "Morning."

"And you're here why?" Grizzard said. Trust Grizzard to go for bad-cop attitude first thing. Maybe he did it with everyone. Maybe he saved it just for me.

"I saw the tracks yesterday in Hartford," I said, dropping into the short simple sentences of cops on a crime scene or soldiers on an Op. "I was wondering if the same things attacked here. Wondered if I could help. You *were* just calling me, right, Sam? Sheriff?" I lifted the cell, which showed a dropped call from this area code.

Sam gave a half smile. We had lifted a few beers the night of Brax's funeral. More than a few, actually. He had gotten totally wasted. My skinwalker metabolism hadn't let me find that kind of release, but I had done my best to keep up with him. Then I drove him home in his own car and helped his girlfriend get him into bed. I hadn't seen him since. He was now wearing a wedding ring and ten extra pounds. "Yeah," Sam said. "Good to see you, Yellowrock."

"You got pics of tracks?" I asked.

Grizzard jerked his head to the side, a command for me

to come on over. With that simple gesture, I was accepted into the search group. My breathing settled and my shoulders relaxed. It was good to be home. I tucked my thumbs in my jeans pockets, leaving my fingers dangling while Grizzard punched some keys on the laptop. A photo covered the screen, a close-up shot of a paw print. I set my spread hand on the table top. "About that wide?" I asked.

"Near enough," Grizzard said. He hit a key and another shot appeared, this one with a ruler beside it. A small test to see if I really knew what I was talking about or was just blowing smoke. "Same thing that you killed in Louisiana? Half vamp?" I shook my head no. "Same thing that attacked that couple yesterday?"

"Likely," I said. "Werewolf." The cops around me shifted. Two put their hands on their gun butts, cop reaction. "There were two wolves at that site. They were trying to turn the girl. The man got in the way. You saw the mug shots, already, I take it."

Grizzard sighed. Betty said, "So it's true? They'll turn into *werewolves*?" Unspoken was the worry that anyone who fought the weres could suffer an injury and go furry at the next full moon. Cops sign up for the danger, but some risks make even the best of them uneasy.

"No." I pulled my phone and scrolled through the text messages that came in during the night. "I asked the New Orleans vamps for a healer. Aaaaand"—I spotted one from Bruiser, clicked on it, and interpreted the text—"a Mercy Blade is coming in tonight from Charlotte. Her name is Gertruda," which might be German or might be a typo.

"What. Some fanghead is gonna bleed the kid? Not gonna happen," the tobacco chewer said. He shifted his weapon in its holster and spat again.

I took note where not to step. "She's not a vamp." Which was the truth as far as it went. Mercy Blades were anzus, feathered birdlike creatures once worshipped as storm gods, now hiding among humans and vamps, under layers of glamours. I didn't tell them that part. They didn't ask. This should be interesting. "I was bitten by werewolves once. A Mercy Blade got to me in time and healed me of the taint."

"Yeah?" Grizzard looked me over as if looking for dog

ears and a tail. "Is she gonna stay a while?" he asked. Meaning would others have access to her services. The people bitten at the crime scene below. Cops in the future.

I texted a short line into the phone. "I'm requesting an extended stay until the weres are brought down." I pocketed the cell and changed topics. "Back to the tracks. Was there another track, a weird one, maybe on top of the were-paw tracks? Like it was stalking them?"

The group exchanged looks that excluded me. Grizzard said, "Can you describe them?"

"Pen?" He placed one in my hand and slid a scrap of paper to me. I was no artist but I could draw grindy tracks. Most any moderately talented three-year-old could. I sketched in the three-toed tracks, the middle longer than the others, claws like sickles. I could tell by the way the small group froze up that the tracks had been found at the crime scene.

"It's from a creature called a grindylow," I said. "Ugly little green thing about four feet tall. It hunts weres that break were-law. If we can find it, we might learn something from it." And I might be able to convince the little creature to join forces with me. Didn't tell them that either. I couldn't lie worth a dang, but lying by omission? I was learning to do that real well.

"We're not releasing that to the public," Grizzard instructed.

"Fine by me. The press is plastering my name and likeness all over the airwaves. They aren't my best pals." I thought I had worked my way into their good graces and so I took a shot. "Can I see the site?"

Grizzard nodded to Sam. "Orson, take her on down."

Relief poured through me. "One last suggestion," I said. "Weres are really hard to kill. Silvershot may not kill them any faster than regular ammo, but silver *will* hurt them. Bad. If they suffer a wound—say silvershot double-oughts—I don't think they can change form to heal until the silver is surgically removed, forcing them to stay in the form they were in when injured. Left in them long enough, it'll poison their bloodstream. If you want, I got a local guy who handloads my rounds with silver fléchettes. I killed several in New Orleans with them."

"You've killed these things?"

"Yeah." I looked into the trees, down the slope. They had nearly killed me, but I left that out too. Lying was getting easier. I waited for some guilt but nothing happened. It was Sunday morning; I should be getting ready for church instead of lying to cops. Yeah. I was going to hell.

"Name? Cost?" Grizzard barked.

I gave him the name and contact info for the guy who hand-loaded my rounds. "I can't tell you the cost. That's dependent on the market value of silver, the amount of silver he uses in the fléchettes, a whole bunch of factors."

"Okay. Take her down. Don't fuck up my crime scene, Yellowrock."

"You're such a softie."

Before he could reply, Sam grabbed my elbow and pulled me away. "You never did know when to shut your mouth," he growled.

I looked down at him and grinned. "You can't hold your liquor."

Sam Orson did a little eye-roll-blow-out-breath thing and pulled me down the hill. On the breeze I smelled blood. Dead meat. Human.

CHAPTER SEVEN

Vigilante Law's Got No Place in My County

The hundred square feet inside the yellow crime scene tape reeked of human blood, werewolf, and dead fish to my sensitive nose. The three humans the weres had feasted on were still near the tents, buzzing with flies. The smell in the campsite had drawn a murder of crows, sitting in trees, watching, waiting. One turned and looked at me, cocking its head to the side in a movement reminiscent of the way vamps move when they aren't trying to ape humanity. Or when they don't care if someone sees their true nature. I held my face still, nonreactive, and studied the scene, walking around the perimeter, viewing it from every angle. Some of the crime scene techs were bagging evidence, marking where each body part or piece of evidence was found. Others were taking photos or making notes or putting down little evidence markers for new physical trace to be added into the bigger picture.

The campers had been attacked in the night, the wolves rushing in from the west, tearing into the tents, then into the sleeping campers. Three had been killed quickly. Three others had run into the woods and been chased. "What did the surviving campers say?" I asked.

"They were chased, knocked down, bitten, and let go."

"All of the live ones were female," I stated.

Sam studied me as I analyzed the scene. "How did you know that? We implied to the press that the one who called for help was male."

"Three tents, three coolers, three bear-bags of food. All the dead and eaten ones are male, but you have female clothing of different sizes scattered all over the site. I admit to an assumption that it wasn't six cross-dressers, ergo three couples." Sam snorted softly. "Also, the werewolves in New Orleans were trying to make mates. Werewolves aren't like other weres. They don't breed true. The only way they procreate is to bite a human." Of all the weres—the Cursed of Artemis—the wolves were the ones still sick, and the disease that made them two-natured and furry also meant they weren't the brightest bulbs in the chandelier. I finished, "Females who are bitten don't survive, or if they do, they go insane and into permanent heat."

Sam sucked in a breath as the words sank in. There was so much I couldn't say to the cops, but the effects on the victims could not be kept secret. I thought about the grainy, poor quality photograph of Itty Bitty: delicate features, big blue eyes, pretty. I closed my eyes, feeling the gritty dryness of exhaustion. "Where did the wolves enter the campsite?" I asked, though I already knew, having tracked the scent on the wind.

Sam pointed uphill. "They came in from a church parking lot, up that hill there, about three miles. Went out the same way."

"Dogs tell you that?"

Sam snorted. "Dogs got all squirrely soon as the handlers drove up. Every single one. Went into full-blown panic mode. One bit his handler. Fu—freaking terrified." I grinned at his careful change of wording. Cops aren't known for their diplomatic language, but Sam was trying. "The handlers took them down to the river after the three-toed thing instead. What did you call it?"

"Grindy. Short for grindylow," I said. "I need inside the perimeter, closer to the vics. Tell me where I can step and where I can't. Then I want to see where the grindy came in from."

"The grindy came from a stream at the bottom of the crevice," he pointed. "I ain't going down there. The fall'll

kill ya," he quoted from an old movie. "And so will the hike
back up."

"Okay. Walk me in." Placing my feet into Sam's footprints, I got close enough to the victims to verify that they
had been dinner. I'd seen a herd of deer after a werewolf
pack tore into them. This was a lot like that. I also smelled
witch blood, and since few male witches survive to adult-
hood, it likely meant that one of the bitten women was a
witch. Itty Bitty was of witch blood. This wasn't coincidence. The wolves had tried turning human women for
mates and it didn't work. Now it looked like they were going for witches.

Sam said, "Turned them into manburger," and chuckled
softly, the way cops do to separate themselves from carnage. It made them colder and harder than other humans,
but it also kept them sane. I understood that, and didn't
respond.

Grindy-marks and tracks were pressed into the edges of
the kill-site, indicating that the little green Yoda-golem-
wolf-killer came upon the site after the killing. Maybe several hours after. The grindy didn't have access to modern
transportation and had to swim, hence the tracks up from
the stream below.

As I worked, thoughts floated through my mind, a free
association that meant nothing until my subconscious
found the linchpin and tied everything together with a satin
bow. Useless, tired thoughts like: *I need to find the grindy
and pair up with him to track the weres, speeding both our
searches. But I have no idea how to find him. I wish I had
access to a dog form by day, to scent-track. But if I shift, I'll
be stuck in the shape until moonrise or nightfall, whichever
comes soonest. And if I come upon the wolves in dog form?
No dog has the natural weapons of a werewolf. I'd be Jane-
burger.* And lastly I noted that the wolves had been particularly grisly in the way they had attacked and eaten the men,
going for maximum impact—leaving a message.

I crossed the crime scene tape again and was back on
the periphery, leaving Sam chatting to a tech, when I
smelled something unexpected. I placed Sam and the
techs—all were busy—before dropping to my knees in the
brush, the small backpack riding up under my arms. I

moved across the ground on four limbs, half crawling. The scent was faint, the reek of old, dried blood, overlaid and almost masked by pungent were-scent. On hands and knees, I followed the old-blood odor to a pile of leaves at the base of a tree. Checked the others again, finding them involved in their jobs, Sam discussing manburger with a tech. I reached in and rustled through the leaves. My fingers encountered something hard and cool. Metal. I palmed it and eased it out.

It was Rick's key chain, the old one the wolves had access to when they had him prisoner. I had seen his new one yesterday, enamel black leopard. This one was plain, on a worn-out biner. I'd seen it many times, but it was best identified by the old scent of his blood.

The wolves dropped it, not by accident, but knowing it would be found. I palmed the keys, putting things together. I'd taken on the two surviving wolves of the Lupus Pack and won, as no human could have, not even with an element of surprise. They had bitten me, tasted my blood. They knew I wasn't human. The weres were goading me, challenging me. *Come and get us. If you can.* And not just me. They had taken down victims, tried to turn them, in the Pigeon River at the bottom of Stirling Mountain. Which is where Rick and Kem were staying. Weres lived by smell, so they knew the were-cats were there. On the surface, the attack had been intended to turn humans. On the underside, it sent a message to me, Rick, and Kemnebi, leader of PAW, the Party of African Weres. I was the one who had brought Kem-cat and Rick here, which made it all my fault. *Crap.* I pocketed the key chain and jogged around the crime scene to Sam. "Describe the bottom of the gorge for me?"

He walked to the edge and looked down the mountain. "Thirty, maybe forty degree slope. Near vertical further down. Dangerous going and damn hard work coming back up. Debris-clogged storm runoff at the bottom."

I thought about my paddler buddies. "Is it something that could be paddled or rafted?"

"Not by anyone sane, sober, or with ten functioning brain cells."

I snorted softly. "Yeah, well, it was just a thought."

"A stupid one."

I lifted a hand and jogged away, back up the mountain. When I reached Grizzard's position, hidden among the trees, he called out, "You learn anything?"

I thought about the key chain in my pocket, and knew Grizzard saw something cross my face. I had never been good at lying, and lying to cops was harder still. "Mmm," I said, and scratched my chin thoughtfully. "I think there are only two, and they're looking to make mates."

Grizzard grunted. "Damn supes."

"Yeah, well. The grindylow is on the humans' side. Tell your guys to be on the lookout for a green Yoda with fangs and claws, about four feet tall. Don't shoot it. It's your friend."

Grizzard's eyes narrowed. "This grindy better not take the law into his hands. Vigilante law's got no place in my county."

I chuckled. "You corner the wolves, and they'll go down fighting. Which means your men stand a chance of being injured and waking up furry. Then, if you do manage to subdue them, you have to put them in a cage strong enough to hold them, then feed them, and care for them, even when they go furry. Werewolves are more dangerous than any other supernatural creature, even a vamp. They're literally insane. Let the grindy do his job. Just my advice."

"I'll take it under consideration. You guarantee that fangheads didn't do this?" He jerked his head vaguely down the mountain.

"Guarantee." I looked at my watch. I had missed church. Dang it.

CHAPTER EIGHT

You Chasing the Big Doggies?

I drove away, pulling up the GIS maps and Google and Yahoo! and MSR Maps, which offered aerial views that could be overlaid with or exchanged for street maps. I found an unnamed access road that might take me partway down, and hoped the MOC's vehicles were as good off-road as they were on. And hoped the extra weight of the armor wouldn't be a hindrance to getting back out. I made it halfway down the gorge, finding a place to execute a tight three-point turn that was more like a ten-point turn, the wheels threatening to slide off the narrow trail and carry me all the way down. I parked facing back up the hill, drank a liter of water, added two more to my pack, and took off, down to the bottom, hoping to end up at the convergence of another creek. It was a harrowing descent, and I worked up a sweat.

The Smoky Mountains are rain forest, creating their own mini-climates at different elevations and disrupting the natural west-to-east trade winds. The temperatures dropped the lower I went, and the air grew progressively more damp. The morning sun disappeared, an afternoon angle needed to warm the west-facing mountain wall. A mist grew around me, wispy and thin in long vertical strips, the mist for which the Smoky Mountains had been named. It stuck to my skin and clothes, cold and clammy. Small rills and runnels formed and merged, splashing down vertical rock faces and cutting into the mountain floor. My sweat chilled and my breath was loud in my ears, my palms growing raw from roots and trees, sliding across bark and rock that decelerated my descent.

Though surely the land had been surveyed, it looked as though no one had been here since the deforestation in the 1920s. I found no human trails, but lots of rabbit sign, deer scat and tracks, and ample bear sign: dead trees clawed for grubs, a honeybee nest high in a tree showing fresh claw marks and bark damage where the bear had climbed. And once I saw what looked like mountain lion sign, old scat, dried and strewn. Beast held me still, a paw on my mind, studying the scat with all her senses. My mouth opened and upper lip pulled back, sucking the scent in through nose and mouth, but my mostly human scenting ability left Beast nearly head-blind. She looked up the mountain, and spotted a tree with vertical claw markings from the ground up to about two feet. *Mountain lion?* I thought at her.

Finally she thought at me, uncertain, *Bobcat. Male.*
When? I asked.
Last snow time. Maybe.

Last year. Winter. I stood still, bringing in the scents of the place, smelling rushing water rising on the breeze, deer, bear, rabbit, opossum and raccoon, numerous birds, the dry reek of snake musk, polecat, and skunk. No large cats. I moved on down the mountain, Beast alert and curious. *Hunting dead-fish-smell green thing?* she asked.

I laughed, the only human sound in the gorge. "Yes."
Kill and eat it?

"No. Definitely not. It's hunting the werewolves."

Beast hissed, deep in my mind. *Kill and leave wolves to rot. Killers of winter food. Thieves of meat. Wasters of meat.* There were few more horrible insults from Beast than *wasters of meat.* She said nothing else, but I appreciated her focus. She often saw and smelled things that I missed or ignored because I didn't know what they meant. Like the scat and the claw marks.

I reached bottom an hour after I left the sheriff, and stopped on the edge on the creek, straddling a downed tree. The movement of water was quiet here, where I sat on the bank in the sun, my feet shuffled beneath last fall's leaves, but I could hear the roar of water just ahead, where I thought the confluence should be, and from upstream, where it obviously took a drop. Hurricane Ivanna was sweeping slowly up the Mississippi River basin and dumping torrents of water to our west. Projections had it turning east, right for us, with forecasts of four to six inches of rain over two days. Soon this creek would be a raging torrent.

Lunch was protein bars, nuts, three brownies, and two bananas. It left me feeling full but not satisfied. I stored the paper and plastic, and tossed the peels high on the bank, knowing some veggie-loving animal would eat them despite the bitter taste. The pack much lighter, I headed downstream, watching the banks for grindy-sign. The sound of water on stone grew and the air was wetter with mist.

I spotted the three vertical claw marks just before I got to the confluence. They were slashed into solid granite, the fresh cuts still bright in the sun. I placed my fingers into the slash marks, finding the stone dry despite the heavy mist. I had just missed the grindy. "Dang," I whispered. Below the slash marks were three-toed prints with claw marks deep in the soil.

I pushed on another twenty yards and stopped in the vapor, above the merging of two creeks. It wasn't a peaceful marriage, more like a shotgun wedding, with noise and complaints roaring. The water formed a violent eddy, the water of the two currents hitting and rising in a foamy wall a foot high. The water churned so hard it flowed upstream for thirty feet in one place, a midsized beaver-gnawed log caught, swirling, and making no headway downstream. Other logs were trapped in rocks, held firm by the push of the water, making a sieve that collected and held everything solid carried by the water. Tires, two-by-fours, a torn mattress, buckets and paint cans, clothing, whole trees with leaves and roots were caught in the maelstrom.

The body of a deer was trapped on the pile farthest upstream, only the haunches and upper rear legs visible, flies buzzing, even in the wet mist. Downstream, the strainers were even worse, the bottom of the gorge filled with logs and human debris.

From my pack, I took a camera and snapped pictures, noting the GPS location. Sam was right. No one in his right mind would navigate the creek, not with the sieves and strainers that clogged the waterway. I had missed the grindy. The only thing I had accomplished all day was to prove to myself that the wolves were responsible for the mauling and killing and that the grindy was on their trail. Which I had presumed from the markings and the attack at the Pigeon River. Disgruntled, I made my way back up the mountain to the SUV for the difficult drive back to a real road. *I could have taken the helo,* I thought. Beast hissed with displeasure.

I was nodding at the wheel by the time I made it back to Hartford, on the Tennessee side of the mountains, but I couldn't stop for the day. Not yet. I called Dave and Mike and both were available for an early supper/coffee/beer, as long as I was buying. Leo had given me a company credit card, and I intended to use it.

The afternoon was hot and airless; the air-conditioning and dim lighting of the Bean Trees Café was welcome. Mike ordered appetizers—garlic cheese fries, homemade onion rings, sweet potato fries. Though Beast turned up her nose at cooked meat, we all ordered burgers, loaded. The guys got beer, microbrewery stuff that I really wanted to try, but knew might make me sleepier, even with my Beast-hyped metabolism. I ordered a double espresso so I could make it back to Asheville without falling asleep. I wasn't a coffee lover, preferring tea, but caffeine was one drug that my skinwalker metabolism did respond to. I was more awake when the food came.

"Most of the creeks between here and Asheville in Buncombe County run east to west across the mountains," Mike said, his voice carrying even over the busload of noisy tourists. "They're confined to the French Broad River Basin and empty into the Tennessee River Basin, and then into Mississippi River Basin."

Meaning that they were attached to the Pigeon River, burbling just outside the café. Got it. He pulled a creased map from his pocket while I wiped my hands on a pile of napkins, swallowing down the last mouthful of Black and Blue Burger. I drank some coffee. And while it was still going down, said, "Okay. So the grindylow can get to most anywhere without ever leaving the water, especially when summer was so wet, and fall looking like it'll follow the same path. Show me the locations of the grindy-marks the creekers and hikers have seen."

Mike, wearing a red T-shirt, with a do-rag of the American flag on his head, unfolded the map with the grindy-signs that had been noted by the paddlers, hair-head creekers, and hikers. There were a lot of them. A *lot* of them. I counted the ones just on the Pigeon and the creeks nearby, and came up with over thirty sites. The grindy was claiming some major territory. I hadn't seen anything like that in New Orleans. But then, there were no rocks there, and I hadn't been looking for trees with slash marks. The guys had compiled the research, saving me time. I flipped open my cell and dialed Bruiser, Leo Pellissier's right-hand blood-meal.

"What, Yellowrock?" He sounded irritated.

"Bruiser. Quick question. When the grindylow was swimming in the fountain at vamp HQ, did it leave any claw marks in the marble? Like the ones in its bedroom when it trashed the place?"

"No. Is that all?"

That was just weird. Why mark now, and not then? "No. The grindy's searching for the wolves. I'm hiring some paddlers and hikers to help me search for the grindy, hoping it will work with me and lead me to the wolves. I'm paying the paddlers twice their going rate to take them away from their businesses. I'll need Ernestine to deposit electronic checks into their accounts. I'll e-mail the numbers to her."

"Fine."

I looked at the cell, thinking that Bruiser was awfully short-tempered for a guy who'd nearly had his way with me in the shower not so long ago. I put the phone back to my ear. "Thanks." I closed the cell. "Okay. Money's not a problem. Name and double your fee for the info you're collecting. The vamps want the weres caught and handled." I ate some sweet potato fries while studying the map and, with the other hand, pointed to three creeks, close to Asheville: Spring Creek, Big Laurel Creek, and Bushy Creek. "This is the farthest east the grindy marks have been seen, and there seem to be a lot of them here, too. Maybe more than up Stirling Mountain."

"There may be more in other places, but they don't get the traffic, even in the touron season," a river guide said from over my shoulder. It was the guide with the silver stud in his tongue. At my curious look, he said, "Tourist? Moron? Touron."

I gave him a small smile. I laid my cell on the table, the fancy one paid for by Leo, the one with all the bells and whistles, including a map-app and GPS tracking. "Here's where I was this afternoon." I pointed to the GPS coordinates. "Is this close to any of these creeks?"

Dave took over, aligning my coordinates with the ones on the map. "That's a feeder creek not far from where Shelton Creek and Laurel merge to become Big Laurel Creek," he said, his damaged voice soft but still carrying over the screams of the tourists' children.

"So, here, here, and here"—I pointed to the places on the North Carolina side of the mountain range—"he's marked several dozen times. And all three creeks are within hiking distance of the kill-site of last night's attack. So maybe the weres have a hidey-hole somewhere in this area too."

"There's hundreds of rental and camping places, and thousands of empty, unused places where someone could squat for the summer," Mike said, "and they'd never be noticed."

"Mmm," I murmured, considering the map, eating more sweet potato fries and licking my fingers free of grease between bites. I tilted my head to follow the overlay of streets and recognized the street where Molly lived. She was at the top of a mountain above one of the grindy-marked feeder creeks. All the blood left my face in a cold rush. A painful tingling started in my fingers. "Crap," I whispered. Two of the smaller creeks were on either side of the mountain ridge where my best friend, her husband, and kids lived.

Beast woke up and rolled to her feet in my mind, a low growl vibrating through me. *Kits,* she thought, hunching as if preparing to leap.

Two of Molly's sisters lived just down the mountain from her. Angie's school wasn't far away either. I stood up and turned the map again. The third creek was near a road that went right by my old apartment, the one I'd moved out of when I thought I'd be staying in New Orleans for a while.

If the grindy was hunting wolves, then the wolves were hunting me. I sat and dialed.

Angelina, Molly's daughter, my godchild, answered. "Hey, Aunt Jane. You chasing the big doggies?"

The feeling of cold spread through me. "Angie Baby, have you seen some big doggies?"

Mike and Dave stopped midmotion and focused on me.

"Yep. Two of 'em. They standed up on two feets and looked in my window. I stuck-ted my tongue out at them and made some black light and they ran away."

Black light. Were's had gotten through the wards on her house, and Angie had used her gift to chase them off, both of which were bad. *Crap. Crap, crap,* crap! In so many conflicting ways. Angie wasn't supposed to be able to draw on her witch gift until puberty, but the little girl had the witch gene from both mother and father, and her gift had come upon her early. Even with her parents binding her gift down, she was scary strong. She knew things she shouldn't far too often, as if the gift was searching out ways to express itself and had found an opening in prescience and in knowing what was happening to the people she loved. But when the wolves got close, she used the gift to protect herself and her family. Which was good. Wasn't it? "Angie, let me talk to your mother, okay?"

"Okeydokey. Mama!" she screamed in my ear. I pulled the phone away. "Aunt Jane!"

"Big-Cat, what's up?" Mol said a moment later.

"Hang up, Angie," I said. I heard the click, though Angelina had ways of knowing what was going on other than eavesdropping. I swallowed, feeling my stomach contents rise. "Did Angie tell you about the dogs at her window?"

"Yeah," Molly said, drawing out the word.

"Could have been werewolves."

There was a long silence, and I could almost see Molly testing the wards on and around her home. "Hmmm," she said, her voice dropping an octave. "We have them set to allow wildlife through. Looks like we need to change a few settings." *Change a few settings* was Mol's way of talking to me about magic. She knew I'd never understand if she used real magic vernacular.

"Mol. They're looking to make mates. Human females

don't survive the werewolf taint. Maybe they think a witch might have a better chance. Tell your sisters. Be careful."

"I saw the mug shots on TV. They followed you here, didn't they?"

Molly was smart. Sometimes too smart for my comfort level. "Could be," I admitted.

"Big Evan will have a cow. So don't tell him. I gotta go, Jane."

She called me *Jane*. Which meant she wasn't happy with me. "Bye, Mol," I said, feeling properly rebuked. She hung up without saying good-bye. Great. I was putting the family of my best friend in the world in danger. Again. If Big Evan found out I was responsible for this latest situation, he'd skin me alive and I'd deserve it, totally.

Weary and sleepy, I tucked the cell into my pocket and ate the last of the sweet potato fries before heading to the parking lot where I climbed into the SUV and sat with the air-conditioning running, thinking. I could drive up the mountain and visit with Rick, but . . . Guilt and exhaustion in equal measure taunted me. Exhaustion won. I wheeled the heavy vehicle out of the Bean Trees lot and onto the interstate. Away from Rick. Chicken, yeah, that's me. I'd rather fight an old rogue-vamp in my underwear, with my bare hands, than deal with relationship problems.

I motored back to Asheville along Highway 70. Along the way I crossed over Big Laurel and Spring Creek where Mike and Dave said there were multiple grindy marks. Because the summer had been so wet, they were running, but only enough to support smallmouth bass, not a boat. The rocks I could spot from the road were smaller than the boulders on Big Creek, the runs looked twisty but easy. But what did I know? Less and less the longer I lived.

Back at the hotel, I dropped off the vehicle with the valet and found my room by feel and smell. Way past exhausted, I showered off the sweat, fell onto my bed, and wrapped up in the sheets; I was asleep instantly.

And woke just as quickly. *Predator in my den,* Beast thought at me. *Human male. Stranger.*

Someone was entering my room. Yeah, there had been knocking. My sleeping mind had ignored it, thinking it was housekeeping. Thinking they'd see the DO NOT DISTURB sign and go away. He hadn't seen the sign because he'd entered from the twins' adjoining suite.

I didn't move, my breathing steady and slow, listening, eyes slanted open a crack. Afternoon light angled through the window blinds. I'd been asleep for several hours and was now lying on my stomach, hair everywhere, pillow pushed away, hands buried under it, thick comforter bunched at my side, hiding me from the sitting area. And obscuring my view of the intruder.

Two guns were on the nightstand, three feet away. I'd have to push upright, roll, grab, off-safety, aim, and squeeze the trigger. If he was armed, I'd be dead. The knives were on the coffee table several feet away. My weapons might as well be in Europe. And there might be people in the next room. Others in the hallway. *Collateral damage.* All I had was speed, bed linens, and pillows. Not much to use against an attacker. I was naked. Vulnerable. Alone. But then, he didn't know I was here, what weapons I might be holding, or were at my sides in the sheets. A tiny point in my favor. Or not. His uncertainty might make him kill me first and ask questions later.

Need claws, Beast thought. *Shift.*

I clenched my hands and relaxed them. Once, and only once, I had brought Beast's claws to my human hands. But I had no idea how I'd done it, and it didn't happen now. *Too far away for claws,* I thought back to her. She hissed, but didn't disagree, so I lay unmoving. Listening. Thinking. Beside the bed was another weapon I could use. It offered no precision, and was more along the lines of brute force, but it might give me time.

My intruder was stealthy, silent except for his breathing. Human blood-servant by his scent. Unfamiliar vamp-taint marked him, but it was old. He hadn't fed from his master's blood in days. He wore soft-soled shoes and unscented deodorant, no cologne. He hadn't seen me yet, hadn't killed me. I appreciated that in a man. But I smelled gun oil and lubricants. Yeah. He was armed. By the movement of air, I placed him. He was at the couch, looking over my weapons on the coffee table, paying special attention to my Benelli M4 shotgun. It was my baby, and was loaded for vamp with silver. If he tried to take it, I'd tackle him, weapon or no weapon. He moved to my clothes, which I'd left piled on a chair. I heard the faint movement of cloth and leather as he went through my pockets and inspected my boots. He needed to turn away before I could move. I felt more than saw when he noticed me. Adrenaline poured into the air, the scent sharp and spiky as cactus. *Now or never.* I drew Beast up into me, pulling her strength into my bloodstream.

In one smooth motion I slid my hands down, beneath me. Pushed up and off the bed, whirling. Grabbing the bust of the founding father, its weight and my momentum continuing my spiral. Seeing the man, turning, raising his arm. Faster than human. I released the statue with as much force as I could power through shoulders, arms, fingertips. Grunting softly with the effort. Slung my hair out of the way. Grabbed the Walther PK380. Had it in hand when the bust impacted his body.

His soft *oof* was surprise more than pain. But it was enough to screw up his aim. The suppressor on his weapon made little spats of sound like books dropping. Mine was much louder.

CHAPTER NINE

Wrong Century, White Boy

I dove hard toward the foot of the mattress and down. Firing twice more as I fell behind the bed. I hit hard, right elbow taking the impact. Fingers going numb on the gun. Rolling back toward the intruder. Scrambling to my knees. Smelling blood on the air. Not mine. Panting.

The doorjamb shattered, the door blown open by sheer muscle power. The twins were in the room. Their movements blood-servant fast. Weapons drawn. One twin held his weapon in a palm-supported grip. One twin with a handgun in each hand. They rushed the guy. He went down, cursing, writhing on the floor, my rounds making him bleed.

Brandon took my gun and set it on the table. Turned me around, looking for blood, evidence of injury. When he found none, he tossed me a robe. Brian dialed 911. Derek and Wrassler raced in to the room. So did hotel security. It was chaos. And soon after, local cops arrived, to drag me down to the law enforcement center. At least they let me dress first.

"So, you don't know who the guy is, why he had no ID, why he was in your room, or why he was carrying illegal, with a mounted suppressor. You don't know anything. This guy just slipped into your room and started shooting at you."

"Pretty much," I said. The Chief of Police, Billy Chandler, liked me even less than Grizzard did, but Billy's dislike was just on principle, not because I'd gotten one of his men killed. Billy didn't like anyone carrying concealed in his town, and he didn't like tall motorcycle mamas with an arsenal and an attitude, guarding troublemaking fangheads in his town. Of course, he'd liked me no more when I'd just killed vamps for a living, and he liked vamps even less than he did me. *Cops.* Can't live with 'em, can't live without 'em. Which brought Rick to mind. I shoved the memory of his scent down deep inside.

"To carry concealed, blades have to be less than six inches long. North Carolina law," Billy said. "The shortest one in your possession is twelve inches."

I almost said, "Penis envy?" but clamped down on my big mouth. I love messing with cops, and one day I was gonna mess with the wrong one. But I was getting smarter. Finally. I couldn't stop the grin, however, and Billy's eyes narrowed as if he'd heard the words anyway. "I wasn't carrying concealed," I said, sounding reasonable and calm. "The blades were on the table." Not to say that I didn't carry them concealed. I did. Often. And if stopped by the cops, I'd use the Vampira Carta as my defense, not that the reasoning would get me very far, but it was all I had.

"And you don't know who he is?"

"Nope." He'd asked me that ten times in the last hour. I'd had enough. I waved at the one-way mirror and pointed at my Coke can. "Can I have a refill here? The service in this joint is awful." I looked at the chief. "No tip, this time, Billy." Back at the mirror, I yelled, "You guys got all my money. Put some into a machine for me, would you?"

Billy shifted on the hard table. He was sitting on the edge, trying to tower over me, trying to use height to cow me. And though I'd never say so, it was working, sorta. I was six feet tall in my bare feet. In boots I was way taller than most men, and wasn't used to them looming over me. So I shrank down lower in my seat, slumping, and stuck my feet out the other side. I held the empty can up again, flicking it with a fingernail, making it tink.

After a long, tinking moment, he said, "You're a pain in the ass, Yellowrock."

"Ditto, Billy. Why don't you sit in a chair. The table has to be making your butt numb. Is my lawyer here yet?" The

B-Twins had promised to send one, when the cops dragged me off.

"He's here." Billy sounded frustrated. Maybe he needed more fiber in his diet; fewer doughnuts, though he wasn't overweight, just soft around the middle. "You're free to go."

"No, 'Don't leave town,' advice?"

"Far as I'm concerned, you can leave town again and not come back. Things are more peaceful without you around."

"Only on the surface, Billy Boy. Monsters swim in the deep dark depths."

He cursed under his breath, and stood as a man entered. I checked the hairline and said, "Brandon." Then it clicked. "You're the lawyer you promised me."

"Graduate of Tulane Law, LLM, in 1946." He pretended not to see the chief's double take, and he smelled of the truth. Brandon really was an attorney. "And while I don't practice in North Carolina, I do have privileges, pro hac vice," he said, as if that meant something to me. "But to make sure all your 'I's are dotted, I brought along a friend."

A female blood-servant walked in behind him, not someone I knew, but she smelled like Lincoln Shaddock's blood, expensive perfume, money, and entitlement. She was taller than me, which made me uncomfortable for some reason, blond with perfect makeup and flawless skin, an innate elegance, and she was wearing a tailor-made silk suit. I crossed my arms over my T-shirted chest and nodded from my slouched position. She nodded from her superior one and twinkled blue eyes at Billy. "Thank you, Chief. We appreciate you expediting the release of Miss Yellowrock." She put out her hand as if she expected him to kiss it.

Billy Chandler blinked and melted even as he sucked in his soft belly and pushed back his shoulders. He took her hand and smiled. "Ms. Mooney, you have always been an asset to this department and this city. Anything we can do, within reason and the law, is always our pleasure. And you pass that along to your mother, you hear? Anything."

Yeah, like he had a chance with the woman. And what was with the royal "we"? And wait. *Mooney?* Shaddock's heir was Dacy Mooney. I straightened and looked the blood-servant over.

"Dacy is well aware of local law enforcement's appreciation for her generosity."

"That in-unit computer upgrade has made a vast difference to the cop on the street."

"We have to protect the boys in blue," she said, twinkling at him, and gently removing her hand from his grip.

"Yada yada," I said, standing. "It's nearly dark, I've had no sleep to speak of for days, I've been invaded, shot at"—*and shot a man,* my heart whispered—"been dragged down to the LEC, and kept without food and water, and I'm ready to get outta here."

Mooney flashed me a wide smile and gestured to the door. I led the way into the hallway, passing by the lady lawyer. She looked like a million bucks. A Paris Hilton, if Paris had unfeigned self-assurance and molecular-deep class. Her suit was form-fitted, her bag was snakeskin, and her hair was twisted up in a sleek French twist. She smelled great. I disliked her intensely for it. Which made me feel all kinds of guilty, and angry for the guilt. "Miss Yellowrock, it's an honor to meet you," she said as I passed.

I swallowed down my retort and the sigh that wanted to follow. In the hallway I turned, tucked my jealousy away into some hidden part of me, and put out my hand. "It's a pleasure to meet you too." I managed not to sound grudging, which was unexpected and satisfying.

We shook and she said, "My car is outside. We can speak there."

I collected and signed for my valuables—except for the gun I'd fired—and meekly followed Mooney outside. Even in the mountains at 2,134 feet elevation, September in the South was sweltering. The muggy heat slapped me like a steamy towel across my exposed flesh. "I know you must be starving," she said. "Let's stop for an early dinner so we can talk." She stepped to a waiting, slightly stretched, black limo, that was, honest to God, a Volkswagen, sparkling in the late afternoon light. I had no idea they even made Volkswagen limos.

Sliding bonelessly into the car, she was as graceful as a swan, and I was all kinds of ungainly clunky as I slid in after her. Brandon closed the door after himself, sat across from us, and the car pulled into traffic, around the loop, and onto College Street.

Mooney said to the driver, "Take us to Mr. Shaddock's place, please, Erving." He lifted two fingers in acknowledgment before the privacy window went up. Shaddock's only restaurant, so far as I knew, was a barbecue joint, and my estimation of the blood-servant went up a notch. Either she was psychic, had deduced by my slouch and my T-shirt that I was a fast-food, meat-and-potatoes gal, or she had researched me. I was betting on the latter. She added, "Two of your security experts will be joining us for the early meal." She looked at Brandon. "Your brother and the others can handle security for the sleeping Grégoire?"

"They can," I answered for him, looking the VW over. The limo rode heavy, as if armored, and it had computer screens and cell phones on chargers in discreet little pouches, champagne and beer in a little glass-fronted fridge, and windows so darkly tinted that a vamp could have taken a ride in the daytime and not been charred. It was clear the limo had been hand-built to order. And best of all, there were holstered guns in the side pockets. Immediately I felt better. I always did around guns, as long as they weren't pointed at me. "May I?" I indicated one particularly interesting weapon that had a grip a linebacker might have used.

"Help yourself." Her lips curved into a secretive smile, the kind an adult gives a kid when they get a new toy, and I wanted to say something snarky, but figured it might get me banned from the lovely-looking weapon. I eased it out of the case, which was a heavy-duty plastic mounting, not a holster as I had supposed. The weapon wasn't something I could casually pick up. I had to lift it from its casing. And when I did, I sighed. It was a S&W, X-frame Model 500.

"Holy Moly," I whispered. The handgun—small cannon— had an overall length of fifteen inches with an eight and three-eighths inch barrel. The cylinder was almost two inches in diameter and nearly two and a quarter inches long. "Holy Moly," I repeated. Carefully, I thumbed the cylinder open and spun it to reveal five charge holes, each a half inch in diameter.

"You'll find them loaded with 50-caliber cartridges—

sterling silver rounds seated in traditional brass," she said. "Hand-packed vamp-killers."

Or werewolf killers, I thought. "This sucker weighs nearly five pounds, fully loaded."

"And yet you lift it with ease."

I'd given away something I still wasn't ready to admit and had no idea how to fix it. I shrugged. "Strong wrists."

Mooney laughed and crossed her legs. Unlike most women she was wearing hose, and they shushed gently with the motion, drawing Brandon's eyes to her legs, as she'd clearly intended. Her smile widened and she gave me a look that said, "Aren't men cute?" Instead of giving that thought voice, she said, "We've never been properly introduced. I'm Adelaide Mooney, blood-servant and daughter in life to Dacy, Lincoln Shaddock's heir."

I didn't want to like the woman—she was too … perfect. Elegant. Ladylike—but I was starting to. Dang it. "Why is it loaded with silvershot?"

She inclined her head, as if I had done something particularly bright, like a dog with a new trick. Or as if I'd passed a test, something set up to prove I deserved to be in charge of security. Her blue eyes tinted toward a delicate shade of lavender, maybe cornflower blue, and were uncomfortably direct. "Your record is exemplary and your eye for weapons is excellent. You come highly recommended by Leonard Pellissier and by my security researcher, who provided a dossier on you in record time."

I couldn't help but be pleased that Leo had said something nice about me. Especially as he'd tried to kill me several times in our short acquaintance. "Let me guess. Reach did my dossier?"

"You use Reach for background?" She sounded gently surprised, perhaps too well bred to sound insultingly startled at what that implied about my net worth.

"Mostly when Leo foots the bill," I admitted. "Reach is a little pricey for my usual budget."

"He is that," she said. It wasn't quite a disgusted mutter, but it came close. "So it's likely that he had your information on file, collated, well studied, and ready, and yet he waited an hour to send it to me, hoping to make it look as though he was doing rapid new research."

I laughed; I couldn't help it. "Sounds like Reach."

"Yes, it does. So. What are you?"

I went still for a long slow moment. Without taking my eyes from her bluish lavender ones, I slowly eased the Smith and Wesson mini-cannon back into the plastic casing. It kept me from shooting her with the big gun.

"As a blood-servant, I have an excellent sense of smell," she went on. "Lincoln tells me you smell of sex and war and rushing water in a deep glen. He's poetic, is our Linc. You don't smell human. So what are you?"

"None of your business," I said, sitting back, the words coming slowly.

"But it is. You are providing security services for a high-level parley that directly affects my current and future lifestyle, and my decision whether to attempt to become a Mithran or remain a blood-servant. Everything you do and everything you are is my business."

"Take it up with Leo," I said.

"I have. He was not forthcoming."

"Because he doesn't know what she is," Brandon said. I had almost forgotten he was there, he'd been so silent and still.

"Impossible," Mooney said.

"Fact. None of the Mithrans know what she is," Brandon said, "though Leo's Mercy Blade may know and simply isn't saying. He calls her the 'little goddess.'"

"I'm not a goddess," I said, sounding disgruntled, knowing I needed to get the spotlight off of me. "But I am hungry." I looked at Adelaide, thinking rude might work. "You said you were Dacy's daughter in life, which, as I understand it, means she had you in the natural human way. Before or after she was turned? How old *are* you? You have to be *old*."

Adelaide laughed, a tinkling amusement that made my own laughter sound like a mule braying. "Leo told me you were direct."

I figured that was a ladylike way of saying I was vulgar, but since I was going that way, I couldn't gripe. I slouched down in the butter-soft leather and waited, watching her.

"I'm in my early eighties. If I want to keep my youth, it would be wise to risk being turned in the next decade.

Which is why I want to know what you are." She was tenacious. A lawyer would have to be. I sighed but didn't answer. Adelaide looked at Brandon. "Elf?" Meaning me.

"Leo says no. Grégoire says no. She isn't elf, were, or anything they know. Though they do scent cats and birds and dogs on her, and she doesn't own pets."

I looked out the window. They were talking about me as if I was tied to a lab table, but I couldn't complain. I'd started the rudeness. They had never smelled anything like me, because the only other skinwalker Leo had ever scented had gone to the dark side and killed, eaten, and stolen the body and life and scent of Leo's own son. Long before Leo ever got a whiff of him again, he smelled like vamp and family. I had killed the imposter.

I leaned to the small fridge and opened the door, taking out and opening a Yuengling Lager, which gave me something to do with my hands besides shooting the two blood-servants with one of the lovely weapons. After an uncomfortable silence, during which I realized I hadn't been offered the beer I'd taken, the blood-servants examined me while I scrutinized the city of Asheville in the afternoon light.

The city is in a valley surrounded by mountains, having expanded its borders in all directions. Downtown, however, is small and close; a silent five minutes later, despite the Sunday afternoon tourist traffic, we were pulling up in front of Shaddock's BBQ. The sign out front showed a picture of two soldiers, Confederate and Union, eating together over a campfire and the remains of a roasted spitted pig. The sign was amusing, as the vamp owner had been turned by a Union soldier vamp on the battlefield of Monocacy, on July 9, 1864. I figured the two soldiers had spent their getting-to-know you dinner over the throat of a human, not a cooked pig, but I'd been wrong before. I climbed out of the car when it stopped and led the way inside, ignoring the sidelong glance shared by the servants. Inside, I took a seat at a party-sized table and watched as Brandon hung his jacket on a hook, revealing broad shoulders and an economy of movement. Clothes were wasted on him. Which was a totally inappropriate thought.

To combat the images of Brandon and his twin posed

half-naked on the cover of a romance novel, I ordered three hogshead baskets (the largest order the place offered) of smothered fries, a large Coke, and a number four—pulled pork with all the fixin's. I was nowhere near finished with the day's activities and I needed protein, fats, and caffeine until I shifted or slept twelve hours. The two servants ordered and then chitchatted about the weather while we waited for fries and my security guys. I learned that a cold front was moving south fast, and was expected to barrel into the region behind the hurricane. We'd have an end-of-summer storm, heavy rain, followed by sweater weather. Beast purred thinking of a hunt in cool temps, and a snarky smile pulled at my lips.

Brandon lifted his brows at the sight. Adelaide repeated the gesture. It had to be a class thing. It was so polite and understated, and yet so superior. I shook my head and waved my snark away.

The fries and the guys all got to our table at the same time, Derek taking the seat beside me, his thigh shoving my chair down the long table. "Injun Princess," he said to me. To the other two he said, "B-twin. Pretty lady."

Wrassler pulled up a sturdier chair from another table. "Legs," he said to me, and nodded to the others. Both men had scoped out the place and everyone in it upon entering. Wrassler instinctively angled his chair to watch the front entrance. Derek sat to cover the windows, the rest of the building, and the street, as I had. Instinctive, hardwired security measures. They placed their orders and then everyone turned to me. Like choreography.

I suppressed a chuckle and said, "Okay. Sit rep. We got two werewolves in the area. They probably chased us here." Derek and his boys had slaughtered the Lupus pack, so my use of "us" was truth. "The grindylow swam and/or hitched a ride on a boat from New Orleans, chasing his master, the were-cat Kemnebi, who is vacationing on the Tennessee side of the mountains."

Brandon went still. "The were-cat is here? And you didn't see fit to inform us?"

Adelaide looked back and forth between us. "This were-creature is dangerous?"

"No. He's a high-level ambassadorial type with the

Party of African Weres and the IAW," I said. I narrowed my eyes at Brandon. "He's sixty miles away and working a monthlong drunk. If you have a problem with not knowing, take it up with Leo. He's the boss. It was need-to-know. You didn't need to know, before. Now you do. Get over it."

I ate several fries while they all took that in, and I nearly moaned with the flavor. The fries were smothered with chili, cheese, jalapeños, red beans, sour cream, and ketchup, like nachos but with potatoes. To die for. Wrassler, the easiest-going guy I knew, had no problem with need-to-know intel, and was making inroads on his basket of fries. Derek was thinking and nibbling on the basket sitting in front of the blood-servants. Who hadn't touched the greasy bit-a-heaven.

"Lastly, and maybe most important, I was attacked by a blood-servant that none of you *claim* to recognize." Adelaide's back went stiff at the implied insult. You'd a thought I whapped her nose with a newspaper. "And if he wasn't one of yours, then we have an unknown vamp interested in the parley proceedings." Which would complicate everything, though complications were nothing new when dealing with vamps.

When Brandon and Adelaide had had time to digest the semi-insult and info, I drank down the Coke and said, "The problems are"—I raised a balled fist, extending a finger—"the werewolves are trying to make the vamps look guilty for the attacks"—I raised another finger—"while simultaneously trying to create mates and rebuild their pack." I raised a third. "The grindy is chasing them to punish them for attacking humans"—a fourth went up—"and the were-cat is drunk as two skunks in mourning for his dead mate." My thumb went up, fingers splayed. "Leo and the IAW want me to hunt down and kill the wolves." I raised the index finger of my other hand. "And that means working at night." I dropped my hands. "All that, on top of a high-level parley Leo has resisted for decades, humans protesting, media attention, and interest by an unknown vamp. I need to know one thing—can y'all handle security without me for a bit?"

Derek said, "We can handle it. If pretty boy knows how to work a headset."

"I was working com units when you were in knee britches, sonny," Brandon said.

"Knee britches? Wrong century, white boy."

"Stop," I said, waving the waitress over when she appeared uncertain about interrupting with our meals. The tension at the table was making the staff nervous. "Can you work together or not? 'Cause if you're going to act like twelve-year-olds, I'll look for other help. Like Chen." I glanced at Adelaide, who smiled slightly.

Derek snorted. Brandon swiveled to me. I raised my brows at him, mimicking his hoity-toity expression, and stuffed a forkful of pork in my mouth, sauce on my lips. Deliberately crude.

"We'll manage," he said.

"Good," I said through the food. Then I chewed and swallowed. "You boys chat. I gotta go to the ladies room." I made my way to the room with the cow on the door, a cow wearing three brassieres with six udders stuffed up high and proud. The bull's room was just as indelicate, but involved something that looked like six feet of horns and a Speedo. I felt, more than saw, Adelaide follow me. *Now what?*

CHAPTER TEN

I Sleep with Vamps for a Living

I did my business, aware that she did the same. I stopped at the mirror, undoing my hair and rebraiding it, waiting on her. Women wearing stockings or pantyhose took longer than women in jeans. The lighting claimed I needed some color. Lipstick. Blush. Mascara. *Some*thing. I braided my hair, watching her feet in the stall. If they spread and braced she might be pulling a weapon.

Adelaide flushed, opened the door—no weapon—and left the stall, meeting my eyes in the mirror; she washed her hands at the sink, standing beside me, still holding my gaze. She was amused, as if she had been betting with herself that I was watching for a gun. I couldn't help it. I grinned back. She said, "You do yank their chains."

"Sometimes," I said.

"As often as possible," she amended.

I gave a head shrug, a tilt of acceptance. "You wow them with your looks and charm, and keep them in their places panting after you. Looks and charm aren't my strengths. I have to make do with moxie and muscle." We still hadn't met eyes directly, the mirror acting as intermediary. But this woman wanted something from me, and I hadn't fig ured out what.

"You really have no idea how beautiful you are." It was an incredulous statement, not a question, and she looked sad.

I snorted, not trying to be delicate. "I know exactly how

beautiful I am. I'm not. I have good bone structure, but striking is the best I can do. Now, when I get all doodied up, and my pal Molly does my face, I do better than striking. But I'll never be beautiful."

"Mmm." Adelaide pulled towels and dried her hands. "They all stared at your backside when you left the table."

"I have a nice butt. Great legs. No class."

"You chose to *display* little class," she amended again.

I leaned my weight on both hands, against the counter, still holding her eyes in the mirror. I let a bit of snarl enter my voice. "Are you trying to be my *best pal*?"

"You aren't making it easy," she said, exasperated. She leaned in as well, her posture copying mine. "Do you know how difficult it is to find a friend who is as tall as I am? Who doesn't make me feel like a lumbering giant? Who might understand the life of a blood-servant? Who isn't *chasing after me to get close to my mother*?" The last was said with a soft undertone of old anguish.

My face fell. *Crap.* She was serious. After a long, silent moment, I said, "Yeah. To the tall part." I studied her cornflower blue eyes. They were earnest, a hard emotion to fake. "So . . . you really are trying to be my friend?"

"And I have no idea why I've bothered. You are a pain in the ass."

I laughed. She didn't. I stepped away from the mirror and looked at her. She stepped back and met my gaze. "Okay," I said.

"*Okay*? Okay what?"

"Yeah. Okay. Let's be friends."

An expression I'd never have expected flashed across her face. Delight. Which was just weird. Weird that someone wanted to be my friend. And not because I was famous—sorta—or different, or killed vamps for a living. But because I was tall. And because I understood.

Even Molly had become my best pal because I'd intervened between her and a pack of witch-haters way back when. Adelaide wanted to be my friend because she was tall. And lonely. And *that* I understood totally. I let one corner of my mouth curl back up. "You do know that I'll never love dressing up like a girl. We'll never go shopping or to the spa for facials and pedicures. We'll never have anything in common."

"Except height and similar awareness of life-with-vamp," she said.

"Yeah." I put out my hand, knowing that this part might ruin the possibility of friendship between us. "Jane Yellowrock. I kill vamps for a living."

She took my hand. "Adelaide Mooney. I sleep with vamps for a living."

Which shot ice water through my veins. I clasped her hand tighter, electricity zigzagging through me, chilling my skin. Her palm was soft and delicate, her fingers long and slender but powerful, holding mine. "You don't have to," I said softly.

"Neither do you."

I felt the grin pull across my face. "I don't want to like you. But I do."

"Good. BFFs. For real."

No one said BFFs anymore, but she *was* eighty years old. It was hard for the older servants to keep up with current jargon. "Okay. Deal." And honest to God, she teared up, her bluish-lavender eyes swimming. "If you cry every time we agree on something," I growled, "it's going to be annoying."

"No, it's not," she said. "We aren't going to agree on much."

I laughed, her tinkling laughter skipping across mine like stones on a lake. "There is that," I said.

Slowly she let go of my hand. "Thank you."

"Likewise. Now. I gotta get outta here. I need to make an appointment and then get a couple hours of shut-eye, and then I have to hunt werewolves."

"Sounds like fun." She produced a card like a prestidigitator. "My transportation service. Tell them I sent you. Set up an account with them and they'll be at your disposal. But just so you know, they'll tell me every location where they pick you up and where they take you. So if it's a secret, don't use them."

I took the card. "I like you. And I feel like that's a huge mistake."

"Ditto," she said. "Be safe." Adelaide left the ladies room while I dialed the number on the card and ordered a ride. Back in the dining room, I finished my pork and then walked out. I had places to be and wolves to track.

*   *   *

Adelaide's service turned out to be a chartered driver company, like an upscale taxi service, but run on retainer. I didn't expect to need it, but who knew? Back at the hotel, crime scene tape had been plastered all over my door. I paused for a moment before entering, shoving the damaged door open, ducking under the tape. A patch of bloody carpet had been removed. The room had been vacuumed by CSI techs. The linens were gone. And my things were no longer in my room. No clothes. No guns on the coffee table. I went to the closet and reached into the back corner, my fingers finding the box with the obfuscation spell on it. I pulled it forward and tucked it under my arm. The contents shifted slightly with the action, a deadened, hollow sound.

"Your belongings and weapons are in our suite." I turned to see Brian standing behind me, yellow tape between us. I hadn't heard him, the carpet in the hotel deep enough to muffle his footsteps. He was wearing slacks and a starched white shirt, sleeves rolled up to the elbows, a tan holster over it. His feet were bare, which was endearing in an odd sort of way. "All except the weapon you shot the man with," he continued. "The cops have it and I rather doubt you'll get it back. *Ever.*" He fell silent, waiting for me to process what he'd said. The cops weren't giving my gun back. Cops don't give weapons back when the victim of a shooting dies. But they had let me go so . . . the man I'd shot had only recently passed on. Kicked the bucket. Died.

Slowly, like a wrecking ball falling, I realized what had happened. I'd killed a human. A thinking, breathing being with a soul. Not a rogue-vamp killing machine. Not a rabid were. I'd ripped him out of existence. And for hours I hadn't thought about him. Not once. A cold mist of shock billowed slowly through me, expanding, filling me with the icy reality. I looked away from Brian, wondering why I hadn't thought about the man I had killed until now. Wondered why I hadn't considered the possibility that I'd killed him. I'd thought him only wounded, and blood-servants don't kill easy. *I killed a human being.* I wrapped my arms around me, the box pressing into my side, staring at the bare patch of floor. There was a faint stain of blood on it. I could still smell the stink of gunfire. *I killed a human being.*

As if he knew what I was feeling, Brian said, "The lead investigator said the guy had no ID on him. Prints came back as a made man out of New York. He disappeared off the law enforcement radar two years ago, possibly going to work as a contract killer for a renegade Mithran." When I didn't reply, he said, "Two hits have been laid at his door in the last sixty days, one in New Orleans." Which meant he had long arms, whoever the vamp master was.

I looked up to see that Brian was wavering. And then I realized my eyes were full of tears. When I managed a breath, the air moving down my throat ached. He continued. "He came in through our room. If we hadn't both been in Grégoire's suite you would have been safe."

"And you might have been"—I swallowed through the tight pain in my throat—"dead." I moved toward him and ducked beneath the yellow tape, closing the door after me. We stood in the hallway, close enough to smell his aftershave. "So, I'm bunking with you guys?"

He hesitated, and I could almost see the possible responses move through him, one sarcastic, one innuendo, one that was simply kind. "Our suite has three bedrooms. The hotel opened the third at no charge." He pulled a card key from a pocket and said, "Leo has ordered a replacement for your Walther. It'll be here in the morning." He had settled on a response a friend might use.

A tear fell and I caught it with a quick dash of my hand. I nodded, took the key, followed him into the suite beside mine. It was decorated in warm grays, cool browns, and dull creams. Soothing colors. I went to my room, a predominately gray room with a silky gray comforter and charcoal pillows, and I shut the door, leaning my back against it. I wiped my eyes. I never used to cry. Never. But then, I never used to have friends. I never used to put them in danger. I never used to kill humans. My life was changing and it was all pretty much sucky.

I took a breath and forced calm into me. The room was tiny, less than half the square footage of the adjoining, bloody suite, but my clothes were in the closet, my weapons on the bureau, neatly laid out, which made me smile through the tears, and my toiletries were in the bath, seen through the open door. I pushed from my perch and stripped, moving through the room, dropping clothes where they landed. I stepped under the shower, the scalding water pelting me. And the tears started again. I was changing and didn't like who I was becoming. I'd never get clean.

How had I killed man and not even spared him a thought? How could I have eaten a full meal, joked and chatted and made a BFF, and not thought once about the man I'd shot. And killed. When the crying jag ended, I dried off and crawled under the covers, dry eyes burning. Beast padded through my thoughts, her gaze golden and steady, her paws silent, weighted, her breath a susurration, almost a purr. Sleep claimed me. Beast's claws milked my soul.

I woke at six p.m. and lay on the bed, staring at the shadowed ceiling. My own scent had filled the room as I slept, the smells no longer alien. I was calm. Rational. Not grieving over the part of me I'd lost. A killer, the blood-servant of an unknown vamp, had come into my room. His death didn't make the danger go away. If he had been targeting me, then I was attracting dangers that might hurt the vamps, making me a liability to the job. If the man had been after the vamps, then the unknown vamp master would plan better next time, would send better quality killers. Either way, grief and guilt were wasted and stupid. I put them away.

The most important and overriding factor was that he'd gotten past security. I'd been sloppy or it was an inside job—someone I trusted had let him in. I needed to tighten security, switch around weapons, methodologies, timing, and personnel. Keep more people on duty, make the guys pull twelve-hour shifts.

I crawled from the mattress and dressed, putting on a black skirt that fell to my shins, a tank with a tight vest, lightweight jacket, and dress boots. Into my boot holster went the six-round Kahr P380 and in the other went a sheathed knife with a ten-inch silvered blade and a deep groove—a vamp-killer, which would work equally well against wolves. I rebraided my hair and wrapped it into a bun, tight against my nape, giving my face a severe, harsh angularity. I selected a tube of lipstick at random—they were all shades of red—and smeared it on.

Last, I pulled the box of fetishes from the closet, opened it, and studied the necklaces inside. A skinwalker's fetish necklaces are made of bones, teeth, beaks, talons, and feathers, each necklace strung with parts from one species. Skinwalkers can shift into most any land mammal or bird, providing we have access to a sufficient quantity of DNA, the coiled helix of genetic sequences specific to each species, each creature, and providing that the mass exchange is close. I'd never tried to shift into a fish, reptile, or sea mammal as Rick had asked, but that might be possible too, I didn't know. Walkers can also shift into smaller creatures, if we're willing to lose part of ourselves, depositing mass to be regained when we return to human-normal. Shifting into larger creatures requires taking mass from something with no genetic material and adding it to the shifting process. All mass transfers are dangerous, and I prefer not to attempt them, fearing I might lose too much of myself shifting into a smaller creature, forfeiting memories, abilities, even part of my body. Fearing I might not be able to throw off mass gained after shifting into a larger creature, ending up with an extra hundred pounds of me. So, most of my fetishes were mammalian—predators or omnivores—that massed about one hundred twenty-five pounds.

I studied the fetishes, thinking, undecided. For once Beast had no comment to make, hunched deep in my consciousness, silent, watchful. If I hunted as Beast, scent-tracking would be working against her natural abilities. *Puma concolors*—mountain lions—are sight trackers, ambush hunters, and I needed something better suited to scent-tracking. Like the bloodhound I had tried once. Excellent nose. But a bloodhound could get so involved with a scent it would forget to eat, drink, or change back before dawn. And no bloodhound had the weapons to fight werewolves if I got lucky and found them. I set the mountain lion fetish in the bag and replaced the box. I unzipped my go-bag, checking clothes, throwaway cell phone, and cash. I picked up my Bible. It felt foreign in my hands. The gun in my boot did not. Something was seriously wrong with my life for that to be so, but I could think about that later. After this job was done.

I called for the valet to refuel and bring around the car I had used last night and then stepped from my tiny bedroom. I stopped and placed a hand on one hip. A chair had been dragged from a seating arrangement and now blocked the exit. One of the twins was sitting in it, dress shirtsleeves rolled up, pants with a razor crease. There was no mole at his hairline, IDing him as Brian. His arms were on the chair arms, one ankle on the other knee, facing my door. Blocking my way out. And one hand held a trank gun.

My thoughts went into overdrive. I hadn't brought any tranks on this job. Tranquilizers were Derek's specialty. Seems like my right-hand man had been thinking on his own, and Grégoire's two right hands had been sharing his equipment. I didn't know how my metabolism would react to a tranquilizer. I'd never dosed myself. Some things I hadn't thought I'd need to know. And so far, neither of the twins knew about me being a skinwalker. He hadn't fired. Yet. I smiled, showing teeth, not trying for sweet. Moving slowly, not taking my eyes from the twin, I set my go-bag and Bible on the surface nearest. A bureau by the height. "Brian. You got something to say? Or do you want to fight me, 'cause it'll come to a fight if you think I'm staying in tonight."

"I know you're not staying in. I don't intend to fight you. I just want to make sure you listen to me." His New Orleans accent dropped in, thick as warm honey, the words slow, the emphasis wrong, like the way a Southern gentleman might have spoken a hundred years ago. Polite, despite being implacable.

"I'll listen better without the trank gun."

"Maybe. Maybe not. Today you killed a man."

My flinch was internal. It didn't show. "And?"

His words took on the lilt of that same old Southern man telling a story. "I killed my first man when I turned forty. A priest and two of his laymen came after Grégoire with a stake and holy water and a necklace of garlic; with kerosene and a pistol for me. It was Brandon's day of rest, and at the time we kept only one blood-servant with him. There hadn't been trouble for decades. We had become lazy." He gestured with the trank gun. "Complacent.

"I was alone in the lair, when the priest cantered up on his piebald mare, the laymen, horsed, at his sides. The house was small, on a bluff overlooking a bayou. It had a hidden room under the floor, the tunnel entrance concealed by a rug. Grégoire's lair."

He shrugged slightly. "Some Mithrans sleep all day. Some don't. Back then, Grégoire slept deeply by day. And the priest, he seemed to know that, he did. Seemed to know where Grégoire would be. To know my master would have only one blood-servant to defend him. I don't know if one of the blood-slaves had told the priest, or perhaps the church tortured it out of someone. But the priest, he had no qualms, not one. He had come to kill a devil and a devil worshipper."

I looked away. Tension I hadn't known I was carrying seeped out of my shoulders. I blew out a breath and took the nearest seat, a corner of the couch. I sat with my elbows on my knees, my hands close to the boot holster. If Brian tranked me, I'd shoot him before I went under. If I went under. But I wanted to hear this.

When I was settled, he went on. "The laymen splashed kerosene over the front porch and walls. I panicked. Killing humans is against Mithran law, and against Grégoire's personal edict. But I had to protect him. I stood beside a table, facing the door, three pistols and a sword at my side, and waited, sweating like the house was already on fire, my heart a thunder in my chest. The priest threw open the door and strode inside.

"I don't know if they got their signals wrong, or it might have been an innocent mistake, but the laymen struck their match too soon. Flames billowed up. The priest fired. I fired. He missed; I didn't. He fell, with flames leaping behind him. He wasn't dead. He crawled for the door, screaming for help. But the house, it was old, the wood like dry tinder. I pulled up the iron trapdoor and crawled through the small opening, onto Grégoire. I curled there, as the heat rose, and the roof crashed down and the priest, screaming, burned to death."

I said nothing, knowing now that he didn't intend to kill or trank me. Knowing that this was a form of intervention, an act of compassion. Some confessions are just that—acts of kindness.

"I might have disarmed him, dragged him down with me. I might have forced him to drink of Grégoire's blood and heal him. But I saved myself and let him burn. And, even now, I hear his screams when I wake in the night. Hear and know that I did nothing to save him. He had been sent to kill me and to kill my master. And so I shot him and left him to die.

"What you did today was self-defense. That man's death might provide short-term protection for my brother, my master, and me. And so I thank you for the sacrifice of a small piece of your soul." I started, hearing words on his lips I'd thought myself, hours earlier. "If you are willing to take the advice of an old, old man, then do your penance, and live—with the memory of your own evil."

I lifted my Bible. "Is there any penance for the death of another?"

"Abel died." His New Orleans accent faded away, his voice now pitiless. "Cain was marked with the mark of the Beast and exiled. But he lived. I confessed to my own priest, who gave me harsh penance, and then he left the country never to return. Mithrans and their crimes were more than a man of God could bear. It took twenty-five years to work off my penance. In the twenty-five years, I found freedom and peace. And you will find peace as well, if you choose it."

Mark of the Beast. Yeah, I know that one. "I'm not Catholic."

Brian smiled then and shook his head. "No. You are a little goddess."

I stood and gathered up my things. "I'm not a goddess. Can I go now?" Brian stood and pulled the chair out of the way. I left the suite.

I drove to a little church I had found—a wooden, white painted, two-hundred-year-old building on a crossroads, tucked into the side of a hill. The steeple rose against a backdrop of dying hemlocks, pointing to heaven where the sun set, a golden, rosy glow. Boulders the size of small houses rose up in the grassy yard all around, one behemoth half as tall as the church itself. The land was unsuitable for farming, but made a good site for a church and, if gifted to a congregation, would be a contribution to be remembered. It wasn't the church I had once attended when I lived here, but a new one, where no one knew me, which said something about who I was now, something that I didn't want to look at too closely. It was the same denomination that I'd attended in New Orleans, though they eschewed the word denomination. This one was called simply Church of Christ, and they were having a revival-type service all week long.

I was early, only one truck parked in the lot, the front doors wide to air out the day's heat, half the lights on, but the sanctuary empty. I went in and took a seat in the semi-darkness, sliding to my knees on the old, wide-plank floor. It had been a long time since I had prayed. And I didn't know what to say to God. I settled on confession, beginning with the whispered words, "Today I killed a man. His death was sudden. I didn't give him time before death to confess. To seek you." Tears started to fall, hot and searing. "I killed a man," I whispered, the words like the breath of hell in my mouth. "I didn't really mean to kill him. But all I can see is his body fall. And fall. And fall. Like so many vamps and weres. And I have to wonder if they were all as precious to you as a human is. I have to wonder if the blood of murder rests on my soul."

CHAPTER ELEVEN

Streams Talking Softly in Mountain-Water Tongue

No one bothered me while I prayed. No one bothered me while the small church filled up and the lights came on, and the heat went up despite the open windows. I stayed through the service, singing with the congregation, without the benefit of instrumental music. I listened to the earnest minister and his sermon on what it meant to be drenched in the blood of the lamb, a topic Beast might have reacted to, but this once, she remained silent, in the background. And I slipped out during the last hymn so I wouldn't have to talk with any of them. It was the chicken's way out, but I wasn't ready to be welcomed into the presence of God's people yet. It was hard enough to try to reach out for the presence of God himself. And I had a feeling that I might find it easier in the silence of the forest and ragged hills, far from other humans.

My Cherokee self, the part of me that had memories from long ago, was damaged. Had been broken by the death of my father, the rape of my mother. Had been further damaged by the loss of my people on a cold and frigid snowy night. By the years I spent as *we sa*, a bobcat, before I stole Beast. And by the hunger times, lived in her form. I had tried to find that ancient, human, Cherokee part of me, to wake it and merge it with who I was now, creating one cohesive self. I felt that if

I did, if I could find my ancient self, I might learn something important, might finally feel whole. But I was fractured, broken, and I didn't have the time, not now, for self-analysis and soul-searching. Someday. Someday.

I glanced back at the small church and started up the truck, driving away as the last notes of the last song poured through the open, stained-glass windows, along with the stained light, I had a search of a different sort to begin.

A half hour later, after a stop at an Ingles to purchase ten pounds of raw steak, a dozen granola bars, and a roll of paper towels, I turned off the paved road near Hot Springs, onto a well-kept gravel road, still some six mountain road miles from the site I had decided to search. It was near the Rich-Laurel Wildlife Area, on a little feeder creek that emptied into the French Broad River. There were no people close by. It was late and the weekend campers were long gone; the few hard-core campers were gathered at their tents, fires burning merrily here and there, easy to spot and easier to avoid in the dark.

I maneuvered out of the campground, parked out of the way, and got out to reconnoiter, leaning against the armored vehicle, the metal warm beneath my skin, wild grasses moving against my skirt and boots. I let Beast rise slowly to the surface, her senses expanding. I could discern her heartbeat, slower when at rest than mine, beating strongly beneath my own, a mystical sensation, powerful in my memory. The night, dark beneath the overhead foliage, grew perceptibly brighter as my pupils widened with Beast-sight. My lips parted and drew in air over tongue and through my nose, the way big-cats scent, though I had no scent sacs in the roof of my mouth like Beast.

Even to my human nose the night breeze was sun-heated and rich with the perfume of the earth, river-wet from the French Broad only feet from me. Fish and water plants. Warm stone and old campfires, turtles, wild undergrowth mixed with escaped garden plants, basil in flower and something spicy-bitter. But no human scent nearby. No human sound or voice carried on the air. I was alone. I started to pant in the warmth. The engine pinged softly beneath my hands.

Good night for hunt, Beast thought at me. *Moon is big, like pregnant doe.*

I carried my supplies to the base of the Paint Rock. The red rock cliff was jagged and broken, rising a hundred feet or more above the French Broad River. It was once covered with ancient paintings, paintings that predated the Cherokee, drawn in red pigments, but time and the elements and the stupidity of man had erased most of them. Humans had spray-painted their names and ancient-looking figures over large parts of the fractured surface. But with the breath of the river flowing across the earth, the place still had power.

I opened the steaks and dropped them on the smooth earth at the base of the massive rock, the meat still chilled from the store's refrigeration. With the roll of paper towels, I cleaned my hands and put the wrapping and foam containers into the grocery bag and sealed them. Carried the trash back to the SUV.

I stripped in the front seat and left my clothes in a pile on the floor, hoping no one would tow my vehicle, but not really caring if they did. Grabbing up my supplies, I stepped from the SUV, barefoot and soundless, my travel pack under one arm. Opening the zipper bag containing my fetish necklace, I set the necklace of the *Puma concolor* over my head. It was made of the claws, teeth, and small bones of the biggest female panther I had ever seen, the cat killed in Montana during a legal hunt, the pelt and head mounted on some bigwig's living room wall, the bones and teeth sold through a taxidermist. The mountain lion was hunted throughout the western United States and thought to be extinct in the eastern states, though some reports said they were making a comeback east of the Mississippi. One could hope. I didn't have to use the necklace to shift into this creature—the memory of Beast's form was always a part of me—but it was easier. I locked the SUV.

Already it felt weird walking on two legs, as Beast moved up from the deeps into my thoughts. Barefoot, the wild grasses sharp and cutting on my calves and thighs, the rough surface of the earth rocky beneath my tender soles. I returned to the Paint Rock and the stack of raw, bloody steaks on the ground.

Beast wanted to lick them. I held her still, though my stomach was rumbling. I was panting, salivating. *Hungry,* she thought. Because Beast is something outside my skin-walker nature—an independent entity who shares my body and, more and more often, my mind—I don't have complete control over her. And I know, in my bones, that if other skinwalkers exist, they don't have a Beast-soul living inside. We had ended up together through an accident, if black magic can be accidental, and thinking about it always left me feeling uneasy.

I pulled the go-bag over my head and positioned my gold nugget on its double gold chain, swinging free. Together, they looked like an expensive collar and tote, making Beast look like an escaped exotic pet. I leaned into the Paint Rock and scraped the gold nugget across a space unmarked with human names, depositing a thin streak of gold. The gold was like a homing beacon, among other things, a way to find my way back, if I was lost after a hunt.

Yesssss. Hunt, Beast thought at me. She was ready to scope out the territory, unfamiliar hunting ground, though it was close to Asheville and seemed like a location we might have explored. Naked, I sat on a sun-heated stone and closed my eyes, feeling the power of the world in this place, the strength of the breath of mother Earth. I shivered in the remnant heat. Holding the fetish necklace, I closed my eyes. Relaxed. Listened to the wind, the pull of the moon, rising above the horizon. I felt the beat of my own heart, and Beast's. She rose in me, silent, predatory.

I slowed the functions of my body, let my heart rate decrease, let my muscles relax, the rock wall against my back, facing the moving water. Mind clearing, I sank deep inside, my consciousness falling away, all but the purpose of this hunt. That purpose I set into the lining of my skin, into the deepest parts of my brain, as I always did, so I wouldn't lose it when I *shifted*, when I *changed*, because oftentimes, right after a shift, Beast had complete control, while my own spirit and mind slept. I dropped lower, deeper, into the darkness within me where old pain and memories swirled in a shadowed world fouled with blood and fear. The night wind on my skin cooled. The river whispered a susurration, leaves moved and sighed. Memories firmed, memories that, at all other times, were half forgotten, both mine and Beast's.

As I had been taught so long ago, I sought the inner snake lying inside the bones and teeth of the necklace, the coiled, curled snake of DNA, deep in the cells, in the remains of the marrow. For my people, for skinwalkers, it had always simply been "the inner snake."

I took up the snake that rests in the depths of all beasts and I dropped within. Like water trickling through cracked rock and down a mountain. Grayness enveloped me, sparkling and cold as winter. The world fell away. I was in the gray place of the change.

My breathing deepened. Heart rate sped. My bones . . . slid. Skin rippled. Fur, tawny and gray, brown and tipped with black, sprouted. Painpainpain, like a knife, cut between muscle and bone. My ear tabs bent and twisted, listening, and my nostrils widened, drawing deep.

She fell away. Night was fierce and bright in mountain hunting place. Crags and cliffs rose all around, with water flowing fast, earth breathing. I drew in air over tongue, a long scree of sound. Scents long remembered filled nose and mouth and mind: thick mist above river, air scented with taste of home. Smell of soil and fire. Plants strong with fall seeds. Old smell of rabbit. Blood from cow, old and cold. I panted. Listened to sounds—music from far, far away, sound of car along gravel road, not close but coming. Streams talking softly in mountain-water tongue, so different from bayou-water tongue. Familiar sound of home. Gathered limbs beneath me and padded to dead meat. I ate.

Later, moon still high, I cleaned paws and claws and groomed face and whiskers free from cold dead cow blood and hot deer blood. Yearling buck walked along road where I ate. Buck had never smelled big-cat before. Was not afraid. Stupid deer. Good meat. Fresh hot blood, good blood from easy hunt. Beast was good hunter. Full belly.

Hunt now? Jane said in back of mind. *Hunt for wolves. Search for scent of grindylow.*

I rose and padded away from wide river, into darker night under trees. Found trickling creek and followed it up-hill, past campground, into wild country. Smelled scent of wolf. They had been here.

How long ago? Jane asked, her thoughts excited.

Two days and two nights. Have not returned.

Can you tell how they came in here? What roads did they use?

Turned and turned, sniffing wind. *Small road is high in hills. Smell of gasoline and man chemicals that poison the earth.*

Can we go there?

Beast is good hunter. Can go where I please. I padded through dark woods, leaping from stone to stone or high into trees, following scent on ground from high in air. Wolves had to walk on ground, and could not hunt from up high. Could not leap as Beast did. I had hunted and killed wolves long ago, wolves who had killed Beast's prey in the hunger times. *Pack hunters,* I spat, hissing. *Hate pack hunters. Thieves of food.*

Found place where man had fouled the earth, dumping poisoned blood of machine onto ground, stink strong in air. Jane had tried to explain about machines. Not alive. Not dead. But machine has blood and hard parts like bone, and sometimes growls and is sometimes dead but not dead, like vampire. Confusing. Man is confusing. Man's world is confusing. And dangerous. Sniffed machine blood. Old and bitter smell.

A four-by-four, off-road vehicle, Jane thought. *They're illegal in the parks. Either the wolves came in on little-used roads and the rangers didn't catch them, or this is private land.*

Trotted farther on flat place along hillside. Smooth like road but grassy under paws.

Old logging road, Jane thought.

Logging humans stole trees from land. Was reason two for hunger times. Fire that followed was three. Killed mountains for many-more-than-five years. No live prey anywhere. Man is stupid. Man is dangerous.

Jane did not respond. Soon found place where wolves changed from man to wolf. Old bloody bones scattered on ground. Cold, old chickens, wrapped in smelly plastic. Blood full of water and smelling rank. Looked back at logging road, thinking. Man-wolves came here on machine, like car but not like car. Changed. Hunted. Came back, got on machine, and left. *Why?* I asked Jane. *I do not smell blood from hunt. They did not bring down prey.*

Jane drew in air like hiss of snake. *They came to make more. They came to turn humans. They entered campground on,* Jane tried to count back days, but was tired and confused, *maybe Friday night.* Crap. *They were here and they bit someone and they left. They bit a lot of people that night.*

And people are gone. Full of werewolf sickness. No way to track who they bit.

Jane cursed. Some words are bad, some are not, but all are just words. Humans are confusing. I headed along wolf trail, following scent and spoor. Found two places where humans had been bitten. One was abandoned house, full of mold and roaches and rats. Human man had been sleeping there, had not bathed, had fouled his own den for days. Jane called him *squatter.* Wolves had bitten him and left. Man had left too, stinking of blood and fear. Outside, smelled where he had gotten in car and driven off.

Impossible to find, now, Jane thought at me. *It's like an epidemic. If he gets away, and he turns furry, he'll try to bite humans. Crap, crap, and double freaking crap.*

Moved on, following scent trail. Other place was campsite near river. Man and woman had been together. They had fought wolves. Both had died and been eaten.

No one had discovered bodies. Humans cannot smell fresh death. Humans do not see when buzzards mark place of the dead. Jane would tell humans. Snarl on face, I left and padded to river to wash old human blood from paws. Dawn was not far off. The mist of river had risen, as if trying to reach up to clouds pushing in through the sky where sun fell at night. I stepped into river and drank, letting water wash paws, cool belly. And leaped onto rock, then to another, and then a hard, strong leap to middle of river, to a boulder larger than the others, gray and brown in the night. Standing high above water, to see world. Good place to see the sun.

*   *   *

The sun was rising over the eastern curve of the river when I shifted back, in the middle of the river. Beast had lain down on a night-cool rock out in the open, the river rushing around the boulder, a soft, pulsing froth. She had watched the sky lighten to a dull gray, her belly still full. Happy. Ignoring my pleas to return to land. And at the last moment, before the sun's rays slanted over the earth, she had let me shift back. And there I was, in the middle of the French Broad River. Naked and exposed. And no way back to shore without a river-swim rock-crawl. Beast thought it was funny, her hacking laughter clear in the back of my mind. I'm not sure if her sense of humor is peculiar to her or is shared by all cats. I have a feeling that it's a little bit of both and that my own sense of justice and making the punishment fit the crime had altered her cat-humor.

The water wasn't high enough to swim, and the light wasn't bright enough to see through the surface. By the time I was back to shore, I was bruised and bleeding from contact with underwater rocks, had a scrape on one shin, and was half drowned from falling into holes with no apparent bottom. Wet and smelling of river, I opened my go-bag, pulled out crushed, wet, wrinkled clothes and flip-flops, and dressed in the golden light, hoping no one was up and about to see me. Dang Beast.

Dressed, wet hair hanging down my back like a tangled skein of wet wool yarn, I made my way back to my car. I was lucky. It was still there, but with a parking ticket under the wipers. It was a whopper, but I'd bill it to Leo, and he'd pay, especially once the dead campers were reported. I found my fetish where Beast had dropped it and scattered river sand over the dried beef blood. Inside the car, I ate granola bars and drank a liter of water before driving back to the hotel, just missing rush hour traffic. Carrying the trash, two fast-food bags of Mickie D's, and my other clothes, I tossed the keys to the valet with a ten. "Keep it handy. I'm leaving in twenty minutes."

After a fast shower, stuffing my face with six McMuffins to ease the hunger of a shift, and changing into more professional clothes—jeans and a tee, all dry, with green snakeskin Lucchese boots that added three inches to my six feet,

I drove to the sheriff's office to report the dead campers. Buncombe County Sheriff's Office was in Asheville city proper, on the corner of Haywood and Carter streets. I walked in, one of the fast food bags under an arm, just after shift change to find the place hopping and looking well funded, despite government budget cutbacks. The tourist trade had been up all summer and tourist tax dollars had helped offset the decreased county and state taxes. Tax dollars that would evaporate if the wolves weren't stopped soon.

I handed my card to a female deputy at the check-in window and asked to see Grizzard. When she looked pointedly at the bag, I thought how easy it could be to conceal a gun in a food bag, so I opened it and let her have a look. I tilted it to her with a little shake, and said, "They were for Grizzard, but he'll never know he's one short. They're a little cold, but have one." I didn't have to twist her arm. Rule number one, if you want a favor from a cop, bring food.

"He's in," she said, buzzing me in, taking a breakfast sandwich as I passed, and giving directions. She was eating when I headed for the stairs and the bowels of the building. I wasn't searched or stopped, and tucked my hands into my jeans pockets, bag smashed under an arm as I meandered, relearning the layout of cop-central. I found the office and stood in the empty, dusty, secretary/receptionist/junior deputy's nook of a workspace, listening through the walls as Grizzard blessed out a deputy and an investigator for a crime scene chain-of-custody failure. He sent them out with two admonitions. "Whyn't you both not be so damn stupid next time." And, "Make sure the assistant DA knows about the evidence problem you pissants made." Our sheriff had such a sweet mouth and easy-going temper.

I turned away as the county cops left, as if studying an old-fashioned corkboard on the wall, and let the men get out of sight before tapping on the door. Grizzard was standing slump-shouldered behind his desk, his belly stretching apart the buttons of his dress shirt. He wasn't getting fat, but it looked as if it had been a while since he worked out. Maybe a while since he slept, by the dark circles under his eyes. He looked up at me, straightened his back, pulled in his belly, and grunted. "Whadda you want. It better be to tell me you found the werewolves."

"Not quite."

He must have seen something in my eyes because he closed his, dropped his head, and let out a pent breath. "What?"

"I was trying to track the wolves last night and I found a house where the wolves bit a squatter. And a campsite—" I stopped, remembering that Beast had wandered through the site. Her paw prints would be there. I closed my mouth. I hadn't thought this through.

"And?" Grizzard was now watching me closely, too closely.

My silence had stretched too long. Except for bald-faced and obvious lies, I had no idea how to explain big-cat prints. Again, I was flying by the seat of my pants, depending on luck. The silence stretched, I flushed, and Grizzard looked suspicious. Into my memory, Beast shoved the bobcat tree markings I had seen Sunday. I had an out. "You have two dead campers," I said. He flinched. "My GPS wasn't working, but I can show you the location on a map. It's just off the French Broad, downstream of Paint Rock, outside of Hot Springs."

"Hot Springs?" Relief poured off of him in an aromatic wave, pheromones that scented of something like joy. Gruffly, he said, "Why didn't you take it to Madison County sheriff's office? You're wasting my time, Yellowrock."

Madison County. *Well, crap.* "Yeah, that's my goal in life, Grizzard. To tick you off as often as possible." I let a hint of a smile out with the words and he grunted again. I extended the crushed bag of Mickie D's finest. "I never met the Madison County sheriff. I have no idea where his office is and no time to hunt it down. I'm giving you the info and you can do what you want with it. And to make your day even better, it might be on park land, so you can split some *more* jurisdictional hairs." My smile fell, as I remembered the campsite. "It was bad, Sheriff."

Grizzard cursed and rubbed his hand over his face. He smelled of old sweat and failed deodorant and, on his breath, rancid coffee and fast food. "And that's the best you can do for a bribe?" He indicated the bag, still outstretched, with a little finger toss, his voice carrying amused remorse—joking, but maybe only a little.

"Yeah. I'll try to make it steak next time. Take 'em." Grizzard took the bag, opened a McMuffin and ate it in three bites. I heard his stomach rumble in relief. "When's the last time you ate a real meal?" I asked.

"Before werewolves started eating people. That takes the joy out of food." He opened another sandwich and took a bite, disproving his own theory about his appetite. "Okay," he said through a bite of my cheap bribe. "Show me." He raised his middle finger to a tri-county map hanging on the wall. I didn't think the middle finger was an accident.

Turning my back to him, which Beast didn't like, I found the bend in the river, the junction of Spring Creek on the far side. I pointed. "Campsite's here somewhere. Away from the river."

Grizzard pulled up an aerial view on his laptop and it was detailed enough for me to find what might be the rock I woke up on at dawn, not that I shared it with him. I pointed to a smaller area, thinking I recognized a tree that was now larger than when the shots were taken. "The house where the squatter was bitten is . . . here." I shrugged when Grizzard tried to pin me down more than that. I wasn't gonna do his job for him, and besides, mountain lions don't do GPS.

"Park land is close, but so are some private parcels," he said, sounding frustrated. He dropped into his chair and dialed an old-fashioned phone, calling the park service, where he spoiled the ranger's breakfast, requesting he drive to the site and check it out. When he hung up, he drummed his fingers, thinking.

I would hate being a cop. The sitting around waiting would drive me nuts.

Next he called the Madison County sheriff, who turned out to be a woman. I heard her voice on the other end of the phone, direct as a drill sergeant and nearly as earthy. Grizzard addressed her as Scoggins, and I had a mental picture of her, with steel gray hair, a muscular body, and the posture of an aggressive alpha dog. Just my nerves talking, but it seemed to fit the voice. She cussed as she took down info and sent a deputy out along Paint Rock Road to liaise with the ranger. She cussed as she arranged radio frequencies so they could manage a four-way chat without being overheard by John Q Public. While they talked and arranged and cussed some more, Grizzard ate, managing to down two more sandwiches.

I brought him a coffee when his voice started to sound dry. The good little helpful citizen, yeah, that's me. I smothered my impatience and waited.

CHAPTER TWELVE

Who? Bit? You?

I heard the park ranger gag when he described the site over the four-way chat line. It was on park land, but just barely. The deputy wasn't much better, sounding young and full of horror.

Then, in the background, I heard the ranger say, "There's fresh cat tracks. Like a mountain lion. Huge paws."

Grizzard lifted his eyes at me, holding me pinned. I tried to look surprised and innocent. "No mountain lion sign in the state," he said, "not in nearly a hundred years. The record kill for bobcats, though, is something like forty-eight pounds." He added thoughtfully, "Lynx have bigger paw pads." He shook his head. "But unless it's got rabies or distemper, no bobcat or lynx attacked, killed, and ate humans. Mountain lions, though—"

I shook my head, interrupting. "Wolf tr—"

"Wait," the ranger said. "I see the wolf tracks. There're everywhere, but older. Settled into the soil." A moment later he said, "Looks like the wolves did the killing and the cat came to investigate. If it's a bobcat, it's got the biggest damn feet I ever saw."

Trying to maintain an innocuous expression, I lied. "Could be. I heard snarling and hissing and, in the distance once, a woman screaming bloody murder." Those were sounds a bobcat makes, especially a female in heat with males fighting over her. Lynx screams sound different to Beast, but no human would know the difference.

"Unless you have some reason to consider putting out traps, forget the cat for now," the female sheriff said, taking charge of her men. "When CSI gets there, have them make pictures of the cat prints and include it in the report.

"Grizzard," she said, her voice tight. "How do we kill those things?"

"Silvershot."

She cursed succinctly. "I can't afford silvershot. My budget's screwed already."

I lifted a finger. Grizzard jutted his chin at me, giving me permission to speak. "I can call a . . . friend or two. See if they'll donate the silver rounds." I meant Leo Pellissier and Lincoln Shaddock. They were loaded. Let them help out the local law, make a few friends in high places. But I also knew not to hide that from the cops. "Vamps," I said.

Scoggins cussed like a sailor for ten seconds, then went silent. Grizzard and I could hear her breathing over the line, harsh sounds like an angry bulldog. "Grizzard? What do you think?"

"Better the suckheads than my men going furry every full moon," he said instantly.

"Fine," she spat. "But tell them not to expect political favors."

"I think they'll be happy if your men don't shoot them with their own gifts," I said wryly, skirting close to snide and sarcastic. "I'll get back to you as soon as I know what they'll do. Can I go now?" I asked Grizzard, not that he had forced me to stay, but I had covered my tracks, found out what the cops were up to, and now had other places to be.

"Yeah. Sure." I went into the hallway and Grizzard called out to me. I paused in the doorway and swiveled to face him.

"Yellowrock, anything you can do for us will be appreciated." The words sounded like they were pulled out of him with red hot pincers. I waggled my fingers to show I'd heard, and took off down the hall, texting requests to Bruiser for phone calls and to the twins for meetings. Sometimes it was easier to go through the human (or mostly so) blood-servants to get to vamps, especially when asking for big-ticket items that didn't relate perfectly to the mission at hand.

Thanks to the miracle of modern tech, I had my day planned in minutes and was left with three hours to kill, which meant I could take a nap or a break. I opted for the one with food. Seven Sassy Sisters' Herb Shop and Café had a booming business, locally and Internet, selling herbal mixtures, teas in bulk and by the ounce. The café served brewed teas, specialty coffees, breakfast and lunch daily, and brunch and dinner on weekends. Homemade soup and breads were available, both to go and to eat in. The menu leaned heavily toward vegetarian fare, whipped up by the eldest sister, water witch, professor, and three-star chef, Evangelina Everhart, a drill sergeant of a woman who terrified me on some ancient, primal level.

In New Orleans, Evangelina had been thrust upon me by Molly over the summer, as my houseguest, during the talks between witches and vamps about reparations for the deaths of witch children and to open communication lines between species. The visit hadn't ended well, and Evil Evie and I still had some things to discuss, a conversation I figured would be unpleasant. She had put what looked like a love spell on George Dumas, Leo's prime blood-servant, in what I assumed had been intended to provide an edge in a game of political maneuvering between vamps and witches, a game where the vamps had all the advantages. I got in the way, and it spilled over on to me, which caused Bruiser and me to end up half-naked in the shower together. I didn't appreciate being spelled, even if it was by accident. And love spells are illegal by witch-law. No matter how I looked at it, Evangelina had been a bad guest. If she hadn't been Mol's sister, I'd have sent her packing with a few bruises to show for her time.

There were two reasons I hadn't dealt with the problem since then: deference to Molly, and the knowledge that Evil Evie was the leader of the sisters' coven. Covens were like team sports, and the leader demanded obedience. She also had the right to draw on the power of the coven's members for group workings. I didn't know enough about witches to stick my big nose in. Yet. I wanted to handle it with tact, which wasn't my strong suit, so I was thinking it through. For weeks now. Ignoring any possibility that fear of Evangelina or fear that Molly would get ticked was keeping me away. No. Not me.

I stood in the doorway to the café when I arrived, sniffing out the place. The café was decorated in mountain country chic, with scuffed hardwood floors, bundles of herbs hanging against the back brick wall, a dozen tables and several tall-backed booths, seats upholstered with burgundy faux-leather and the tables covered with burgundy and navy blue check cloths. Today there were ten patrons at various stages of breakfast, not as many as usual. The kitchen was visible through a serving window, proving that Evangelina wasn't in today, which relieved me immensely, restoring and sharpening my appetite. Not that much ever dulled it. I strode in.

Carmen Miranda Everhart Newton, an air witch, newly widowed and with a baby in one of those portable car-seat thingies resting on the counter by the register, squealed, rushed around the counter, and threw herself at me, hugging me. She smelled of milk and talcum powder and other people's cash. And baby. I couldn't help my smile. Beast purred deep down inside. *Kitssss,* she thought at me. We had saved Carmen's life and, by extension, the baby's life, before it was born. Of all the sisters except Molly, she liked me best. I patted her back, feeling like a giant next to the tiny woman.

The wholly human sisters, Regan and Amelia, and two other witch sisters, twins Boadacia and Elizabeth, ran the herb store, which wasn't open yet, worked at the café as waitstaff, and doubled as cooks when Evangelina was off. The witch twins were the babies of the family, fearless, gorgeous, and always getting into trouble trying spells they shouldn't have. Dual screams announced Cia and Liz just before they tackled me. All four of us staggered back against the door, laughing. Which left me in the middle of a giggling, chattering pack of females. It made me feel all mushy inside. The hugging felt weird. I wasn't a hugger. I patted shoulders knowing I should be doing something else. Something more. I met Molly's eyes over her sisters' heads, and was surprised to see tears. Molly was happy I was here. The mushy feeling spread through me, unaccustomed, unfamiliar, alien. And wonderful.

The witches smelled of bread and cooked meat and herbs. Despite the Mickie D's, my belly rumbled. The girls laughed at the sound and pulled me to the family's corner booth near the kitchen. I usually avoided booths from an ingrained security standpoint, but I didn't say no. The Everharts were the closest thing I had to a family, the group of sisters having practically adopted me when I brought Carmen out of a vamp's lair alive and well. They had hair in various shades of red, eyes of blue or green, and names with character, strength, and something like poetry.

Feeling warm and content, I allowed myself to be pushed into the booth next to Molly and took Little Evan on my lap where he stood, squealing. His sneakered feet bounced on my thighs and he tried to climb onto the table, his little denim-covered bottom up in the air.

"He's into everything," Molly said over the ruckus. "Ten times worse than Angelina ever was." At my inquiring look, she said, "Angie's in school."

"Which feels so strange," one sister said as they all tried to cram into the booth with us, all talking at once, and over each other until I couldn't follow who was saying what, not while trying to hold on to Little Evan.

"Angie Baby's so grown up."

"The next generation of Everharts is going to be huge."

"Cia's boyfriend wants six kids."

"I'm trying to talk him down."

"We'll take better care of this batch."

"No deaths with ours. Never again."

"No runaways, no losses, no disappearances."

"Good health and happiness. From now on," Molly said. It sounded like a blessing, and when the others repeated the phrase in unison, "Good health and happiness!" I knew it was—a blessing for family, in the ancient way of blessings, words spoken with purpose and power.

"Amen to that," one sister said. The ones with mugs clinked them together.

"Janie, you want the usual?"

I craned around looking for the speaker and said, "Yes, please," in my best Christian schoolgirl's manners, figuring I'd never be heard. But a rasher of black-pepper maple bacon, cut thick, fried crisp, and a half loaf of seven grain bread appeared on the table as if by witches' conjure. A pot of fresh tea followed. One sister took Little Evan, and I started eating, knowing I wore a goofy smile, as much because of my feelings as for the food. Everhart sisters' hips crushed against mine; the chatter was almost deafening. Six eggs scrambled hard and a stack of pancakes with blueberry syrup found places between the arms and hands and mugs, the two sisters on duty keeping food and drinks flowing to customers seated around the café, too.

"Anyone figure out what Angie's dreams mean yet?" Cia asked, pouring tea into my cup and topping off the four other mugs.

"Deer could be some sort of anthropological, Celtic, mass-memory."

"Dead deer in a big pile. Blood and bones. No horned ones. Not a Celtic thing."

"A warning?"

I couldn't help with dream interpretation. If I dreamed of dead deer, Beast would be eating them. I grinned wider and dug in as one sister upended a canister of whipped cream, squirting a mountain on top of the pancakes and another poured on blueberry syrup. The New Orleans French Quarter had nothing on the Sassy Sisters' menu. The chatter grew as customers departed and the sisters settled in for a visit. The baby's car seat landed in the middle of the table, the baby asleep, and cute in a drooling-snoring-bald-toothless way. And my heart expanded until it might explode. Yeah. If I'd grown up with a family, this was what I would have wanted it to be like: noisy and loving and demonstrative.

And then, right in the middle of the meal, the chatter, the girlish exuberance, something changed. I felt it, like a heated breeze across my skin, a warm, rosy intensity from the doorway. *Crap*. Fork in hand, I half rose and craned to the entrance.

Evangelina stood there, outlined by morning sunlight.

She was wearing jeans and boots, a tee with a long purple scarf, a stylish cotton jacket. And a murderous expression. Beast rose and hit my bloodstream with her energy. I leaped over the table. Landed. No weapon but the fork.

Evangelina's face instantly morphed into a beautiful smile. I stopped, blinked. Had I seen that—that whatever it was? She advanced, arms out to me. She looked happy to see me, which was a stunner. Evangelina had seldom been happy to see me. She also looked pretty, slender, as if she had lost twenty pounds, and, more important, she looked twenty years younger. *Kill,* Beast hissed. *Danger.* I tensed, confused by Beast's reaction, not sure why I was standing there holding a fork. Evangelina pulled me into a hug. Her rosy glow covered me, damping my worry.

It's okay. This is good. Feeling foolish, I lowered my fork and hugged her back. Hugging felt fine. Good. *Normal.* She released me and pulled me to the table, my left hand in hers. I went with her. Retook my place as the sisters reorganized for me, and started eating, my left hand still over my head, lifted back over the booth seat behind me, clasped in hers. The pancakes were so good. I stuffed several mouthfuls in at once. Sweet. Fruity. Fabulous. *Oh. My. God.* Flavor flooded my mouth and exploded inside me.

Evangelina let go of my hand.

Beast's claws tore through me. The rosy glow ripped away, slashed with a claw-strike. I gasped, heart racing, and started to sit up. Beast held me still, pulling the fork to my mouth. The food in my mouth was suddenly just . . . food. I chewed and swallowed. Again. Eating. Eyes on my plates. Not looking up. Not letting Evangelina notice that the spell she was using was no longer working on me.

Crap. Spelling people without their knowledge was against witch-law, but the dang witch had spelled me again, using the same freaking rosy glow spell she had used before, the time I had nearly ended up having wild, crazy, hot, out-of-control sex with Bruiser in my shower. This time, instead of sex, I felt hunger, flavor, and the intense joy of family. I looked around, chewing. The girls were all watching Evil Evie, over my shoulder, behind the booth, laughing, hanging on her every word. Evangelina was telling about the cookie baking class she was planning. Spelling us.

Little Evan, who had been passed from sister to sister during my meal, crawled across the table to me. No one stopped him. They were all too entranced by Evangelina, who was listing the cookies she wanted to teach the locals how to bake: sugar, lemon-lavender, snickerdoodle. Evan Jr. pushed my dishes out of the way and crawled into my lap. Moving with the clumsy, belly-and-diaper-in-the-way motor skills of a child, he stood on my thighs and stared into my eyes, forcing me to sit upright. I had never noticed that his were bluer than a Carolina sky after rain. I had never noticed his hair was more fiery than either of his parents'. I had, in fact, never noticed Little Evan except as a funny little kid. And if it was possible for a toddler to be worried, he was.

"Aun' Jane," he whispered, putting his cheek against mine. Though Little Evan had been talking for months, I had heard him say less than ten words. And he had never said my name before. Never. "Aun' Jane!" He grabbed my braid and yanked, insistent. The last of the rosy glow dissipated from my mind. "Aun' Jane! He'p!" I put my arms around the kid and he wound his around my neck holding on for dear life. Choking me. He wasn't spelled. And he knew I wasn't spelled. And he knew his mother and aunts were. "Heee-yup! Pwease."

This was bad. Evangelina had ensorcelled her sisters. She was putting out some kind of whacky energy that spelled nearly everyone she met. She was spelling herself. Beast's claws pushed into me, painful. I tightened my arms around Little Evan and whispered in his ear, "I know. It's okay. I'll fix it." *Somehow.* He nodded fiercely; his cheek was wet against mine. Little Evan was crying. *Oh crap.* I hugged him hard and passed him to Molly. She took him absently, never looking at him. Little Evan looked over his shoulder at me, straining against Mol's hold. Beast settled her claws into my psyche, painful, sharp. I saw a vision of a doe, tall grass between us. And the feeling of sudden, violent movement. The taste of hot blood. *Yeah. Gotcha,* I thought. *Ambush.*

Slowly, I lifted my knee and put my right foot onto the burgundy seat. Beast poured strength and hot speed into me. I pulled in a breath, swiveled around, rising, grabbing the high back of the booth seat. Time slowed, heavy as wet sand. Evangelina stopped midsentence, eyes wide, and still I kept rising, bending over her. Fastfastfast. She started, shocked, one hand lifting, slowly. I leaned in, gripped her scarf, twisting, pulling her to me. The heat from her spell slid over my hands and away. Her face lifted, her hair falling back. And everything I thought I knew about witches, and this witch in particular, went up in smoke. There were pinprick spots on her neck.

"Who bit you?" I demanded.

Her lips parted. And I smelled another scent on her, like the bottom note on a cheap perfume, overloaded by the fresher ones, dying fast. I bent over her, twisting my other hand into her red hair. It felt like silk, like something from a dream. Beast growled deep inside me and I heard it spill from my mouth. "Who? Bit? You?" I demanded, not expecting her to answer.

"Lincoln Shaddock," she whispered.

"Blood-whore," I whispered back.

Evangelina's hands came together and up, separating as they passed through my arms. Slammed outward. Ripping her scarf over her head and her hair from my grip. Suddenly she was on the other side of the booth. I turned, following her, still holding the purple scarf and strands of silky hair. She hunched her shoulders, her hands like claws, her nails blunt and painted pink. "I am none of your business!" she shouted. "Leave me alone!" Her hands formed a bowl and pink sparkling energy flashed from them. It washed over me, a heated wave of scented light, smelling like funeral flowers and old blood. Trying to spell me. Trying to make me accept and forget.

When I spoke, it was an octave lower and full of threat. "Stop. Now," I growled.

The light washed past, feeling oily and flat-sharp, faceted. I could have sworn I heard it hit the brick behind me and shatter. Realizing her spell hadn't worked, Evangelina shouted, "What the hell are you?" She raised her hands high, screamed with rage, and stormed out the door.

The silence in the café was acute. Every person was staring at me. I was frozen in place, standing in the booth seat, Beast so close to the surface, I could feel her breath pant in my lungs. I felt a tug on my jeans. Harder. "Aun' Jane. Aun' Jane." I looked down to see Little Evan holding on to a belt loop, his pudgy fingers yanking. I let him pull me to the seat. My arms went around him when he crawled into my lap. I was gasping, panting, desperate for air. The pinkish glow was fading, evaporating like the odor of strong perfume when the wearer is gone.

Liz muttered, "Big sis is her usual charming self." The others laughed.

Pulling on Beast-sight, letting my heart rate slow and steady, I studied the witch sisters. Their eyes weren't blank, but they also weren't reacting with sufficient shock at seeing me pull Evil Evie's hair, and their coven leader and elder sister storm off. Clinging to the sisters was the faintest tinge of shell-pink, the spell still active. And if I managed to figure out how to stop the spell—like punching Evangelina in the mouth—would that make things better or worse? Would it break the spell or make it unstable, dangerous? Disrupted spells sometimes caused a magical backlash that would physically or psychically harm the witches.

"Molly, did you know Evangelina was spelling you all?" I asked.

Molly's lips lifted with unconcern. "Would you like more tea?"

I shook my head no, my neck muscles so tight they nearly squeaked with the motion. Little Evan pulled my arms around him. "Hug, Aun' Jane." I tightened my arm, cradling him and sipped my cooling tea. The girls' chatter surrounded me. They had already forgotten Evil Evie's outburst, all the sisters, the customers, everyone except Little Evan and me. What should I do?

Spelling herself to become younger and prettier was only against witch-etiquette. Letting a vamp drink from her was against witch-history but not illegal. She had been around another supernatural being, not something I recognized, not anzu, not grindylow, not the sick, infected werewolf taint. The creature smelled like woodland and rock and empty places. It screamed of danger. Demon? But that wasn't illegal according to witch-law either, only stupid. The spell-over-her-sisters *might* be an infraction. If I handled the situation with Evangelina wrong, I would make things worse. I pulled the strands of rich red hair caught in my fingers, twisted them into a tight spiral, and folded them in the purple scarf. One-handed I tucked it into my shirt, not sure why, but it seemed important. I had some thinking to do.

The door opened. The morning air flooded into the room, tinged with exhaust and the scent of fresh hay. A voice said, "Morning ladies. Can anyone here feed a hungry man?" *Rick? Here?* Why would he be *here*, without me?

I lifted my head from the baby's and met Rick's startled gaze. "Hiya, Ricky Bo," I said, letting a hint of threat into my voice. "I think we need to talk."

CHAPTER THIRTEEN

Tag Team Sex? That's the Best You Could Come Up With?

Rick sat across from me looking caught and guilty and happy, which was a weird combo of emotions even from a were-cat who couldn't shift yet. We had moved to a corner table for privacy, and the sisters who were off duty had broken up, going about their own business, including Mol.

"Talk," I said, sounding a lot less mean than I intended. Maybe because he was just so pretty. Black hair fell over his forehead and ducked into his collar, waves catching the overhead lights. His eyes, Frenchy-black in New Orleans, looked Cherokee black here. And his cheeks were glowing with that "please touch me" look men had when freshly shaved. I curled my fingers under to keep them beneath the table and tried to look stern.

The two witch sisters brought Rick's breakfast when it took only one, and I didn't have to grow up with them to know they wanted to get close enough to touch, as well as hoping to overhear something juicy. Rick turned his hundred-watt smile up at them, the one he uses when he's trying to woo his way into a girl's pants. They both melted under the look, and I kicked him under the table. He laughed, slanting a teasing look at me. The girls giggled and departed with dual requests. "You need anything, you just holler." And, "Any. Thing. At all."

I shook my head. He grinned, sipped his coffee, took up knife and fork, and ate four bites before he complied with my request. Order. Whatever. And the pauses, gestures, and small torments were so familiar that they brought an ache to my throat.

"I miss you," Rick said. My heart did a rollover-skip that I kept off my face with difficulty. "I miss human female company." Of course he did. So much for the heart gymnastics. "I miss any company that's sober, not grieving, and not vanishing some nights to hunt, coming back to the tent site smelling of blood. A scent that makes my stomach rumble. But mostly, I miss you."

My heart went back to happy Pilates. "And?"

He sipped and ate some more, keeping me waiting. After he swallowed he sat back and gestured with his knife. "And I've had some very interesting phone calls in the last twenty-four hours, all of which I can respond to by spending time with you and the witches."

"What calls? Who?"

"First, no one had my new cell number. Except you."

I went still. "Crap." Leo gave me the new cell a few weeks ago. I knew he could track me with the cell's GPS. I hadn't thought about him being able to read my cell phone history. That was a rookie mistake. "Leo," I said. I explained about the cell and Rick nodded. "I'll get a new throwaway phone," I promised.

"Yeah. Let me know the number. But that doesn't explain how everyone *else* got my number. That has to be my *host*." The way he said host was like smearing the syllable into a toilet. Rick and Kemnebi were a strange pairing, no matter how I looked at it, and the fact that it had been my idea didn't help. "It started yesterday. Jodi—who did *not* have this number—called to check on me, and told me this guy would be contacting me. No name. Just 'this guy.' Which sounded like The Man."

"You're The Man," I said, putting it into caps as he had done. Jodi was his up-line boss at the New Orleans Police Department. If she told him to do something, like watch me, or sleep with a witch, he would. He always had in the past.

"Not anymore," he said. I started before I realized he

was responding to *The Man* comment, not my thoughts. "Even if I don't shift at the full moon, I'll never be human again. I'll be a supe in hiding. Like you. Law enforcement work is going to be nearly impossible." He stuffed a forkful of egg into his mouth and I went still, thinking back over his words, listening for anger or grief. I picked up only resigned acceptance and a kind of wry self-condemnation. But then, cats don't grieve like humans or dogs do. It's different with cats. Beast called it blood-grief, or hunt-grief, and it was violence incarnate. Or they get drunk for a month, like Kem. I nodded for him to continue and picked up my tea, sipping, keeping the cup in front of my mouth, my fingers wrapped around it for warmth. Rick went on, "Today, I get this call from a Mr. *Smith Jones*, who offered me a permanent job, of sorts, with an agency yet to be named."

I sat back, thinking. It wasn't NOPD—totally out of their jurisdiction. That left FBI and The Psychometry Law Enforcement Division of Homeland Security. The agency had fingers in every paranormal pie in the country except for the witches, most of whom grew up together, related by blood and heritage. Witches were a hard nut to crack even for PsyLed.

"I accused him of being PsyLed," Rick said, letting me know that we were thinking alike. "When he said no, I could hear the lie. Seems I have cat ears now, to go along with the improved sense of smell and vision." Rick sipped his coffee and bit into a homemade biscuit.

"Even if I don't shift at the next full moon my life is going to suck three days a month for the rest of my unnatural life. It won't be like I can hide it. No agency or department would have me except undercover with African black were-cats, none of which will exist in the U.S. when Kem sobers up enough to go home. Even if there were were-cats here, I'd have a hard time infiltrating. Their sense of smell is too acute. They'd pick up on any hidden agenda and tear me apart. So my life as a cop is gone unless I admit I've got the were-taint and join PsyLed as an outted supe. Half supe. Like that." Rick shrugged, eyes on the coffee in his cup. "Anyway, that's a decision for another day. *Smith Jones* had a job for me. He asked me to make contact with you, see if you could get me close to the vamps. He wants me to join your security team."

My heart went cold as a stone. Deep inside, Beast chuffed with laughter, which made no sense, as anger shot through me like frozen lightning. "You son of a bitch," I murmured, without inflection, setting down my cup. "You want to use me to get close to Leo."

Rick laughed and a tension I hadn't consciously recognized left his limbs. He sat back in the booth and met my eyes. "I told him no." My mouth opened and closed with a snap. "I'll always want to be a cop," he said, "but my life is different. Forever. So, no cozying up to friends and lovers to find out info. Except for one thing that might be important."

"And that is?"

"Why did Evangelina leave talks that were progressing so well between the vamps and witches and come back to Asheville? The vamp and witch parley has stalled. Jodi told me no new meetings have taken place since she left. Why did Leo finally agree to an MOC parley? Two questions that ended up here, together." Rick leaned back to his plate and ate several more bites. One of the girls refilled our cups, lingering, as if for an opening in the intense silence to chat with pretty boy Ricky Bo. When she wandered away, her disappointment was an odor on the air. Softly, Rick said, "A small group of New Orleans vampires kidnapped and killed witch children for decades. *Centuries.* And Evangelina Everhart walks out on restitution talks? Not in a manufactured huff she could use to get concessions from vamps who want to settle. But just wanders away." His fingers walked through the air as if floating.

PsyLed was worried about the same things I was, which was just weird. Of course, I knew about Amy Lynn Brown's miraculous recovery, and they didn't. But weirder was Evil Evie's display of spell casting, which Rick didn't know about. She had an agenda. I sipped. Rick ate. I offered my thoughts as far as I could. "She knew about the parley for MOC status." Rick nodded as if that was obvious. And it was. There were only just so many people she might be here for. I was pretty sure she hadn't followed the twins or Derek and the security types. That left Rick and Kemnebi, but she wasn't hanging around the Tennessee side of the mountains. And so that left Grégoire and me, here in Asheville, though as far as I could tell, she had gotten here before either of us. "Do you, or Jodi, or PsyLed have any idea why Leo chose Grégoire, specifically, to handle this parley, over his own heir?"

"Initially, Leo was supposed to come himself." When I raised my brows, Rick shrugged, "It's scuttlebutt. Leo trusts Grégoire. They were lovers in France before they emigrated here. Maybe for a century." He laughed at my expression. "Leo swings all ways—human, vampire, bi. I just heard about it. That info just got added to the woo-woo files yesterday when a photocopy of Magnolia Sweets' diary was delivered to NOPD, no fingerprints, no return address, so it could be fake, but it makes sense."

I wanted to bang my head on the table. Magnolia Sweets had been Leo's primo once upon a time, his prime blood-servant, before she was bitten by a werewolf and went all furry. Maggie Sweets was the bitch who had tortured Rick, and she was dead now. Her death could be laid partly at my door. Her death was also the reason the two lone wolves were chasing me and trying to rebuild a pack by biting humans and witches. It made sense, except for the part about who had found and sent the diary. That was a puzzle.

As to the Leo-and-Grégoire-lover part, Grégoire had supported Leo when the master of the city's back was against the wall, when he was being challenged by the vamp who was now the MOC's heir, and had stuck around when Leo was in the dolore—the whacked-out grief suffered by vamps when people they love die. And Evil Evie, who was not acting like herself, had left restitution talks and come home to Asheville. For Grégoire? For me? Or Leo? Had she heard he was considering coming here himself? I blew out a breath. *Okay*. She found out about the parley and could further some sneaky, evil end better if she was here, drawing on her coven. "And Jodi doesn't know why Leo agreed to Lincoln's parley, after denying his petition for so long?"

Rick scraped his plate and sopped up the greasy egg remains with a hunk of biscuit. "Nope." But he didn't meet my eyes and I was guessing that he had ideas even if no facts.

I said, "To answer your question, I don't know why Evangelina left New Orleans." I didn't tell him about the spell or the vamp bites or the werewolf scent she carried. I couldn't. Rick was being courted by PsyLed. If he took the job, he'd be my enemy. The Everharts' enemy. And now that I knew he could smell truth and lies, I couldn't tell him a bald-faced one, maybe not even fudged-truth-lies. Things to think about. I fished in my pocket for my keys.

"Don't you want to know about the other calls?"

I stopped, pulled my hand free from the denim. Rick smiled slightly, his eyes crinkling at the corners. I'd kissed him there several times, his eyelashes tickling my lips. Pain moved through me like snakes of fire.

"George Dumas called." When I didn't say anything, Rick said, "He wants to know if we're seeing each other. He wants to 'court' you." Rick waited as if expecting me to say something. But I had no idea if we were seeing each other or not. I had no idea if Bruiser was serious about wanting to "court" me, or was looking for a way to keep an eye on me, or had been told by Leo to sleep with me for some nefarious Leo-reason. My life was way too complicated.

I stood and pulled out my keys. "Thanks for the warning."

Faster than a human could ever move, Rick's hand slashed out and grabbed my wrist. His grip was crushing, were-strong. "Don't you want to know what I told him?"

I looked back and forth between his eyes, seeing nothing there that I could read. The reek of big-cat heated the air, the smell of jungle, and murky water, and musky male. "Not really." I jerked my hand to the side, away from his palm, against the weaker pressure of his fingers. Broke his hold. I dropped thirty bucks on the café's counter and walked outside. As I got into my SUV, I tossed Evangelina's scarf and hair into the passenger seat. The first patters of rain made little splats against the windshield as I took the wheel, feeling the leather give under my grip.

Molly might be in danger. Might. Maybe. I had no idea

how witch magic worked, except that interrupting a spell or a working was dangerous to both spell caster and spelled. I had no idea what to do and I wasn't used to feeling helpless. I needed to research spells and stopping them. I needed to go after Evangelina and knock some sense into her. I needed to be *doing* something. Instead I started the vehicle and backed away from the café, useless.

I spent the next few hours in my room, researching spells and how to interrupt them. There was precious little on the Internet about the subject and most of it was contradictory. When I ran out of info, I talked on Leo's fancy cell with the paddler, Dave Crawford, who had organized the creekers—adrenaline-junky-kayakers who took the most dangerous, steep whitewater runs—to look for grindy markings, and aligning the newest sightings on a map. I was pretty sure where, within twenty-five linear square miles, the grindy was holing up. When I took into consideration the folded terrain inside that twenty-five square miles it was more like a hundred square miles. It was a huge amount of area to search.

Frustrated, I pulled on tight exercise clothes, black spandex, and went looking for a sparring partner. Wrassler, standing guard in the hallway in front of Grégoire's room, told me how to find the hotel's fitness area, his smirk ringing bells in my mind. I jogged downstairs, and took it in fast: the small room and blood-servants. The B-twins had cleared space, machines pushed to the side. Some tinkly Oriental or New Age music played over the speakers. The twins were dressed in black cotton martial arts uniforms—traditional karate Gi tops with kicker pants, and were still warming up. The clothes told me a lot about the martial forms they practiced. We had the place to ourselves. Wrassler had known they were here, of course.

The door closed behind me with a soft whoosh. The twins paused in their stretches and I grinned at them, letting Beast rise in my eyes. They stepped apart slowly, facing an opponent. My heart started to pound, a fierce, hard rhythm. "How quickly does vamp blood heal you boys?" Brian laughed and shook out his hands, setting his feet, carefully balanced. Brandon bent his knees, finding his own perfect readiness position, one hand fisted in a defensive posture. With the other, he made a little "come and get it" motion. I leaped.

It wasn't play. It wasn't practice. It wasn't sparring. It was the closest thing to real combat I'd had, outside of fighting for my life, in years. I proved to myself that longtime blood-servants were faster than humans, stronger than humans, and sneaky as cats. They didn't play by TV rules, attacking one at a time. They played by fire ant rules—swarm and destroy. Punches, open handed and fisted, kicks, sweeps, blocks that disguised punches, kicks that hid more kicks, attacking from both sides and from front and back, holds better suited to judo or the wrestling mat, and moves that were strictly illegal in the fighting ring came at me. I loved it.

For nearly half an hour, they attacked, the beating we were giving and receiving growing in speed, force, and complexity, until we moved in a blur. The scent of vamp blood, their blood, human sweat, testosterone, and big-cat musk-and-blood filled the space; faint lust pheromones added to the wonderful stench. We overwhelmed the air-conditioning, our body heat condensing on the door and windows. When I cheated, using momentum and the Gi tops, throwing one brother into the other, both men lost the tops, fighting bare chested. Which made Beast pant with delight. I took two hard punches, one to the face, before I got her back into the brawl.

We fought hard, pulling no punches, and I gave as good as I took. It was painful, swift, and exactly what I needed, bruises, strains, sprains, blood on the mats, and all. When we were exhausted, sweating, and breathless, I heard a sound that pulled me out of the fight. The door to the fitness room closed with its soft whoosh.

I bounded out of Brandon's fist-punch-range and into Brian's space. Brian's arm went around my waist, pulling me against his sweaty chest and abdomen, steadying us both, stopping the bout. Brandon whirled toward the door. We went still. Two of my security boys were inside the room, sitting on equipment, as if they had been there a while, dressed in workout clothes but looking lazy. Derek was standing in front of the door, his heels twelve inches apart, legs braced, hands clasped behind his back as if at Marine parade rest. He was dressed in baggy workout clothes. But his eyes were hard and predatory. Derek Lee was seriously ticked off.

I started to say something. Started to try to explain why I was faster than a blood-servant. As strong as one. Make that two. But Brian's arm tightened on me in warning. I clamped my mouth shut. Brandon turned to me and said, "Nice bout, Yellowrock. Rematch. Soon. And we take the gloves off for that one."

"Yeah. No more Mr. Nice Guy. No more holding back to protect the little lady." Brian pushed me away from him as if I burned his skin and picked up a towel. He tossed one at his brother and they moved toward the door. I fell in behind them.

Okay, I got it. Act as if nothing had happened. Riiiiight. "You boys weren't holding back," I said. "You gave it all you had and I busted your butts. But if you're gluttons for punishment . . ." The twins pushed past Derek and out into the hallway. Derek didn't try to stop them. He didn't reach out and grab my arm, to hold me back, but I could feel his eyes smoldering holes in my spine. He murmured, "You're as bad as the suckheads. Maybe worse. At least they don't pretend to be human."

I blinked but didn't give away that I had heard, though a heated shock flushed through me. I was in the hallway, the door wide open behind me, still talking. ". . . I'll be happy to provide the fists and feet to teach you to respect the weaker sex."

"If it's sex you want"—Brandon said, wrapping his arm around me and pulling me along as Brian punched the elevator button—"we can oblige on that score too."

"Ever heard of tag-team wrestling?" Brian asked. "We can make you scream for more until you're begging us to stop."

And we were in the elevator, the doors closing on us. I fell against the elevator wall as the unit moved, my eyes closed. "Crap," I said.

The brothers chuckled, twin sounds of amusement. An unwilling grin pulled at my mouth. "Tag-team sex? That's the best you could come up with?"

The door dinged open and we stepped into the hallway. "Admit it, Legs. You have mental images right now. We know. Your heart rate sped up. Blood-servants can tell."

I walked between and past them, feeling their eyes on me in all my sweaty glory. But I was not going to reply. Not. Going to.

"All you can think about is how big the bed is in the master room of the suite."

"And how big we are."

I couldn't help my grin but I wasn't about to let them see it. "I can be titillated without being tempted. Thanks but no thanks."

We entered our suite and moved through the common space; I went into my room and shut and locked the door, hearing them laugh in that securely masculine way that makes a girl's heart race and mental images dance around in her head. I leaned against the door at my back and re-membered to breathe. I would not be tempted. I would not. Beast, however, had other ideas and a good imagina-tion. Even better visual skills about things she wanted. I made it to the shower and turned it to scalding, stepping under the spray fully clothed. Just as quickly, I switched it to cold and leaned into the tile. Cold water sluiced down me. Very cold.

Dang blood-servants.

I got a much needed nap, followed by a half hour on the Internet again with a more refined search on breaking a coven leader's spell without killing everyone involved—which couldn't be done from the outside, apparently—and was dressed and ready for work as parley security chief, early. Tonight I was wearing tights, knives, and a split-skirt dress that went to my ankles, sterling silver stakes in my bun as hair sticks. A new Walther, delivered courtesy of Leo, rested at my back. Lipstick my only makeup. My eyes looked feverish, my cheeks bright with blood flush.

Hungry, ignoring the twins, I checked my com equip-ment as I stalked through the suite and down to the Black Bear Grill, where I ordered fried green tomatoes, orange glazed duckling, and the cowboy bone-in rib eye, with grilled asparagus and stag fries with truffle oil and cheese.

And a bottle of wine. I didn't once look at the prices, knowing that I could feed a family of four in Bangladesh or sub-Saharan Africa for a year on what I was letting Leo pay for one meal. I was a hedonist. I was evil. I needed to get down on my knees and beg forgiveness for everything. Instead I downed a glass of wine on an empty stomach and let the alcohol flood my system, knowing the sensation would last only minutes, but wanting the buzz, however fleeting. I tore off a hunk of bread and ate it with my second glass of wine. I felt, more than saw, the twins enter.

They flowed through the room, around tables and chairs and the other patrons, and they sat at my table. Silent, they helped themselves to my wine, looking at the bottle with disdain. They ate my fried green tomatoes when the order came. They ordered meals and salads and more appetizers. Brandon chose another wine from the list. In French. With a perfect French accent, of course. When the waiter left, I rested my arms along the chair rests and stared at them.

"We're sorry," Brandon said. Which was not at all what I expected them to say.

"We can't do a job if we're all in the sack together."

"We can't think straight if we're thinking about you."

"We can't protect Grégoire if we're thinking about protecting you too."

"We might try to keep you alive instead of him."

"If push came to shove."

"We apologize."

"We hope you'll accept our apologies and lack of professionalism."

It was sorta like watching tag-team wrestling. "Fine. You're forgiven."

"Good. Now let's eat. We have a long night ahead of us."

We ate. We chatted. And when the meal was done, we stopped in the hotel lobby to meet Gertruda, the Mercy Blade of the MOC of the Raleigh-Durham area. She had been in town all day, moving between patients in the hospital, using the healing magic and skill of her race, and this was my first opportunity to meet her. She swept through the doors, imperious. And totally unexpected. She was a plain woman, steel gray hair pulled back in a bun, wearing a denim dress with a frilly shirt underneath. She was homey, a little stout, grandmotherly. She was as unlike the other Mercy Blade I had met as it was possible to be, and she wanted nothing to do with me.

She glanced over us all, greeted the B-twins by name and ignored me totally. Lifting her nose at my proffered hand, she pulled her skirts aside and went to the elevator. "Well, that was lovely," I said, my face burning.

The twins laughed. "Gertruda thinks women should be properly covered, with long skirts and no adornment. And no guns. It isn't ladylike. Don't worry about her."

"We like you just the way you are."

"She thinks I'm trashy," I clarified. The twins shrugged, still amused.

We made our way back to Grégoire's suite. The meeting was to take place there tonight, and Derek was already set up and waiting in the central seating area when we entered. He looked at me once, his expression telling me that we had things to discuss, but I knew it would be later, not when the package—his word for Grégoire—was at risk. The current phase of an ongoing job came first, before anything more personal. Derek was a pro.

Grégoire's suite made the B-Twins' suite look like a dollhouse, twice as big and three times as sumptuous. We checked the placement of eyes and muscle: one across the street watching the small crowd of protestors and the front door; two in the lobby where they could see the door, elevators, stairs, restaurant, and front desk; Wrassler was in the hall outside the suite. At ten to midnight, Grégoire left his bedroom and came into the common room. He looked relaxed, languid, and so beautiful he would melt the heart of a demon. No wonder Leo and he had gotten friendly. Grégoire was dressed down tonight, in pants and vest the color of port wine and a white silk shirt. He sat on the couch and crossed his legs. Okay, I got it. The formal parts of the parley were over. Now they were into the brass-tacks part.

The twins took position at the window and door where they wouldn't hit each other with crossfire, but unless they were good shots, they might hit Wrassler through the door. I tapped my mike and told him to reposition.

Minutes passed. At twelve thirty, Lincoln Shaddock was half an hour late, a pretty dang big insult to Leo's representative unless there was a bigger problem than I knew. I caught Derek's eye and gave a minuscule head jerk, excused myself and stepped into the hallway, Derek on my heels. Into the mike I asked, "Who's on tracking and traffic update?"

"That'd be me," a voice answered. It was Angel Tit, a nickname based on a Vodka Angel's Delight. Until recently, I hadn't been trusted enough to be given the guys' real names, but security on this gig required deep background checks, so I knew them all now. But the monikers we'd used in the past had stuck with us. "No problems, Legs. Traffic is clear. The rain has made some creeks rise, but not enough to be a danger."

Rain? Right. It had been raining this morning when I left the Sassy Sisters. The hurricane had arrived in all its wet glory, another indication that New Orleans and its problems had found me again. I pulled my phone and punched through contacts for Adelaide's number; I had input it during computer homework. When she answered, I said, "Where's your boss?"

"With yours, I would hope."

"He's a no-show." A shocked silence settled between us, sharp and electric.

"I'll make some calls." She clicked off.

I looked at Derek and Wrassler. "Any chance the wolves attacked him en route?"

"Anything's possible," Wrassler said. "But that one's not likely to have caused Shaddock anything but a mild discomfort. Not a half hour." Before I could continue a list of possible attackers, he said, "The protestors are all accounted for." At my questioning look he said, "We got trackers on the vehicles and they're all at home, out front, or at work, according to Angel."

I nodded. Ten long minutes later, my phone vibrated and I answered Adelaide. "Tell me something good."

"I can't do that, I'm afraid," she said, her words stiff. Embarrassed. She told me where Shaddock was, what he was doing, and added, "Shall I meet you there?"

I pulled the phone away from my ear and stared at the

screen, eyes unfocused, thinking. And then it all started to come together. "Crap," I whispered. When I put the cell back to my head, I said, "Twenty minutes," and hung up.

I looked down at my dress and then at my men. "Call for two vehicles to be waiting around front in five minutes. Derek you're with me. Wrassler, pick a guy and follow." I stuck my head back inside Grégoire's room. "The parley talks are off for tonight." Grégoire's eyebrows went up slightly. Before anyone could ask, I said, "I'm not quite sure why, but I have an idea. It's possible that Shaddock was attacked. I'll call back when I know more. I suggest you stay within the confines of the hotel until you hear from me."

Without waiting for a reply, I backed out and closed the door. "I've gotta change. You guys need to be in jeans and well armed."

"Vests?" Derek asked, meaning flak jackets. Combat clothes.

"No. But weapon up. We're going to Shaddock's barbeque joint for dinner and dancing."

CHAPTER FOURTEEN

You'll Be True-Dead.

A bump-and-grind Country Western number could be heard out in the street, even over the steady patter of rain, an oldie goldie about a funeral in a bar, the singer propped up by the jukebox, dead. Which fit a few of the people inside, some of whom weren't breathing and had no heartbeat to speak of. When we walked in the door, the place was mostly deserted of normal human customers, but there was still a crowd composed of vamps and the hangers-on of the vamp community, blood-slaves and junkies. Oddly, there were no blood-servants. If I didn't already have alarms going off in my head, that alone would have spelled trouble. The place smelled of cooked meat and the dry, herblike scent of dead meat. Vamps. I tucked my three silver crosses into my shirt as Beast rose in me and peeked out, curious.

Only one couple was dancing; it was a version of the two-step, but with way more pelvis action than the song or dance style warranted. Lincoln Shaddock and Evangelina Everhart had their legs entwined and their faces close together, whispering, laughing. I smelled vamp and witch blood and sex on them, heated from the dance. And the pink spell covered them both.

I already knew that Lincoln Shaddock had bitten her, leaving two constricted pinprick spots on her neck, but I didn't know why. They had lived in the same area for years.

Nothing in my research suggested they had been together before. So why now? Why was Evangelina spelling the region's most powerful vamp? What exactly did the pink rosy spell do? As I watched from the shadows, I saw a red mote of spell-light flash out of Evil Evie and zip around the room like a bat out of a hellhole. It whipped around and disappeared into Shaddock's chest. "Crap," I whispered. I'd seen that before. To my muscle, I said, "Do you see a pink glow on them?"

"No, but they need to get a room or turn around so I can get a better view," Derek said.

Before the witch noticed us, I pulled my men into a shadowed corner table. I'd had my share of booths with their restricted sight design and problematic body realignment options. We sat, my jeans stuffed into Lucchese boots with ash wood stakes exposed at the tops, each of us loaded with enough concealed guns, knives, and silver to bring true-death to every fanghead and human in the joint. I spotted Chen, standing at the end of the bar, his face like a slab of granite and eyes black as midnight. He inclined his head slowly, and moved toward the back, disappearing into the shadows. I figured that was tacit permission to do whatever I needed to his boss.

When a perky waitress came we gave cola orders so we could keep sitting at the table. "Drink nothing, eat nothing," I said, thinking of knockout drinks to disable us, or poison to finish us off.

"Copy that," Derek said.

I studied the scene. The vamps were all sitting, lounging actually, on long booth seats, one or two to a booth, their human blood-meals gathered at their sides. Blood-drunk slaves were smiling vacuously while being dinner or were working as security, cooks, waitstaff, bartenders, and busboys. Once they looked us over, they returned their attention to the dancers, a security lapse no blood-*servant* would ever make. One-handed, I checked the placement of my hair stick weapons: six wood stakes and a slender-bladed, sheathed knife. With my other hand, I pulled my cell and dialed New Orleans, ignoring the way my heart tripped when it rang.

The connection opened, and I heard R&B/island music

in the background, the signature sound of the new house band at the Royal Mojos Blues Club, a bar and dance joint owned by the vamp master of New Orleans. "Good evening, Jane. How are you?"

I pulled in a slow, calming breath. "Hiya, Bruiser. I'm good. You?"

"Do you need me?"

I thought about that for a moment and decided to go with pretending there weren't a dozen innuendoes in that one question. "I need you to run an errand for me." I ignored his "Pity" and went on. "I need you to go to my bedroom and into the closet. I need you to pick or smash open the weapons cabinet in it, and look for a black velvet bag. If it's there, I need you to open it and pour the contents out on a table. Don't touch it. And call me. Will you do that?"

"Why?"

"I need to know if Evangelina stole something from mc."

"I can think of far better things to do in your bedroom than play smash and grab, but yes. I'm only a few blocks from there. I'll call you shortly." The call ended.

Lincoln had his hand under Evangelina's shirt. Public displays of affection were not Shaddock's style; I didn't like what that said about his state of mind. As for Evil Evie, she was once the most stuck-up, inhibited, repressed woman on the planet. Now? Not so much. I set the phone on the table, wondering how much power Evangelina was siphoning off her sisters and if that was more dangerous than interrupting the spell. I studied Shaddock and his dance partner, thinking about what I'd just set in motion due to the red mote I'd seen.

When Bruiser got to my freebie house in New Orleans he would know I hadn't planned to return. My belongings were in cardboard boxes on the floor of the closet, packed for shipping. They had Molly's address on them. They had postage attached. I didn't know what Bruiser might say or do, but I figured it wouldn't be pretty.

While we waited, I saw movement among the vamps as two powerful walking dead stepped into the restaurant. They weren't powerful as in physically imposing, but they were formidable. Commanding. Dominant. Compelling. Dangerous. And, *crap*. They had decided to pay us a visit.

They surged toward us across the floor with the boneless, nearly gravity-defying grace of the hunting vamp. "Heads up," I said. "Dacy Mooney and Constantine Pickersgill at the door. They want something." But then Lincoln's heir and spare would do *nothing* unless they wanted something. "They'll smell the gun oil and ammo."

As they neared, I felt the crosses under my shirt start to glow. The vamps draped themselves into chairs at our table, Dacy wearing a beaded buckskin fringed jacket and dark brown jeans with boots. She had feathers woven into her blond hair. On her, the look worked. Seeing the glow on my chest, Dacy laughed low, as if crosses didn't scare her. Her fangs snapped down with a small click, one and a half inch bone-white killing teeth. Beast huffed in delight, which always surprised me. She liked sane vamps too much sometimes.

Pickersgill said, "Are you boys here to try your hand against Linc?" There was insult in the word *boys*, as thick as if he'd used the N-word. But it was threat in the tone that my guys reacted to, pulling weapons, the light gleaming on silvered blades, the smell of challenge rising.

"Hold," I said. I stared at Mooney's eyes, blue as her daughter's, not vamped out, but in control. "I'm here to send the witch packing and Lincoln to Grégoire on his knees, quaking in shame and fear."

Dacy smiled. "You'un Leo's enforcer?" Her accent was pure Tennessee, probably poured on thick to keep from sounding like the threat she undoubtedly was, but the heavy accent sounded weird coming out of a vamp's mouth. I didn't reply. I had seen the term in a codicil of the Vampira Carta, and read over the language an enforcer used to establish control over vamps, but I hadn't really studied it. I didn't fully know what *enforcer* meant in vamp terms, and I didn't want to get stuck with any nasty duties I hadn't already signed up for, not unless agreeing kept my people safe. So I shrugged, which was universal for, *Call it what you want.*

"No need for violence, y'all," she said. "If I'da wanted you'uns dead, you'da been hamburger sixty seconds ago. As it happens, however, my little girl says I can trust you, Jane Yellowrock, even if you do hunt my kind. And if you're speaking the truth, then I'll be happy to stand aside and let you"—she tapped her cheek as if thinking of the right phrase—"*interfere* with my master's *plans for the evening*. He's actin' foolish, which ain't like him a'tall, and is unworthy of us'ns." She stood. Over her shoulder she said, "Try not to hurt him too much," and winked. I laughed, letting Beast show in my eyes.

Pickersgill followed her to their table. It was easy to see who was heir and who was spare: Dacy was firmly in charge, with political savvy, brains, *and* power. Pickersgill was smart, but in the power department, he was her shadow. As they settled, the outer door opened, and Adelaide entered. She was dressed in slim casual clothes and a pair of Italian leather boots that likely cost more than my entire wardrobe. She cast a fast, evaluating look around the restaurant, met my eyes and let her lips curl up on one side. Then she walked to her mom's table and slid in.

Derek was watching me. In the past, I would have pulled Beast back down and tried to pretend that nothing had happened when Dacy and I had our little dialogue, but lately I didn't bother. I was getting tired of the angry, wary condemnation in his eyes each time I proved I wasn't purely human. Or maybe the irritation was Beast, flexing her claws. Cats didn't care who liked them, as long as everyone else knew their place—at the cat's feet, under the cat's claws. Derek sat forward, his body tensing. Before I could act on that subtle dare, my phone rang, Bruiser's number on the display. I punched a button. "And?"

"When were you going to tell me you were leaving for good?" His voice was emotionless, empty as a vamp's.

"When I made up my mind for good," I said, stuffing guilt down deep and out of the way, "which I haven't. What did you find?"

"Several things. Magnolia Sweets' old trunk, open, the contents strewn, a locked weapons cabinet, and an empty velvet bag." I closed my eyes. I had known Evangelina was a thief when I saw the red motes in her spell. She had stolen the pink diamond, the blood-diamond that carried the sacrificial power of hundreds of dead witch children, the black magic amulet or relic used by the Damours—witch-vamps. I had taken it off the Damours when I killed them, and researched it, learning its name and some of the myths that surrounded it. The *blood-diamond*. The weapon that was at the heart of the witch negotiations with the vamps in New Orleans.

"Hmmmm," I said, thinking about Magnolia Sweets' photocopied diary. I'd had her trunk for a while, and had never gotten around to digging into it. Once the werewolf had died, it didn't seem like a good use of my time to take a blast to the past. I was betting Evil Evie had opened the trunk and sent the photocopy to Jodi at NOPD. "Thanks. I'll get back to you. Lock up on your way out, would you?"

"Jane?"

"Yes?"

"I want you to come back to New Orleans. This time without a spell between us."

"That's problematic right now," I said, "because Evangelina Everhart is using that spell on Lincoln Shaddock. And I'm getting ready to intervene."

"Between a witch and a bespelled Mithran? Do you have a death wish?" He sounded pretty close to dumbfounded.

I chuckled and ended the call. I left the cell on the table, and tossed silver crosses to the men at the table. They caught them, the silver glowing. "Hope you boys are ready to play," I said, letting my hands drop to the stakes in my boots as I stood. Ash wood, no silver, weapons for wounding not killing, unless I was very unlucky and hit Lincoln's heart. In that event, I figured I'd be dead at Dacy's fangs before he hit the floor. And she'd be the new vamp in the talks with Grégoire. I wondered which ending Grégoire would prefer. "Follow my lead, and I'll leave you an immobilized vamp to restrain. Then I'll take the witch."

I moved ahead of my guys toward Lincoln, who was facing me, dancing with his eyes closed, leading Evangelina into a quarter turn. Beast poured her strength and speed into me. I flew across the floor. Hit the couple. Heard Evangelina's breath grunt. The vamp and witch separated. Bodies moved back and away as my own rammed between them. The pinkish glow of the spell prickled over my skin, scattered. And now that I knew what it was, I smelled witch blood and black magic, tart and burning, like fire, heavily banked but killing-hot.

Lincoln snarled, vamping out. Fangs dropping. I staked him fast, hitting him in the abdomen, low enough for the watching vamps to recognize a deliberately nonlethal strike. Trusting the men to handle him, I whirled on Evangelina.

She flailed for balance, feet scuffling. I followed her down, grabbing her arms. Pulling them wide, out from her body. Pushing her. Stepping over her, a leg to either side, riding her down. I let gravity do my dirty work, feeling her hit the floor, and the air whoosh out; I landed on her abdomen as if straddling a horse, my feet on her arms, my hands at her throat. "Hiya, Evie," I said. "Let him go." And I let Beast slam through me, eyes glowing golden, a growl low in my throat, "or I'll kill you where you lie."

"You won't steal this from me," she gasped. "I won't let you." She rocked hard, more power in her limbs than a human should ever have. The pink glow of the dark magic built beneath her skin.

But the I/we of Beast was coursing through me, and no witch could hope to win. "Yield," I said, my voice the lower pitch of Beast. *"Yield!"* I showed her my teeth and she drew back against the floor, chin down as if to protect her throat in my hands. "Say it. Say you yield," I said. I don't know what she was seeing, but Evangelina went limp.

"I yield," she whispered.

"Release him. Say the words."

"Bíodh sé saor, le m'ordú agus le mo chumhacht."

I had heard Molly speak Irish Gaelic and this sounded something like that, mellifluous, melodic, and full of poetry. I wasn't sure what to do, until I heard Shaddock curse.

"To me! To me! Scions to me!" His power rippled over me like a blanket made of cactus thorns. And suddenly there were blood-slaves everywhere, and the snicksnick-snick of semiautomatic handguns readying for fire, followed by the familiar ratcheting sound of shotguns.

All thoughts of killing Evil Evie were pushed aside. I just wanted to get out alive and stop a small war. "Lincoln Shaddock and all his scions," I shouted over the sudden si-

lence, knowing I was about to get myself in trouble. Just
knowing it. But we were on the brink of something deadly.
"Bow to the enforcer of Leo Pellissier, Master of the City
of New Orleans and Blood Master of the Southeastern
United States. Bow or die!" I shouted, using the language
from the codicil to the Vampira Carta. The lines sounded so
Hollywood I wanted to laugh, but when I felt a knife blade
stroke my neck just under my bun I stifled it and added
more softly, "By the command of Leonard Pellissier's enforcer, the Rogue Hunter, stand down!" The rogue hunter.
Who was me. And man-oh-man, didn't that sound weird, to
command by my own title.

"Listen to her," Adelaide said, pleading, commanding.
"Lincoln, master, listen to her. She is here to help."

"Hold, scions," Shaddock snarled. That unnatural silence fell on the restaurant again. I captured Evangelina's
gaze and held it. She swallowed, suddenly seeming to realize that she was in a spot of trouble. She opened her mouth
and I tilted my head in warning. Her lips sealed shut. The
blade disappeared from my neck. A cold sweat prickled
down my spine in belated reaction.

"Do not hurt her," Shaddock demanded. "She is mine."

Crap. He had claimed her? Like a blood-servant? I had
only moments before I had to deal with Shaddock, and
strangling his pet witch before his eyes was not the way to
keep this parley moving forward. Killing Evangelina might
tick Molly off too, once she came out of the spell, and if she
survived its ending, but I really wanted to hurt the witch. I
tightened my fists against her windpipe, lowered my face to
Evangelina's, and murmured against her ear, "You stole
something that was entrusted to me." Her body tensed, her
fingers curling into protective fists, thumbs inside. Stupid
move. She would break her thumbs if she hit me. "You've
been using it, spelling your sisters, draining their power,
making yourself prettier, younger, thinner. Drawing people
to you. Making them feel and do what you want them to.
You used it on Bruiser. You tried it on Leo. And now Lincoln Shaddock."

"My ends justify the means," she whispered. "I'll kill you
for interfering."

"Get in line," I said, my mouth a vibration on her cheek.

I pulled back just enough to see her eyes. Strands of hair crossed her face, a red so intense and silken that it looked artificial, altered by the spell she had cast. Her eyes were bright and lovely, her skin so perfect it glowed. "Black magic," I said, softly, "powered by the blood of witch children."

Evangelina's face flushed a florid, almost painful red. She sucked in a breath to speak a spell. I raised up and came down hard, butt on her belly, boots on her forearms. She gagged with pain and I smelled stomach acid and acrid sweat. "Stop fighting. I know what you've been doing, but for the safety of your sisters, we'll deal with that problem and for the return of *my property* later."

"Not yours," she said instantly, though it was more a reflex than actual thought. "But, *deal*." I stepped off her arms and stood up. Evangelina rolled over, to hands and knees, and was out the door nearly vamp-fast. So much for taking the witch with me.

I whirled to Shaddock. Only moments had passed, but the vamp looked older and weaker, oddly withered. He had a wooden stake buried in his middle, and three humans in black jeans and tees holding him down. He wasn't fighting. His scions stood around him empty-handed. "I yield," he said tiredly. "I yield."

"You will call Grégoire, Leo's emissary," I said, "and offer apologies." I pulled every formal word I could think of and said, "You will grovel at his feet in shame and fear, in dishonor and ignominy. And this once, I'll back you, by telling Grégoire that you were under attack by enemies of the parley. *This once.* After that, I'll slit your throat, cut off your head, and toss your body to the human protestors. And hope Dacy is better prepared to resist a pretty face. You'll be true-dead. Do you understand?"

"I do." He looked at me, his fangs clicked back, his eyes human, or nearly so. Confusion flooded through him, so strong I could smell it. "What happened? What did I do?"

Crap. He really didn't know what he had done. "You let a witch spell you. And I've saved you the one and only time."

I followed Lincoln back to the hotel, where I guided him to Grégoire's suite, his elbow firmly in my grip. Inside the suite, he fell on his face, prostrate, and begged the forgiveness of Grégoire and Grégoire's master in language so flowery and archaic, I didn't even bother to try to understand it. The delicate elegant vamp looked at me in utter surprise. I managed a small smile and tilted my head, suggesting with body language that Grégoire accept the apology. He stood, snapped down on his vest points, bent at the waist, and pulled the taller, heavier vamp to his feet as if he weighed two pounds. Grégoire was an elder master, and size was no indication of might in an old vampire. He looked at me.

"He was attacked," I said, trying to think how I could make this part sound as formal and fancy as I needed, to maybe save the negotiations and Shaddock's butt. "He was spelled by a witch, with an amulet created by Renee and Tristan Damours and their brother. It's black magic powerful enough to cloud the mind of a master vam—Mithran. The . . . culprit"—yeah, that was a good word—"will be dealt with."

"Is this so?" Grégoire asked Shaddock.

The tall, craggy-faced vamp looked at me in surprise. In spite of my promise, he hadn't been expecting me to defend him. "Yes."

Grégoire focused on me, his eyes slowly bleeding black in scarlet sclera. "I charge you—when this parley is over, you will find this culprit and bring her to me."

A cold chill I had been fighting all evening shot through me. I was so screwed. And Evangelina was so dead. But if I disagreed, Derek would be given the job; Derek would bring him Evil Evie without a qualm, and when she died, the spell she had snared her sisters in would implode. Molly might die. By agreeing, I was sealing my own fate and destroying my friendship with Molly forever. She had forgiven a lot over the years, but turning her sister over to the vamps for punishment would be the last straw. Already trying to find a way out, I nodded.

Grégoire stared me down—quite a feat for a vamp a foot shorter than me, and I realized he was waiting for me to do something. *Like bow?* I narrowed my eyes at him. *No way am I going to—*

"You may set your minions on the financial search," he

said. His words were clipped but there was an amused twist to his lips, as if he knew what I was thinking. Maybe he did. I texted Evangelina's particulars to Reach, my research guy when I could afford him, with a vamp request to provide a financial background on her. With what Reach charged vamps for info, he could plan a trip to the Caymans on the proceeds from this one job.

The rest of the night I watched the proceedings in Grégoire's hotel suite, dressed in jeans and boots and drinking tea by the potful to stay awake. The remnant of the hurricane crashed outside the windows. The hired help was jumpy, sliding their eyes away each time one met my gaze, obviously remembering everything I had done in the last twenty-four hours that a human couldn't. It was sad, and likely to be a problem in the future, but there was nothing I could do about it. I wasn't human. I never had been, despite the times I had tried to deny it to myself. I was having to deal with it, so Derek and his men could too. A much bigger worry was how I could convince Molly that her eldest sister was doing black magic, when Evie had a coven master's rights over her. I wasn't certain about any of the particulars. I knew only one thing. Evangelina had to be dealt with. Somehow.

By dawn, I was beyond exhausted. Back in my room, I showered, dressed in a pair of boy-shorts undies and a tank, and curled into the mattress, pulling the thick comforter over me. Rain pounded at the window. Wind pulsed like the cold breath of the devil.

I was about to close my eyes on the world when I remembered to check the Weather Channel so I could adjust security considerations for the rain. Instead, the TV came on with local a.m. news. A pretty young announcer was saying, ". . . claims he found a campsite deep in the Pisgah National Forest that had been attacked by predators. The teenaged hiker claimed that the site was an old one, with the remains of at least two people, located in a deep declivity with a narrow feeder creek at the bottom. This description matches the previous attack sites enough that the sheriff department and park service has sent out searchers.

So far, however, park rangers have not found the site, and some are calling the claim into question, wondering if the allegation was something the teenager dreamed up for attention."

The shot changed to a sign for the Pisgah National Forest, rain slamming down, making a spray with its force. The voice-over said, "This latest mauling and gruesome death is said to be older than the previously discovered campsites, but isn't far from the campsite at Paint Rock. In each of these cases, the campers were all killed."

Adrenaline tried to spurt into my system, but instead of increased heart rate, I felt only dispirited apprehension, the anxiety like a sore tooth rather than a raging fight or flight response.

The TV camera shot expanded to reveal the entrance to the park, and focused in on a group of drenched backpackers, who were clearly leaving. The shot changed again to a close-up of three twenty-somethings, the rain-soaked man in the middle speaking for them all. "You expect some element of danger any time you camp, man, but this is worse than anything I ever faced out west, and I used to camp in grizzly territory."

The girl said, "Yeah, we're outta here. My parents said if I didn't leave, they'd come up here and drag me home."

The announcer came back on and said, "Park and county officials have suggested that campers leave, and are making sure that every camper who stays understands the risks. They had already instituted a check-in system for every hiker and camper, every day, and the numbers of new campers have dwindled to nothing. Until the marauding creatures are trapped and destroyed, the tourist dollars in Buncombe and surrounding counties will dry up to nothing."

I muted the TV. Groaning, I rolled out of bed and to my feet. So much for sleep today. As I dressed, rain and wind beat at the windows. *Oh goody.* A hunt in the middle of a hurricane. I didn't have that misery even when I lived in New Orleans. This was sooo gonna suck.

It didn't take much to obtain Grizzard's permission to join the hunt. The sheriff looked worn and wan and beaten, his body odor telling me that he was running on adrenaline, caffeine, and not much else. He'd have given me permission to join if I'd shown up dressed in a chicken suit, he was that tired and that worried. He gave me his personal cell phone number and a GPS unit and waved me off just as the downpour increased intensity.

I ignored the teenaged hiker's directions and started down the mountain at a different incline from where the other searchers were working. The kid had gotten confused getting back to the park path, but the stench of his fear and the putrid scent of old blood and rotten meat led me down at the proper angle. I hadn't expected to be hiking in the rain on this gig and hadn't sent my water-resistant clothing ahead to the hotel. Torrents of water cascaded from the sky, aiming directly down my collar. I was soaked to the skin in minutes, grousing under my breath. *This is Leo's fault. Totally Leo's fault. And Bruiser's. Yeah. His fault too.*

It took me an hour to backtrack through the woods and mud and laurel thickets until I hit werewolf scent. It overlay the reek of fetid, disintegrating bodies and took me directly to the campsite. There was a lot of gore and parts of three bodies. Maybe four. The camp was so strewn it was hard to tell what was what. The tent was in shreds; scavengers had been at the site, dragging things around; belongings were scattered. I moved back uphill until I found a cell signal and called Grizzard, giving him the coordinates before returning to the kill-site.

The rain made it hard to make sense of anything, and not just because the ground was mushy and the downpour was spilling down my neck. Not just because the cold front was pushing in fast on top of the dying hurricane, changing temps into early fall. The storm had washed all the scents downhill to meet the feeder creek the campers had pitched their tents beside. The creek was now a rushing torrent clogged with trash, brush, and body parts, the roar a violent white noise that drowned out every other sound.

I had seen a lot of gore in my day. I'd made a lot too. But this was beyond anything I had seen, a sensory overload, further complicated by the scent pattern. The wolves had been here more than once, their newer scent overlaying the older one like open wounds, infected and dying. And, of course, the grindylow had paid the place a visit, leaving his fishy trace. I learned one important thing—the woman killed here had been a witch, like Itty Bitty. No coincidence.

I crossed my arms and hunched my back against the cold, but, despite my faster metabolism, the dropping temps were seeping into my bones along with the wet. Standing under the partial protection of a big-leafed Royal Paulownia tree, I studied the site. I didn't know what was driving the wolves beyond revenge and sickness. The level of violence here made no sense at all. The wolves had rampaged, killing all the campers, even the one woman, in an attack that appeared frenzied and irrational, even for werewolves. I looked out over the campsite, trying to see it from the viewpoint of whacked-out wolf. Rampage. Violence. Bloodlust.

Beast huffed and sent me an image of a spotted kit chasing her tail. There was mild insult in the image, and I chuckled, despite my misery. *Moon madness,* she thought at me. *First shift after losing pack. No purpose but bloodlust.*

That made sense, so I worked the timeline backward. Jail, the loss of their pack, then the full moon, had made the wolves unstable, uncontrolled. This site, though new to me, was the first attack site, made soon after the wolves got to the mountains. The attack site with the dead couple on the bank of the French Broad had been the second. The pieces began to click together like dominoes falling into a pattern. When the wolves finished with the campers on the river, they had gained control, and bit the squatter at the abandoned house, leaving him alive. The attack on Itty Bitty, the first site I'd seen, had been the fourth attack, and the place where the three women had all been bitten but left alive, was the last and most recent wolf attack. There had been none since, which might just mean that the wolves had gotten smarter.

If the wolves had made any mistake, it was here, when they weren't thinking at all. I needed to track them back to where they had shifted to wolf and then back to human. I needed to understand it fully. Shivering with the dropping temps and immobility, I moved up under the laurel, against a rock face, protected from the rain, and found werewolf tracks. By the smell and the number of tracks, they had slept here in wolf form in the last few days. It was evidence. I moved out again and, for another hour, growing colder, wetter, and more frustrated, I stood in the increasing cold, under the unreliable protection of the Royal Paulownia, waiting for the searchers to find my GPS location. I was spinning my wheels, getting nowhere. With the rain, I wasn't going to be able to track on this one, not without a better nose than I had in human form. And I wasn't going to shift in front of humans. That left very few options.

Looking over my shoulder, I spotted the searchers sliding down a steep incline, led by the sheriff. I smelled coffee and cigarette smoke and sweat from the group behind him. Grizzard was not gonna like this. Not at all. "Hey, sheriff," I called out. "You like cats?"

"You mean like the big-cat that walked all over my crime scene yesterday?"

Oh crap. I'd forgotten about the Beast prints. "Um, not exactly," I said. After that, my day went into the toilet.

CHAPTER FIFTEEN

Be Polite to the Nice Pussycat

That the sheriff allowed me to bring in Kemnebi while we waited for the state crime scene techs to arrive and set up, proved he was reaching the end of his rope, but the fact that he agreed to allow the black were-leopard to hunt with us in big-cat form, showed just how stressed the county officials had become. All it had taken was my comment that the wolves had been back to the site recently, since the rain started. The fresh wolf tracks under the small ledge had been all the evidence Grizzard needed to consent. Even the park officials agreed that a tracker with claws and fangs of his own was a good idea, if I could keep him under control. I also knew that the officials would be making casts of any black were-leopard prints they found, to compare to the Beast prints. I figured that would clear Kemnebi from any possible suspicion in the killings, but it wouldn't make the county and park powers-that-be any more satisfied.

Wet to the skin, chilled, I waited in my SUV at the access road, the heater running. I checked my e-mail, answered phone calls, and took a much needed nap, stretched out on the SUV's leather backseat. Before noon, I heard tires on gravel and sat up, yawning. Rick, driving a borrowed, dented pickup, pulled in beside me and cut the engine. I was surprised to see a black leopard sitting up high in the passenger seat. Somehow I had expected Kem to shift on site. He swiveled his head and met my eyes. Hissed, showing killing teeth in warning.

Beast stirred. We were alone, parked far from the law enforcement vehicles, upwind from the scent of old death. Beast thought at me, *Want to hunt. Want to hunt with Kemcat.*

"Not gonna happen," I murmured, as I climbed from the vehicle, shut the cab door, and tucked my hands in my damp pockets. "Not now, not ever." She narrowed her eyes at me, deep in my mind, flicked her long, blunt tail, and slunk away, sulking. I leaned against the wet SUV.

Rick exited the pickup and walked around the truck toward me, moving like he was half leopard already, with a liquid and predatory grace, despite the water repellant jacket and layers beneath. His hair was blacker than midnight, his eyes blacker still, and something warm and heated flowed down my body and settled in my lower belly. Despite the rain and the chill on the wind and stink of old death, a smile pulled at my mouth.

Rick opened the passenger door and Kem stepped out, a slow, four-pawed slink. The spots beneath his black coat weren't visible in the dim light, and he looked pure black with gold-green eyes, round pupils wide. He shook once and hissed, looking up at the clouds, shoulders hunching. Black leopards are good swimmers, surpassed only by tigers in their love of water, but getting rained on was evidently different from taking a leisurely swim in a cool pond on a hot, jungle day. Kem had seen me once, from a distance, in Beast form, and he looked at me now, remembering. He hissed again, pulling his lips back, wrinkling his snout.

Rick held out a steel-prong dog collar, the kind that, when the leash is pulled, extends prongs into the dog's throat. The collar style is used to control dangerous, aggressive dogs, and was the one concession Grizzard had insisted upon for a black leopard on the day's hunt.

Kem hissed in warning, showing his insult in the way that cats the world over do, by passive aggressive behavior. When Rick bent to put on the collar, Kem jumped to the hood, then the cab roof, and off the other side of the pickup. Without looking back, he started downhill, directly toward the kill site, tail in the air like a modified, upraised, middle finger.

Rick slanted his eyes at me and let his mouth quirk up on one side. "He's pissed because he's sober in daytime. He's worked hard to avoid that state since we got here."

I thought about Kem knowing me in my Beast form. About Grizzard and the gun-happy deputies. "He's not going to let you use the collar at all, is he?"

"Nope. Not without a fight none of us can hope to win. And, speaking of fights, he told me that the first time I shift, he's going to challenge me to personal combat and kill me for sleeping with his wife, which I didn't do."

The breath left my lungs as if I'd been socked in the gut. *Mine,* Beast chuffed, shoving her claws into me. *Mine!*

"Yeah, that's the way I felt about it too," Rick said, as if he'd heard her claim, but reacting to my facial expression. "He says were-law doesn't allow him to kill me until then. And since I won't know how to fight, won't even know how to stand on four legs, I'll be dead before dawn. Fortunately, the full moon is a few days away, so we can find time to say good-bye."

"Not gonna happen," I said. "I'm his alpha. I won't let him."

Ignoring my reply, he handed me a fleece shirt and a Gortex jacket, both dry. "Here."

I curled my fingers into the warm clothes, thinking of Rick and Kem, fighting. Kem would kill him slowly, playing with prey. I pulled the clothes to my nose and inhaled Rick's scent, warm and masculine and satisfying. "Thanks," I said. I looked down the hill for Kemnebi, who was mostly invisible, moving in the shadows of the slope. I kept my eyes on the forest as I said, "I'm still his alpha. Remind me before the full moon. I have a feeling that my Beast might have a thing or two to say about some black leopard killing you."

"Beast?"

I laughed softly. "Yeah. Beast is what I call my cat-self."

Beast hacked at the words. *Not Jane's cat. Beast belongs to no one.*

"Of course, once she kills or chases off Kem-cat, she'll likely flay your hide off with her claws for cheating on her with the wolves."

"Uhhhh . . ."

To give myself something to do while he floundered, I pulled my wet shirts off and tossed them to the floorboard of the SUV's cab. They landed near Evangelina's scarf with a wet plop. Warm, dry clothes went on over my chilled skin; I was pretty sure he was looking, and I shivered once, hard. To the cold, I assured myself, not in reaction to Rick. I felt so much better inside the warm clothes that I sighed as I locked the door. "Come on. First things first. We gotta catch and dispatch some sicko werewolves who are killing and eating humans." I moved into the brush and under twisted, tangled laurel. Rick slid into a backpack and followed, silent and thoughtful.

The searchers stopped and watched as the black were-leopard circled the kill site. Kem-cat walked with a fluid, feral grace, leaping across the terrain; he made no sound, a killing shadow crossing cloud-dimmed ground. He was beautiful, wild, and unafraid for humans to watch, which was more in keeping with human thought processes than big-cat thinking. Leopards, like mountain lions, are solitary, hiding by day. That he showed himself with such balletic abandon said it was deliberate, part of his job description as the leader of the Party of African Weres.

If his purpose was to disarm the humans, it worked. The searchers were staring in awe, seeing something feral and wondrous, rather than a creature who could bring them down with single snap of powerful jaws. Fortunately, now that he was sober, Kemnebi wasn't going to yank their chains and do something that would cause the well-armed men and women to shoot him.

Rick eased up behind me, nearly as silent as Kem-cat, standing with his shoulder to my back, checking out the searchers and the tree line. Grizzard moved slowly to me, always facing Kem-cat, his movements showing he was aware of predator/prey response to quick movements and turned backs. When he reached me he muttered, "What about the collar?"

"You put it on him," Rick said. He held out the leash and Grizzard looked at it, then at Kemnebi, and frowned. Kem moved around the campsite, feet lifting and falling with careless precision. He sniffed and hissed and avoided body parts, his rounded ear tabs flicking backward and forward. Rain pelted on him and on us, but I was half-dry— the top half—and so I didn't care. As we watched, Kem stopped and put his nose to the wet ground, sucking in air in a scree of sound.

Grizzard started, his hand moving to his weapon before he could stop himself. "What's he doing?" he asked. "What's that noise?"

"Flehmen behavior," I said, not taking my eyes off Kem. "Cats have scent sacs in the roofs of their mouths. When they scent-search, they pull in air through nose and mouth, over the tongue, past the scent sacs. It's noisy."

"Gross," said a searcher standing near enough to hear. "That's why I keep dogs."

Kem turned toward us and hissed.

"Mmmm," Rick said, amusement in his tone. "Better be polite to the nice pussycat."

Kem hissed again, this time at Rick, who laughed low, the sound taunting. It didn't take a genius to tell the two men had a dysfunctional relationship. Of course, Kem's threat to kill Rick took dysfunctional relationships to entirely new heights. I hoped my being Kem's alpha would keep Rick alive and healthy. I'd have to rethink my plans come the full moon.

Kem made two circuits around the campsite and one to the ledge where the wolves had slept before he moved away, into the woods, up under a laurel thicket. He reappeared minutes later in another spot, and then in another. He was mapping the wolves' ingress and egress, and when he was satisfied, he padded quickly to Rick and sat, tall and pretty, front paws crossed and greenish eyes on Rick as if he were prey. He hacked, opened his mouth, showing killing teeth.

Rick asked, "You done?" Kem nodded once, a strange-looking gesture on the big-cat. Rick pulled out an old fashioned spiral notepad and flipped pages. I hadn't seen a paper pad like that in years, but it was a smart move. Most electronics would have been ruined by the rain. If the pad was damaged, a buck and change would replace it. Rick located a list of questions, clearly ones they had worked out before they got here.

"How many wolves?" Rick asked. Kem patted one paw twice. "How many times did they come here?" Kem again padded twice. "How many times did the grindylow come here?" Kem padded once. "Is the scent wrong?" Kem nodded once, his eyes intent on Rick.

I had no idea what the question or answer meant, but now wasn't the time to ask.

"Did the wolves enter the campsite from the same direction each time?" Kem shook his head no. "Can you track both trails?" Kem nodded, but ducked his head slightly, raising his shoulder blades. "One trail is going to be harder to follow?" Kem nodded. "The older one," Rick said. Kem nodded. "Now?"

This time Kem didn't answer. He turned in a single sinuous swirl, leaped over his own shoulder in a motion that appeared to defy the physical laws, and headed into the laurel thicket. I looked at Grizzard. "Coming?"

"Not this time." He turned hard eyes at Rick. "You're that cop from New Orleans, the one PsyLed called me about." Rick's mouth tightened but he nodded, the gesture oddly like Kem-cat's. "You'll know what I need to see, if anything. For now, I have a crime scene to work up. If you get something, call. I'll find you." Grizzard turned his back and stamped through the wet, his shoulders rounded with fatigue.

"PsyLed called him?" I asked.

"First I heard about it. Come on. We have a cat to chase."

By four p.m. I was tired, cold, wet, hungry, and probably permanently deaf. The constant rain was a white noise that drowned out every other sound, a steady, deadening, deafening roar that only got louder when we had to cross swollen streams and cascades. The falling temperatures had made everything miserable, with a low-lying fog shrouding the ground like heavy gauze, hiding puddles, runnels, holes, roots, protruding rocks, and ruts. Laurel and rhodo thickets had meant crawling bent over like the Hunchback of Notre Dame, and my palms were torn and blistered and wrinkled up like raisins. The wind was traitorous, delicate and warm one moment, buffeting us with cold the next.

Not even Gortex is designed to resist a hurricane, and my boots and jeans had failed the stream-crossing test. Even my underwear was sodden. Rick had brought several pounds of raw steaks in his backpack for Kem, and a jumbo-sized pack of high-cal trail mix for us. If not for the nuts, coconut, and dried tropical fruit, I'd have been tempted to try to steal from Kem-cat, which would have been gross *and* stupid.

To make the experience more wretched, as far as I could tell, we were lost. I had no idea what the leopard had discovered. We hadn't seen a real road—one paved in the last century—in hours, and we had crawled up and down steep slopes until east and west were alien concepts, even for me. If Kem wanted to lead us out into unknown territory and leave us to die, he couldn't have found a better place for it. Grumpy. That was me. Ahead, I saw two dark mounds emerging from the fog. Once we were upon them, they resolved into our vehicles. I lay across the hood and panted, my relief so strong I wanted to weep.

"Big, bad vamp killer, reduced to a whining mass of female flesh by a little water," Rick teased. The look I gave him shut him up and he backed away, palms open wide in a mock protective gesture, eyes laughing. The first time we'd been alone together I'd taken him down, but something about the way he backed off, with a confident swagger I hadn't seen before, suggested that now I might not have it so easy.

I crawled into the SUV and turned the seat warmers on high, the heater on max, and the windshield warmer on. I sat in a miserable heap and shivered until the interior was toasty and my core temp started to warm. Then I crawled around in the back for anything that might keep me warm, coming up with a tire iron, a tool box, a ragged fleece blanket, and a pair of cargo pants left balled in a corner by God-knows-who. The scent wasn't familiar and the pants were none too clean, having been used as a towel to wipe a mechanic's greasy hands, but I stripped and pulled them on, hoping I wouldn't get body lice or worse. The blanket, I ripped a head hole in with a screwdriver and tore a ribbon off one end to use as a belt. I was just barely presentable when a human-shaped Kem and Rick got into the vehicle with me, Kem in the passenger seat, his feet on my soaked clothes, and Rick lounging in back. Rick, wearing dry clothes, looked me over and laughed before passing me a king-sized Snickers bar. After the laugh, I should have refused on principle but I took it and started chewing.

Kem wasn't impressed either way, though he accepted a Snickers as well, and ate it in huge, half-chewed bites. He opened another, gesturing with it in what sounded like a non sequitur in his elegant African accent. "The grindylow no longer function according to its previous and proper purpose. It should be able to track the werewolves once it has taken their human and were scents, and it should have killed them long before now. It isn't, it hasn't. Its scent pattern has change in ways with which I am not familiar. It appears to be moving much more slowly than normal, spending long moments in one place, doing what appears to be"—he stopped, as if unable to find the right word—"*nothing*. Perhaps it is . . . *resting*."

The emphasis on the word resting made it sound foreign to the little green-skinned grindy. "They don't rest?"

"No. Never. Not as long as human is in danger. Perhaps it is . . . ill." But he didn't look fearful, Kemnebi looked ecstatic at the prospect. The grindylow had killed Kem's mate for trying to infect Rick. Kem hoped he'd die.

I frowned, adjusted the blower at my midsection, and ate another candy bar, curling one leg under my butt for comfort as I angled myself to face him. "The grindy didn't stop the weres in New Orleans from repeatedly biting Rick. Torturing him." Rick went utterly still, and I could suddenly smell the stress and fear-memory leaching from his pores. He was remembering.

Kem's lip curled at the smell. He slanted a look to the back, at Rick. "The grindylow was beleaguered in New Orleans. His mistress broke were-law with this *human*." Kem's eyes took on a voracious glow at the word. "He knew that were-law required her death. He . . . *loved* Safia. Her death was painful to him and was responsible for the delay in tracking the wolves."

"Yeah?" I remembered the state of the grindy's room at vamp central. It had been shredded, as if in a rage. Or in frustration. Another of the dominoes fell. I cursed softly, and Kem turned away when he saw the understanding in my eyes. "Coulda been that. Or, you caged him in his room so he couldn't get out and stop the werewolves from torturing Rick."

Kem turned hot golden-green eyes back to me. His beast eyes peered at me in threat. I wondered what I'd learn if I pushed at the cat. Beast stirred, flowing up through my veins and nerves, intrigued by the big-cat. It almost felt as if she had been waiting for this moment, primed for some action she expected. Wanted. Heat and power flooded through me and she stared back at the leopard, her claws unsheathed and painful, holding me down. When I spoke next, it was her thoughts I spoke. "To punish Rick for Safia. She was going to leave you. To mate with him."

Kem growled. Time did a shift and seemed to step sideways, slowing into overlays of still-shots. Kem's lips drew back. Revealed fangs. Male big-cat musk saturated the air. Claws burst through the tips of Kem's fingers; black fur sprouted on the backs of his hands.

Beast slammed through me. Pain cut through my hands and mouth like razors. My jaws ached and I tasted blood as big-cat canines pushed through my gums. She hissed, showing killing teeth. I pushed up with the foot beneath me just as Kemnebi launched himself across the cab. One claw swatting at my face.

My leap lifted me over the swipe. Golden-furred hands tore into Kem's neck. My hands, Beast's fur and claws. Blood spurted. My fangs tore into his throat. Latching to either side of his esophagus. I bit down, not hard enough to tear out his throat, just enough to cut off his airway. His claws ripped into my middle, catching on the fleece and the belt, hooking deep.

Behind Kem, the door to the cab opened. Rain and wind swept in. I got a glimpse of Rick. We tumbled backward, my body over Kem's, to land with a splash on the watery earth and sink into the mud. Beast took over my mind. Kem could get no air. He thrashed. And went still.

CHAPTER SIXTEEN

Is This a Proposal or Something?

Battle was over. Kem, trying to pant, lay back his head. His claws retracted. Forelegs spread, his belly exposed to me. Accepting Beast/Jane dominance. I/we shook him, teeth tearing through tissue only a little. To wound, not to kill. Kem relaxed even more. Proving his submission.

Kem fights like human in leopard skin. The I/we of Beast fights like puma inside human. Better hunter. Better killer.

Beast. Pull back. Let him go, Jane thought.

Will not *harm my mate.*

Okay. I'll tell him that. Just . . . Just let him go.

Fights like human. *Humans cheat with dominance. Will let go when he gives up.* Soon, Kem-cat's stomach muscles relaxed. His legs went limp. Finally, really, giving up. *Now.* I let go and Jane stepped up and aside. Pain raced through me as big-cat teeth and claws reshaped and reformed to human mouth and hands. *Painpainpain.*

I lay on the hood of the SUV, on my back, the rain pelting me, panting with agony. Oddly, the first thing I thought was that I was once again soaked to the skin. I laughed, the sound chuffing, half puma. The second was, "Oh crap." I lifted my hands. They were human, but they hurt like I had boxed a brick wall barehanded. I put fingers to my face, to my teeth. Human and human. I was still wearing pants, so I hadn't shifted totally. If I'd shifted into Beast in daylight, I couldn't shift back until night or moonrise, whichever came first. So . . . I hadn't known Beast could do a partial change. And Rick had seen it. *Crap*.

I rolled over, fast, to my hands and knees. My hair was undone, hanging in long wet strands to the engine. It was still running beneath my body, an unvarying, uniform purr. Rick stood a little ways off, Kem once again in black were-leopard form at his side. A leash was around his neck, the prongs pressing into the flesh of his throat. Blood coated his throat and chest, watery in the rain. He was lying on his belly, head down, eyes looking up. When he saw my stare, he crouched lower. A moment later, as if he thought his crouch was not enough, he rolled over again, giving me his belly.

Prey response. Accepts my alpha for now, Beast thought, *but will still try to take what is mine.*

Rick stared at me, a wry look on his face, amused despite the blood washing over his feet. Rain pelted down on us all, Kem's fur matted. Rick's black hair lay against his skull like a coat of paint, his black eyes so dark they looked as wide as vamp pupils. I looked down at myself, my blanket shredded with long swathes of skin showing through. I put a palm to my belly. I was completely human. I was healed, though I remembered Kem's claws striking my middle. *You did this once before,* I thought at Beast. *Half shifted.*

Yes. Will not accept beta place to Kemnebi, black leopard with ugly skinny tail and stink of human. Smell of strange hot country.

I chuckled beneath my breath. To Rick I said, "I'm going back to the hotel. I'm out of clothes. We'll talk later." I raised my voice, "When Kem-cat becomes human again, tell him if he kills you, I'll kill him. You belong to my Beast."

Rick's mouth curled up higher on one side. "I'll do that. Is this a proposal or something?"

My stomach plummeted. "Something." But I didn't know what. "Later." I slid into the cab, pulling the doors shut. With a crunch and splash of tires on rock and mud, I pulled away. I was halfway to the hotel when I had to stop at a drive-through for food. I consumed a bucket of regular recipe Kentucky Fried Chicken and six biscuits. And I couldn't stop laughing, a breathy, half-hysterical sound, a soft note of dread and pain in the depths. I was still laughing when I dialed the twins' room.

Back at the hotel, Brian met me at the curb, wrapping me in a white robe and carrying me through the lobby, dripping. A small crowd was sitting at the fireplace, flames licking the air as we passed. They clapped, as if this was an *Officer and a Gentleman* moment and I was being carried by my prince charming, up the elevator. I laughed, still with that wild ringing note, and Brian kissed the top of my head like he might a small child's, appreciating the moment.

When we got to the suite we now shared, he lowered my feet to the carpet and took in my bedraggled state, his eyes glued to the wet skin beneath the soaked blanket and the bundle of wet clothing in my hands. I shivered hard, despite the time to warm up and the food. I said, "Hot shower. Three double stuffed potatoes and a two pound steak, so rare it's still mooing. Please." I shut my room door in his face.

Half an hour later I was warm and mostly dry, my hair braided and wrapped in a towel. I had looked at my reflection in the bathroom mirror and decided not to do that again. I looked as if I had lost ten pounds, and as if I hadn't slept in weeks. My eyes had dark circles, my cheeks were sunken. The half-shift had taken a lot out of me. *Better than dead cat,* Beast thought at me. She had a point. In the common area of the suite, I sat down at a small table and dug into the food, eating with a steady precision more suited to a robot than a hungry human. The twins watched me with hooded eyes, nearly as still as a vamp, except for the whole needs-to-breathe thing.

When I was done, Brandon said, "You look like something the cat dragged in."

I grinned. Beast hacked deep inside, amused. "Yeah." I picked up my cell, keys, a leather jacket, and the scarf I'd taken from Evangelina. "I'll be back in a bit. I have to see a witch about a problem."

"Does this problem have to do with the parley?"

"Yeah." I left the room, calling for the SUV on the way down.

I drove into Molly's driveway and parked in the false dusk of the storm. It was still raining, but now there were breaks in the downpour, moments when sprinkles pattered down, moments when it stopped altogether. The sky was variegated, darker to the east where the storm was fleeing, the clouds piled on top of each other as they rushed from the cold front. I turned off the engine and sat.

Molly's house was different since I'd been here last. Big Evan and Mol had added on a garage with a man-den over it, enclosed the old carport, added a bathroom and a master bedroom out back. The addition had doubled the size of the house, but they had maintained the quaint 1920s mountain style of peaked gables and arched windows.

I hadn't been invited over since I'd been back. Not once. I remembered a time when Mol, Evan, Angie Baby, and I had dinner here several times a week. But the invitations had stopped when Molly had been put in danger on my watch, when Angie and Little Evan had been kidnapped. It didn't take a rocket scientist to figure out that I had become persona non grata in Big Evan's eyes. His car was in the drive; there would be no slipping in and out without him knowing. I had no idea if I'd be welcomed or told to leave, especially once I reminded them of that recent danger. I hadn't finished my jobs by killing off all the werewolves, and destroying the blood-diamond, bringing danger back to haunt them again. My insides felt hollow, despite the proteins, fats, and starches I'd eaten.

The house sat on the crest of a mountain at the top of the world, and the views were spectacular. The front yard was lush with fall plants, mums of all colors and sizes, a burgundy-leaved Japanese maple as centerpiece; maple varieties were grouped everywhere, some whose outermost leaves had begun to go salmon or yellow in the chill. The backyard would rival any garden anywhere, with fruits and veggies so tasty and big they looked like mutants. Mol's an earth witch and her gift is herbs and growing things, healing bodies, restoring balance to nature.

Legs like lead weights, I got out of the SUV, pocketed the keys, and moved up the paved drive. On the chill breeze, I caught a whiff of werewolves, but the scent was faint, distant, and quickly gone as if it had never been. But it was real, not a figment of my imagination or fear.

The new door in the middle of the old carport opened and a small whirlwind flew through. "Aunt Jane! Aunt Jane! Aunt Jane!" she squealed, the high pitch nearly bursting my eardrums. I stooped to catch her and Angie Baby threw herself into my arms with enough force to make me stagger. Her arms went around my neck, choking, her strawberry-blond-streaked hair whipping in the gusty wind. I smoothed it down with one hand and looped the other arm under her bottom to support her weight as I carried her toward the house. "I missed you," she said.

My heart melted into a big puddle of goo. "I've missed you, Angie Baby." I batted away tears that gathered any time I was near her. "You've grown two inches, at least."

"I'm a big girl now." Her voice dropped to a whisper, "Daddy's at the door and he's mad. Why is he mad at you?"

I didn't lower my voice when I answered, but spoke in a normal tone, my booted feet bringing me closer to the glowering man, knowing he could hear me. "Because I let the Big Bad Ugly vampire witches steal you and nearly kill you. Because I put your mama in danger." Big Evan's glower turned uglier, colder. I thought about werewolves in the mountains near this house, killing people. "Because he loves you all so much that he'd fight anything to protect you. Your daddy's doing the right thing, Angelina. He is." I handed her to him.

The big man took her in gentle hands and set her down behind him, his body a barrier between us. I thought my heart would break. "Go back to the movie, Pun'kin," he said.

"Okay, Daddy." Her footsteps tapped away.

There weren't many men who made me feel little, but Big Evan was one of them. He stood six feet six, and weighed over three hundred pounds, mostly muscle. He had red hair, a full red beard, and brown eyes so hard they could cut stone. He crossed his arms and braced his feet. Waiting. I pulled the damp lavender scarf out of my pocket and held it out to him. "Tell me what you smell. If you think it's important, we need to talk. You, Molly, and me."

Evan took the scarf and held it to his nose. He breathed in. Evan is a sorcerer, one of the few alive anywhere, and still in the witch closet, to protect his kids from unwanted attention. His eyes flew down to mine. Widened. He inhaled again. "I smell Evangelina and blood magic."

I nodded. Evan knew about the witches in New Orleans and the diamond. Of course, he thought it was still safe and *in* New Orleans. "She stole the pink diamond from my weapons safe," I said. "She's been using it on vamps, bloodservants, and me. She's using it to grow younger and prettier. Though she has the right to draw on her sisters' magics, they haven't noticed the changes in her. Which means she's not just drawing on them as coven leader, she's spelling them too."

"That bitch is spelling *my wife*?" he snarled. Evan's eyes narrowed, calculating, putting together what he might do to stop it. When he reached the end of his ruminations, he said something vile under his breath. "And I can't interrupt the spell without serious consequences. Why didn't you destroy the relic?"

"How?" I asked. "How do you destroy something that absorbed the energies of dying witches for hundreds of years? Drop it in the ocean? In a volcano? What happens to the energies in any of those cases? They don't just wink out, poof, it's gone."

"You've brought nothing but evil to this house in years. I don't want you here."

Tears burned in my eyes, but he'd never see them. "Fine. You figure out how to handle it." I yanked the scarf away, swiveled on a heel, and stalked back to the SUV.

"She lost some weight." It sounded like the words were dragged out of him. I stopped, staring out at the curve of the world. The sky was bright, a patch of blue showing in the west. "Evangelina has. And"—he blew out a breath that sounded like a small storm—"at least fifteen years."

I clenched my hands and turned back. "Her hair is silky as a child's," I said, "something adults' hair loses by the time they're forty or so. If her skin glowed any more we wouldn't need lights. She let a vampire feed from her. I saw the wounds. When I accused her of it in front of her sisters, I don't think they even heard the words."

"This is your fault."

"Accepted."

"You better come in."

I took a breath to steady my nerves and entered the house. The new door opened into a great room. The former carport's back brick wall was now a fireplace with merrily burning gas logs and a hidden laundry room. Bump-out windows were on the western side, Molly's orchids on display. Some were in bloom, including a heavenly vanilla. Big Evan stood still, mentally checking the house wards, eyeing the locks. "No opening the doors, Angie," he said.

She nodded without looking at us. A kiddie film was on the TV screen, and her attention was fastened on a princess and a pony, her small body curled into the seat cushion of an Evan-sized, leather couch. She yawned and pulled an afghan over her, looking sleepy.

Little Evan was standing in the door to the kitchen, bare-chested, wearing footie jammie bottoms. He stared at me, eyes wide. I patted him on the head as I climbed the steps into the kitchen. The small intimate space had been expanded into the old family room and now housed a larger table, a pantry, and a central island as well as skylights for Mol's herbs, growing in a bay window. But the heart of the kitchen was still the old Aga stove with bread baking in the oven, beef stew bubbling on top, the teapot on perpetual simmer, and copper pots hanging over it all.

Molly was leaning against the counter when I came in, wearing a denim smock and dark red blouse. Her hair was up in a ponytail, and she wore garnet earrings. She clutched a fist between her breasts and her eyes were hesitant, sliding back and forth between Evan and me, nervous. "What's wrong?" she asked. I cringed to know that, when my best friend saw me, the first thing she thought was trouble.

"Evangelina," Evan said, "is dabbling in black magic."

Molly's eyes seemed to lose focus for a moment; then she smiled brightly. "I have hot chai on the stove. Evan, would you get the mugs?"

Evan looked like he'd been poleaxed. He had expected Molly to agree or deny or get angry, not act as if the words had never been spoken. His eyes on his wife, he opened the new glass-fronted china hutch and hooked fingers through three teal mugs. Molly took them and started setting up for tea. Evan said, "Evangelina is practicing black magic."

"I have homemade gingersnaps and snickerdoodle cookies. And I know Jane wants whipped cream in her tea." She opened the fridge and Evan took the spray can from her. He closed the door, cupped her head in his huge hands and tilted her face up, in what was the most tender gesture I had ever seen. He smiled down at his wife and she smiled back. I heard mumbled words, likely some form of Gaelic, saw his lips purse and heard him breathe out as he blew at Molly's face.

I thought for a moment he had broken the spell on Molly. But she jerked back, strong emotion flushing through her, so hot I could feel it across the room. She whirled to me, pain and hurt on her face. "You never liked Evangelina," she said. "But you don't have to make up things about her."

"Make up—"

"You never liked my sister. I tried to give you time to get to know each other, to become friends. And instead, when she met a man she liked, you took him away. How could you do that?"

Bruiser. She was talking about Bruiser. "She used a love spell on him, Molly. That's wrong."

"A love spell?" Evan asked. I nodded and he released his wife's arms, stepping back, his shoulders drawing together. He was watching her the way a doctor watched a patient he was diagnosing. I just felt sick to my stomach.

"All I did was tell him he'd been spelled. I didn't take him away," I said gently.

"You always treated her like she was less than you, unworthy of you!" Mol said, as if neither of us had spoken. As she slipped past Evan, he made a circular motion with one hand, indicting that I was supposed to keep Molly talking. I didn't think that would be hard to do.

"I'm scared to death of her. Doesn't mean I hate her," I said, "or look down on her."

Tears gathered in Molly's eyes. "My sister has suffered more than any woman should ever suffer, and all because of *them*," she nearly spat, "the *things* you *work* for now." She advanced on me, one finger pointing, her arm out straight like a wand or a staff, a weapon of destruction. Tears coursed down her face. "They took her *family*!"

Oh crap. A vamp turned Evangelina's family? I vaguely remembered she had been married long before I met Molly, but thought the hubby divorced her and got custody of their daughter. But then, I hadn't been friends with all of them until just before Carmen's baby was born, and I didn't know much family gossip about Evil Evie. Behind Mol, Evan looked confused, as if he'd never heard that vamps took Evangelina's family. With a tiny head-shake, he put that bit of news away for the moment and blew up a pink balloon. The sight of the big, bearded man blowing up a girly balloon was comical, but then it hit me. Evan was an air witch. He was using what he had on hand to construct a spell on the fly. "Why did Evangelina come home from New Orleans?" I asked, trying to guide Mol to safer topics.

Molly hesitated, "To get away from the vampires. The things you're helping to—"

"She's dating a vampire," I said. "I saw the bite marks on her—"

"No. That's a lie," she said. Behind her, I saw Evan pause in the balloon blowing and sip something from a flask. He then blew the fluid into the balloon, the liquid a mist coating the inside. "You never liked my sister. I tried to give you time to get to know each other, to become friends. And instead, when she met a man she liked, you took him away. How could you do that?" She had just repeated herself, word for word. The phrases were part of the spell on her.

"Evangelina is using the blood-diamond, the relic I took from the vampires, Molly. It's powerful, made with the unwilling sacrifice of witch children. She spelled you."

"You never liked my sister. I tried to give you two time

to get to know each other, to become friends. And instead, when she met a man she liked, you took him away." Molly was caught in a continuous loop of suggestion and I had no idea how to help her break free.

"Mol?" Evan placed one hand on her shoulder. Molly stopped. Turned. And Big Evan popped the balloon. The sound was loud in the confined space. Molly inhaled quickly, a gasp of surprise. Instantly her eyes closed and she slumped. Evan caught her as if she weighed less than Angelina. He carried her out of the kitchen back to the new master bedroom, leaving me alone.

I looked around the kitchen, at loose ends. Should I let myself out? What if that set off the wards? I didn't cook but I checked the bread in the oven. There were six loaves, all golden brown. I found the knob that said OVEN and turned it off, then found a cloth and removed the loaves, setting them on the counter, totally out of my comfort zone. I turned off the stew.

Evan still wasn't back, so I went to the great room and stood in the doorway watching the children. Angelina was asleep, her face scrunched up in dreams. Little Evan was holding one of his sister's dolls, raising and lowering the arms, making little engine noises like a Transformer. They were safe. Happy. Watching them, some of the tension left me.

Angelina sucked in a breath. She sat up, her eyes wild. She screamed. "Deerdeerdeer!" I raced down the short steps and grabbed her. "Deerdeerdeerdeerdeerdeer!" she screamed over and over. I sat on the couch and rocked her, whispering sweet nothings of comfort as she screamed, the cushion warm from the heat of her sleeping body. Suddenly she was sobbing. She twined her arms around me and held on. Little Evan abandoned the doll and climbed up beside us.

"Dewerdewer," he said, trying to imitate his sister.

"What's wrong with the deer?" I asked her, wishing Evan would come back and help. But the doorway remained empty.

"She's killing the deer. She's eating them." Angie looked up at me. "It was still alive, Aunt Jane. Its eyes were open. I saw it."

My breath tightened in my chest, an involuntary pain.

Beast ate deer. Was she seeing memories of Beast's last kill? "Who is killing the deer, Angie Baby?"

"The frog. The big frog."

I wiped her eyes on the afghan, trying not to laugh at the image. "It was a bad dream, Angie. Just a bad dream."

"She's been having it a lot," Evan said from the doorway. "We've been letting her watch too much *National Geographic*. Her frog has teeth and it's feeding live prey to its frog babies, like foxes and coyotes do, to teach their young how to hunt." I looked at him and he added, "Mol's still spelled, but sleeping."

I stroked Angie Baby's hair, holding her trembling body. "If I hit Evangelina over the head with a baseball bat to distract her, can you break the spell?"

Big Evan almost smiled. "As happy as it would make me to see that, no. I've never disrupted a coven power-ring. Let me study on it a while." Which went against my every instinct.

Evan looked at the door, and I knew I was being given the bum's rush. Quickly I asked, "What happened to Evangelina's family, her husband and daughter? Why did Mol say the vamps were involved?"

"They disappeared years ago. The daughter and Evangelina didn't get along. Marvin took off and he took the girl with him. They vanished. Evangelina followed up leads for years. Never found them." He shook his head. "I don't know why Molly said that about her family."

"If Molly is spelled, could Evangelina have put that in her mind?"

Evan looked worried, his mouth thinning, lips hidden by his beard. He said, "Yeah. But I'll have to deal with that later. Come on kids," he added. "It's time for dinner, and Mommy's taking a nap." He met my eyes. "The wards are down. You know where the door is."

"Yeah. I do." I sat Angie on the couch and opened the door. On the night air, I smelled . . . wolf. My hackles rose, Beast's pelt rising against my skin. "Did you and Molly adjust the wards on the house to exclude werewolves?"

"You mean the werewolves that followed you from New Orleans?" he said, his words harsh.

"Yeah," I sighed, "those werewolves." Once again, in

Evan's eyes, I had put Mol in danger. And I was just about to make that worse. "They're trying to make mates and I think they've discovered that witches might work better than humans."

Evan cursed foully under his breath. I walked out of the house into the night. Alone.

CHAPTER SEVENTEEN

And if the Fangheads Kill Them?

I stopped at the herb shop and parked in the shadow of a massive flowering plant. The big leaves were elongated, heart-shaped, and, this time of year, the entire small tree was covered with odd flowers, dark fuchsia, sharp-pointed petals, with dark blue centers. Molly had told me its scientific name, but all I remembered was Japanese butterfly bush. Today, the long, limber branches were trailing the ground, heavy, bent by rain. I brushed a straggling branch and it sprang back like a kids' weapon, nature's squirt gun, scattering water all over me. I grimaced up at the dark sky. "Thanks. I needed another drenching."

Before I went inside, I walked around the café and shop, sniffing. A wet breeze danced in the dark, lashing my face and body with overgrown shrubs while the muddy earth sucked at my footing and roots and vines tried to trip me. Around back, a small ditch funneled rainwater down the steep hill, gurgling. Rising on the breeze, I smelled werewolf. It wasn't fresh tang, but the wolves had been here recently. I had been too distracted to notice when I came for breakfast, or I'd have caught the scent. The dang dogs were everywhere. I had smelled them at Molly's, now here. Maybe it was more personal than targeting witches for mates. Maybe they were deliberately targeting my friends. In the electronic age, it wouldn't have been too hard to discover who I cared about.

I went inside, to stand on the mat just within the shop, keeping my muddy feet off the floor. Regan and Amelia, the human Everharts, were working, Regan at the cash register ringing up a final sale, Amelia mopping up muddy footprints. They acknowledged me with matching grins. When the customer left, Amelia said, "We missed you at the café. It's good to see you, Jane."

Regan offered me a bakery treat and the last cup of a flavored tea. I pulled off my muddy boots to keep from messing up the clean floor, and sat at a table while the girls worked around me, closing up the shop, chattering about college and term papers and Amelia's new boyfriend. I ate and drank and nodded. When I was finished with the mega-muffin—lemon-poppy seed, bigger than a softball and Oh My Gosh delicious—I told them about the wolves, concluding with, "They're trying to rebuild their pack and trying to make mates. And even though you're human, you smell like witches, females who might be able to survive the wolf bite."

The girls, who had gathered closer as I spoke, looked at one another and got this *look*. I never had a sister, but I knew what silent, instantaneous, nonverbal communication looked like, and this was it. Almost as one, the girls swiveled and disappeared behind the front counter. They popped up with guns. Big honking guns. I started laughing.

Amelia was holding a perfectly legal 12-gauge shotgun, and Regan was holding two very different semiautomatics with matte black grips. Regan said, "The handguns are loaded, of course; this one"—she held up the H&K—"with silver nine mils for vamps, but I hear it works well on weres too. This one"—she held up the S&W—"is loaded with hollow points for humans and robbers."

My brows went up. Hollow point rounds explode just after impact, and when they hit anything made of flesh, that explosion shreds everything in its expanding path. They are for killing, not stopping. And not something I ever expected an Everhart to own.

Amelia patted the shotgun, "Molly sent us to the guy who hand-loads your silvershot and this baby holds four of the silver fléchette rounds. That's all we could afford."

Regan said. "But we got plenty of regular ammo for robbers."

"Rapists."

"Kidnappers."

"And drunken good ole boys."

"We been robbed once," Regan said, her eyes narrow. "Never again."

Still laughing softly, I finished off the tea, debating whether to tell the humans about the predicament with their witch sisters. I decided against it for now, and stood, pulling on my boots. "Stay safe. Don't shoot the good guys." They turned the lock when I left the shop, and it fell with a clunky, defiant finality. Molly's sisters were an interesting bunch. Dangerous as heck. But interesting. I was in the SUV, trying once again to get dry, when my cell beeped. I smiled when I saw Rick's new number in it. "Hey there," I said.

"You know where Henrii Thibodaux's Bayou Queen is?"

"Yeah. I ate there once."

"I have a gig playing here tonight. And I smell something familiar."

I got a sick feeling in the pit of my stomach. "What?"

"Werewolves. Get over here."

I walked in to Henrii Thibodaux's restaurant, just off Highway 25, in the middle of the dinner hour. I smelled wolf instantly, even over the delicious aroma of fried seafood and grilled meat. I walked around the dining room, sniffing, checking out the men's room, sticking my head into the kitchen just in case a wolf might be working as busboy, then made my way to the parking lot, where I lost them, their slightly sick-smelling scent hidden under the wood smoke billowing up from the cooking vents. They had been here, but they had been gone for a while. Standing alone in the lot, I made a couple of calls and went back inside.

I placed an order, joined Rick at a table and dug into beef ribs with Texas Two-Step sauce from Henrii's sauce bar. Rick had already finished boudin balls with Black Voodoo sauce and two beers—Cajun food in the mountains. Only in America. All I'd done all day was eat. If I didn't shift and hunt soon, I was gonna start gaining weight. I was also bruised, sore, and banged up, but the healing of a shift would have to wait.

"So." He picked up a half-empty beer bottle and sipped. "Last time I saw you, you were half cat, half human."

I paused, a rib halfway to my mouth. *Oh crap.*

"Kem calls you a Qora, or a Bouda. A shape-changer. He says only the most powerful ones can do the half shift."

I sighed and bit all the meat off the rib in neat little nips, thinking. When I was done, I wiped my fingers and said, "You don't look weirded out about this."

Rick laughed, an incredulous note mixed with the humor. "I'm plenty weirded out, Babe. But you reach the point where your ability to react emotionally to all the new shit being tossed at you is gone."

I ate another rib, watching him as he drank a third beer. He didn't look inebriated. His shape-changer nature had affected his metabolism. Rick would find it hard to get a buzz. "I've never done that half-change thing before. What did it look like?"

Rick shook his head and drained the beer. The waitress brought him another, which he opened and sipped. "It was . . . bizarre. Grotesque and beautiful all at once. Wild and feral. It looked painful. The movies don't do it justice."

I nodded and finished another rib. The silence between us was far more comfortable than maybe it should have been. I was waiting for the other shoe to fall.

"The bikes were riding off when I got here," Rick said, returning to business, "and the place reeked of wolf. Could you smell them?"

I nodded and licked my fingers; he pushed his food basket away and leaned back in the booth, stretching. He was wearing a T-shirt I'd seen before, a thin black weave of silk knit that revealed as much as it hid, when the light hit it just right. My eyes were drawn to the mass of white, slightly ridged scars on his shoulder and swiped across his abdomen, and then to the long play of muscles down his side and the ripple of abs.

He was watching me, a small smile on his lips. I closed my mouth and remembered to chew. But, Oh. My. Gosh.

Fortunately, before I could react beyond a sinking, spreading heat, he said, "They're chasing you to get even, chasing me to finish killing me. What else?"

"Trying to rebuild a pack. But they aren't smart enough to do it in any kind of order. They'd be easier to catch if they *were* smart. Stupid is harder to predict. Random instead of logical. And"—I swallowed—"I'm not sure how they knew to come to Asheville and the Pigeon River in the first place." That thought seemed important, though I didn't know why. Yet. We chatted for a bit, almost like a real date. Until Billy Chandler, Chief of Police, walked in with two cops trailing like sycophants or servants, which they might as well have been. "I called them," I said at Rick's surprised start. "How do you want to play this?"

"In bed would be nice, but not with cops present." I grinned at that and he went on, "I'll say I saw them on their way out." Rick was the only one in town, besides Grégoire and me, who had actually seen the wolves in person and not just in mug shots, so his strategy would work. I drained my Coke and watched the cops approach. Chandler had a mean look on his face. Easy to tell I wasn't his favorite person.

"Spill it Yellowrock," he said. "I don't have time for your shit."

"Maybe you got time for mine, Billy." Rick slid farther down in the bench seat, almost lounging, and his eyes were slit like a lazy cat's, revealing only the lower half of dark irises and a slit of pupil. His tone held a warning, as if telling the chief to be polite. To me. A different kind of warmth filled me. No one had ever tried to protect me. Not ever. With my height and muscle build, most men figured I could take care of myself. Which I could, but still . . .

I hid a grin, stood, and went for a refill. When I got back, I heard the tail end of the conversation. Rick said, "Henrii has security cameras. The manager pulled the footage and burned a copy." One hand went to his shoulder and the scars there, faintly visible beneath the thin fabric of his shirt. "Without a warrant," he added slowly. "And you can thank Jane for that." He smiled slightly, watching Chandler. "You owe her."

This was news to me. And everything about that statement was sooo unlike Rick. It was the kind of taunt a cat might make to a dog. *Crap*. The full moon was growing closer and Rick's new cat nature was peeking out. The chief turned to me, standing in the aisle. I smiled sweetly at him and nudged him aside to retake my seat. I lounged back too, my Beast automatically mimicking Rick's insolent body language. *Mine,* Beast murmured, her eyes on Rick. She had liked him as a full human, but now that he was part big-cat, Beast seemed entranced. Billy's frown deepened. I ate a cold fry and licked a drop of sauce off my index finger, and let my grin widen.

"Let's see this security footage," Billy said, voice gruff. It wasn't a thank you, but it wasn't an insult either. Rick and I unfolded ourselves from the seats and we all trooped upstairs into the small office. The manager had left the disc in the system, and Rick hit a button. I sent him a look questioning the readiness of the equipment and he shrugged slightly with one shoulder. I guessed that working as musical talent in a place like Henrii's gave the help some leeway.

On the laptop we saw grainy images of two men entering the restaurant, shaved heads and faces, one in glasses. My heart thudded. It was the two wolves I had left unconscious and bound for the cops in the hotel room where the pack had held Rick prisoner. It was easy for my mountain lion self to accept their reality by scent alone, but my human half had a visceral reaction to the sight, electric, toxic. So did Rick, a faint reek of fear leaching from his pores, though his body posture didn't tighten or appear to react. More and more like a cat.

I focused on the screen. One of the wolves was bigger than Big Evan and solid muscle. I'd nicknamed him Fire Truck. The other guy looked little next to him, but probably stood between five feet seven and five ten. It was hard to tell next to the mountain of Fire Truck. The smaller guy moved fast in the digital footage, seeming to jump through the intermittent progression of frames. He had squinty eyes and bulges under his hoodle that were likely weapons. He looked weaselly, which became his new name.

We watched Fire Truck and Weasel disappear inside, trailed later by a woman wearing a granny dress and old-fashioned boots, an open umbrella over her. Rick pressed a button and the digital footage again showed the woman leaving, her gait ungainly in the boots, followed by the two werewolves. The time stamp indicated that sixty-two minutes had passed. Another button showed us the parking area and the wolfmen helmeting up, starting bikes, and cruising out onto the street. An instant later, Rick entered, and the footage stopped.

"Again," Billy said. When the bikes roared off, we got a glimpse of the license plates, enough to know they weren't North Carolina plates. He looked at Rick. "You're sure these two are the ones who kidnapped an undercover cop, held him prisoner, *tortured* him"—Billy's eyes looked Rick over, as if searching for werewolf taint—"and tried to kill him."

"Yes," Rick said, not rising to the insult in the look.

"Before you go thinking Rick might turn into a werewolf and bite your men, you should know that the vamps' Mercy Blade took care of any possibility of that," I said. "He's not a werewolf." Rick laughed and the sound carried a bitter note. Yeah. No werewolf. Of course he might go big-cat-furry. And soon.

Billy frowned. "I'll upgrade the BOLO on the bikers to include stills from this video, and list them as armed and dangerous, with orders to locate but not approach." Chandler looked at me, unwillingness clear in his eyes. He didn't want to be asking me anything. "If we find these guys, what are we supposed to do?"

"Call me," I said. "I'll bring the vamps."

"And if the fangheads kill them instead of apprehending them?"

"You'll have some paperwork to fill out," I said, and pushed through the cops into the hallway and down the stairs. Outside, I sloshed through puddles to the SUV and roared out into the street. I had a lot to think about.

I do my best thinking when I'm not actively pursuing a thought. Ideas are like small prey, scuttling into corners when a cat tries to chase them, coming out to play when the cat sits silent and unmoving. Back in my room, I studied topo maps, maps of rivers and streams, and once again studied the map of the grindy sightings and the wolf attacks. I noticed a place I hadn't hunted before, one that looked like promising terrain—not as steep as big-cats liked, but composed of shale too steep for human activity. While I packed a small backpack as a go-bag, I gave the security team instructions for the night, and orders to call Leo if the vamps resisted the plans. I texted Bruiser with two lines, telling him I'd be hunting and that the vamps were not to leave the hotel due to security concerns. He'd know to put Leo on it my guys called him.

I also discovered a recent voice message from Angie Baby. I punched in the code and listened to her soft voice say, "Aunt Jane. You got to come back to see me. Okay? Mommy's not actin' like she's supposed to. You gotta come."

Guilt wormed its way into me like a steel barb. It sounded as if Mol was still spelled. But Big Evan was on the job, and I had promised to give him time. "Soon, Angie Baby," I murmured.

I set the cell Leo could use to track me on the table and left the hotel wearing clean jeans, running shoes, T-shirt, and a light jacket. I took off in the SUV I was coming to think of as mine. I bought a new throwaway cell at a strip mall and stopped at an Ingles for food supplies before driving up 70, a patch of road I was getting far too familiar with.

Almost everything about this gig seemed to point to the road between Asheville and Hot Springs: the wolves' kill-sites, the grindy sightings, the wolf scent stalking Molly and her family, and even Lincoln Shaddock's house and hunting territory. I didn't believe in coincidences, and had seen little evidence to shake that faith. But there were a lot of them: Evangelina going to the dark side, Lincoln Shaddock under her spell, werewolves ending up in the area, to name a few. They had to be tied together, but how? I needed to try something new to shake things up, including my own thinking processes. Instead of hunting the wolves where they had killed and departed, I needed to hunt where they had hunted and not killed. In Beast form.

I parked down the mountain from Molly's, in a little-used driveway just as rain started again. The chain guarding the drive was old, rusted, but solid. The lock holding it was rusted through and broke apart when I took a tire iron to it. I drove up the drive, weeds scraping the undercarriage, and parked around a bend where the SUV wouldn't be seen come morning.

Sitting in the front seat, I stripped naked, rolling the clothes I'd been wearing around the throwaway cell and into my large travel bag. I packed light when I hunted as Beast, when I had territory that I/we claimed as ours. Or in summer. In New Orleans. Or when I was just hunting and could stay in Beast form if dawn caught us far from home. Tonight it was cold, with an unseasonably early frost warning. I had no idea where I'd end up by dawn. I might have to shift back to human someplace far off and hike to the nearest road. Maybe hike until my cell worked. I couldn't stay in Beast form all day and do my job.

I wrapped a new fleece blanket around my shoulders. Someone had kindly replaced the small one I'd destroyed. Naked but for the miniblanket and a pair of cheap flops, carrying the go-bag and my mountain lion fetish necklace, I walked down the drive, the last of the hurricane's sporadic rain pelting me. The path descended sharply before I came upon an old mountain house from the thirties or forties, roof caved in, asbestos-siding walls bulged out, burned windows like eyes into the underworld. It once had a view down the mountain, but saplings and scrub had grown over and obscured any vista. In the scrub, I found the rounded top of a boulder and cleaned a space around it, pulling vines and briars. I hurt my hands but the shift would fix that.

I scraped the boulder with the gold nugget I wore, to give me a way to home in on this location, and folded the blanket for a seat before sitting on the rounded stone. Cold stone can freeze a bare bottom fast. I put the backpack on around my neck and adjusted it to Beast-size, closed my eyes and breathed in, held it, and let it out, slowly. Again. And again. Tension I hadn't known was there flowed from me like the rain. I relaxed and stretched my shoulders. The fetish necklace in my hands was comforting, a known in the midst of the unknowns of this job. I slowed my heart rate, breathing, letting my mind calm. And I thought of Beast.

*   *   *

Jane was gone. I lay still, smelling, listening. Water from sky, water running on ground, water falling from leaves was scent/see/taste/feel-on-skin. Scent of roebuck, skunk, lizards, and snake was strong. Mice and rats lived in ru-ined man house. Many-more-than-five birds and squir-rels, smelling wet and cold, in tree-nests, asleep. Tasty but hard to catch. One mouthful crunch. Not worth the hunt. Twitched ear tabs. Heard waddling pads of raccoon moving down the mountain. Smell of man nearby, the stinky breath of cars always on air, old smoke, sour wood, and rot from man-den. Beast-sight made everything clearer, brighter, sharper than Jane eyes. Mountain curved on both sides, into trees. Saw house far off, lights dim and flickering, like TV pictures. Saw car moving on distant road. Heard trucks far away.

I rose from rock and stretched, pulling at muscles, stretching out chest and spine and along legs. I picked up necklace and blanket in mouth and padded back to car. Ugly car. Liked Bitsa, bike with roaring voice and nose in wind. Hunger pulled at stomach. Ache of hunger times, like claws. Jane woke up, deep inside.

Crap. I forgot to get the steaks out of the car.

I chuffed, cat laughter. Set necklace and blanket on ground and braced on side of car. Curled out claws. Opened door. *Good hunter. Will eat cold dead cow and then hunt for wolves. Eat deer or rabbit if I find them.*

Well, I'll be a monkey's uncle. When did you learn how to do that?

Beast is smart. Drew down flesh above eyes, thinking. *Jane does not have monkey necklace.* Jane laughed. I did not know why. I set necklace and blanket on seat and jumped inside. Took cow package in teeth and jumped out. Tore through plastic and ate cold dead cow, taste old and watery. Wanted to hunt and eat live cow, fresh blood and hot meat, sound of cow cries, in pain and fear.

You are not hunting cows. They belong to people.

Raised lip to show killing teeth. *Beast is not owned. Even by Jane.* She was silent.

Sat beside car and finished meat, cleaned paws and face with long tongue, raspy and coarse, pulling blood and meat bits off of jaws and paws. Stomach satisfied, I stood and closed car door. I moved down mountain, smelling for wolf.

Moon was high and small, bright against cloudy sky. Rain fell in spats. Man lights were few here, many stars filling black spaces of night. Trees were covered in moss, dark and green and silver in Beast-sight, leaves rustling with breath of earth. I jumped over small streams. Saw trout in one, sleeping under rock. Trout tasty. But water was cold. Heard animals move, sounds Jane could not hear in Jane-form, could not see in Jane-form. Jane was slower than Beast, yet Jane had killed many wolf. Jane was good hunter with man gun and man claws of steel. The I/we of Beast was better than Jane or big-cat alone. Good hunter. Threw back head and screamed challenge into night. *Beast is here. This is* Beast's *territory.* Raced down hill. Found wolf scent on cool breeze. Wolf smell was fresh. I set nose to earth and sniffed, long scree of scent-taking. Beast brain not good for nose-to-ground-hunting. Beast brain not like dog brain, not like bloodhound Jane had once been. But Beast could hunt this way if hungry. Had learned in hunger times. Had lived when other cats had died. Nose to ground, I started to run.

Found wolf scent on road. Found wolf-kill of big buck. Old blood, old flesh. Ate from old kill, claiming it. Beast's kill now. Licking muzzle clean, followed wolf scent again. Long time passed.

I/we smelled Molly. Smelled Angelina.

CHAPTER EIGHTEEN

Molly Can Kill Cow?

Raised head to sky and screamed, this time in warning. *Mine. Mine, mine, mine. Kill wolves who hunt Molly's den.* Sound of territory-claim echoed through hills. Raced ahead of scent, to yard with trees and flowers, house in middle of grass sparkling with witch wards. Blue wards, bright with light, covered house. Molly and Angelina-kit and Little Evan-kit were safe inside. House was dark. Molly would not see Beast. But she would know our scream. Know we were here to protect.

Padded silently around Molly's house, outside of wards, magic tickling on pelt and whiskers. All were safe. Molly was good mother of kits. Evan was good protector. Evan made Jane claw of steel, favorite vampire knife. I spun and raced after wolves. *Will kill.*

By the time dawn turned sky gray and chased away small stars, I had hunted all night. Followed wolves far. Ate from old deer kills. I had chased wolves to Molly's witch sisters, little houses warded by blue lights and purple lights, some smelling like pumpkin or melon or stinky herb, each sister's magic different in color and scent. Hunted wolves downhill to river and along creek. It was full, roaring with water-voice, claiming place in creek bottom. It ran fast, splashing cold on pelt. Rain- and mud-smell were everywhere. Smell of grindylow was strong in creek, but was different here in

mountains. Better. Not dead-fish stink, but fresh-fish stink.
Grindy had marked rocks and trees with claws.

Smelled Evangelina. Leaped to big rock in middle of
creek and saw big house on hill above creek. It was Evangelina's den. Stacked den rooms, three stories high. Many-
more-than-five pointed tops above many windows and
many colors of blue and green paint. *Gables and dormers,*
Jane murmured. *An old gingerbread-style house. The Everhart family home, maybe?* Wolf-stink was strong here, but
ward was up, bright and burning Beast-nose like sting of
bee. *It should keep out the wolves,* Jane thought. I crouched,
watching, listening.

Many-more-than-five kinds of flowers and stinky herbs
grew on hill. Many trees with hard nuts. Vegetable garden
with yellow squash and pumpkin and other plants Jane
might eat. Beast would not eat. Beast was hunter. Did not
smell catnip. Liked catnip herb. Ward around Evangelina's
house went off. I sniffed. Magic still in air, stinging in nose.
Wards always on during night. Off now. Smelled . . . Tightened feet together, ready to pounce. Smelled wolf, close!
Hate wolves. Thieves of meat.

They're here now? Jane thought, fear in her heart, wanting to run. A bright spot came on inside house. *Candle?*
Jane asked, seeing through Beast-eyes. Small light moved
through house, bright in windows, light then dark. Door
opened and Evangelina walked into yard carrying small
lantern and a covered bowl made of clay, painted blue.
She's naked, Jane thought.

Breathed with silent laughter. *Jane is naked,* I thought,
when we become big-cat.

Door closed behind Evangelina with soft click. Saw short
straight handle, like limb, on door. Jane said, *Lever handle.* I
leaped to land on bank and crouched, pawpawpaw, silent up
steep bank. Found place under thick bush to watch.

Evangelina had a witch circle on the ground, round
trench dug out and lined with white quartz stones as big as
Beast-paw. She lit little lanterns at four points of circle,
flames flickering. Smaller stones made lines inside circle,
like words Jane reads.

Compass points, Jane thought. *But not English words. I
can't read it. I don't know what it is.*

I moved into shadows and crawled across cold ground, belly low and shoulders hunched, closer to house. Two leaps from house, settled into tall stalks, flowers up high, moving in breeze.

Evangelina was sitting in middle of circle, facing lines that were not words, legs crossed, bowl in her lap. Pink diamond rested on stone before her. Glamours and spells misted over her, bright pink and color of blood in Jane-sight. Not easy to see red with Beast eyes. Black lightning flashed through the mist, which grew like storm clouds in sky, bigger and bigger, out of nothing. Sparkling mist seemed to flow through the air, over diamond, and back, breathing through witch's body as if alive.

Evangelina said a word. It sounded like, "Ansuz." A ward came up, billowing from the mist around her body, blood-colored and dappled with black clouds. The clouds sparked and snapped like electricity, as the ward curved over her and closed. Evangelina sighed.

The witch removed lid from bowl; it was full of blood. Much blood. Evangelina said strange words, not in Jane's language. "Fayhoo. Eeesaw. Fayhoo. Eeesaw. Fayhoo. Eeesaw . . ." Chanting. She put hand in bowl of blood and raised it, cupped. Dripped it over the pink diamond. Her chanting grew softer. Sleepy-sounding.

I panted silently as heart rate sped. Jane cursed inside of mind. I watched house. It was dark and empty, windows looking at world like dead eyes. Gathered limbs tight, eyes on porch. *What are you doing?* Jane asked. I leaped. Landed on bare patch of ground. Leaped again, landing on porch. Whirling around, long powerful tail whipping for balance. Evangelina was still chanting the two words, her back to house. She poured blood over her own head. Foolish witch, like kit with first kill, climbing inside to eat. Hard to clean pelt after.

I sniffed. Blood did not smell of witch. Nor of anything Beast knew. *Strange blood.*

Spelled blood, Jane thought. *She's done something to it.*

I lifted a paw and unsheathed claws. Hooked lever. Lifted. Door opened. I liked lever opener of door. I raced inside. Door closed quietly behind me. I raised up and looked out window. Evangelina was still sitting in circle, her naked body running with blood.

I padded through the house, food room, eating room, sitting television room, room for computer with table for writing. Two rooms with beds, one with faint smells of many humans, one for Evangelina. It was large with big bed, dead trees at corners, tent top above. *Silly to have tent over bed in room with ceiling.* Jane laughed. Chair, bathroom, closet, clothes everywhere on floor. I stood at door, pulling in air through mouth in soft screeing hiss. Stopped. Tasted air again. *Vampire Lincoln Shaddock and much blood and sex.*

Crap. Molly's going to have a cow, Jane thought.

Beast wants to hunt and eat cow. Like bison but easier to kill. Jane says no. But Molly *can kill cow?*

No. Molly won't— Jane made air breath sound in mind. *Never mind. Upstairs. Quick. Please,* she added. Jane was trying to be good beta when Beast was alpha. I turned and padded to stairs, long tail bumping hallway. Raced up stairs. Doors closed up here, but were levers in dark metal. *Bronze. Period reproductions,* Jane thought. I opened doors. One room piled high with things, dusty, old. One room was bedroom, dusty, not used. Bed had tall tree posts like Evangelina's and tent on top. *Canopy,* Jane thought. *Decorated in pink and lavender. Curled photos around the mirror. An old laptop. CDs. Jewelry in a pile.* Crap. *It's a teenager's room.*

Pulled door closed. Room for bathing and cleaning body was dusty too. Big house-den for one witch woman. Waste of den space. Last room at end of small hallway was different. Smelled scent from this side of door. Blood. I sniffed, learning scent. Male. Blood many years old. I pressed lever with paw and door opened. Room had wood floor, couch, table, TV. Smelled of cigar smoke. And old newspapers. And dead human.

Stepped carefully, slowly, inside. Blood was on floor, smell oldoldold. Chemicals had been used on it. *Clorox,* Jane thought. *Detergents.* I padded to back of couch and found rug there, against wall. Rolled up. Sniffed at end. Dead human was inside. Jane cursed, fear in her heart.

Beast is not afraid. Beast is not prey, I reminded her. I turned and left room, pulling door shut with paw until it snicked closed, hiding dead man in rug. Checked other doors. All closed. Padded up to third story. Door at top had round handle, not lever. *Will not be able to go here.*

Ran down stairs. Saw door at bottom, not able to see going up. Low light came from around edges. Opened door to see stairs leading down. I stopped. Tasting, testing. Air sparkled like taste of lemon. Taste of onion. Bad taste, like sting of bee. Remembered bee landed on food. Ate it. Hurt for long time. Could smell nothing here but bee smell. Nose curled. Hacked. Sneezed. Bad taste/smell. Heard soft groan. Sound of breathing, snoring, came up stairs, with light from room at bottom. But stairs were dark. Unlit.

Good thing we aren't in a bikini, Jane thought, *or this would be seriously dangerous.*

Did not understand Jane's laughter or Jane's fear. Stepped over threshold. Checked door handle, to see if I could get out. Good lever handle on both sides. Started down stairs. On wall at end of narrow stairs I saw a picture in frame. Jane slowed to study it. I let her be alpha. Jane thoughts flooded my mind.

I drew on my human sight. The painting was a depiction of a witch circle with a pentagram in the center; there were adults standing at the points of the pentagram. The female participants were dressed in belled skirts, big sleeves, and corsets that came to a point below the navel. The males wore knee pants, lace and satin, big-buckled shoes, and white wigs piled up high. And all had fangs. Lying in the center of the pentagram were two human-looking children, naked and bound. One of the wigged and goateed men held an athame over them. On his chest he wore a gaudy, heavy, gold chain set with a thick casing holding the pink diamond—the blood-diamond—the casing shaped of horns and claws. It looked barbaric, brutal, and powerful, an artifact from a distant time and place.

I knew this painting. It was a depiction of a black magic art ceremony intended to bring vampire scions out of the devoveo, the state of insanity they entered into when they were turned, and which they endured for ten years or so, until they found themselves again amidst the bloodlust of vamp-hungers. I nudged Beast down the stairs, slowly. As we moved, more paintings appeared on the white-painted basement wall ahead, all hung at the same level.

I had stolen these paintings from the vamps who had killed witch children. There were fifteen, a batch of seven from one century, the fifteenth century, I thought, and seven from the sixteenth century—or maybe it was sixteenth and seventeenth century. The only thing that mattered was that this was art from two time periods that had been used to chronicle experiments of black magic—blood magic. I had given them to Evangelina to destroy or store. Not to use.

Beast padded into the basement room. Whoever was breathing and snoring, wasn't in here. There was no furniture, no washing machine or dryer, nothing except walls and ceiling, which were painted white, and the floor, which was painted black . . . and the white witch circle in the center of the room. The paintings on the walls were equidistant apart, and were arranged according to century. Though the fashions changed, the people in the paintings did not. They were the vampire witches, the Damours, Renee and her brothers—and husbands. She had married her siblings. I'd helped kill them.

In the earlier paintings, the female vamps wore high-waisted, slender dresses showing a lot of cleavage, delicate shoes, and lots of natural-colored hair. The adult Damours were depicted through the ages, and sometimes their whacked-out teenaged children. In some paintings, the teens lay in the center of the witch circles and pentagrams, vamped out and clearly raving; in others, they were outside the circles. And there were always the sacrifices. In several paintings, the sacrificial witch children were dead, their throats cut, lives forfeited in the pentagram's center. In others, they were being drunk from as they died.

The experiments had changed in each depiction. In some, the circles and pentagrams were made by cutting into the earth, as if with a spade. In others, the circles were made with other things: powder or flour, feathers, flowers, broken stones, pebbles, shaped stones, bricks. The sacrificial athames in the older depictions were steel. The most recent ones were silver. One painting showed the long-chained teens ripping out the throats of the sacrifices and drinking them down. In another, the husbands and their two children were inside the circle, savaging a second man. Two younger, fangless children were being sacrificed by Renee Damour, the mother, a silver knife held high.

The fourteenth painting was different from the previous ones. In it, a vamp raced downhill, white dress flying back with her speed, eyes blazing, holding a flaming cross. Sabina Delgado y Aguilar, the vampire priestess, coming to the rescue, vamped out, her face in a rictus scream of pain, her arms on fire, flames licking toward her body. The vamps in the circle were running away, faces full of terror.

The fifteenth and last painting came from the 1970s, just before the advent of digital cameras. Vamps hadn't had the use of silvered mirrors or silver-based film, so, until recently, if they wanted to see themselves, they had to pay for art. I had killed the Damours, the original owners of the blood-diamond amulet, to keep them from killing Angelina and Little Evan. I had done what seemed wise in giving the paintings to the strongest, most ethical witch I knew, the children's aunt. And she had stolen the diamond and reunited it with the paintings. But Evangelina was not a vamp with vamp children, and she was no longer ethical. What was she doing with all this? Nothing made sense. The snoring grew softer as I stood there. Monotonous. It seemed to emanate from the back wall, from a thin, dark line, a narrow crack.

Beast took the last step to the black floor and stopped, paws together, neck outstretched, facing the white-painted witch circle in the center of the big room. The outline of the circle on the floor was covered in salt, sealing it, indicating that, when Evangelina left, she left a working in progress. As we stared, Beast took another step, and I felt a quiver pass through us, electric and painful. The ward over the circle flared, bright and sharp, red as blood. Stinging.

Beast hissed. The shock settled low in our belly, deep in our joints. And tugged. The room went brighter, whiter, as our pupils dilated. Beast took another step forward and stumbled.

Crap. Beast? Black lightning and scarlet motes flashed through the ward, much like the *hedge of thorns*, a protection ward Molly had once made for me, and similar to one

Evangelina had made for Leo, back when she was still part of the witch/vamp negotiations. But Leo's had been built like a cone which had stopped just short of the ceiling, and it hadn't worked perfectly. This one was bowl shaped, a far stronger ward.

Beast took another step. Something dark flowed up from the center of the circle, like smoke, but cohesive. Like a shadow, but three dimensional. It threw itself at the ward. The lightning coalesced at the impact point, blacker than night, flickering with purple and blue lights. Scarlet motes swarmed out and around the ward, as if looking for escape. The shadow fell back, expanded horizontally for a moment before reshaping. It looked vaguely like a person, one with extra-broad shoulders. Something about its form also looked angry and, maybe, hungry. The ward returned to its bloodred color and the lightning resumed its flickering.

Beast's breath sped up, panting. Hunger lanced through her stomach and bowels. She took another step toward the *thing* inside.

I realized that she had been spelled by whatever working was taking place in the circle. *Beast!* I shouted into her mind. Another step brought us within feet of the circle. *Beast!* When she didn't react, and took another step, I reached out mentally and put my hands and feet into her paws. Balance was different. I'd never been in control of Beast and I/we stumbled. I sat us down, her body listing drunkenly. The floor had a chill to it on Beast's backside, like bare stone. But at least we weren't moving forward anymore.

I could still feel the call drawing Beast closer, and knew I had to get us back from the working, but I didn't know how. Extending her claws, I pressed them against the floor lightly, as I studied the thing inside. It seemed to study me, though if it had eyes I couldn't make them out and I had a feeling that I shouldn't look for them. The thing was amorphous, or maybe multimorphous; I could see through it as it moved around the periphery of the circle, like a dog might walk around a cage, not touching the ward. It had a tail. Or a leash. As if part of it was being spindled out and anchored to the floor in the center of the circle.

On the floor, where the trail of darkness ended was something shiny and gelatinous. It had to be blood, though

I couldn't smell anything over the tingly magic. I didn't know much about witch magic, and I knew nothing about blood magic—what many called black magic—but I was pretty sure, based on the blood and the way Beast was acting, that this was a summoning spell.

And that meant the thing in the middle might be a demon.

Crapcrapcrapcrap!

The snoring changed pitch, breaking into my awareness. It had been so regular I had forgotten it. And perhaps the thing-in-the-circle had forgotten it too, because at the change, it whirled and raced to the far side of the ward. It grew horizontal again, and I realized it was spreading wings, diaphanous as mist. It snapped its wings closed and raised its head. I could see a shadow beak, like a hawk's, open with a cry.

Maybe the thing-in-the-circle had begun to affect me as well, because I could suddenly breathe easier. I pressed down with a front paw, pushing against the floor. My body moved back, sliding. I pulled that paw to me, using the other paw to apply pressure to the floor. Slowly I pushed Beast's body away from the thing-in-the-circle and back toward the steps.

Jane? Beast thought at me, sounding disoriented.

It's okay. I got us out. Can you walk?

Beast yawned and shook her head before flowing into a stretch, the kind cats do after a nap. *Can walk. But not close to lightning.*

The wall on the other side of the room isn't solid. There's something on the other side. Can you get us there?

Beast stood, her balance only a little affected. I released control of her body and pulled back, away from the centers of her brain used for motor control. Being in charge of her body—that had felt seriously freaky. Beast walked around the room, her right side sliding along the walls as if she were scent-marking them. Beast pressed a paw against the back wall. It opened with a creak; the section of the wall was a hidden door. Scent spilled out, as if it had been spelled to remain inside, but opening the door broke the ward, releasing it. The thing-in-the-circle thrashed; the sizzle of electricity as it bounded around its cage was like the sound of searing meat. I drew farther into Beast's mind and let her take over.

Wolf den, I thought to Jane. I growled. Dropped head, showing teeth. Room was dark, dim light spilling in from behind. Wolves did not attack. I looked back, to see caged thing hitting ward, black lightning sparking. Looked again into room filled with wolf smell. I was smart hunter; would not enter place of darkness. Saw white place on wall, switch for light, and raised up. Lifted switch with paw pad. Light filled room, faster than sunrise. Room was full of big cages, stacked along wall. Like cages in place for doctor of dog.

Only if the dogs are big as ponies, Jane thought.

Only two cages were full. Werewolves. I hacked with laughter. *Werewolves in cages. Good. Catch wolves. Cage them. Kill them.* I gathered for leap.

No, Jane thought. *No killing. Well, not yet.*

I hissed. *Want to kill wolves.* Wolves were in human form. Big hairy male, the one Jane called Fire Truck, and smaller male—Weasel. Sleeping.

Naked again. What is it about Evangelina and nudity.

Smell blood. Wolf blood. Padded close, to see cuts on wolves' bodies, gaping open, not healed. I stretched out neck, nose to cage, opened mouth. Sniffed/tasted. Smell of poison.

Not poison. Something else. I sniffed again. *The cuts won't heal because she used silver to make them. And the wolves didn't fight back when she did. They let her. Oh crap. She slipped them a Mickey. Evangelina was the woman with the umbrella at the Cajun restaurant. She tracked them and took them down somehow and brought them here.*

Smell vampire blood too. Smell Lincoln Shaddock.

Jane was silent, unable to speak, thinking too fast for Beast to follow.

Spell in witch circle is to summon two-natured, moon-called, I thought. *Tried to summon us when we got close. But we are Beast. Better than Jane or big-cat alone. Better than wolves, better than Lincoln vampire.* Tilted head. Thought for a moment, thought like Jane. Thinking like Jane hurt. *Lincoln Shaddock was dead and undead, two-natured but not two-natured. We are two-natured, but not two-natured.* Shook head as if flea nipped at ear. Magic was confusing.

She's had Shaddock in her bed and basement, wolves in cages, a body in a rug. Jane made blowing sound again, frustrated. *You're right. Perhaps a summoning affected him. Vamps are dead and undead. With the whole being-alive-at-night thing, maybe they're moon-called too. Weres are two-natured and full-moon-called. Why summon either?*

Jane went quiet. *Unless she expected* Leo *to be here. Rick said it was scuttlebutt, and maybe she had heard the rumors. Maybe getting Leo here, where she would be at the center of her power and he was cut off from his clans, was her intention all along.*

Thoughts for daytime. We spend too long in Evangelina den, wolf den. Must go. I turned, walked to door and pawed switch off. Wolf den with cages went dark. I walked into room with witch circle, leaving door open. No lever handle to pull it shut. Felt pull of spell on floor. Jane put hand on my mind, held off summoning.

Thing-in-the-circle stared at us. I could sense its . . .

Bewilderment, Jane thought. *It can't understand why we aren't being drawn inside with it.*

I moved around wall, back to stairs, and up. Summoning spell weakened. Was gone when we reached top of stairs. I pushed Jane away. *Beast is alpha.* Closed door behind us. Went to window. Evangelina was still in circle, body covered in blood. She was lying on side. Sleeping. I opened door and slipped through. Raced off of porch and leaped across brush, to land, silent, on rock and pebble path. Looked over shoulder to see Evangelina, bloody, asleep. Another leap took us deep into shadows under low tree. We turned again to look at witch, sleeping, covered in blood. Hacked softly. Stupid kit mistake.

Let's shift, call Adelaide's driver service, and get back to the hotel. I have a lot of research to do. On demons.

CHAPTER NINETEEN

Want to Play?

Back at the hotel, I picked up my cell and made a few calls, the first to Evan—and he actually answered even though he had to see my number on the readout. I described the scene at Evil Evie's and he said, "I need to think about this. You will not interfere, do you understand? Break the spell at the wrong point and you could kill Molly."

"Sure. Whatever." I hung up, ticked off, though I knew he could handle the demon situation better than I could any day.

I left a message for the sheriff that the wolves were currently caged and no danger to the public. I deliberately didn't leave any details, and figured that would irritate him—I enjoyed baiting cops. I punched END with a little grin, turned on the gas logs and the laptop, curled on the bed, and went Internet hopping.

There were a gazillion sites about demons on the Internet, most stupid, but maybe a half gazillion that could offer something to me. I refined my search, adding in beak, wings, moon-called, werewolves, and started a list on a pad. There were demons of all kinds: Christian, pagan, Jewish, tribal, ancient, fictional, mythical, modern, European, American tribal Indian, Eastern, Middle Eastern, Asian. I began a list, trying to ignore the weird feeling that a predator was standing across the room with its eyes on my neck. Just nerves, but still. Demons were scary.

When I had a page full of demon names, I closed the laptop and leaned back on the bed, pillows piled behind me. This wasn't working. There were too many possibilities. The gas fireplace cast both heat and flickering shadows, warming the room enough for me, even wearing only boy-shorts and a thin tank top. I should be desperate for sleep, but I was too wired to close my eyes, and the sunlight that poured around the edges of the blackout blinds assured me I should be up and around, not exhausted and depleted. All I could see was the demon in the circle as I/we walked away from it.

I wasn't used to sitting on my hands, doing nothing, but charging in to Evil Evie's basement and attacking the thing in the circle would likely cause more harm than good, and maybe release a demon to wreak havoc on Earth. I could call the cops, but that would just endanger humans. I could call Leo. And if he came and killed Evangelina, any hope of future parley between vamps and witches was ended for this generation because the witches would hold all vamps accountable for the death. It would be the next generation before younger witches would be willing to try again. In all honesty, that didn't bother me. But if Leo interfered, and the spell went kaboom, it might hurt Mol. Or, I could go to the café and tell the sisters but that was going to be a problem no matter how I might phrase it. "Hi, girls. Your crazy-as-a-bat sister—the one screwing a vamp—has kidnapped two werewolves, stored them in cages in the basement, drained their blood, and summoned a demon. Oh, and she's sleeping outside buck naked, covered in spelled blood, and has a dead man rolled up in a carpet in her house." Yeah. Like that was gonna work. Not.

Worse—Evangelina had stolen Shaddock's blood as well. What did the mixture of were and vamp blood do to a spell cast by a water witch who had a demon in a magical cage? As usual, I was in the dark and flying by the seat of my pants. I dialed Molly and was shunted directly to voice mail. I hung up without leaving a message.

I was between a demon and the deep blue sea. I was screwed no matter what I did. I'd have to depend on Evan to handle it. I curled up and closed my eyes. Despite my worry, I fell asleep.

*   *   *

The door opened and Rick walked in, shutting the door behind him. I was dreaming, that kind where you know it's a dream but you're paralyzed, unable to move, unable to participate. He stood in the firelight for a moment, his eyes adjusting, before he dropped his jacket to the floor and toed off his boots. Pulled his T-shirt off. His pants slid to the floor.

Naked, he crawled onto the bed. Toward me. "Want to play?" Shadows danced over his body as he crawled, cat-like, up the mattress, looking long and lean and somehow deadly. I had never seen Rick by firelight. It warmed his olive skin to golden, shadowing and highlighting. The planes of his face were sharper, his cheekbones leaner. The muscles of his chest and abdomen were ridged muscle. He was bruised purple and green across his ribs, but in my dream, he wasn't sore, his movements smooth and effortless. Big-cat claw-scars crisscrossed his chest, looking too white, smooth as old marble. I could feel the heat of his body as he crawled up over me, hands and knees to either side, straddling me, trapping me beneath the covers. His dark eyes seized mine, a reflection of fire in his irises. His hair fell forward over his face, black and wavy, curling on the ends. He looked oddly like Leo in a long ago dream.

Slowly, he lowered his face and touched his cheek to mine, sliding along my jaw to the other side and back. Scent marking motions. I pulled in a breath that tasted and smelled of man and cat. I struggled to move, snared by the dream, my hands sleep-paralyzed beneath the covers. His lips brushed my chin and up to my mouth, featherlight, soft as a kitten's fur. I chuckled. And the sound woke me. And he was still here.

Heat flooded through me. It wasn't a dream. I raised my head to meet his mouth, but he pulled away, teasing. Heat became irritation in a flash. I dropped my head and pulled my arms free, my limbs now obeying me. I set my palms to his chest, pushing him way. Rick's hands captured mine, pulling my arms to the side, pinning me to the mattress with his weight, the comforter separating us. He was much stronger than before, and although I jerked, I was held in place. "No, no." His mouth touched me again. His breath warm, soft puffs. "Not until we talk."

"Talk?" He wanted to talk *now*?

"We can only play," he whispered, his words brushing my face. "I can infect with sex, maybe even with protection, so nothing more. Just play." His voice dropped to a low growl. "I've missed playing with you, Jane."

The growl melted my annoyance away like water on hot stones. Beast raised up and looked through my eyes, hungry for the mate she had claimed. She showed me an image of two cats hissing at each other, a large male and a young female. He smelled musky and strong. She wanted him to chase her. She swiped out at his muzzle, drawing blood. Spun away. He lunged. She let him catch her.

I chuckled. Rick traced my jaw with his lips, teeth nipping gently. "Sounds nice for me," I said. I tilted my head back so he could nuzzle my neck. His blunt human incisors bit down gently over my carotid and jugular, my pulse caught in his teeth. He bit down harder. Just to the edge of pain. I gasped. "What do you get out of it?" I managed.

He slid lower, taking the comforter with him. And sucked my nipple into his mouth. My gasp became a moan, the texture of my tank top abrading my skin, heated and wet. Sucking hard, he pulled more of my breast into his mouth. Arched his back, pulling his head away, maintaining the suction, elongating breast and nipple, his teeth grazing as he released. His mouth descended again, this time taking mine. His mouth punishing hard. My lips opened. His tongue plundered before sucking mine into his mouth. I wanted my arms around him. When I tugged them away he pressed them harder, into the mattress. His chest brushed mine, my nipples tightening painfully. I moaned into his mouth, and he laughed. Pulled away.

"I get a lot out of it. I get to follow Kem's orders," he whispered, releasing my hands, sliding his fingers up my arms, "*and* spend part of the day in your bed." He brushed his hands down my sides, along my breasts, close, not touching the sensitive peaks, one cooling and wet.

"Oh." I licked my lips; they were bruised and tender. "What orders did Kem give?"

He shoved the comforter away and gathered the hem of the tank. Pulled it from me. The air, though warm, was still cooler than Rick, and I tightened as it swept over me. His hands skimmed lower, warm, calloused fingers sliding into the top of the boy-shorts. "Later," he whispered. And I forgot everything else.

Much later, Rick was lying beside me, his head braced on one arm, the comforter pulled half over us. The firelight still dancing with the shadows, I stroked my fingertips up and across his chest, across the bruises old and new that discolored the flesh over his ribs. "Explain," I said, pressing gently in the center of one blacker than the others.

Rick flinched slightly. "Kem in a temper." I frowned. Rick shrugged. "I heal fast now."

I didn't dispute that, but Kem was full were. Even in human form, he'd be hard for Rick to defend against. Slowly, I traced across his ribs, up his chest to his shoulder with the mountain lion and bobcat tattoos and the scars that marred them. He tensed when my fingertip traced the mountains in the background, almost pulled away, but reined in his reaction. My fingernail scraped lightly across his bicep and up to his collarbone, back down to circle the eyes of the mountain lion. Rick stilled, watching me with the intensity of a hunting leopard. Curious, rapt.

The eyes of the lion and the bobcat, and globes of blood on their claws, were the only unmistakable things left of the exquisite tattoo. In the mass of scar, warped design, and distorted colors, I could make out the shape of the teeth that had bitten him, the werewolf bitch trying to tear the tattoo from his flesh. Firelight lit on the irises. I touched one. My fingertip stilled as the texture of witch magic tingled up from his skin. The eyes glowed hotly, as if throwing back the flames, a molten gold, and seemed to look at me. The taste of magic sparked, tart, citrusy.

I lifted my fingertip and the irises returned to the gold of expensive ink. I tapped it again and the glow returned. The tattoo had been put into his flesh by a witch, a spell that had been interrupted, but I didn't know the whole story. "The witch who made this, who put a spell into your skin using a tattoo." Rick made a hmmm of encouragement, the sound half purr. My heart hammered unsteadily. How could I ask this without sounding needy or whiny or stalker-nuts? "Was she a seer?" Which was marginally better than asking him if she saw me in his future. How else would he have my two cats on his body? I wondered if—

"I don't think so."

My heart plummeted. Of course not. That was stupid.

"Her name was Loriann. She was doing the dirty work of a half-crazy vampire named Isleen, one of Katie's get."

I settled deeper in the pillows and pulled the comforter higher, thinking, *Okay, I don't get some kind of proof that we belong together. But then no one ever does.*

"Isleen wanted scions, but there was something wrong with her blood. Hers either never rose or died while chained. So she found herself an old witch, a crone, living out on the bayou with her two grandchildren, and tried to force her to create a spell of binding. When Gramma refused, she killed the old woman in front of the kids and told the eldest, Loriann, she'd kill her brother, Jason, if she didn't do the job."

I flinched slightly. One side of Rick's mouth quirked up with an expression that said, *Yeah, life's a bitch.* "Then she fed from Jason and took him away. He was seven."

I watched his face. "She fed from a child?" A first feeding was almost always sexual in nature, vamp saliva tightening all the pleasure centers in the body and working on the brain like a drug. Feeding from a child under twelve was against the Vampira Carta.

"Yeah. She did. Couple nights later, Isleen and I met up in a bar. And I spent the next few days in an abandoned horse barn, stretched out on a black marble square, chained inside a witch circle as Loriann's spell was built into me. Then, just like in the movies, at the ninth hour, I was saved and Isleen died."

Rick had been tortured before, long before the wolves got to him. But he wouldn't want pity. His eyes hold mine, and the breath I took was steady and slow as I forced my emotional reaction to his tale deep inside. "You were saved?"

"Yeah, I was partially free by day and I managed to

make some stakes. Isleen and I fought, and I was losing just when Leo and Katie blew the barn doors in and finished her off."

"Spells of binding. Rick, that's why the moon can't call you. You're already partially bound to something else." At his expression I said, "And you knew that." He nodded. "But did you think that Molly and her sisters"—I stopped for a heartbeat. *Not Evangelina. I have to be sure of that.* I found my place with only a bare hesitation—"might be able to break it for you?"

"It crossed my mind. But I might go furry, and if the spell goes active when I change, it might keep me in cat form, which is not how I want to live my life. At this point, I'm waiting it out. See what happens at the full moon," he shrugged mildly, which was false body language. Had to be.

I thought about that for a while, about not knowing what your body might do, about living forever in Beast form. I had spent over a hundred years as Beast, and it had changed me. "Okay. I can see that. So. What did Kem send you to do? Buy beer?" Instead of answering, Rick lowered his head and touched my lips with his. I sighed into his mouth and pulled him over me. "I like playing," I murmured. Rick laughed again, the amused vibrations throbbing through me.

By late afternoon, I was exhausted and lethargic and energized all at once. I watched from beneath half-closed lashes as Rick dressed and left the room. I heard him speak to one of the twins on his way out, and caught the tenor of the exchange, one of those manly tones that said they knew what we had been up to for the last few hours, which they would. Blood-servants can hear better than humans and we hadn't been trying for silence. We'd been playing. Yeah. For hours. Still smiling, I rose and made my way to the bathroom for a hot shower.

I was still steaming when my phone rang. "Yellowrock," I said, cutting the water.

"I understand that you believe you have located the grindylow's lair," Kemnebi said.

"Yeah. Pretty much." I had told Rick I had a good idea

where the grindy had holed up. It hadn't taken him long to report back to the black were-leopard. "Do you wish for me to go with you to track him down?"

I pulled my hair to the side so it would drip into the tub instead of on the phone. "Yes."

"Provide me with the coordinates. My cat will lead the hunt. My . . . associate," he spat the word, "will assist us."

I figured that the associate was Rick, the man he planned to kill as soon as Rick shifted. Which was not gonna happen, even if I had to start a supernatural international incident to prevent it. "Fine by me." I gave him the location, an address in Hot Springs where he could leave his car. "I'll be there in ninety minutes," I said.

"Excellent." The call ended, and so did my long steamy shower. I dressed and dried my hair with the hotel's blow dryer, braided my hair out of the way into a fighting queue. Slid vamp-killers and wood stakes into my clothing and hair, made sure I was wearing crosses. Last thing, I double-checked that half of my ammo was silver and half was regular. The sun would set in a few hours, and there was no telling what might happen after dark with a pissed-off black were-leopard and empty hunting territory. Into a zippered pocket I placed a mountain lion tooth, my backup emergency tooth for shifting into Beast.

Dressed for hiking and hunting, I found three more messages from Angelina, messages I couldn't deal with, not and let Big Evan do things his way. But I was going to have to make an appearance at Molly's. Soon. I exited my room, texting instructions to Derek, not thinking about the blood-servant twins with big ears and bigger libidos. I made it five feet into the common room when Brian was in front of me, nearly vamp-fast. Leering. I almost dropped the cell.

"I just earned twenty from the ugly brother," he said. I didn't respond except for the blush starting somewhere below my waist and quickly spreading up my chest. It suffused up my throat and into my cheeks. Brian's smile widened. "You *are* a screamer."

I pursed my lips to keep in an instinctive retort, and pushed past him. This was just teasing. Or jealousy, which made me grin. I was closing the door to the suite when I heard him say, "Derek retrieved your SUV. Do you want to tell us why it was hidden in the driveway of a burned-out homesite?" I didn't. I closed the door and sent a second text to Derek, thanking him for getting the vehicle back and thinking of all the uses of GPS and how they could trip me up. I had to do better about arranging recovery of my own vehicles. I was getting complacent in the world of vamps, weres, humans, and tech. I needed to take better care.

A little over an hour later I was parked a mile downstream from Evangelina's, and ready to hunt. The battered, rusted, red pickup truck pulled in beside me, rolling through the mud, with Rick driving, Kem sitting pretty on the front seat. Minutes later we were on the hunt.

The day was warming up enough that I carried my leather jacket through the straps of my backpack, and extra water bottles attached by biners to loops on my hiking pants. Layered T-shirts could be pulled off one by one as needed to cope with warming temperatures. Even in the mountains, the temps could change from cold to warm fast; it was the South, after all.

A frost last night had turned the dogwoods scarlet, started the other deciduous trees into a color change, and shriveled the kudzu. Plants that flowered in fall were budding, opening in fast forward. If the chill held, in two weeks the mountains would be a riot of red and golden hues.

Rick slid a backpack onto his shoulders and we moved down the hill to the noisy, rushing creek, and upstream. Even in human form, the scent of the grindylow was pungent and potent, fishy, with a base scent that now smelled like blood. Kem-cat leaped from rock to rock, Rick and me scrambling to keep up, communicating by hand signals rather than voice to be understood over the water's roar. We might both have better reflexes and speed than humans, but no human could keep up with a big-cat on the prowl. And there was no doubt that Kem-cat was on a scent.

Like the *Puma concolor*, the black were-leopard was a solitary hunter, seldom seen in groups larger than three or four, and most often spotted alone. They were the most adaptable of all the big-cats, and unlike their spotted brothers and sisters, lived most often in deeply forested areas, where their dark coloring was most effective. They'd eat anything meaty, storks, baboons, wildebeest, jackals. They liked the taste of domesticated dog. If they could kill it they would eat it. But they were also preyed upon by other big-cats, most commonly the African lion. Ever since finding out that Kem intended to challenge and kill Rick, I had been doing my homework, looking for weak spots in the leopard's defenses. So far, not many had presented themselves.

I can be male sabertooth lion. Beast hacked deep in my mind, watching Kem leap nearly twenty feet across the rushing stream. *I can be big. Beast will protect mate.*

Which I knew. And which scared me to death.

The creek was still running high, twisting and turning, carving a deep gulley into the earth. It curved back on itself, and then back again, like a snake in a hurry, whipping back and forth. Where a larger river had the power to cut through obstacles, slowly straightening its path over decades and centuries, small creeks were left to search out the path of least resistance, and this creek had done just that, resulting in a surprisingly compact switchback carved between high banks into the base of the mountain. We passed Evangelina's house, and Kemnebi stopped on the rock in the middle of the creek. Sniffed the stone. I knew he was smelling Beast when he turned to me and hissed, his golden-green eyes knowing and taunting.

Kem-cat knows we are Beast, she murmured to me.

I didn't react, except to stare Kem down. *He knows we're* something, *but doesn't know quite what,* I thought. As with wolves, a big-cat stare was a challenge, and the hair across Kem's shoulders rose, a prickling black ruff. He lowered his head in threat, stretched his back, and depressed his rib cage below his shoulders. This time when he showed his teeth and hissed, there was real menace in it, heard over the sound of the rushing water.

Beast shoved down on my mind, her claws sinking deep. My shoulders and head moved forward. I/we drew a steel claw with each hand and hissed. Confrontation and challenge sparked between us, almost alive in its intensity. The pheromones of conflict rose on the moving air, so strong I/we could taste them. *I am your alpha. Do not forget.*

"Jane?" From the corner of my eye, I could see Rick looking back and forth between Kem-cat and me. When I didn't answer he said, very carefully, "Did I miss something?"

After a long moment, Kem looked away, staring into the trees. His ruff settled, claws retracted. Beast withdrew and I found myself. I managed a guttural, "He's my beta. He wants to kill you. I'm just letting him know it won't be easy." Rick was silent, weighing my words. I straightened, sheathing the weapons. I moved along the path, showing Kem I wasn't afraid of him, but not being dumb enough to give him my back either. The air around him was musky and sour with loss of face as the pheromones of anger faded. Keeping Rick alive was going to be difficult. Two leaps later, the leopard was again ahead of us, his long ropy tail held high, showing me his butt, proving that two could play the game of taunt-the-cat.

I followed, watching Kem-cat move upstream, muscles bunching beneath his skin, Rick close on my trail. The path quickly narrowed between thigh-high weeds, briars, poison oak and ivy, native plants and ones that had escaped from gardens, flowering with yellow, purple, and shades of pink and red. It was rocky going, the soles of my hiking boots gripping and releasing. We worked up a sweat, despite the cooler temps near the water.

We had been on the path for a couple of miles when Kem rounded a curve of the creek and disappeared, melting into the shadows of midday like smoke. When Rick and I got to the curve, we discovered a feeder creek, a foot or two wide and only inches deep, with a ten-foot waterfall that was breathtaking. And a pile of scat, marking Kem-cat's territory for us to step over. The smell of grindy was so intense here, I was sure he was right around the corner, but Kem had trodden through mud and leaped up the ten foot height. He was crouched beneath a laurel, staring down at us, a predator estimating the weight and danger of prey.

Beast slammed into my mind again and glared. Growled. Kem blinked. A moment later, he slid into the shadows. I

looked at Rick who was watching me, amusement, specula-
tion, and something warmer hiding in the deeps of his eyes.
He held out a hand, indicating the nearly sheer wall, wet
with falling water. "After you."

I grabbed a root and gave a tug. It held. I started the
climb. At the top, a fresh breeze slapped me in the face. It
was heavy with the stink of old blood and rotting flesh.

CHAPTER TWENTY

Get Your Own Damn Shoes

Two miles and sixty minutes of hard hiking later, we were in a narrow cleft of mountain, far from any path. The temps had fallen, and I was wearing my jacket; my feet, even in my hiking boots, were again wet and icy from walking in the only place a human could—the rill of water. I was out of sorts, the lack of sleep was catching up to me—that and the constant smell of death on the breeze, as if the entire mountain breathed with the stink of rot and grindylow. The hair on the back of my neck went stiff, as buzzards soared overhead, ghosting through the rising air currents.

The way ahead was blocked by dead trees; one gigantic white oak had come down, taking half the saplings on the mountainside with it, and together, they had blocked the cleft and backed up the creek, except for the small rill we had been following.

I started yet another hard climb, using the shattered limbs lodged with stone. I heard Rick follow, and knew he had put me ahead so he could catch me if I fell. It was totally unnecessary, and so sweet I couldn't keep the silly grin off my face, in spite of the putrid stench and buzzards soaring. Hand by hand, I pulled myself up the dead-tree-and-rock wall and reached the top.

The water was backed up into a pool about twenty feet long, less than ten feet wide, brown with tannins from decomposing leaves, but clear. On the far slope were corpses.

Deer corpses, bones and hide in a jumble, in various stages of decomposition; the most rotten ones were at the bottom; a well-picked, fresh corpse was on top. Maybe four deer, all small. There were also fish bones and several turtle shells. Buzzards lined the tree limbs staring at Kemnebi and the human intruders, alien emptiness in their eyes. Mixed with it all was the smell of the grindy. And an occasional whiff of something like the stink of sour cheese, if you first mixed it with dead fish and added in some vomit. Yuck.

"Dead deer," I murmured, thinking of Angie Baby and her nightmare. Beast-fast, I pulled blades. If she were seeing my future, then something bad might happen here. If.

Kemnebi lay only feet away on a downed tree, his belly off the ground, staring at the corpses across the small pond. He was breathing too fast, a shallow pant, his muscles tense, shoulder blades up high. He looked like a scared cat. I licked my lips.

"Cave," Rick said.

Beyond the pile of deer was a slice of blackness. The Appalachians were riddled with caves: limestone, mines through solid rock, narrow places where underground creeks once ran. Hundreds had been mapped. Hundreds more had yet to be discovered. And when they were, they were often hard to access. The mouth of this one was clear of brush and detritus. A well-trodden path led up to it, to the pile of bones, and to the water. It was covered with the three-toed and three-clawed paw prints of the grindylow. The entire area was covered with grindy markings, slashed into rock and trees.

I looked at Kem and back to the cave. The vamp-killers felt good in my palms as I stepped up and around the small pool toward the cave entrance. The jumbled bones were covered in flies. Maggots—not my favorite bug—crawled everywhere, big, small, totally gross. A buzzard spread its wings and flapped, irritation in every feather. I'd interrupted their feast. Rick at my shoulder, I stood at the entrance to the cave, letting my eyes adjust, drawing on Beast's speed, vision, and hearing. Adrenaline flushed through me. Something brushed my thigh. I daggered downward. Jerked to a stop. The tip of the blade was buried in the shoulder hair of Kem-cat, just touching the skin over his scapula. He looked up at me and growled softly in warning. I showed him my teeth. My look promised challenge. Later. He looked into the dark before us. Together, we stepped inside the cave.

It was an underground microcosm of the cleft in the mountain, almost mimicking the shape of the pool. Twenty feet deep and ten wide at the entrance, it narrowed to a point overhead and at the far end, a slash into the heart of the world. Stone slabs composed its walls. The roof was fifteen feet high at the entrance, lower at the far end. The floor was dirt, covered with fresh fir branches. More fir branches lined a small shelf at the back, about three feet off the floor. And on it was the grindy, curled tightly in a protective ball. When I'd seen him last he had been wearing baggy human-style clothes. Now he was naked. Around him were green balls of fur, shocking bright, almost neon. One moved. And mewled. "Holy crap," I whispered.

Rick said, "He had babies." *He* was a *she*.

The grindy woke, moving from balled up asleep into fighting mad and protective-mother-predator in half a heartbeat. Standing over her litter, she showed us long killing teeth, her arms out, claws spread, legs wide, her head forward, like any predator in danger. Multiple teats like a nursing dog's hung on her belly, and when she shrieked, it was a high-pitched squeal, her eyes wild, not recognizing us at all.

Kem turned with a liquid grace and leaped from the cave. I backed away, not taking my eyes from the grindy, Rick's shoulder touching mine. He was holding a nine mil, safety off, ready for firing. I felt better just seeing the gun. I had seen what the grindy's claws could do to a boulder, and my flesh wasn't nearly that tough. I also wasn't immortal. If I lost my head I was done for. If I received a mortal blow, and didn't have time to shift before blood loss took me, I'd be dead. My father had died that way, too fast for a shift to save him.

In the daylight I blinked at the sight of Kemnebi, on a log, still staring at the cave. He looked at us and patted the log twice with his left front paw before whirling, front feet leading his body, taking off up the hillside. "And that means, what?" I asked Rick, still processing the sight of the grindylow with babies. Babies with neon green fur. Angie had seen this. How weird was that?

"He's hunting. We get to wait."

"How about we do that upwind of the bone pile." We trudged uphill, pulling our way with trees and roots when needed, until we found a stone outcropping overlooking the grindy's lair, but upwind. We sat, our feet swinging over a seventy-foot drop. Rick opened his backpack, revealing apples, raisins, and nuts. I opened mine, showing packages of jerky made from three types of meats and six Snickers bars. "So how long do we wait?" I asked, taking off my shoes so my feet could dry.

A cat-scream and a roar sounded, echoing through the folded earth of the mountain. I jerked my gaze up, following the sound. The roar rang out again, followed by the challenge of a big-cat. Snarling. It was a fight. "I'm thinking Kem is trying to kill a bear. So not long," Rick said, his tone wry. He took my feet in his hands and began to rub, his eyes watching out over the mountain below us. The sloppy sentimental thing called my heart did a little somersault.

Want to kill a bear, Beast thought at me, flooding my system with longing and my mouth with the remembered taste of hot blood and fat. *Long time since I hunted black bear.*

"Not today," I said aloud. And shook my head when Rick looked at me curiously. I bit down on a strip of turkey jerky and chewed while Beast prowled the back of my mind, pouting. And Rick rubbed my cold feet. This was turning out to be the weirdest job I'd had in a long time. Moments later I was asleep.

Rick said, "He's back. Wake up, sleepyhead."

I sat up and yawned, spotting the dark shadow that was Kem, far below us on the opposing face of the mountain. He was moving erratically, jerking and sliding, backside first, dragging a black bear down the mountain. It looked like two hundred pounds, maybe two fifty. Beast couldn't have dragged the bear. She hissed in displeasure, but it was true. Beast could drag a hundred fifty pounds, but not much more. Leopards have excellent musculature in head, jaw, neck, and shoulders, and superior climbing ability. They can even climb down a tree headfirst. The leopard could probably drag the bear up a tree, which is where leopards keep their dinners, safe from other predators or scavengers. Kem dragged the carcass inside the mouth of the cave. I looked at Rick. "I thought Kem was ticked off with the grindy for killing Safia."

He shrugged. "Instinct is hard to resist. I've seen him feed the grindy while fighting the urge to kick it. He says the two species are linked, I'm guessing on a metaphysical level."

I shook my head and put my cold, wet boots back on. Together, Rick and I descended the precipitous hillside, mostly on our butts. When we got to the bottom, Kemnebi stepped from the cave in human form. Naked. I averted my eyes. Rick opened his backpack and tossed Kem some clothes and a bag of nuts. Kemnebi dressed without the slightest sign of embarrassment, and ate the nuts, while I tried to affect a bored expression, pretty sure I wasn't succeeding. Rick tossed him a package of granola, the kind with M&Ms in it. Kem ate that too. Then he walked barefoot toward us with that deadly-looking, catlike grace. Without preamble, he said, "They give birth only once a century. I did not know she was female, nor that she was carrying young." I wasn't sure how he could not know her gender, and he answered almost as if he had heard my thoughts. "They have very little external genitalia. They are very private creatures. I put her life in danger by bringing her to this country." His voice was toneless, but his eyes were heavy with guilt and sorrow. He looked around the steep hills and back to the cave. "She has been deeply stressed by her inborn imperative to hunt down feral weres, while carrying young. She did not hunt enough for food, did not gain enough weight, and her litter is small. The bear will feed her baby-hunger for the remaining days of her nursing."

I remembered the teats. I'd thought the grindy was an amphibian, not a mammal.

Without looking at Rick, Kemnebi held out a hand, imperiously. "Shoes."

Before Rick could react, I jerked the backpack out of his hand and stalked to Kem. Far too close, inside his per-

sonal space. I felt his cat flinch at the intrusion. Beast huffed
in defiance. "He's not your servant. He's not your slave.
He's not your punching bag." Kem's eyes went golden
green so fast I didn't even see the change. But I wasn't finished. "And he isn't yours to challenge or to kill. He's *mine*.
Get it?" I tossed the backpack into the pond. It landed with
a splash. "Get your own damn shoes."

I grabbed Rick by the elbow and yanked him downhill.
"Yours, huh?" he said, sounding entirely too satisfied. I
growled at him. "You do like to play rough, Jane Yellowrock. I like that about you." I ignored him, dragging him
along, Rick laughing under his breath, shaking his head.

I shook my head and hid a smile. "Shuddup."

Back at the parking lot, I let the men go off in their borrowed, battered truck and I headed back to Asheville. I was
cold, wet, exhausted, and really, really, *really* needed a nap.
Which I got. Finally. Even though sleeping meant I still had
not called Angie back.

By half an hour after midnight I knew there were problems,
I just didn't know what kind or how bad. The evening's talks
had been scheduled to begin at twelve, but Shaddock was
late. Again. No one answered at the clan home. No one answered anywhere. It was like Shaddock and clan had been
sucked out of the universe, and thinking about the thing in
Evil Evie's basement, the bite marks on her neck, and the
pink spell, that might be possible. I just hoped he wasn't
stuck in the basement ward. If he was, I'd need Evangelina's sisters to free him. And maybe a howitzer.

Grégoire, insulted, retired to his suite with his twins,
having a midnight blood-snack and a massage, leaving me
with orders to find Shaddock. Things weren't going well for
the local vamp, and if Grégoire's expression was indicative
of the future, Shaddock wasn't going to be master of any
city, anywhere. Ever.

Back in my room again, I closed the door behind me,
stripped off my fancy jacket, and opened my cell. There
were no voice mail messages or texts from Molly. No calls
from Evan either. Nada. Nothing. They wouldn't call now,
not this late. There was also nothing from Rick.

I was closing the cell when it rang, startling me. I flipped it back open, my heart in my throat, but it wasn't Mol. I narrowed my eyes at the number on the screen. It wasn't one I wanted to hear from right now. "Yellowrock." I let my tone show my lack of pleasure.

Bruiser hesitated as if reading my emotions from the single word. He said, "Leo is dispatching the Rogue Hunter to the service of Lincoln Shaddock." Bruiser was sounding all formal, which he did when he was acting strictly in Leo's behalf, and not entirely with his own approval. When Leo wanted me to sleep with Kemnebi, Bruiser had used the same tone.

"Yeah? Would this have anything to do with old Linc being a no-show? *Again?*" I asked.

"There has been a disturbance. You will provide him and his clan all reasonable service."

"I don't sleep with Leo's pals," I reminded him.

His voice was warm, a low burr, when he said, "You *have* been remarkably resistant to my charms."

Ooookaaay. I opened my mouth and closed it. Not gonna say *anything* I was thinking.

"Now," he went on, his tone sharpening, "Leo hears rumors that his pet Rogue Hunter has claimed the title of his Enforcer. Is this true?"

"Ummm?" I got a sudden bad feeling. "Maybe."

"Brilliant." But I could tell he really meant *stupid.* "The Enforcer is a titled position in a Master's household. Have you drank from him? Have you drank from *any* Mithran?"

"Nooooo." I drug the word into three syllables.

"Don't, for a period of two moon cycles, unless you want to be bound to that vampire as an Enforcer—a top blood-servant similar to a primo. One sip of blood will seal the contract." I let a breath go, a long exhalation he couldn't hear. *Not a problem.* I had no intention of drinking from any vamp, ever. "Please . . . *attempt* to be less foolish," he said. The call disconnected.

I was still holding the cell when it rang again. I was a popular gal tonight. "Yellowrock."

"Jane. It's Adelaide. We need you at the compound." Adelaide, tall and blond, the blood-servant lawyer who wanted to be my gal-pal. Before I could respond she said,

"Lincoln's chained scions have been let free of their shackles. They killed—" Her voice shut off as if someone had garroted her. I heard a breath drawn, full of tears. "They killed Sarah. She turned twenty-two yesterday. She was just a child." There was a sob in her voice. She had liked Sarah.

This was why Leo had turned my services over to Shaddock. Young rogue-vamps who killed humans were staked. By me, if they got out of the scion lair; opening a scion lair with unchained rogues was a near guarantee that some would get out. I chose my words with care. "Why hasn't Lincoln handled it? Or Chen?"

Her voice changed, growing stilted and sharp. "Mr. Shaddock isn't on the premises at the moment. He is not available. And Chen is elsewhere employed."

"Ah." *Crap.* Shaddock was missing from more than his parley talks, and Chen was hunting him. "And the person who set the rogues free?"

"We have the event on digital video, and the perpetrator is *contained.*" Her emphasis on the word *contained* made me think her culprit was not in the best shape.

"I'll be there within the hour." I tossed my vamp-hunting gear on the bed, catching sight of myself in the long mirrors as I moved. I was no clotheshorse, but I looked pretty good in harem pants, boots, white silk shirt and short vest. Too bad I wasn't going to get a chance to show the outfit off. While I talked on the cell—ordering the supplies I needed, and my SUV brought around front—I stripped and pulled on leather studded with silver. Weaponed up, stakes in my bun, and every vamp-killer blade and gun I owned. And strode toward the door to the hallway.

It opened, my hand still above the knob. The smell of vamp swept in. I had a hand on a stake before I could catch myself, and met Grégoire's gorgeous dark blue eyes. His delicate brows lifted, his gaze resting on my hand and the stake, unamused. I released it as if it burned. "Oops." Grabbing a stake in the presence of a master vamp wasn't smart.

Grégoire laughed. Waving one hand as if he were dismissing the gesture of violence, he moved into the suite, graceful as a ballerina. His forward motion alone backed me up, his blond hair loose about his shoulders, his scent like aromatic lilies tonight. Grégoire was wearing midnight blue silk jammies that probably cost more than everything I owned, the shirt unbuttoned to reveal a pale chest, hairless and smooth. And he was barefooted. I don't know why, but the sight of a man's bare feet can make me melt. Of course, if a vamp wanted to get the drop on me, he would come at me just like this, looking innocent and harmless. I backed up fast, my hands off my weapons. "Grégoire."

"Rogue Hunter." The matching bookend blood-servants stepped in behind him and shut the door. They were wearing even less than their master, silk pajama bottoms hanging low on their hips and twin looks of expectancy that sent warnings through me like lightning. "My master sent a gift for you," Grégoire said. "I have been instructed to give it to you prior to your activities tonight." He extended a black velvet box six inches high and fourteen square, like something from an expensive jewelry store.

"Ummm." One can't be too careful accepting gifts from vamps. Sometimes they thought it meant they owned you. Not that I'd ever received a gift from one, if I discounted the sabertooth lion bones Leo had given me once and the cell phone. And the guns. And I discounted all that because it was business. But this wasn't. "Okay. What is it and what does it mean?"

"I have been assured that it is an indication of his satisfaction with your expertise and service, and to replace something lost in his labor. A boon, with, as you Americans say, 'no strings attached.'"

I took the box gingerly, as if it might explode, and set it on the coffee table in front of the couch. Grégoire sat in a wingback chair and waited, the twins at his back, eyes on the box. I took that as my cue to open the gift. I sat on the couch and raised the hinged lid. The inside was black silk, and on the silk was a jewelry display shaped like the neck and shoulders of a woman. No head. The shoulders were covered with a black silk scarf, lightly draping and partially obscuring a piece of jewelry beneath. I hoped the MOC wasn't sending me jewelry. Or a promise that he wanted to take my head. There were all sorts of ways to interpret a headless mannequin.

With a gesture suitable to a magician's stage, Grégoire leaned forward and swept the scarf away. Beneath it was a mesh of interwoven rings. Leo had replaced my broken vamp collar, the one a werewolf had destroyed, crushing it with his massive jaws. I breathed out slowly. It was beautiful, made of three different sized rings, hooked together in an intricate weave. There were tiny, faceted stones attached, all in tawny gold colors, the shade my eyes flash when Beast is near the surface.

"The collar is composed of two layers, which may be worn together or separately. The lower layer is made of sterling silver over titanium, for better strength and protection than the collar you lost to his service. The upper layer, which attaches so"—he indicated a delicate latching mechanism—"is decorative. Twenty-four carat gold rings with chocolate diamonds and citrines scattered across the surface. My master had it created especially for you so that you might wear it even when working in a formal gown and yet be safe."

I blinked. And ran his words through my mind again. *Sterling, gold, and diamonds?* This thing must have cost a fortune.

"The silk scarf is my small contribution." He flicked it smoothly over my arm. "It may aide you when you hunt at night. It secures over the collar to hide the gleam of metal, and to assure that no rogue Mithran will recognize a weapon around your neck prior to an attack."

I looked up at the twins and licked my suddenly dry lips. "Is this okay?" Meaning, can I accept it without prejudice or would acceptance be a promise to hop into Leo's bed?

"When a master of a city offers a boon to a servant or employee," Brandon said, "it's exactly as my master has said—a gift only, a reward for a job well done."

Suu-weet. I reached to take the necklace but Grégoire's hand was there first, vamp-fast. I yanked back my hand. Slammed back into the couch. He was standing in front of me. And I didn't see him move from the chair. *Crap*. This was payback for reaching for a weapon in his presence—being taught that he was way too fast for me to kill. Having it shown to me that sane master vamp beats stupid vamp-hunter any night. A cold sweat broke out on my flesh and Beast was oddly absent, not bragging to me that she could win this fight.

Grégoire lifted the necklace and removed the upper

gold layer, setting it aside. He unclasped the silver fighting necklace and *moved*. That air popped and I felt the wind of his movement on my face. I tensed. My jacket was pulled back, the jerk hard enough to make me gasp. The silver necklace settled around my shoulders, cold, and tightened on my neck. Grégoire's fingers were no warmer than the silver. Grégoire's fingers were touching the silver. *Crap. A vamp who can handle silver. He had been silver poisoned recently. Surviving that might give him immunity.* Thoughts fast and desperate.

I heard the faint snick when the latch caught. And suddenly Grégoire was in front of me again, leaning over me. His hands on my throat again. I was inches taller than Grégoire, and pounds of muscle heavier, better trained, way better armed. And yet, if he wanted me dead, he could snap my head around and pop it right off. I had once fought Leo. I knew how hard masters were to beat. Gently, he pulled my leather jacket in place. Raised the zipper with a metallic ratchet. "Do we understand one another, *ma chère*?"

"We do." I forced myself to meet his eyes. They were dark with rage, pupils wide, as if he were slipping into his vamped-out state, yet held himself in check. He had that much control, was that strong. I took a breath, slowly, carefully. And drew on my Christian school girl manners, hoping it might be enough. "Please assure the Master of the City of New Orleans that his gift is received in all . . . humility"—I searched for more words— "and delight."

"And?" Grégoire asked.

I swallowed. *And? And what?* "And . . . um . . . and the scarf is beautiful." But that wasn't what he wanted. "And . . . please assure that I meant no offense to the blood-master's most trusted and beloved adviser and scion."

Grégoire smiled sweetly, almost angelically, and patted my cheek. "You have not brought me the witch who bespelled Lincoln Shaddock. And now he is missing again. Still bespelled?"

"Probably." I admitted.

"I gave you a charge. Fulfill it." He vanished with a whirlwind and that pop of displaced air. The twins were looking at me quizzically, and I realized that they hadn't seen me almost pull a stake on their master. I sank back in the couch cushions and tried to remember how to breathe.

I managed three insufficient breaths and stood. I needed out of here. "I'll report back by sunrise." They nodded, still confused, and I walked around the coffee table, the headless mannequin, and the golden collar, and out the door. Sometimes all a girl has is moxie, and when her knees are knuckling and her heart's racing and she's sweating drops of pure fear, that's a good time to draw on that feminine talent. That and prayer. Yeah. Prayer might be a real good idea about now.

Crap. Grégoire had handled pure silver. Just like Leo could. Had Leo been silver poisoned once? And he was fast. Maybe faster than Leo. So why was Leo the Master of the City of New Orleans, and not Grégoire? And how was I gonna get out of killing Evangelina if Lincoln was trapped in her basement with a demon?

CHAPTER TWENTY-ONE

Things Had Just FUBARed

I was at Lincoln Shaddock's place in less than the time I had allowed myself. Unfortunately, so was Sheriff Grizzard and a strange woman. They both looked royally ticked off. He met me at my SUV and looked me over as I opened the door. As I climbed out, my eyes caught on the folded scrap of purple on the passenger floor. Someone had folded Evangelina's scarf. I'd have to tip the valets well. They were going beyond the call of duty.

I closed the door and Grizzard took in the array of weapons, most illegal. The woman stood at his shoulder, her hand on a pistol grip under her arm. *Cop*. Rather than defend my weapons, I pulled a blade and handed it to Grizzard hilt first. I pretended not to hear his shocked breath at the sight of the naked blade glittering in the moonlight. He took the hilt and turned it to the dim light while I unstrapped the blade sheath. "It's a vamp-killer. German steel overlaid with sterling, hilt and blade all one piece. The hilt is molded over with high impact, crosshatched plastic for a better grip. The blood groove is extra deep. Killing vamps is bloody business."

"I hear their blood is like acid," the woman said.

"Some of them. Some not. Depends on the bloodlines."

"They're talking about licensing these in Congress." He looked up at me under bushy brows. "Talking about licensing vampire hunters too."

"Congress is always talking." I gave him the sheath and tucked my box of supplies under one arm. "The sheath attaches to your belt and upper thigh. Consider it a gift. Who are you?" I asked the woman.

"Loretta Scoggins, sheriff of Madison County."

The drill-sergeant-sheriff who cussed like a sailor. I handed her a blade too, considering it a point of good PR. Leo could replace them. Grizzard and Scoggins started working on the straps and I led the way to the door. "Pickersgill tells me Lincoln is missing," he said.

"Yeah. And I have to go save him from the wicked witch of the west. But first we have to restore order to the chained ones."

"Is that gonna be hard?" Loretta asked.

I laughed, the sound too dry for real humor. "It can be."

Pickersgill was standing at the entrance, the two and a-half inch steel door held open. Soft light filtered out, illuminating the shrubs at his side. He was a slight, nondescript man, not nearly as pretty as most vamps, which means he was brought over because he had something to offer his maker. With his history, that meant his military and political smarts. I nodded to him; he nodded back and shut the door behind us. "You came alone? Not with your boys?"

"You were insulting last time. How bad is it?" I asked.

"They tore into her. Drained her dry. I've called in all the help I could find on short notice—four Mithrans and a dozen blood-servants. I even tried to get Gertruda, the Mercy Blade, but she's spending the night at the hospital, healing the humans of were-taint. Sheriffs," he said, shaking their hands. He pointed to a security consol. On a screen was the scion lair. Blood was splattered everywhere, centered on a girl lying on the cold stone. She looked dead. Rogues were racing around the room, as if chasing imaginary prey. Others were standing in the corners of the room, immobile. All the cages were open. Pickersgill punched a button and said, "The human came in to feed them, and the Mithran came in behind her." On the screen, the door opened and Sarah entered, a sweet-faced girl with balletic movements, as if she danced to songs only she heard. Behind her a tall vamp entered, moving fast, creating a fuzzed-

out image on the low-quality video He hit the girl. She spun
away, and before she fell, he had opened the first cell.

"Now all of them are unshackled," Pickersgill said, returning us to the current feed, "and one is the blood rela-
tion of a Mithran who is here to help." Translation—the
vamp would resist if I had to kill his kin. Lucky me. More
vamp politics, which I sucked at.

"I want to see the vamp who let them loose."

Pickersgill frowned, but led the way down the stairs into
the windowed room, our reflections moving like underwater undulations, the way they might look in bullet resistant
glass. Last time I was here, I hadn't realized they were bul-
letproof. Which translated to freaking expensive.

The place smelled of vamp and barbeque smoke, heavy
on the sage. Someone had come straight from the restaurant. We reached the lower level and I looked over the
vamps and blood-servants clustered in a sitting area. They
were all dressed in jeans and leather. The servants were
wearing silver chain mail armored vests with high collars,
leather and silver cuffs over each wrist. Not bad, and totally
unexpected in a vamp's household.

At a gesture from Pickersgill, they parted, revealing a
vamp curled in a fetal position on the floor. He had wood
stakes in his belly, immobilized and bleeding onto a plastic sheet, which struck me as neat and tidy, or way too
prepared. He had silver shackles on his wrists. And a pink
glow all over him. *Crap.* Evangelina had spelled him to set
the chained ones free. What was the witch *doing*? *Trying*
to get herself killed? "Keep him shackled, but take out
the stakes. I have a feeling he was spelled to set them
free."

"Evangelina," Pickersgill said. It sounded like a curse.
"My master has placed her under his protection. We cannot
harm her."

I sighed and lifted a shoulder. "Don't worry," I said.
"Grégoire has ordered me to bring her to him." A truly vi-
cious smile grew on Pickersgill's face. Grégoire outranked
Shaddock. He could do anything he wanted to the witch.
"Let's get to work," I said.

"They *ain't* gonna be injured," one of the vamps said. It
still surprised me to hear a vamp speak with any accent

other than European, and the country drawl was jarring,
not that I let on. I acknowledged the heir and her daughter
and looked at the speaker, an emaciated woman with collar
bones sharp as plow blades. She looked stubborn. Angry.
Desperate. I asked, "Is your true child one of the escap-
ees?" Meaning born from her body in the traditional human manner.

Her head tilted, that birdlike or snakelike motion they
do when they forget to act human. "Her name's Roseanne,"
she said, her expression full of resolve, eyes narrowing at
me. I was pretty sure that determination was her intent to
kill me if I tried to stake her child. I addressed Pickersgill.
"Is there any chance the victim can be turned?"

"If there's a spark of life left in Sarah, yes. But it doesn't
appear likely."

I stared them down, sliding one hand into my surprise
supplies. "If she can be turned, then it isn't murder. If she's
dead, I don't care what you want."

The vamps swiveled to me almost as one, like pack hunters sighting prey. Grizzard took a slow breath as fear pheromones laced into the air from his skin. Scrawny's eyes
bled black in an instant. A young vamp touched her arm in
warning. "Mom. Don't."

Without taking my eyes from Scrawny, I took in the
young female. It was Amy Lynn Brown, the miracle vamp
who came out of devoveo in two years time. I inclined my
head at her and went on. "Any of the chained who get away
from this house get staked when I catch them, even if the
human woman *can* be turned, so it's in your best interests
to keep them contained. I won't risk letting them kill a human. *Another* human," I corrected.

Scrawny's fangs snapped down. I stared down at her.
"You have a problem with my methods, call Leo Pellissier."
I held out my cell. "Speed dial seven." Scrawny breathed
deeply, which she didn't need to do, but it seemed to calm
her, that and her daughter's hand on her arm. She closed
her eyes and stepped back from me, her pupils shrinking
when she opened them again. Maybe it was the thought of
talking to Leo. Or maybe at the thought that I talked to
Leo. Or called the MOC by his first name. Or Amy Lynn's
insistence. Whatever. It worked.

I looked at the sheriffs. "Unless y'all want to take them in for murder?"

Scoggins said, "Hell no."

Grizzard said, "What am I gonna do with crazy-ass vamps, begging your pardon, Constantine, Dacy, ma'am. If they signed the papers, then they're treated accordingly. That's the law as it reads right now. Of course that may change if the Supreme Court decides to look at the Vampira Carta before the Congress gets around to making a decision on citizenship."

"Yeah, yeah. But all they do is talk," I reminded him. He chuckled and gave me that hale-fellow-well-met political grin. I turned back to the vamps and told them how the situation was going to be handled, drew out a map of the scion lair, and walked them through it twice. I finished with, "Adelaïde, grab a fire extinguisher." She looked puzzled but went to the corner of the room, returning with a red extinguisher.

To the others I said, "When the door opens, close your eyes, turn away, and cover your ears. Understood?" I looked at Scrawny. "If you can immobilize your child, you can appeal a death sentence to Leo." Her eyes filled with bloody tears. *Crap*. A weepy vamp. Which made me feel all kinds of guilty. Sometimes I forgot that they used to be human, and still have humanlike emotions. Amy Lynn patted her arm.

From my box of supplies I pulled two silver mesh nets and unfolded them. They were designed after a net I'd once seen used to immobilize a vamp. That one had been constructed of sterling, interlocking crosses, which burned and scarred most vamps on contact. Mine was made of silver-plated steel rings with tiny sterling barbs all over them. They weren't sharp, and so wouldn't hurt humans, but they were extremely painful, almost incapacitating, to vamps. I'd had the nets made, at Leo's expense, when I discovered I was going to be security on this gig. They were for close-in work, useless at any range, but perfect for this job.

I gave one to Grizzard, and one to Scoggins, explaining how they worked. "Have you ever used a fishing net? Throw it out and pull it back in? This is just like that. When you throw, you hold the silver and this rope. When it lands on a vamp, or a vamp and a human, you release the silver and yank the rope. It pulls the silver mesh taut and encircles them. It's painful but if the net is removed quickly, the wounds can be healed by a master's blood."

I pulled out a grenade, and saw every eye land on it with reactions from curiosity to fear to humor. Grizzard chuckled under his breath, teeth showing. "Now, why didn't I think of that?"

"This is a stun grenade, called a flashbang," I explained to the vamps. "Unlike grenades designed to maim and kill, these are nonlethal incapacitants, designed to temporarily neutralize enemies in combat. When detonated in a closed space, the concussive blast and bright light is enough to overwhelm the enemies' ears and light-sensitive cells in their eyes, making them temporarily deaf and blind." I stopped. Flashbangs had been designed for human combatants and there were no studies of them being used on vamps. Vamp eyes were different from human eyes, and while I didn't *think* the devices posed a permanent danger to vamp vision, I didn't know it for sure. It wasn't like I'd been able to experiment. Until now.

Other than blindness, my biggest concern was that the flashbangs had been known to ignite accelerants, and the myths said that vamps burned fast and hot. One of Evangelina's paintings depicted a master vamp with her arms on fire, and she had survived, so I didn't know for certain if the myth was true or not. But I saw no reason to take chances, which was why I had Adelaide standing by with a fire extinguisher.

"Okay. Pickersgill, you and Scraw—the mother of the true child inside, yank open the door fast, I'll toss in the stunner, and you slam it. They'll likely throw themselves at the door, so be ready to muscle it closed. Once it detonates, with any luck, they'll all be down, but I'm not betting that they stay down long. Yank the door back open. I'll enter first, followed by Grizzard and Scoggins. Adelaide comes in next to put out anyone on fire."

Scrawny blinked at the phrase as if deciding how to react to its coarseness. I shrugged. It was what it was. "The rest of you follow, but don't expect to see much. There will be a lot of smoke that's painful to breathe and hurts your

eyes. Try to hold your breath." Right. Tell vamps to hold
their breath. "Humans, I mean.

"Dacy," I located the heir's blue eyes and delicate form.
She was like a doll, but a powerful master. Her eyes were
bleeding to black in a slow, controlled manner, the sclera
brightening to red at the same cautious speed. "If the girl is
still alive, you start her transformation. If she's gone"—I
looked around—"then we'll need these." I passed out
wooden stakes. "A belly thrust will immobilize them. Then,
if Lincoln Shaddock, Blood Master of the Shaddock Clan
wants, an appeal can be made to Leo for mercy. Or old Linc
can stake them. If they get off the property, I'll handle it
alone."

Dacy looked away, her eyes brimming with tears. Great.
Now I was making them all cry. "If Lincoln was master of
the city," she said, "we would have a Mercy Blade to help
us. We wouldn't have to—" She stopped, and drew in a
breath thick with tears. "We wouldn't have to hurt our scions, risk their deaths." She dashed a hand across her cheeks,
leaving blood smears.

"Dacy," I said gently, still holding out the stakes, "Mercy
Blades don't chase down freed young rogues. They only"—I
searched for a kind word—"*help out* with the long chained."
*Help out. Right. Help out as in stake and behead them while
they lay chained to a bed.* But I didn't say it. Go me. "If your
chained ones killed a human, then they're rogues. But I
won't kill them if I can help it." She stared at me in surprise.
As slowly as a human, she took the stakes and passed them
to the scions, her motions reflected in the huge windows to
my right. I handed more to the humans, reminding them to
belly thrust.

I led the way into Lincoln's bedroom and jutted my
chin, indicating the hidden door. Scrawny and Pickersgill
took up position, Pickersgill at the side that opened,
Scrawny on the hinged side, which I figured was smart. If
Scrawny had a chance, she might get in my way. "Turn off
the lights inside. And be sure to turn them on after the
flashbang goes off." I thought for a moment, wondering if I
had left out anything. Probably.

"On three," I said. I rotated my head on my neck and
stretched my throwing arm. "One." I reached deep, draw-

ing on Beast-speed and strength. Pulled the pin. "Two." I reared back. "Three." The door opened so fast I didn't see it move. The flashbang flew, ballistic, into the unlit room. The door slammed shut with an explosive gust of air. I covered my ears, just in case. So did the others. We could hear the detonation and the resultant screams even through the heavy door. Vamps who are dying, or think they are, give a piercing, eardrum-bursting shriek, like the love child of a screech owl and a mountain lion on crystal meth, amplified like a seventies rock band. Drawing two wood stakes, I said, "Open." The door opened even faster than before, the lights blazing overhead, turning the noxious smoke inside into a thick cloud.

I launched myself into the scion lair. Smoke stinging my eyes, burning my nose. A naked form rushed out of the smoke, vamp-fast. I swept a leg forward and around and followed the rogue down with a belly stab, midcenter, deep enough to hit the descending aorta. Vamp blood sprayed out over me. I braced for a burn, but there was no chemical sting from the splatters. He was down. I left the stake in his belly and pulled another. I caught a flash of silver as a net was tossed over a female form. Three rogues came at me, vamped out, small fangs snapped down. Their pupils were smaller than a human's at noon on a desert. They were effectively blind, but their nostrils were wide, sniffing, their breathing fast. I stabbed, took a step, thrust, pulled a new stake, stepped, thrust.

I'd taken down six, with eight stakes, when I realized that I should have counted the chained or thought to ask how many there were. *Crap.* Stupid, rookie mistake. I slammed my back against a cage, facing two vamps who came at me in concert. It wasn't the usual mindless action of a rogue. These two were older than the others, their fangs longer, whiter. And they could see. They hesitated a fraction of a second, half a heartbeat. One dodged in. The other kicked out. I blocked the first one. Took the kick in the knee joint. Something popped. The world tilted. I went down.

A net flashed over the one who'd kicked me, glittering silver. He squealed like a pig being slaughtered. The other one fell on my injured leg. I smelled his hunger, his need. I was out of stakes. Training and instinct took over. I stabbed up with a vamp-killer, into the notch below his sternum. And remembered midstrike that I wasn't supposed to kill him yet. I adjusted aim halfway in, trying to avoid a heart-thrust with the silvered blade. He grunted and slid from me. Curled up on the floor in the fetal position. Panting, mewling. I took a breath and started coughing, even as I pulled more blades.

Overhead, fans and the AC had come on, sucking out the smoke and the reek of vamp blood, filling the room with clean but frigid air. As the smoke cleared, I could see. It was all over.

Naked vamps were lying everywhere, most curled into the fetal position, bleeding profusely, their blood running across the stone floor to the central drain. Scarlet had been sprayed over the ceiling, walls, and cell bars like some kind of postmodernist paint job. Three blood-servants were down, all getting blood-sips and healing tongue-laving from the scions, which creeped me out, even though I'd been on the receiving end of healing laves and knew their benefits. One scion was holding his back as if he'd taken a tumble. He was feeding off Pickersgill, the two men in an embrace that made me feel like a voyeur. Scrawny was in a cell feeding a vamp, Amy Lynn cradling them both like babies. The girl was the one who had been weeping when I was here last. Now, her needlelike fangs were buried in her mother's wrist, getting an infusion of vamp blood from mommy dearest.

I swiveled to my butt, and stretched out my right leg with both hands. It had been kicked and slashed by vamp claws, and it *hurt*. Blood coated my palm, not pumping, thankfully, so not arterial, but still a lot of blood. Some vamp-baby had hit a big vein. I wouldn't be walking on it. Not until I shifted. But all the scions were down, all were alive, and miracle of miracles, the girl, Sarah, was being fed Dacy's blood. I could make out a pulse beneath her ear, weak and too fast. She swallowed. I blew out a laugh and remembered to breathe. Pain radiated up and down my leg. *Crap. This is bad. Good for the vamps. But bad for—*

"Jane! The front door is open." Grizzard stuck his head into the scion lair.

Dacy looked around, counting. "One got out."

"Thomas." There was dread in Pickersgill's voice, and I couldn't imagine what might alarm a vamp who had lived through the cold war, the Cuban missile crisis, and the death of President Kennedy, as well as all the post 9-11 stuff.

I really didn't want to know, but I asked anyway. "What's so bad about Thomas?"

Pickersgill said, "He was Lincoln's primo blood-servant until he was injured in the line of duty and Linc brought him over. He's been sane for three years, but he . . . uh—"

"He's a Naturaleza," Dacy stated tonelessly. "We didn't know until he came out of devoveo."

"Well, crap," I whispered. The Naturaleza believed that they had a *right* to hunt and kill humans, just because they were at the top of the food chain. They were way more dangerous than any rogue, because they were thinking, intelligent, sociopathic killers, often with resources like safe houses and bank accounts their masters didn't know about. If Shaddock had known, Thomas would never have been turned. He would have been allowed to die a normal human death, or been put down. If he was sane, and hadn't yet killed a human, then he didn't fall under the category of young-rogue, therefore he wasn't mine to hunt until I was asked, and I wasn't sure who *was* supposed to hunt him. Things had just FUBARed. I pulled a length of leather off a thigh strap and bound my injured knee, almost gagging with the pain, but the bleeding slowed. I rolled to one hip, pulled my phone, and speed-dialed Leo. He answered on the first ring.

"Things did not go well," he said. The MOC was prescient. Maybe he read tea leaves. Or blood stains in the bottom of his glass. Or maybe he had access to the security system here at Shaddock Central. He had access to the cameras in all his Louisiana vamps' clan homes, so why not here as well?

"No. They didn't." I considered Leo. Yeah. The MOC may not know much about computers, but Leo's wealth could buy all the knowledge and expertise he wanted. Smart money said he had access to everything. "They had a sane vamp in captivity, a Naturaleza. He got free."

Leo breathed a string of French curse words into the cell, then broke off right in the middle, and laughed. It was one of those silky laughs they do when they have you over a barrel, a gotcha laugh that made my skin want to crawl into a hole and curl protectively around itself. "It is my understanding," he said, "that you are my *Enforcer*." He capitalized the term, saying it the way he did Rogue Hunter, making it a title.

Titles and Leo's delight meant that I was in trouble. If I said no, then I had lied to the vamps. If I said yes, then I was agreeing to a relationship with him. Which meant that I had to drink from him. And to Leo, drinking and sex went hand in hand. Or fang in vein. Leo had tried to kill me enough times while he was seriously whacko for me to avoid *that* like the plague. *Crap.* A dozen possible responses flashed through my mind. I settled on, "Not . . . officially."

"Not . . . officially," he repeated, as if tasting the words. "This is correct. I would advise you to choose your words with more care in future, when you claim to be something you are not." I took a breath. I had dodged a bullet. "Yet," he added. *Ooookay.* Maybe not so much dodged as still in the laser sights, but the trigger hadn't been squeezed. "For now, I confer upon you the temporary entitlement to pursue and dispatch this Mithran who holds the Vampira Carta in such disregard. Allow me to speak with the sheriff."

Yep. Ol' Leo had access to the security cams. "How much?" I asked.

"Pardon?" he said, going all Frenchy on me. Leo knew what I was asking. When I didn't reply, he sighed into the cell, and said, "I will meet your usual terms, plus twenty percent, as this Mithran is no young-rogue, and will be more difficult than others to dispatch."

I thought about that for a long moment and nodded, though he couldn't see it. Except in the cameras. I looked up at one and said, "Thirty. And you pay for any and all research and hazard pay for any backup, assuming I need them."

Leo laughed, a low caress of sound that brought a flush of heat to my face even from hundreds of miles away. "Your terms are acceptable, my *Enforcer*." The endearment flowed over me like a caress. Vamps, the really old ones, can do that—affect the pleasure centers of the brains with just their voices. Dang it. "Compel Pickersgill to heal your leg," he added.

Yep. Leo was in Shaddock's system. "I'll make sure I'm healed," I said, skirting an honest acknowledgment. I needed to shift to fix my knee. No vamp was gonna get his tongue on me if could help it. The mention of my leg brought the pain in it hammering to the surface.

I called Grizzard over and handed him my cell. I was just about to be assigned carte blanche to execute a thinking killing machine, and the local law was being told to stand down and let me do my job, all under the auspices of a clause under the Vampira Carta that was tenuous at best and down right illegal at worst. My only other choice was to let him go on a killing spree and allow the sheriff's men to try and take him down. Between a rock and a hard place. Again. Go me.

CHAPTER TWENTY-TWO

You Are Dead Meat

Working the accelerator and brake with my left leg, I sped down 70 into a low-hanging fog, a bag of ice strapped on my knee with a length of flex. Using the speakerphone, I made calls as I negotiated the curves, the first to Reach. Fortunately Leo was paying for his services. "Jane Yellowrock," he answered, "my most interesting client. What can I charge you for today?"

"This goes on Pellissier's tab."

"My favorite words," he said. The tab had just gone up by a huge percentage. Reach would work for anyone, but his prices were on a sliding scale and vamps had to pay more. I could hear keys clicking in the background. "Work order name?"

"Thomas Stevenson, formerly—"

"Lincoln Shaddock's primo, turned just after 9-11, and still chained."

"Not anymore. Sane, psycho, and free."

"Sounds like a fun search. And because he's crazy and hungry, you need it fast. More money for me. You need all pre-turn financial records including tax info, banking both on and offshore and in numbered accounts, real properties in his name, and a quick run through of friends, family, and acquaintances. Probably need a list of any properties they own as well."

"Good. And while you're clacking around in virtual

space, see what you can find on a history of Evangelina
Everhart. I want deep background. If she potty trained
early or wrote a poem in third grade, I want to see it."

"I have the financials on the witch collated, and am
sending them over now. Anything else?"

Dollar signs were dancing a tango in my hindbrain. This
was gonna cost Leo a fortune. The fog thinned and I gunned
the engine, only to hit a thicker patch that forced me to
brake hard. "Probably. If so I'll call. Send the records to my
e-mail. Anything hinky, call."

"Will do."

The call ended and I slowed again as the white closed in
around the SUV like a blanket. I dialed Derek twice before
the call went through, the atmospheric conditions ripe for
interference. On my third try he said, "Go ahead."

Short and sweet. That's Derek. And if his attitude was
anything to go by, I'd either be finding new help or taking
our problems to the boxing ring. Maybe literally. "I'll be
away a while. You're in charge of Grégoire."

"Fine." He hung up with a resounding click, hard to do
on a cell.

Rain splattered against the windshield. I needed both
hands on the wheel, which meant I needed hands-free calling. Next on my wish list from Leo. More urgent, I needed
to get to Evangelina's, and see if Shaddock was there. And
I needed to help Big Evan find a way to wake Molly up
from Evangelina's spell, if he'd let me. And then I had to
find a way to . . . *Crap*. Again, I was flying by the seat of my
pants and had no idea how I was gonna accomplish the job
and still keep my friends safe.

The phone rang and it was Molly's number. Again. I
punched the call button and heard crying. *Angelina*. The
guilt and worry I had been shoving away rolled over me
like a tsunami. *It's the middle of the night. What is she doing
up, using her mother's cell?* "Hey, Angie Baby."

"Aunt Jane, you need to come see me. Now. Mommy and
Daddy won't wake up. Come now. Come *now!*"

My heart did a cartwheel that left me breathless. "I'm on
my way." I switched to my right leg, pressed the accelerator
to the floor and fishtailed around a curve. The road disappeared as the headlights illuminated only fog in a roiling

wave. I compensated and braked, depending on the anti-lock breaking system, before easing the accelerator down. "I'll be there in less than a hour. Can you let the wards down?"

"Yes. I can let them down. I'm a big girl."

But I could still hear the tears. "Are you okay? Is Little Evan okay?" My leg was throbbing and a wet warm sensation gathered under me. I was bleeding again. I didn't care.

"No. I'm sick. And Little Evan throwed up in his crib." The call gave a staticky silence and picked back up on her words, ". . . urry, Aunt Jane. Hurry."

"I'm coming as fast as I can, Angie. I need you to talk to me, so you can stay awake. Okay?" I took a tighter curve and passed an eighteen-wheeler with no room to spare between it and whatever lay in the white shadows off the road. When Angie sniffled agreement, I said, "Tell me how long your mama and daddy have been asleep."

"They went to bed before dinner. I can't wake them up. And you wouldn't call me back." She was crying in earnest now and my shame was stabbing deeper. She sounded so sleepy.

I had to keep her awake. "I'm sorry. I'm so sorry. I promise from now on, I'll always call you back. Always. Angie are you there?" When she mumbled a yes, I said, "Angie, I need for you do something for me. I need you to go into your mama and daddy's bedroom and see if anything is spelled. Like a present Aunt Evangelina gave her. Can you do that?" Maybe if I kept her moving, I could keep her awake.

"You mean like the earrings she gived to Mama?"

My hands tightened so hard the steering wheel gave with a soft squeak of damaged rubber. But I kept my voice neutral and calm. "Yes. Like that. Go look at them and tell me if they have a spell on them, okay?"

"Okay. But don't touch them, right? My angel said not to touch them."

"Right." I could hear snoring over the cell, the low rumble of a bear in hibernation. Big Evan. "Do you see the earrings? What do they look like?"

"Mama's wearing them in her ears. They are pink and

gold. And they got pink sparklies on them." She yawned hugely. "I'm sleepy, Aunt Jane."

Crapcrapcrap! I didn't know enough about magic to make a decision. *What to do?* "Okay. I want you to get Little Evan out of his crib and let down the wards. Then I want you to climb into your mama's van with a blanket and wait for me." When she didn't answer, I said, gently, "Angie?" I took a curve and the call stuttered. I heard Angie say something. And then silence.

"Angie! Angie!" I had lost the call.

I didn't have the other Everhart sisters' numbers on my cell. But I did have Reach. I pushed the number and when he answered, I said, "I need assistance."

"I'm not your servant."

"A little girl and a toddler are in trouble. You gonna let 'em die?"

"Like I said before, you are my most interesting client. Profit-making, too."

"Yeah, whatever. This is on my tab. I need you to look up the numbers of the Everhart sisters, dial the numbers, one by one, and when someone answers, put me through. Start with Boadacia and Elizabeth. I think they live together."

"Secretary. I'm playing secretary," he grumbled. But I heard keys clacking and a moment later, an automated answering message invited me to leave a number. Several clicks later, another message answered, this time with Elizabeth's voice. "Leave a number and I'll get back to you." *Crap.* Why weren't they at home? Unless they were there and spelled. The fear sucked at me, pulling me down, drowning.

"Try Carmen Miranda Everhart Newton," I said.

Following more clacking and more silence, Reach said, "No answer, no message. Just rings."

"Regan and Amelia Everhart."

Regan answered on the second ring, sounding groggy, as if waked from deep dreams. Relief slammed through me, almost painful. "Regan, this is Jane Yellowrock. Wake up. Your sisters are in trouble."

Regan didn't want to believe me when I told her that her witch sisters had been spelled by Evangelina, insisting that it was probably a group working gone wrong, but she and her sister did get out of bed and start the drive up the mountain to Molly's. The girls had no power of their own, but they had been raised among witches and the manipulation of energy, so I was hopeful that they could guide me in freeing Molly and Evan. Unfortunately, I beat them to the refurbished house on the top of the mountain.

The peak was shrouded in dense fog, no outside lights were on, and the house was darker than the armpit of hell. I didn't reweapon. If there was danger here, it wasn't something I could kill with stakes, blades, or even my M4. Beast padded just under my skin, lending me her night vision, her strength and speed tingling just under my skin like her pelt rising. A snarl lifted my lips and my jaw ached, as Beast's killing teeth strained to break free. I slid from the SUV.

My leg was cold where the blood was cooling, and the wound felt like fire, a burning throb of pain. I limped to the house, moving slowly, silently, trying to see the ward before I ran nose first into it. Bumping into Molly's wards tended to result in a siren loud enough to deafen. But the siren didn't sound, not even when my palm bumped something dark. The thud sounded dull, hollow in the encasing cloud. My fingertips touched metal, cold and wet beneath the fog. Molly's van. Hope detonated through me like mini fireworks and I found the passenger door by feel. It opened easily, and mist puffed in. The interior light came on, too bright, making a halo around the vehicle.

Angelina and Little Evan were cuddled on the seat, wrapped in a blanket, asleep. I picked them up in my arms and jogged back to my SUV, the grass and ground crunching beneath me. I crawled in to the front seat and closed the door, settling them on my lap to wait. I pulled Angie Baby close, nuzzling her head, her hair soft as angel wings against my face, breathing in her scent. Her hair smelled of baby shampoo, sleep, and warmth. Little Evan smelled of dirty diapers and milk. The throbbing in my leg eased, even as my blood wicked into their blanket.

Kits, Beast murmured deep inside. *Safe.*

But I had put them in danger. Again. As usual, when I

was dealing with the children, tears came easily; one scalded its way down my face.

"Aunt Jane? Am I a big girl? My angel said I was a big girl."

A sob escaped before I could catch it. My words stuttered through the tears. "Ye-yes, Angie Baby." I hugged the children closer, careful not to use Beast's strength that still stalked just beneath my skin. "You are a very big, wise, strong, good girl, and I am very proud of you." Headlights cut through the night, illuminating little more than the fog. A tiny four-wheel drive car pulled up behind me. The lights went out and two car doors slammed, the sound muffled. My SUV's back doors opened and closed, Amelia on one side, Regan on the other. They leaned into the front seat, heads close, whispering together.

"The wards aren't up."

"Are the kids okay?"

"What's happening? I called around and nobody's answering."

"This is bad. I can't even get Mom to answer."

There wasn't time to reply or to fill them in. I said, "One of you has to stay with the children." I gathered up the kids and drew my injured knee into the seat, ignoring the agony that shocked through my system. Pushing off with my other foot, I straightened up and over the seat, holding the children. The sisters' eyes widened, and I knew I had given away something of my nature with the movement.

Too strong for human Jane, Beast thought at me. *Beaststrong.* Something else I could worry about later. At this rate, my later-list was going to need its own filing cabinet.

The girls' eyes fell on the blanket. "Why are they bleeding?" Amelia asked.

"My blood. Not theirs," I said. Amelia held out her arms. I stretched over the seat and settled the children in her lap. "See if you can keep Angie awake. Regan, you come with me. I need you to figure out how to remove Molly's earrings. Evangelina gave her a gift and Angie said there was a spell on them."

"I still don't believe it." Regan said.

Rather than answer, I stroked my fingers down Angie's cheek, softer than any rose petal, and got out of the vehicle.

The slamming door was tinny, the sound soaked up by the fog. I looked at Regan. "I don't know anything about witch magic. The little bit Molly tried to explain just sounded like gobbledygook. But I do know we can't just pull the earrings out of Molly's ears."

Regan looked grim and pulled the lapels of her jacket together, an action that looked more nervous than cold. "No. We have to stab her first."

A totally inappropriate laugh puffed out of my mouth. "Aw righty then." I indicated the dark house. "After you."

Regan led the way through the fog, seeming to drift in and out of the dense, wet cloud, a ghostly form explaining as she went. "It's not so weird. Only with the receiver's permission can another witch make a spell and set a charm on her. She has to accept it, which is why gifts work so well. If you give a witch a pair of gloves or a scarf, then the spell tied to the gift is activated the moment the witch puts it on. For it to be strong enough to work long term, it has to be keyed to her blood, meaning that the practitioner has to have some genetic material to work with, like a hair with the root still on, or a fingernail clipping with some cells caught underneath.

That made sense. Spells against witches needed the snake in the heart of all animals, the double helix of DNA, the same material I used when I changed into another animal. "Okay. So how are you going to stop the spell?"

Regan looked back over one shoulder, her face mostly shadow. "I'm not." I was confused, but I figured Regan knew that. I also had to assume that she knew what she was doing.

The door in the former garage was unlocked and Regan preceded me inside, turning on lights. The house looked cheery and homey, not like two people were under a black-magic spell in the master suite. There was a pile of blankets in front of the TV in the great room, as if this was where Angelina had nested, holing up to wait through the long hours when I hadn't bothered to call her back. Because my life was so much more important and my problems so much more urgent than hers. Guilt stabbed me again, poking another hole in my soul.

I hunched my shoulders and followed Regan into the

new room at the back of the house. She turned on the light and stood in the doorway, studying the scene. Big Evan was wearing a T-shirt and oversized boxers, lying on his back, one hairy leg and a strip of belly exposed, snoring loudly, one arm out toward Molly. The knuckles of his closed hand grazed her cheek. Molly was curled on her side, facing Evan, most of the covers pulled to her side of the bed, her feet drawn up, hugging a pillow.

Regan stepped to the side of the bed. "Help me turn Mol to her back." She threw back the covers, exposing Molly's pale blue nightgown and sock-covered feet. The smell of sleeping bodies, sweaty and too long unmoved, fluffed into the air. Regan turned Molly's shoulders and head; I straightened her legs. I lifted her hips and positioned them in alignment. It was like moving a freshly dead body. The thought made my chest ache and I slid my hand around Mol's foot, just to be making some small contact. I stared at the garnet earrings in her ears. They were the same pair Molly had been wearing all week. Regan said, "Now I have to stab her."

"You were serious?"

"Yeah. If you're right about Evangelina, then she used blood magic on Molly and only blood will undo it." She looked me over, her brows going up, and her tone wry. "I see I don't have to go looking for a knife." She held out a hand.

"Every blade I have is silver-plated," I said, placing a short, narrow-bladed throwing knife into her hand. "Only the edge is steel."

Regan shrugged. "I'm not a witch, so I can't tell you if there's a difference, or which metal I should use. I just know I have to use the pointy part." She uncurled Molly's fingers and extended her index finger. Regan adjusted her grip on the handle and stabbed down, one quick prick. Molly didn't wake. She didn't even flinch. Blood rose in a shimmering button at the tip of her finger. Regan raised the finger and smeared Mol's blood all over the earrings front and back, leaving blood smears on her sister's lobes and several fresh drops on the musty-smelling pillowcase. Then Regan removed the earrings. She dumped a glass of water into an orchid blooming on the bedside table, and squeezed more of Molly's blood into the glass where it thinned in contact with the remaining water. Regan dropped the bloody earrings with a soft clink of stone-on-glass and carried them from the room.

I pulled a small, delicate chair over and sat gingerly on the pillow-top seat, afraid my weight might break it. Molly's finger was still bleeding and I wrapped it in a corner of the sheet, applying pressure. She looked exposed, vulnerable, and I pulled the linens back up, covering her. Holding her hand, I looked around the room. The new bedroom was painted a soft blue-green, the color of the water around the keys in Florida. The comforter was deep teal with peacock-toned shams, and throw pillows in shades of aqua, mint, and teal. The room was pretty without being frilly, the kind of room a woman decorates when a man shares it. Orchids were in the windows, all blooming, as if she kept the best for this room.

Molly murmured and rolled over. I let her hand go. A moment later she groaned. And sat up. Blinked. And looked at me. "Son of a witch on a stick," she said, her voice rough.

Beside her, Big Evan rolled over and got to his feet, lumbered to the bathroom, moving stiffly, mumbling something about needing to, ". . . piss like a racehorse."

"Jane," Molly whispered, her eyes on me, going wide. *"Regan?"*

"Get dressed. Meet me in the great room," I said, and I moved quickly out of the room. Which sounded much nicer than to say I scurried like a rat. Big Evan hadn't closed the door to the bath and there were some things I simply did not need to share.

I went out to the SUV and carried the children to the house. Amelia took Little Evan to his room offering to change his diaper, thank God. I went to the guest bath and added a pad of washcloths beneath the strap over my wound before settling with Angie on the oversized couch, holding her to me, rocking back and forth. Thinking. The motion caused me a good deal of pain, but it seemed an appropriate price to pay—a penance of sorts. Though I had been raised nondenominational protestant, not Catholic, guilt is something all Christians understand.

I felt Angie waken, a slight change in her breathing, a speeding of her heart rate. "You came," she whispered.

I wanted to kick myself. I said, "When I agreed to be your godparent, I made a lot of promises to your parents, and I made you some too. I promised to take care of you if something happened to your mom and dad, to raise you the way they wanted, and I promised to be there if you needed me. I promised to keep you safe. Yesterday and tonight, I wasn't there for you. I broke my promises." Angie took my fingers in hers. There was blood under my nails; I hadn't noticed it in the bathroom. "I'm sorry, Angie Baby." My voice was breathless, weak with unshed tears. I took both of her small hands into mine. "I promise on my honor, that will never happen again. From now on, I'll take your calls no matter what. If I miss a call, I'll call you back the moment I hear the message, I'll be there for you. I'll do a better job of being your godmother."

"It's okay, Aunt Jane." My heart did a twisting backflip of shame. It wasn't okay. Angelina stood on the couch seat and put her arms around my neck, leaning her small body against mine. "I love you."

I hugged her to me.

"Here. Watch this one too," Amelia said, dropping Little Evan on my lap.

I couldn't help my gasp and her eyes were drawn to my thigh. "You're bleeding all over Big Evan's couch," she said, taking the toddler back. "You are dead meat."

I looked up as a shadow darkened the doorway to the kitchen, Big Evan standing there, filling the opening, scowling. Thankfully wearing pants. "I tried to find Evangelina to make her take the hex off Molly, but she's gone to ground, like she vanished off the face of the earth." His voice dropped in pitch, "Did she spell my whole family?"

I nodded once, slowly. His glower darkened. Likely trying to find a way to make me responsible.

Regan said, "You mean she spelled the *whole family*? Siphoning your power and using your gifts against your wishes?"

"That's against witch law," Amelia said. "Against every protocol witches have."

I shrugged and Angie's fingers tightened around my neck.

"Tell them everything," Evan said, nodding to the sisters, "from the beginning."

I started with the *hedge of thorns*-like spell and the werewolves trapped in Evangelina's basement. Leaving Regan to take mental notes, Amelia took the children to bed as I talked, rightly thinking that they were too young to hear all this. I finished just as Molly joined us, her hair wet and braided down her back. "And there's something dark, a shadow with wings, trapped in the *hedge*."

Molly drew in a horrified breath. Evan's face darkened. "My sister-in-law is consorting with demons."

CHAPTER TWENTY-THREE

Bloody, Damaged Jeans and Nefarious Intentions

"Can you take photographs of the spell in Evangelina's basement?" Molly asked. "That will tell us what kind of spell—"

"And what kind of demon," Evan interrupted.

"—she's using," Molly finished. "And yeah, that too. You should be safe enough from the demon as long as you don't set it free." My eyebrows went up.

"Just keep back from the ward containing it," Evan said.

"Uh huh. Ducky," I agreed and headed out, having learned one important thing before I drove away from the Trueblood house—never kick a hornet's nest. The witches and their human sisters were making battle plans, gearing up to rescue the other members of their witch family. Once everyone was safe from the power-draw, they would meet to discuss what to do about Evangelina. Battle by committee. It would take forever. The girls still didn't want to believe that their elder sister was the cause of the sleeping spell, but with Big Evan on my side (and hating every moment of knowing I was right) and the other witch sisters not answering their phones, they were coming around.

First I had to shift and heal the wound in my thigh. The pain was now a constant throb, and I was feeling light-headed from blood loss. I needed to shift and heal, hunt,

shift back, get some food into me, and check in on Grégoire, Rick, Kem, and Derek—a lot to do in the few hours
left to me before dawn. I didn't like it when my personal
life and my work life overlapped; it just complicated everything. But there it was, a perfect description of my life—
complicated—and Evil Evie was using my job of guarding
the parley to make it worse.

I pulled my vehicle off the road onto an overgrown
track I had spotted several times while making the run
from Asheville to Hot Springs. The fog was more dense
than before, sending down splatters as rain condensed out
of the clouds. I stripped in the front seat and slid naked
from the SUV to the ground, my body instantly wet and
chilled, as the mist curled cold fingers around me. I found
rock easily and lay out on it, shivering, blood loss making
me feel the cold with an unaccustomed intensity. I didn't
have my fetish necklace, but I had my emergency cat tooth.
I lay my head on my arms, closed my eyes, and thought
about Beast. The pain hit.

I shook pain away. Growled low. Jane did not leave cold
dead cow meat. I *hungered*. I sat up, front paws together,
head high, and listened/smelled/looked, tasted the soggy,
white air, felt it wet my pelt. Night was silent. Empty of
prey. Heard only mice moving in grasses. I tilted ear tabs
from side to side. Far away, heard dogs moving in night,
loud, chasing away prey, following a female who was in
heat, too focused on mating to hunt.

I lay on stone, hungry, angry at Jane. Licked at healed
wound. No blood on pelt. No scar on Beast-leg. With head
bent back, heard faint sound of chewing down mountain,
away from dogs. Rabbit? Mouth watered, stomach gripped
in claws of hunger, hurting. *Empty*. Many rabbits. *More-
than-five* rabbits. Rabbits are good food. Silent, following
sound, I moved down mountain, pawpawpaw. Angled into
slow breeze to keep big-cat smell from rabbits. Beast is
good hunter.

Later, I sat in grassy field, parts of three dead rabbits at my
paws. I licked hot blood from my jaw and muzzle. Good
taste after good hunt, chasing, killing rabbits. With killing

teeth, picked rabbit paw up from ground. Crunched hard and swallowed. Good hunt. Belly full. I put a paw on rabbit ribs and licked, rough tongue pulling bits of flesh from bones. Good hunt.

Yeah, and the gardener will be happy you ate his pests, Jane thought at me. *Can we shift back now? I have work to do.*

Jane needs to mate. Play with Ricky-Bo was good, but Jane needs mate who is big and strong. Will take Bruiser. And Leo.

Jane made stuttery thoughts, too fast for Beast to follow. *And what about Rick?*

Will take Rick too. I stood and padded into trees while Jane thought about that. Back to car that was truck. Ess-u-vee. Silly name for truck. Liked Bitsa. Liked Fang. Ess-u-vee was ugly.

The fog was starting to thin and dawn was close when I came to myself sitting in the front seat of my vehicle, buck naked, shivering, starving, the mountain lion tooth jabbing my thigh. I dressed and drove back into Asheville, checking my messages as I maneuvered the road. One was from Bruiser, "Call me ASAP."

I was sleepy, tired, no longer in pain, and starving. One thing I missed about Louisiana was the little mom-and-pop eateries scattered everywhere throughout bayou country, serving fried delicacies like boudin balls and fried squash and fried green tomatoes. Beer and colas. Spicy fries. Here, if I didn't find a Mickie D's or one of its nationwide contemporaries, I'd have to wait until I was back in the hotel for room service. Luckily, I found a Cracker Barrel open early and pulled in for a pre-sunrise breakfast with the truckers. Triple orders of pancakes with sides of eggs over easy, sausage, bacon, and ham filled the ache in my belly. I pretended not to notice the sidelong glances of the truckers at the quantity of food I ate. It was hard work keeping up with the caloric needs of shifting, but the energy of shifting had to come from somewhere, and I didn't have access to magic, so food it was. Lots of food.

Over my fourth cup of tea, I returned the call to Leo's

line in the New Orleans' Clan Home. I was pretty much living on the cell and the Internet these days. I was becoming a modern kinda girl at thirty. Or however old I was.

"Jane," Bruiser answered, warmth in his voice. "How are you?"

Beast, sat up inside my mind, attentive. *Interested.* "Bruiser," I said. I should have done the obligatory small talk about health and the parley situation, but, despite sounding like an ill-bred heathen, I got to my point. "I got your message."

"Yes. Leo has given me permission to tell you about Evangelina Everhart."

My tone careful, I asked, "How is Leo?" We both knew that my question referred to Leo's state of mind. Since getting his Mercy Blade back, everything indicated that the dangerous dolore state of grieving had passed for the Master of the City of New Orleans. And though he had sounded perfectly sane when we chatted, with vamps, I always have doubts.

"He is well. He sends you his best."

Uh huh. Sure he does. I made a noncommittal sound.

"Lincoln Shaddock did not arrive for tonight's parley," he said. "Do you know where he is?" When I didn't reply. He went on. "Do you remember the defensive spell the witch sold Leo as final protection for his day-lair?" I grunted in the affirmative and poured more tea, Evangelina had provided a spell of protection to Leo, the odd-shaped *hedge of thorns*, during the witch-vamp parley that she had walked away from. The fact that Bruiser was bringing this up, indicated that he, too, was beginning to think that Evie was a big part of our current problems.

"It was defective," he said. "It should have been spherical, but it was cylindrical." I had noticed the unusual shape, and sipped my tea, thinking about Evangelina and the witch/vamp problems in New Orleans. "For reasons unknown, it appears that Evangelina was working with the werewolves in their campaign to destroy Leo. He banished her from his city and the negotiations are ongoing with the local witch covens."

Leo banished her . . . ? I sat up slowly. "That is something I should have known before ever coming to Asheville, before I agreed to head up parley security." *Dang vamps and their secrets.* "How did you discover she was working with the wolves?"

"When Leo found that you were going to attack and take down the wolves to save Rick LaFleur." Bruiser's voice went empty, as if he knew I was not gonna like what he had to say next. "He instructed me to contact Derek privately." Derek Lee and his men—my men, supposedly—went with me to save Rick. I felt cold all over, as if I'd fallen into a snowmelt stream. "Once they had LaFleur safe, and you were on the way to the Clan Home, they captured a wolf. They brought him to us. Leo . . . convinced him to tell us everything."

They had taken an injured wolf to Leo, and no one had told me any of this. "*Convinced* him," I said, the word grating. Bruiser didn't reply and I knew that the convincing hadn't involved happy drugs and good liquor. It had involved painful coercion. Maybe much worse. "Is the wolf still among the living?"

"No."

No. And no apology for torturing a werewolf to death, either. I breathed out slowly. Yeah, the wolves should be put down, but not like that. "Do we know why she was after Leo?"

"No. Our wolf didn't know why, only that she was willing to work with the pack."

"Thanks for the information."

"Come home, Jane. When this is over. Come back with Grégoire. To m- . . . To us."

To Leo the torturer and Bruiser, his secret-keeping helper. I closed the phone and drank my tea, staring at an old sign for shaving cream, hanging on the wall. Not really seeing anything.

Foolish kitten, Beast thought at me, superior and insulting, as if she swiped a paw at an importunate kit. *Bruiser would be good mate. Strong.*

After dawn on Friday morning, I parked down the road from Evangelina's, studying the old Everhart place, when I saw her shadow against the curtains. Heat zigzagged through me like lightning, and I pulled a vamp killer. I could go after her, right now, and take her down, tie her up, and haul her to Grégoire. I would have to hurt her, maybe hurt her bad, to get her immobilized before she called a demon onto me. If she could even do that. I didn't know. Maybe if I cut her, a leg wound. *Yeah, that'll stop her. Not.*

Indecisive, I hesitated a moment too long, and the lights inside went off. Evangelina left the house, looking about twenty, slender and curvaceous, wearing a floaty, diaphanous dress in a maroon floral print and little three-inch heels, red, with open toes. Not clothes for working at Seven Sassy Sisters. Her wardrobe had once been conservative. Now there was no hint of the matronly, stern woman she had been. Evangelina got in her little red sports car and drove off. *A sports car? When did she buy a sports car?*

I waited long enough to be sure she hadn't forgotten something, before leaving my vehicle, my camera and cell in my pockets. I stuck my hands in my pockets with them, trying to look as inconspicuous as possible, for a six-foot-tall Cherokee girl with bloody, damaged jeans and nefarious intentions. But I passed no one before I turned down the narrow street and melted into the greenery. I studied the witch circle in the ground and the lines that marked the inside. There was no pentagram, just the odd broken lines, lines that looked half familiar but meant nothing.

I snapped a few pics and stepped onto the porch, expecting a ward to be up at the house to keep out intruders, but I felt nothing until I touched the lever handle at the back door. The desire to go inside hit me like a padded baton. I *wanted* to go inside *Needed* to. I pushed the door open.

Beast pressed claws into my mind and growled. I paused, and she bit down with her canines, the pain like knife blades inside my skull. I gasped at the sudden headache and was able to pull my hand from the lever. But it was hard. As soon as my fingertips cleared the metal, the compulsion left me and I remembered to breathe. I took a step back. "Crap," I whispered. The door, already open, swung inward in welcome, a pretty little trap for anyone wanting to steal. Getting inside was gonna be easy. Getting back out might be a problem.

Good thing I hadn't rushed in to try to take down Evangelina. It was possible that I'd have been inside too fast for

Beast to save me. A chill sank talons into my spine at the thought.

I walked back to my vehicle, head down, scrutinizing my boots. Thinking. I remembered the scarf folded so neatly on the floor of the SUV. Blood magic—likely two different spells with the same power source, the blood-diamond—was being used against the two-natured and against the Everharts. And unless the helpful valet had shaken the scarf, I had some red hairs from Evangelina's head at my disposal.

I carefully unfolded the scarf and found twisted hairs caught in the weave. I refolded it to keep from losing them, and carried the scarf back to the house. Standing on the back porch, I could hear the gurgle of the creek at the bottom of the hill, see the sunrise brighten the garden. The dogwoods were already turning, leaves tinged with crimson. Using the scarf, I opened the door. I felt nothing of the compulsion. "Sweet," I murmured.

I entered the house and stood inside the door, closing it after me. Magic danced along my skin like static electricity, hot and pinging, as if the air was too dry, superheated just to the point of pain. Though humans might not have been able to see it, the interior of the house was illuminated with a soft pink glow, magic permeating the walls, floor, and furniture. Careful to touch nothing that might be holding a magical charge, I gripped the scarf in both hands, using it to open the door to the basement.

The lights weren't on downstairs, but a bloody glow lit the walls of the stairwell, and illuminated the painting at the bottom. It seemed to move, as if it were a TV screen, with active participants instead of a static surface painted hundreds of years ago.

I turned on the lights and made my way down. Stopped at the bottom. The *hedge of thorns* trap was still glowing with red and pink energies, scarlet motes bounding around it, the magic smelling tart, acrid. Black and scarlet sparks fluttered through it, but now they were stronger, more numerous, racing over the surface of the ward. Some areas of the ward were totally black, like heavily smoked glass, with no trace of the red energies. The demon was more substantial, easier to see, half man, half bird, or half man, half fallen angel. He had human calves and feet, torso and sexual organs, with a bird chest, wings with fingers where they might have been had the wings been arms, and a half-human, half-bird face. Human eyes over a raptor beak, but pinkish, with red lids. And inside with him were the two wolves.

I had no idea how Evangelina had kept the demon in the ward while she put the wolves in with him. But considering the compulsion spell, maybe they just walked inside without disturbing the outer ring. Like a one-way valve, allowing in anything that wanted to cross, but letting nothing inside cross back out.

The demon had been eating the wolves. While they were still alive. Gorge rose in my throat. Blood coated the floor of the circle with a gummy, gelatinous residue. The wolves were smiling about it, holding hands, staring into one another's eyes like goofy teenagers in love. The big guy, Fire Truck, was missing chunks of thigh and buttocks. The little guy was missing an arm and chunks of muscle, but the lethal wounds had healed. Sort of. Which meant they had shifted, even with the silver wounds from Evangelina's ceremonial knife. The wolves clearly hadn't been given food or water to make up for the caloric drain, and they were emaciated, loose flesh hanging on their frames. I stuffed the scarf under my arm and took a dozen digital photos of the trap and the thing inside with its dinner. I didn't know if it would photograph at all, didn't know if digital cameras would go all pixilated near witch magic. I checked the shots, and was gratified to see that most came out, and tucked the camera back in my jeans. I took some more shots with my phone, and sent them to myself.

This close, I felt the compulsion of the come-to-me spell and gripped the scarf tightly. The demon stared at me through the scarlet and black energies. I knew not to talk to demons. I knew that to engage them in discourse was stupid, but I did it anyway. "She's making you solid, isn't she?"

He gestured, a tossing motion with his human-looking hand, as if what his captor wanted was unimportant. He had talons on the end of his fingers, black as a raven's and twice as sharp. "She thinks to control me." His voice was guttural, as if he didn't speak often. And his accent was odd, as if he came from elsewhere, or from nowhere, mangled by the beak. "She thinks to use me for her vengeance." He breathed in, the action like a man inhaling an expensive perfume.

"You are *Tsalagi*," he said. "You are of the blood of The People. I have fed upon the *Tsalagi* for many centuries. No one controls me. Not even . . ." he breathed in again, as if scenting me. "Not even your grandmother, little yellow-eyed child."

I jerked, the muscles of my shoulders twitching, my hands twisting the scarf. He smiled, which was just plain horrible. There was dried blood on the beak. His tongue darted out, like a sapsucker, tasting the air.

"They called you *Dalonige'i digadoli*, when you were born with golden eyes like your father and *tsa lisi*, your grandmother." Horror swept through me. And longing. He knew me. From before. I put out a hand and Beast slammed down on me, biting me so hard I felt her teeth pierce my skull, creating the mother of all headaches. I had taken three steps toward the trap and I quickly stepped back. The demon laughed. "Yes, I was there when you were born, watching, waiting to see if your mother would survive or if I might take her." He tilted his head, birdlike, fast. And he whistled, a raptor's hunting call, long and piercing, but not one I had ever heard before. "There was much rejoicing when you opened your eyes that first time."

My heart was thudding. He had known my family? Or just plundered my fractured memories and woven a story? Was this why no one should indulge in conversation with a demon? Because they knew everything you did, everything you wanted, and weren't averse to lying and twisting truths to get you to do what *they* wanted? Yeah. That felt right. I took a breath, steadying myself. And shifted my foot back a step. Another. Toward the stairs.

He went on as if I weren't making my escape. "But when you were five summers old, your grandmother, who was *Ani gilogi*, panther clan, tried to tie me into the skin of one of her beasts, the pelt of the *tlvdatsi*. To avenge herself on the white soldiers who killed her son." I swallowed, and my throat was as dry as sandpaper; the muscles ached with the

motion. "She was a fool," he said. "I left her to die in the
snow, her blood black in the moonlight. I thought to find
you, but you had vanished into the night and the cold, and
I was free. So I took the lives of many of the *Tsalagi* that
night, and many more over the next weeks. I took the days
they had left to them, had the white man not forced them
on to the long march, and I left them dead. With their days
as my own, I walked as human for many years, taking what
and who I pleased."

My breath was too fast, my heart pattering, rabbitlike.
This *thing* seemed to know everything I had lost about my
past. I vaguely remembered the Trail of Tears, when the
U.S. government broke its covenant with the Cherokee
and forced us onto the long march west. So many had died
of the cold, of hunger, and illness. Or to the claws of this
thing.

He also knew what I wanted—to fill the empty places
in my past, in my soul. I *wanted* to listen to him now, and
he knew it. His eyes were the black of The People's eyes,
dark and wise and kind, and he gestured with the fingers
of one hand, to come closer. I didn't. He said, "I have all
the secrets you desire to know. All the truths you have
forgotten."

I pressed the scarf against my mouth, smelling Evangelina in the weave. Tasting tears I hadn't known were falling.
Beast bit down. Shattering pain took me, and my vision
went white for a moment. I put out a hand and my elbow
bumped the wall behind me. I staggered and swore, and
caught my balance. When the pain cleared, I could breathe.

"Go," Beast snarled. *"He is part of the hunger times. He
is part of the fire times. Run!"*

"Come to me and I will tell you what you desire," the
demon said. I backed to the left. My heels bumped the bottom stair. "I knew your father. I can tell you—"

"Jane?"

I stopped. Lincoln Shaddock? I heard metal clinking.
Lincoln rose, a ghostly image seen through the *hedge of
thorns*. Metal clinking louder, he stepped around the ward.
The smell of vamp blood hit me. And sickness. The stench
of infection cleared my head. Lincoln was wearing rags.
Blood coated his lower legs. He was wearing silver shack-

les, the bindings made in such as way that any movement cut into his skin. Black and red streaks ran up his calves, infection from the metal poisoning. "Listen to me, girl." As he spoke, some of the desire to listen to the demon passed. "Tell Leo, I'm mighty sorry. Then get him to safety."

"Why?" I asked, my voice dry and breathy.

"Because when Evangelina sacrifices me at moonrise on the full moon, the demon will be bound and will come after him."

I nodded once to show I had heard, my movement erratic. "How are you avoiding the call of the spell," I asked. "You're two-natured. You should be walking inside the ward."

"The summoning and binding aren't complete. Blood from a living-undead Mithran will complete it, but only on the full moon."

"Okay. Got that," I whispered. "Why does Evangelina want to hurt Leo?"

"All I know is the word Shiloh." Lincoln dropped, landing with a hard flat thump on the black floor, his hands barely catching his weight before his head banged down. "Ask the right people," he whispered. "Ask the right questions." He collapsed with a short sigh and closed his eyes, the sun outside and the silver taking their toll. He was asleep, in the undead sleep of vamps. He'd be hungry when he waked. I should have tried to set him free, but that would have meant getting closer to the demon. *No freaking way.* I turned and ran, stumbling up the steps. Falling. Catching myself on my forearms, bruising. But the pain cleared my head, and I held the scarf like a lifeline as I made it to the top of the stairs and out of the house. Only when I was back at my car did I remember that I'd left the lights on and doors all open. But I didn't care. I wasn't going back in there. Not for nothing. I sat in the sunlight in my SUV, in the warmth created by the sun through the windows, clutching the scarf that had saved my life. And trembled.

When I could think more clearly, I drove to a little store, bought three bottles of ginger beer, which was like ginger ale but dark and sharp-tasting, and four homemade pastries, consuming them standing at the counter, needing the

calories, and ignoring the anxious glances of the propri-
etor at my bloody, torn clothes. When my shakes had
passed and I had my head on straight enough, I sent the
pictures to Big Evan's phone, and was careful not to look
at them for fear the desire to go back and learn more may
take me over. By the skin of my chinny-chin-chin I had
gotten away from the big bad wolf. Or the big bad raptor—a
demon of The People.

I couldn't fight this thing alone. I needed to call in the
cavalry, but I didn't know who to call, who I could trust to
keep Molly alive. With the heater on high, I drove back to
Asheville.

I made my room without running into anyone I knew,
stripped, and climbed into the shower. I stood beneath
the scalding water and let it parboil me, trying to thaw the
cold in my soul left by the nearness to the ancient evil.
When I was warmer, I dressed and went to the drawer
holding my Bible and crosses, the only defense against
evil I knew. I put on three silver crosses, held the Bible on
my lap, and turned on the gas fire with the remote control
as I scrolled through my phone contacts for Aggie One
Feather's number.

Guilt wormed under my skin like bamboo shoots under
fingernails. I hadn't told Aggie—my Cherokee teacher, the
elder who was helping me find my past—that I was leaving
New Orleans. I hadn't said good-bye. I was a coward and an
idiot. And if the thing in the circle had claimed to be anything other than a Cherokee demon, I'd go on being a coward and an idiot. I checked the time on the cell—nine
a.m.—and hit send. Aggie answered on the second ring.

"Hello. How can I help you?"

I thought about that for a moment. Only an elder would
answer the phone like that, knowing the odds of it being a
solicitation call. "Aggie One Feather." I paused. "*Egini
Agayvlge i*, in the speech of The People. This is Jane Yellowrock," I took a breath, "*Dalonige'i digadoli*. Yellow
Eyes Yellowrock. I seek council."

"How may an Elder of The People assist?" There was no
snark in the words, no sarcasm.

I swallowed and said, "First of all you can forgive me for

acting like an idiot and taking off without telling you I was leaving."

Aggie laughed, the sound soothing. "There is nothing to forgive, *Dalonige'i digadoli*. You have a life outside of my counsel, outside of the sweathouse."

I do. I did. But it was way more than that. It was the parts of my life staring at each other across a chasm of decades, across a sea of cultures and religion and history. Parts of myself that were bifurcated, broken, torn. Parts that didn't know how to heal or how to accept the other.

I could almost see Aggie, sitting at her kitchen table, a plate of fresh baked cookies and a bottled Coke frosted with white before her. Her calm reached out across the airwaves and settled around my shoulders like a warm blanket. I relaxed, only now aware that I was tense. I took up my guilt in both hands as if to strangle it, and said, "I haven't been back to see you since going to water. I ran away from your guidance and took a gig in Asheville to put space between us."

"No," she said gently. "You accepted the job to put space between the parts of yourself. The Christian child with the white man's upbringing and the *Tsalagi* and our ancient ways."

Crap. I was so totally transparent. I looked down at my hand in the firelight, at the shadows and light that moved across my skin. I was at war with my selves and I didn't know how to knit me together into a single whole. Aggie knew this, even if she didn't know what I was, or where I came from. "Yeah. Change is hard. Acceptance is harder."

"You will find yourself, *Dalonige'i digadoli*. You will like what you find at the end of that journey. You will like being whole, though the way of the Christian may have to work hard to accept the way of the *Tsalagi*. How may I help you?" she asked gently.

"It's pretty heavy stuff." When she didn't reply I said, "A mostly Irish Celt witch has trapped a demon in a binding circle to summon and drain the two natured to accomplish—I don't know what. The witch is looking younger, prettier, and a lot less stable. The thing in the circle is black, misty, has wings and claims to be Cherokee. Do you know what it is?"

Aggie One Feather took a slow breath between her teeth, the sound shocked. "No. But I will ask my mother."

"I need to know how to kill it."

After a long moment, she said, "If it is a true demon, they cannot be killed. They can only be bound and banished." Aggie's voice sounded calm, steady, not like she wanted to run from me and my problems. Kudos to her for that. I didn't think I'd sound so serene in her place. "And the ceremony to banish a demon to the underworld is lost in time. No one knows of it. I cannot help you *Dalonige'i digadoli.*" I hadn't really believed it would be easy, but a heavy misery flowed over me at her words. "But I will ask others. Give me your numbers. I will call when I know more."

I gave her the number to my fancy cell and to my throwaway cell, the one I used when I didn't want Leo to have access to me. Of course, if Leo could listen in on my conversations, then giving out that number meant he had it now, but it couldn't be helped. Modern communication came with a price: total lack of privacy from anyone with the money to buy the access, and with the will to listen.

When I hung up, I opened the Bible at random and started reading. I hadn't read anything holy in months. I hadn't wanted to. But now, with the coercion of the demon and my own emptiness, I needed *something*. Something to fill me. To protect me. Because I was close to being . . . afraid. Yeah. Afraid. The emptiness inside me was a yawning maw with killing teeth and I was poised on the lip of the darkness. The scripture I opened to in Deuteronomy six wasn't exactly comforting.

Ye shall not go after other gods, of the gods of the people which *are* round about you;
(For the LORD thy God *is* a jealous God among you) lest the anger of the LORD thy God be kindled against thee, and destroy thee from off the face of the earth.

A cold sensation swept through me, like a frozen wind. Had I done that? Gone after other gods? The gods of The People? The gods of my own life, my job, my friends, my own wants? Yeah. I had. I wondered if God would forgive me for that. Before I closed the Bible I flipped to the New Testament at random and read in Luke six:

> Judge not, and ye shall not be judged: condemn not, and ye shall not be condemned: forgive, and ye shall be forgiven:

"Okay," I said aloud, not sure what I was reading, but willing to accept it. I closed the Bible. "Okay, I can forgive. Forgive what?" Instantly I saw the face of *yunega*, the white man who killed my father. I saw the shadows on the cabin wall as the other *yunega* raped my mother. I felt the chill of the cooling blood as I painted my face in promise of retribution.

I jerked out of the memories and put the Bible down, staring at it, the worn pages looking ordinary, powerless, in the dull light seeping around the blinds. "Okay. Not so easy, then," I murmured. I hadn't forgiven the murderers and rapists, even after more than a hundred years.

I closed the old Bible and went online. Reach had sent me some files, a huge one on Thomas Stevenson, Shaddock's scion who had gotten free and was probably hunting humans for dinner. I didn't bother to open it. Instead I opened the one labeled Evangelina Everhart Stone. The file was full of info pulled off the Web and other places, and it mentioned her in a lot of contexts: her graduate and postgrad work at the University of North Carolina; a stint at UNC Asheville as a part-time professor; in Charlotte at Johnson & Wales University's College of Culinary Arts; a few years teaching at Shaw University; the opening of Seven Sassy Sisters' Herb Shop and Café; a newspaper spread about her cooking classes at the restaurant, which had been before I knew her. She had returned to UNC Asheville as a full professor, and married a professor named Marvin R. Stone, and they had one daughter, Shiloh Everhart Stone.

I remembered the body rolled in the carpet behind the couch. And the girlish bedroom, dusty and closed off. Neither husband nor daughter had lived there in years. I did a search for Stone but he had disappeared off the map. So. Hubby might be wearing a carpet, but he wasn't alive.

Reach had provided me with a file on Shiloh. The contents were thin. Shiloh had been a mediocre student, better at art and poetry than math and science, and had disappeared at age fifteen. And reappeared in New Orleans, in a shelter for runaway teens. *Crap*. Shiloh had run to New Orleans—Leo's city. The chill I'd been fighting settled in my bones.

Shiloh disappeared from the shelter before her mother could get to her. The police report said three of the girl's friends had watched as she was yanked into a dark car, maybe a Lincoln or a Park Avenue. The car squealed off before the friends could do anything. Shiloh had been kidnapped. In New Orleans. In Leo's main power base.

Quickly, I minimized the screen and opened a different file, one provided by NOPD, listing all the witch children who disappeared in their city, kidnapped and never found. Shiloh E. Stone was on the list. I compared the date of Shiloh's kidnapping to the dates other witch young had vanished. Three others had gone missing in the same month. "Oh crap," I whispered. I knew what this case was about, now. As with most things vampy, this situation went back a lot of years, the originating event buried beneath the weight of time. But now I had the single thread that tied the disconnected parts together. Shiloh Everhart Stone.

I opened more of my own files and discovered that the policeman who had taken the report was R.A. Ferguson; he had filed the report as a runaway, not as a kidnapping. Shiloh was a witch kid. He hadn't cared about a nonhuman child who disappeared, had, in fact, hated them. I had met Ferguson, just before an ancient vamp had rolled him and sucked the hatred out of him along with his blood. I hadn't tried to stop the vamp.

Evangelina had lost a witch daughter in Leo's city, in Leo's territory, likely to the vamp witches who were sacrificing witch children to the pink blood-diamond. They'd been trying to create a cure for the long-chained—scions who never found sanity. Evangelina had known that. She had claimed that her appearance in New Orleans was for parley—to negotiate peace between vamps and witches, and compensation to the witches for the loss of their children, not that there could ever be sufficient compensation for the loss of a child. But she had really gone there to kill the man she held responsible for her child's death. Leo Pellissier.

Evan hadn't known about Shiloh running away and being kidnapped, which meant it was likely that Molly hadn't known either. Evangelina had kept it all secret until she spelled her sisters to enact vengeance on Leo. Shiloh had run away from home. Had Evangelina killed Marvin by accident, later? Or had Shiloh seen Evil Evie kill her father and then run away? *Crap.* I'd never had a family, but as an investigator, I knew that family secrets were the very worst. They destroyed so much. Sometimes they destroyed everything, as if, after decades in the grave, the dead reached out to shatter the living.

Molly had never told me the story of Shiloh, so Evangelina had likely not told her sisters. Probably because she had killed her husband. I called Evan and left the info about Shiloh on his voice mail. He needed to know. They all did. But for some reason, I didn't mention what I feared had happened to Marvin Stone. Coward. I was a coward.

CHAPTER TWENTY-FOUR

Eat Humans When They Go to the Dark Side

Staring at the computer screen, I put it all together. Evangelina knew that Leo's now-true-dead scions killed Shiloh. The witch was trying to get back at Leo for the decades of murders, but she wasn't stupid enough to try to kill him in open confrontation. She had appeared in New Orleans, allied with the wolves, tried to help them kill Leo in his lair by creating a modified *hedge of thorns* that let the wolves in. Unrelated, but associated, I took a gig in my old hometown and came to Asheville. When the weres got out of jail, they had followed me here from New Orleans to exact their own brand of vengeance. Evangelina—who had been kicked out of New Orleans by Leo—found out that weres had followed me to Asheville and lured them to her home, her place of power. And there she created a spell or upped the power on an existing one, with their two-natured blood. The spell was intended to kill Leo, who was dead and undead—one of the two-natured. It all made sense.

I dialed Bruiser. When he picked up, before he could say more than hello, I said, "Tell me who suggested to Leo that Lincoln Shaddock was ready to be master of his own city." When he didn't answer, I said, "Was it you?"

"Yes." He sounded bewildered, and just a tad defensive.

"I recommended that he go to the Appalachians and meet with Lincoln. Amy Lynn Brown had come out of the devoveo in record time. It was a good call. Why do you ask?"

Instead of answering, I asked a question. "And Leo was going?"

"At first, yes. Then he changed his mind. Why. Do. You ask?"

I closed my eyes. "I ask because Evangelina had you spelled and open to suggestion. She set this whole thing in place, to get Leo here, in her hometown, where her coven gave her power to draw on. And she thought you could force the issue." The main reason Leo had agreed to the parley was because of the location of her coven, though he never knew that.

I heard Bruiser's slow intake of breath. I almost *felt* his shock through the airwaves. My cell beeped. It was Molly's number. "I'll get back to you." I cut Bruiser off and said, "Hi."

"I'm sorry," Molly said. Before I could reply she went on. "For not believing you about my sister. For not trusting that you knew what you were doing. For not standing up to Big Evan when he was an ass about you."

I heard Evan in the background, say, "Hey. No fair."

"Jane is my friend. You were an ass. Don't let it happen again," Molly said, her words muted, her mouth turned away from the phone. I heard Evan grumble in the background. To me she said, "The ass says he's sorry." I didn't believe that Big Evan had apologized, but I would accept it.

"My sisters and I are meeting at two p.m. at Evangelina's to take a look at the demon she trapped, and bind it back to darkness if we can. Evangeline is teaching a cooking class at the Biltmore House all day, and won't be back until after dark. Big Evan analyzed the photos you sent and he thinks that daylight is the best time for us to neutralize the working. Can you be there?"

I thought about taking Derek and the boys to take Evie out, and about all the collateral damage that might result if she fought with demon-backed witch spells. I discarded the idea. "I'll be there at one forty-five," I said. "And Molly? I used Evangelina's hair and one of her scarves to get inside without the spell taking me over."

A long silence followed before Molly sighed into the phone. "I still can't accept that she used blood magic," Molly said. "But if you got in with her genetic material then, well. Oh hell." Her voice was clotted with tears. "See you soon, Big-Cat."

Satisfied that I had done all I could, I set my phone to wake me by twelve thirty, pulled the covers from the foot of the neatly made bed and fell asleep. Hard.

I sat on Fang under the blazing sun at Evil Evie's and sweated, smelling the stench of old blood, sickly sweet and rotting. The early cold spell had melted away into Indian summer, and the jeans and denim jacket were too warm for the high eighties and humidity, but were much preferable to the riding and fighting leathers I would have needed for a vamp hunt. I wasn't sure what Evangelina's witch-magic problem would require, but protection from vamp fangs wouldn't be one of them.

I hadn't wanted anyone to be able to track me, so I left the cell and the SUV with their GPS locator devices at the hotel. I had no idea how the sisters would banish the demon in the basement and free the weres and Lincoln, but it would involve lots of magic, and I wondered if there would be anything left of the old homeplace when they were done.

I studied the odd lines inside the garden's witch circle. The blood-splattered rocks looked like broken alphabet letters, something archaic. It hit me. *Runes.* Evangelina was using *runes.* I felt really stupid. Lots of witches used runes; their ability to craft raw power into something useful had some special reliance on runes. So if I took a tree branch and batted away the rocks that made up her circle, and knocked the runes out of place, it might—

Molly's van pulled up beside me before I had a chance to try it, which was probably a good thing for my state of health. Witch magic that got interrupted might go bang. I pulled off my jacket, tossed it on the seat, and set Fang's kickstand. Boots crunching on the gravel, I stood by Mol's open window. Her face was grief stricken, her eyes on the witch circle with its coating of dried blood. She took a breath, and her throat tissue quaked audibly as she swallowed, tears in her eyes. I patted her shoulder through the window, knowing the gesture was not nearly enough.

"Blood magic," she whispered, shaking her head. "Son of a witch on a stick." Visibly, she gathered herself and opened the van door. From the passenger seat, she handed me a heavy wicker basket covered with a kitchen towel. I held it while she climbed from the van, her face now set and resolute. When the van door closed, she tilted her head, the motion reticent. "Evan told me about Shiloh. About how she was kidnapped in New Orleans. I think . . . I think I knew it, already. I think Evangelina told us when she spelled us all."

I almost told her about the body in the rug upstairs, but something stopped me. She'd had enough bad news today. "Where's Evan?" I asked, instead.

"The kids are napping. He's watching them. I don't need him for this." Which was a lie. Major witch workings required five witches. They had only four. But I didn't argue. This was her sister they were going up against, the leader of the Everhart coven. They would handle it alone. "Turn off your cell," she added. "It might interfere with the working." Which was news to me. I'd have to be more careful.

Two all-wheel Subarus pulled in beside the van, and the other sisters got out, Carmen Miranda carrying a basket from the blue car, the twins Boadacia and Elizabeth from the green one—Cia with a small trunk, Liz with a weighty cloth tote over one shoulder. Molly looked at me. "Do you have the scarf and hairs?" I nodded. "Cover your head and shoulders with the scarf and stick the hairs in a pocket. Stay here."

Molly didn't issue orders often, but when she did, I listened. The sisters converged on the witch circle in the garden and I turned off my throwaway cell, pulled the trapped hairs from the scarf weave, and pocketed them just as Molly had required. Feeling stupid, I covered my head with the lavender scarf and watched as the sisters stepped clockwise or sunwise, each taking her place where a pentagram point would have touched the circle had one been intended for a group working. Boadacia and Elizabeth sat with their backs to me. Molly and Carmen faced me. That left one spot empty, the one pointing at the house. That spot faced the rear door, the location from which I had seen Evangelina's back when she was pouring blood all over herself. The place where she entered the circle and closed it before working with blood. How the sisters knew where she had sat, I didn't know, but they all stared at the spot she had been sitting. I hadn't told them. It was sorta eerie, until I realized they could see where the dried blood was thickest. Maybe the outline of Evangelina's body.

They got the implements for a working out of their containers. Carmen was an air witch, and she lifted a necklace of wing feathers and leaves out of her basket. Molly was an earth witch with an unusual affinity to death, meaning that like most earth witches, she could influence plants and some animals, could draw power for workings directly from them, but unlike most earth witches, she could also sense dead things. Mol took a rosemary plant out of her basket and set the pot at her feet. One of the twins was a moon witch, her magics tied to the lunar cycles, and would be particularly strong this close to the full moon, but only when the moon was high. She looped a long necklace of huge moonstones around her shoulders over and over. Cia was a stone witch—minerals were her gift—and did the same thing with a necklace made of mixed, faceted gems in shades of purple, yellow, green, and clear. They sparkled in the sunlight.

Each of the women were wearing flowing dresses, and in unison, they sat on the ground outside the circle, in half-lotus positions, dresses covering their knees. They closed their eyes. Molly placed her rosemary in her lap, and I could smell the rich sun-heated scent. The one empty place looked like a hole ripped in the reality of their family. Evangelina was a water witch; with her the sisters had once been part of a perfect coven. Without her they were weakened.

I sat on the ground, in the shade of a tree, sweat trickling down my spine under my tank top, and waited. The women didn't look like they were doing anything, and the lack of sleep pulled at me. My eyes fought to close and I ground my molars together to keep alert. Watching the Everhart sisters was like watching paint dry or grass grow.

Ten minutes later, about the time my jaw started to ache, I heard a faint explosion of air, like a vamp disappearing from a room at supersonic speed. A pop-whoosh. I blinked, wondering if I had missed something. The sisters stood as if nothing untoward had happened and started kicking the stones that composed the circle, scuffing at the little trench, throwing the rocks that made up the runes. I caught Molly's eye and stood, grabbed the ends of the scarf to hold it in place over my head, and walked to the circle.

Molly cocked her brow in question. "That looked easier than I expected," I said.

"It *was* easy. We just knocked out the ward that protected the circle and deactivated the circle she used to draw power from us. Now," Molly started toward house, "is the hard part." I moved in front of her and opened the door with my scarf-covered hand. The interior of the house glowed with magical energies, the air itself seeming covered with a pink haze, snapping with black sparks. The smell of the magic was so strong I rubbed my nose. The working was getting stronger, even with Evangelina not here. Even with the circle outside deactivated and physically displaced. Still holding the scarf over my head, I led the way to the basement.

With each step down, I felt the pull of the demon below, the thing that knew my darkest wants and fears and needs. Willing me to join him in his witch-spelled cell. Beast woke, pressing down on me with her claws, watching through my eyes, not happy that I had come back here. *Jane is foolish kit. Silly kit. Stupid kit to come back here, to den of bird predator.*

I know, I thought back. *But I have to be here for Molly.* Even though there was nothing I could do to help Molly deal with what she would find in the basement. Nothing to lessen the impact. But as her friend, I could be there first. Leading the way, I turned on lights to dispel the strength of the *hedge of thorns'* red, bloody glow. I was first in the basement, the electric sparks of the *hedge* pricking over me. The first to see the demon inside.

He was sitting on the floor of his cage, nibbling on the smaller werewolf, beak tearing and ripping flesh. I was pretty sure the were was dead, as there was more blood sloshing in the circle than there was inside of him. What skin he still wore over his muscles and viscera was bluish. The man was missing both arms and most of one leg. What is it about supernatural creatures needing to eat humans when they go to the dark side?

The larger werewolf, the one I called Fire Truck, looked as if he'd lost a third of his considerable body weight. His ribs were clearly visible beneath his thin skin and thick body hair, breathing, smiling, eyes closed, apparently napping in the congealing blood of his wolf-buddy.

The demon stood as I entered, wings half spread as if to cover and protect his dinner. His similarity to an anzu was marked, yet wrong somehow, as if an anzu had mated with a shadow and given birth to this monstrosity. His beak opened and he trilled softly, as if pleased to see me.

Molly stopped at the foot of the stairs, her eyes wide. Carmen stopped behind her, mumbling air witch curses damning storms and fire winds. Behind them, one twin was crying, the other was red-faced with anger. The angry one said, "Evangelina should be whipped for this. Cast out."

Cia said, "Evangelina should go to *jail* for this."

I hadn't told them about the body rolled in the rug upstairs. But eventually I'd have to report it to the police. Even if he'd died of natural causes, I rather doubted he'd rolled himself in the carpet and tucked it behind the couch first. So the cops were in Evangelina's future one way or another.

"Come to me," the trapped demon said to Molly. "I will show you true freedom, true power."

"Don't talk to that thing," Carmen warned.

"Your sister has found freedom and power with me," he said.

Molly whispered, to her sisters, not to the demon, "Our sister has been cursed. Not freed." To me she said, "Where is the vampire?"

I walked around the room until I could see the back of the *hedge of thorns*. Lincoln Shaddock lay on the black-painted floor—sleeping the sleep of the undead, or maybe really dead—against the wall that led into the kennel. I nudged him with my foot, but he didn't react. He didn't look so good; he looked true dead, pasty, shriveled, and maybe a little blue. I bent over him and took a sniff. The usual vamp smell of dry herbs, bark, flowers, and earth was missing. But so was the smell of death. He smelled like . . . nothing. Part of the room.

I walked back to the other side and realized that the sisters were already sitting on the floor at the points of the pentagram that was painted inside the *hedge*, their talismans in laps or around necks. "Molly?" I asked, alarmed.

"Black magic works best at night and is weakest with the sun overhead." She checked her watch. "We hope to bind the demon and send him back to the place he came from."

"Where's that?" I asked.

"No idea," Molly said. I didn't know much about witch power, but I did know about evil, and you didn't go up against pure evil, absolute, not-of-this-world evil, alone. You needed help, big help. Better-than-human help. They needed faith and a full coven.

"Some things we don't need to know," one of the twins said.

"Don't want to know," the other twin said.

Carmen Miranda pulled a silver cross from her shirt and dangled it over her chest in the necklace of feathers and leaves. "It's someplace without air and warmth. Someplace without light. Without the sun. Without the breath of life. Without *God*."

With the last word, the demon threw himself at the *hedge*. Light exploded out, bloody, and cloudy, murky black. A boom sounded, slapping off the walls. I jumped back, hitting the white wall. A mushroom cloud of heat blossomed out. A painting fell, dislodged by the concussion of sound and my body. I reached out, Beast-fast. Caught the corner of the frame as it tilted out into the room. Toward the *hedge*.

I dropped my body and shoved upward, high, hard. I landed on the floor with a dull thud, stabilizing the painting in both hands. Balancing. Lifting even as I rolled beneath it. Gingerly, I set the painting against the wall, where it couldn't break the circle. The room was hot and stank of a sulfur compound.

I twitched my head around, my hair scraping on the

floor, and met Molly's horrified eyes. There was a red place on her cheek, as if she had been burned. Carmen was worse off, blisters rising on her skin. The twins were out of place, standing in the corner, holding hands. Fire Truck, inside with the demon, was shifting into his wolf, reddish hairs sprouting, bones sliding with sickening cracks and pops. Eyes open, he screamed. A crack, black and sooty ran down the sides of the dome of the *hedge. The demon had damaged it.*

"Get out of here," I whispered.

The demon threw himself at the *hedge of thorns* again. The crack spread, a dirty, dull crack in the energies that caged him. A widening fracture filled with darkness, a dripping blackness. The sound was a sonic boom, tearing air from the room. Heat crazed along my flesh, burning. Scalding. Branding. The scent of burning sulfur ballooned out. I screamed. My spine bowed, lifting me from the floor, only my head and feet touching down. *"Get out!"* I screamed to the witches. "Get out!" They ran up the stairs, feet pounding.

My bones slid. Skin abraded, splitting. The gray light of the *change* slid over me, sparking with black lights. But mine sparked like black diamonds reflecting the sun, my own bright magic called forth. Pelt spilled out. Killing teeth erupted from my gums. The magics of the *hedge* seared and singed pelt and skin. I screamed. Pushed out of my clothes, claws ripping cloth. Still shifting, I leaped free.

My Beast magic shoved back at the rift in the *hedge*'s energies. Bright and cool as a mountain stream. Beast filled my mind.

Beast is better than Jane, better than big-cat. Beast knows what to do. Spread claws. Swiped a paw down Lincoln Shaddock's arm, drawing vampire blood. Not two-natured. But powerful.

I/we threw undead blood at crack in *hedge of thorns*. It landed like spats of water on hot stone. Black light blew out. Beast was thrown like kit swiped by mother's paw. Into air. White light shot out. Pulled crack in ward together. Beast hit wall. Paintings fell. Frames cracking. But none fell into *hedge*. None broke circle.

Demon inside circle threw back beak and screamed. I shook head and snarled. Gathered feet under body and backed away, pawpawpaw, silent. Good hunter. Backed to stairs. Stood and studied demon. Studied reddish wolf in ward of *hedge*. Sleeping wolf. Skinny with hunger.

How did you know? Jane asked. Fear filled her mind. Kit fear, afraid of shadows, leaping at leaves as if at prey. *How did you know how to stop the hedge breaking? How did you know when I didn't? And why aren't you being pulled toward that thing?*

I backed up stairs. Whirled, to face up stairs, tail spinning slow for balance. Landed facing away from trapped death. Raced up fast. Hunger tore at belly. *Need to hunt!* I raced through Evangelina's house. Out open door. Into light. Eyes blinked against sun, dazzling in garden.

Witches were standing in garden, staring at house. Staring at Beast. Hands out, fingers spread like killing claws. Power built in their hands. Against Beast. Black storm cloud in Carmen's hands. Cold air gusted through garden, around her, into her hands. Leaves and trees talked with leaf sounds. I chuffed. Warning.

"No!" Molly said. "It's okay."

"No it's not. It's a were-cat," twin Liz said. "It'll bite us!"

I showed killing teeth. Snarled. *Not were! Am Beast!*

Twin Liz shaped her power, sparkling like gems. Twin Cia shaped hers, glowing like face of hunter's moon. Twins spun energy like balls of power, captured in hands.

"She isn't a were!" Molly shouted. She stepped between witch sisters and Beast.

Carmen blinked. "No. She isn't." Smell of surprise, shock, fear—flight or flight scent—and something human filled garden. Awe? Didn't understand human awe, but Jane felt awe sometimes. It smelled like this. "It was you," Carmen said. "In the cave. You saved me."

Twins stopped spinning power. Carmen's power blew away like mist in sudden breeze. "That's Jane," she said. "What is she, if she isn't a were-cat?"

Molly tilted head. Looking into Big-Cat eyes, wanting to hide Jane secret. To hide Beast.

Inside head, Jane sighed. *Crap, crap, crap.*

"Sorry," Molly whispered. To sisters she said, "Jane is a skinwalker. And she has magic of her own." To Beast, she asked, "Did you stop that thing?"

I hacked and sat down, backside on porch floor. Retracted claws, front paws crossed like housecat. *Beast is no pet,* I thought. *Is not owned.* But I closed lips on killing teeth. Looked safe to prey. Twin witches stepped back, opened hands. Power blew away like dust and shadow.

Heard roar from far away. Loud. Tilted head. Car coming. Noisy engine.

Molly looked at her watch. I looked at sky. Much time had passed. Looked at road.

Molly whispered, "Evangelina. She must have felt it when we disrupted her garden circle. She's home early."

CHAPTER TWENTY-FIVE

If He Moves, You Can Eat Him

I trotted to edge of house, under plants and herbs, more rosemary like Molly's, but bigger. Smell was hot, spicy, green. Earth was warm under paws. Hunger clawed at belly. Needed food. Needed to hunt.

The car Jane called *sports* roared around corner. Back of car swept back and forth like fish's tail. Sounded alive and angry, charging bull. But car was not alive. Jane said so. Wheels shot small rocks like weapons into trees. Good car for hunting. No roof. Good for chasing prey and leaping out of. Could chase bison in car.

Evangelina sat in car, face in snarl. Witch energy was like thick cloud around her, pink and black, like sunset and rain clouds. Angry power, racing with red motes. Car roared toward witch sisters, coven master coming. I growled in warning, hunger twisting belly tight.

Time did not change for me, as it does for Jane when she fights. *Fight or flight.* Body reacted, instantly. Claws came out. Pelt stood up across shoulders. Snout opened, pulled back to show killing teeth. I growled.

Molly smelled of fear, fear of sister, fear of coven master. Reached out with both hands. Pulling power from garden, from trees and plants. Rosemary shriveled and dried, leaves stinking, falling on big-cat in brown rain. Liz dropped hands to earth, to draw from minerals in dirt and stone, her face white. Cia reached to sky, to draw from moon; moon

far away, not in sky until dark. Carmen closed eyes and
laughed, drawing in air. Wind swept through trees, growing
strong. But not fast enough.

Sports car growled, slowing, tires blacking road, squealed
like prey, bumped into drive. Many small rocks flew from
tires. Car rocked. Stopped. Many things happened fastfastfast.

Evangelina gathered ball of pink and black energies in
hands. Stood on car seat. Threw energies. Pink light and
black shadow flew through air. Scarlet motes flying with
ball, trailing it. Carmen mouth opened in shock. She pushed
at air. Wind flew from her.

Liz picked up stones.

Pink ball of energy wobbled through witch wind. Hit
Carmen in chest. She made strange sound, grunting, and
fell back. Landed in bushes. Bounced to ground.

Molly threw small ball of light at Evangelina. It spread
like web, like net. Landed over her. Evangelina screamed.
Stabbed at net of light with fingers. I crouched. Hissed.
Evangelina made same sound as Beast. Tore hole in net,
blacked edges stinking like burned bodies. Charred.

Carmen made mewling sounds like hurt kit. Pink energy
spread over her. Scarlet motes sank into her. Her clothes
smoked. Flamed. Her skin was red and blistered beneath it.
Burned. Body started to twitch, red motes flashing under
skin.

Liz threw stones. First one hit Evangelina in hip hard.
Angry witch caught second one. It was white, a stone from
witch circle. Stone grew in her hand. Liz mistake, to spell
Evangelina's rock. She heaved it back at Liz. Harder.
Faster. It grew in the air, like boulder. Molly formed another net, hands working fast. Liz dove to side. Threw
handful of spelled sand into air. Big white rock crackled,
passing through sand. Followed Liz. Hit her. Threw her
across dirt.

Molly tossed new net of light and life, this one green.
Flowers in garden, fruits and vegetables, trees and shrubs
withered, browned. *Died.*

Molly is stealing life, Jane shouted inside head.

Molly's net landed over Evangelina. Net was bigger

than last one. Liz fell to ground. Lying under big rock, heavy. Molly's net wrapped around angry Evangelina witch, like arms of octopus on TV. She screamed. Hurt.

Carmen rose onto elbow. With one burned hand, pointed at sports car. Air swept up. Gathered dust and dirt and stones and dead plants. Whirled like tornado. Hit car. Air wrapped around Evangelina. On top of Molly's net of light. Carmen lay back. Chest heaving. Smelling broken. Singed, burned blood.

Pink and black energy gathered around car. Scarlet motes flashed through mist of power. Grew thicker. Shadows formed spears, black and cold as iron, dark as night sky. Spears tore at layered nets. Burned holes in magics.

Cia held hands together, clasped. Spread fingers and separated hands. Moonlight, soft and glowing, filled space between them. Stones in her necklace split and broke as power came from it. She was making a net. But moon was far away. Slow magic by day.

More dark spears gathered. Facing at sisters. Spears narrowed. Grew barbs. Sharp.

Witch sisters were trying to trap Evangelina in cage of magic. Evangelina was trying to kill sisters to take their power and blood. I gathered limbs tight. Shoulders high. Raised head. Screamed challenge. Shoved off with all paws. Leaped.

Molly shouted, "Jane! No!"

Long leap through air. Paws passed through spears. Burning. Burning. *Hurt. Hungry. Angry!* In midair, I snarled. Hit Evangelina in chest. Claws hooking into witch flesh. Witch body falling. Out of car. Rode body to ground. Killing teeth locked on witch throat. Tasted blood.

Jane wrenched at body. Tried to be alpha. Something touched Beast-mind.

Everything in world went silent. No noise. No sound. No sight except for angry fearful witch eyes. No smells except for witch blood. No taste but witch blood. But did not bite down. Did not tear out throat of enemy prey. Wanted to. Was *stopped*.

Felt heart of prey beating fast under paws and chest. Panting breath of terrified prey. She was afraid. Smell of fear was good. Tried to bite down. Could not. Blood taste was delicious. Hunger clenched at belly. Needed to bite down. *Needed!*

Hand touched my head. Human hand. Little. I tilted eyes up. Angelina stood beside us, one hand on Beast head, one on Evangelina chest. Little witch moved dress and found necklace on Evangelina. Pink diamond, gold chain. Angie wrapped blood-diamond in little fist. Black sparks flashed out between stubby fingers. Dark life, black lightning. Sparks landed on Beast pelt, burning. I growled. Black sparks were sign of Angie-magic. Had seen them before. Bright sparks did not burn Angie Baby's hand. Scarlet motes flowed up Evangelina's skin. Almost as if alive. Like mites racing, like rats running from floodwaters. Flowed up and out of her. Into gem.

I looked at Evangelina's eyes. She was angry. Was *stopped* like Beast.

Frozen, Jane thought. *She froze us.*

Am not cold, I thought back. *Stopped.* Not *frozen.*

Molly and Cia knelt on either side of downed witch, Cia holding ball of moonlight. Molly unhooked Evangelina's necklace and left it in Angie's fist. Cia lay glowing ball on Evangelina's chest and opened fingers. Net spread out from them, wrapping angry witch. Glowing trap like spider's web. Breath eased in angry witch's chest. Heart slowed. Her eyes closed.

"It's okay, Aunt Jane. She's asleep now," Angie Baby said. "I'll let you go, but you can't bite her, okay?" I growled. Angie made small fist and thumped my head, between ear tabs. Jane laughed deep inside and I growled again. "You can't bite her," Angie said, "biscause I won't let you. And that might hurt you."

I hissed again, but lips covered teeth. Relaxed body. Showed submission. Unhappy. Wanted to kill witch. *Wanted* to. Felt Angie Baby let me go. Felt Beast-power flow into body. Narrowed eyes at little witch. But let go with teeth and pawed away from fallen angry sleeping witch. Sat near Molly-van, grooming pelt and burned places on paw pads. Licked away flavor of witch. *Tasty.* But Beast not happy. Jane not happy. Jane couldn't shift into Jane until night. Part of Jane skinwalker magic—unless death threatened, could not shift until night. Beast was alpha in daylight. Felt happier at thought. Could sleep in hot sun. Maybe could hunt bear!

Looked at witches. Still unhappy. Molly crying, trying to get phone to work, but magic had ruined phone. Cia trying to roll stone from Liz. Carmen trying to breathe, breath from lungs smelling burned. Scarlet motes still raced under her skin. I/we had seen this before. Was magic of pink diamond, magic of witch vampire who Jane killed with sliver of BloodCross.

Padded to stone lying on top of Liz. Braced paws into dirt. Shoulder onto boulder. Pushed. Stone wobbled. Cia called, "Molly! Help here!" I waited until Molly was at stone. "On three," she said. Which was good. Beast could count to three. "One. Two. Three!" We all pushed. Stone wobbled. Liz made broken sound. Rock rolled off of her.

Sisters were crying. *Silly kits.* I padded to Angie Baby and sat beside her. She was still holding pink diamond. Red motes ran fast over her fist like bugs on burning ground. I dropped head and nudged her toward Carmen, witch with burns. Witch with red motes under skin. Angie looked at me, prey eye to predator eye, unafraid. "What, Big-Cat?" she whispered. I huffed, amused. *Big-Cat* was grown up name. Angie Baby was not allowed to use it. I nudged her again.

Jane peered out of cat eyes and saw red motes and burned Carmen. Molly, still shaking phone, trying to fix it, was holding hose, as if thinking about washing burned Carmen with cold water. Cia was hugging Liz, crying. Crying loud. I nudged Kit witch, but she did not understand.

Oh, Jane breathed. *Of course. But, crap. I can't tell her.*

I opened mouth and placed killing teeth around Angie's wrist, close to fist holding gem. Teeth gentle. Careful as with own kit, not to break skin. Pulled. I led her to Carmen. Lowered head and placed fist onto Carmen chest.

Red motes raced across Carmen's flesh and dove into the diamond. Carmen gasped. "Coolio!" Angie said. "Mommy, look! See? I was smart to hide in your van!" I bent over hurt witch, smelling burned flesh and burned breath from her mouth and lungs. Carmen was in danger. She had no beast to shift into to heal. I huffed. Carmen might die. Jane made sound as if her kit or mate were injured. I walked away, tail low. Sad. Hungry. Jane was grieving.

Went into house of sleeping angry witch. Hooked burned paw around door handle of cold-food-place. Pulled. Inside, found many clear plastic dishes, some smelling of cooked pasta, cold and slimy. Cooked brown rice, cold and sticky. Cooked beans. Cooked fish! Using killing teeth, I pulled pasta and fish from cold-place. Tore into dishes, spilling food to floor. Settled to eat. Not hot witch blood. Not fresh blood of prey. Not bear or deer or rabbit. But enough for hunger clawing at stomach. Good fish. *Lemon sauce and capers,* Jane said. *Oh. My. God . . . this is so good.* Jane looked at kitchen floor. *And this is such a mess.*

Back outside, I groomed pelt and claws and watched witches pull injured sisters into shade. Molly talked to Angie about healing. About how body worked. Angie was too little. Was confused. *Molly should just draw on Angie's power to heal them,* Jane thought, watching, intent.

Kill kit, like she killed garden, I thought back. *Take too much life.*

Jane looked around garden with cat eyes and said word for sex. Didn't understand why dead garden made her think about sex. Bruiser and Leo and Rick made Beast think about sex. Humans were confusing. Lay head on ground, tilted so sun would warm ears. Closed eyes.

Time passed. Heard familiar sound. Raised head and huffed warning at Molly. She looked up. I huffed again and stood, turned head to road. Old car came down road, old car with rattling insides, not alive, but near death, black smoke for breath. Stinky. Big Evan's old car.

"Thank God," Molly said. I snorted. Big Evan was not god. Evan parked dying car and got out. Took Molly's and Cia's hands and put them on hurt sisters. Burned smell began to go away. Mewling sound from Liz stopped. Evan was good healer with air magic.

Long time in sun later, injured witches were better, enough to take to hospital. Boadacia—Cia twin—drove Molly-van to hospital. Big Evan carried Evangelina into house and

I raced to follow, curious. He dropped her onto rug. She landed with bumping thuds. I hacked, amused. Big Evan looked at me and shrugged. "Oops." But looked satisfied. Angry. Witch Evangelina was once leader of coven. Was zeta bitch now. Least in pack-coven.

Evan put Molly and kits down for nap on Evangelina's couch and went into basement. Beast followed big male witch, mate to Molly. Stepped over Jane-clothes and claws. Evan stood at bottom of stairs with hands on hips, studying room. Saying things low, under breath. More sex talk about mothers. Humans think of sex at strange times. Jane laughed. I did not understand.

Evan pulled things from pockets and threw into room. His magic was dust on air. It smelled like bee sting, hurt nose. But magic of summoning the two-natured faded. Gone. Big Evan had good magic. Wanted to watch Evan. He studied salt circle and *hedge* and things inside it. The wolf blood in circle was gone. Demon looked hungry. Smelled dead wolf death-stink under bee-sting-magic-smell. More of small wolf was gone, eaten. Alive wolf looked sick. Afraid.

Sitting as far from *hedge* as silver chain would allow, Lincoln Shaddock was awake. His flesh smelled sick where silver touched him. Big Evan went upstairs to stinky, dying, rattly car and got rattly metal box. Beast followed like dog. Don't like dogs, but curious about Big Evan. Stayed by his leg, full of many questions. Back in basement, Big Evan took things from box and put metal square with teeth against shackle. Said to Shaddock. "You try to bite me when I set you free and I'll use one of Janie's little knives to make sure it's your last meal. I made her this one." He lifted knife sheath that Jane had worn. Pulled vamp-killer; held silvered blade to light. Handle was made of carved elk horn. Jane's favorite knife. "And I know how to use it."

Evan pulled wooden handle back and forth across shackle. Made ugly sound, loud. I lowered ear tabs to protect ears. *Hacksaw,* Jane thought. *Now why didn't I think of that? Except that I thought the shackle was spelled.* Big Evan used big hands to bend shackle open. And pulled Shaddock to corner of room. The two males talked softly, but Beast heard.

"Why didn't she put you in the circle with the wolves?"

"She did. Most scared I've been since I died the first time. Woulda crapped my britches if I still did that kind of thing. It bit down with its beak, took a taste, and spat me out. Told her I tasted like spoiled milk and rotten cheese." Lincoln was watching Big Evan's neck where pulse beat. But he didn't bite. He put the back of hand over his mouth and pressed. I smelled vampire blood. Did not smell like bad cheese; smelled tasty. I did not understand demon and cheese. Was confused.

Lincoln took a breath and said, "It's looking for something it can possess. It wants something capable of being two-natured, which it plans to kill, and possess just at the moment of death. Bring it back without the occupying soul. But the weres are already two-natured, and they don't die like it wants. Every time it brings them to the point of death, they shift instead of dying. It doesn't want a maimed host, but it's getting frustrated. Impatient."

"Go on," Big Evan said, his voice rumbling, like a growl.

"Humans are single natured, useless to it. And as far as it's concerned, I'm dead." Lincoln grinned up at Big Evan, who was staring at demon in circle. "So it wants a witch."

Big Evan's hands curled into fists bigger than Beast-paws. He looked at Lincoln with death in his eyes. Big Evan would be good hunter. Was good strong mate to Molly and kits.

"Don't re-kill the messenger," Lincoln said. He laughed. "Actually it wants Evangelina."

"If it wasn't for Molly fighting me every step of the way, it could have her."

"Maybe not. It wants to possess someone with power, power that can be used in this world with no cost to itself—possession without the fight against the resident host soul. Witch magic to burn. Evangelina feeds it with her blood." The vampire pointed with long finger to the *hedge*. "Look close. That thing has a tail tethered to the floor in the middle. That's where she put her blood. When she wants in or out, she cuts her hand and drips some into a bowl. Holds it in front of her and crosses over the salt ring into the circle. The thing stands in the back of the circle until she's done whatever it is she wants to do. Then she pours her blood onto the middle of the floor, and the tether gets bigger, stronger. And she leaves."

"The demon talks?" Big Evan asked. "Can it be killed?"

"Evangelina understands it. I can make out some words here and there. Ain't English. Not exactly. And it's immortal, or so I've been led to understand."

"So we have to find a way to bind and banish it again."

The demon trilled a challenge. It did not want to go back to its place of darkness.

"You should ask my angel, Daddy."

Big Evan whirled. Was suddenly holding Jane's claw, her knife. And was standing between hungry vampire and kit. I hacked. Amused. Big Evan was nearly as fast as vampire. Good, *good* hunter. I padded slowly between Big Evan and Angie Baby. Sat on bottom step, on Jane clothes, that had ended up there, during shift. Flexed claws out and in and out. Showed Lincoln killing teeth. *Will kill you like liver-eater. Will kill you like deer. Will kill you like male big-cat that killed my young, if you try,* I thought at him. I let him see his death in my eyes. Growled low.

Lincoln looked at Molly's mate. Looked at me. Thinking. "I have enough control left to not make a meal out of your little girl. Or out of the witches outside. Or the baby and your woman upstairs," Lincoln said. His head tilted, like a snake. He looked sly. "Even poisoned and drained, I can wait until dark to hunt and feed."

Angie Baby came to bottom step and put her arms around Beast. I rubbed jaw along her head, scent marking her, staring at vampire. *Mine. Will protect.*

"Ask my angel, Daddy. His name is Hayyel."

At sound of angel name, demon screamed and fell to floor. Attacked dead body with beak and claws. "Hayyel, eh?" Big Evan said. The demon repeated his noise; he was afraid. "Let's go upstairs, little girl. We have to talk about you stowing away in Mommy's van. I was worried."

"Okay, Daddy." Angie Baby put blood-diamond into Jane jeans pocket. Gold chain was sticking out. Angie looked at Beast and smiled. Put finger to her lips and blew. "Shhhh."

"Upstairs," Evan said. Angie pushed away and scampered up the stairs. He looked at Beast. In predator eye. I growled low. *I am Beast. Do not challenge.*

"Jane, will you stay here and keep an eye on the vamp? If he moves, you can eat him."

I hacked in laughter. Lay on step, like limb over path to water. Stared at Lincoln Shaddock. *Dinner.* Big Evan stepped over me and went up stairs. Magic tingled down stairway as Big Evan set a ward into air. Would make noise if vampire went up stairs. *Good hunter. Good mate for Molly. Good mate for Jane?*

No! Jane thought. *Molly and Evan are mated for life.*

Big-cats do not mate for life. Stupid to mate for life. I blew hard, clearing nasal passages. Stared at vampire. Hoping he would move so Beast could eat him.

CHAPTER TWENTY-SIX

Sharing the Moon-Call

Heard voices up stairs. *Good acoustics,* Jane thought. *Listen.*

"Tell your mama and me about this angel, Angelina."

"He takes care of aminals, him and Thuriel, Mtniel, and Jehiel. He's my protector, my guardnan'. He's right there." Voice grew sad. "Don't you see him? Why not? Oh. He says you can't see angels anymore. Or hear them. Why not?"

"Mmmm . . . Evan?" Molly sounded confused. Worried.

"Tell us what he looks like, darlin'."

"He's got black skin and golden eyes like Aunt Jane and golden wings with brownier, redder spots on them. Like the hawk mama likes. He likes Aunt Jane biscause he takes care of the aminals. I mean an-i-mals. He's her guardnan' angel too. Weeell. He was her guardnan' first, and then my guardnan' angel biscause of what she prayed when she became my godmother."

"Oh, my God," Molly whispered.

"And this angel—"

"Hayyel."

"Hayyel. Will he help us bind the demon?" Big Evan asked.

"Yeeees." The word was drawn out into many notes like a song.

"What do we do?" he asked.

Moments passed, and Angie Baby laughed. "It's easy.

Aunt Jane and me puts three drops of blood into a glass and you dip the knife into the blood and say, '*Bíodh sé daor, le m'ordú agus le mo chumhacht.*'"

Evan's voice sounded choked. "That's Irish Gaelic for, 'Be he unfree—or bound—by my command and power.' And I know before all that's holy that she has never heard that before."

Angie laughed. "Hayyel thinks you're funny."

"D-Do we have guardian angels, honey?" Molly asked.

"Daddy does. He has two. You used to, Mama, but you stopped believin' in 'em and they left." Smell of grief came down stairs. Molly grieving loss of angels.

Loss of faith, Jane thought at me. *Molly's faith in God has suffered. So they left her.*

Lincoln raised his head and opened his mouth, scenting-tasting Molly's anguish. His killing teeth snapped down with little click. Long fangs. Longer than Beast's fangs. I growled low, held him with my eyes. *I will kill. I will eat. I have not hunted.*

He seemed to understand predator stare. Fangs slowly went up into Shaddock's mouth. So slow no click sounded. "Nice kitty." I hacked and hissed at him. He closed his eyes and lay down on the floor. "I'll be good. I am, after all, a *guest* in this here demon-ridden place."

"Okay. The angel will helps us," Big Evan said. His voice flowed downstairs like echoes down cavern walls. "And we have the ceremony. All we need is enough to make a coven."

"Cia will be back shortly. That gives us a full coven . . ." A long silence trailed Molly's words. "If we use the children." Her words sounded sad. *Resigned,* Jane thought.

Big Evan said slowly, "Angie hasn't been totally bound by our wards in months. She's used her gift several times, even untrained. But Little Evan—"

"Is asleep. Maybe he'll stay asleep. We can put his car seat in place and rout power through him."

"If we wait until dusk, Cia will be at her strongest."

"So will the thing in the circle," Molly said.

"But I bet angels are stronger than demons."

Molly sighed. "Yeah. I guess I'll have to rethink my growing lack of belief, huh?"

"Up to you, darlin'."

Kissing sounds came down stairs. Lincoln made snorting sound but did not open eyes.

"And what do we do about your sister? And the were-wolf in the circle? Assuming he's still alive when we get to him."

"Leave her asleep until we get the demon bound. Then we have to turn her over to the witch council and—and I don't know what they'll do to her. For the wolf, we can call Jane's friend Kemnebi to take care of him."

Kem-cat not friend, I thought.

"I have his number written down somewhere," Molly said. "Evangelina's landline phone is still working. Only the cells are ruined."

"This day is turning out to be an expensive one," Evan said, growl back in his voice.

Just after sunset, Kem and Rick drove up in their rattletrap truck. Within minutes, Boadacia parked behind them, van headlights casting odd shadows in the dead garden, which was still shedding desiccated leaves.

I was back in human form, my long hair loose and in the way, wearing some of my own clothes, and some things Molly had scavenged from Evangelina for me. I didn't like wearing her clothes, but I liked even less wearing jeans shredded by Beast's claws and showing a lot of leg. I was in my own tank and undies, and Evangelina's elastic-waist, green and yellow skirt. It was a sixties granny skirt and looked weird with my boots, and I had no idea how I was getting home on Fang in a dress, but that was a problem for later. I was also wearing various knives strapped to my thighs under my skirt, and felt better for their presence. The jeans and the thrice damned blood-diamond were in a confiscated travel tote, hidden under the couch. Not a safe place, but it was all I had.

I was starving and shoveling in brown rice and grilled veggies from the fridge while cleaning up Evangelina's kitchen. Beast had made a mess. I had washed and put the ruined plastic in the recycle bin, and was mopping the floor while eating when everyone came in.

Rick wandered over to me, staring while I ate. His long black hair waved and curled around his jaw, his black eyes sparkled with amusement, and his lips pressed together, twitching. "Shtop ih," I said, through a mouthful of rice. It was seasoned with something wonderful, bits of herbs and stuff, and it tasted delicious. I spooned in another scoop, chewing, mopping.

"You shifted, didn't you? Kem eats like that after a shift." When I grunted in affirmation, he said, "You're cute."

"Nah cue." I swallowed. "Too tall and gangly to be cute."

He took the mop from my hands and finished the floor while I finished off the meal. He was wearing black jeans that cupped his butt like happy hands, and a white tee. The eyes of his cats seeming to glow through the knit. Beast rose and stared as I ate. She approved of a man who could look as sexy as a calendar model even with a mop in hand. He jutted a chin at the floor. "Your cat did this?"

"Yeah. She was hungry. And Molly wouldn't let her eat Evangelina." When Rick arched an eyebrow at me I shook my head and said, "For dinner, Ricky Bo."

"Of course." He wrung the mop out in the sink and set it aside.

He moved to me and pushed the food away. Took my hips in his hands, his thumbs on my lower stomach, turning my body to his and pulling me close. "I have ideas what you can eat for dessert." He kissed my jaw. I laughed silently as his lips nuzzled along my jaw, and up to my ear. Heat moved in the wake of his lips, spreading and settling low in my belly. His cheek brushed back and forth along mine again, scent marking me. Cat-like.

I tilted back my head to give him better access to my neck, wondering if he even noticed what he was doing. My laughter faded, and the warmth in my belly grew heavy, thrumming, where his thumbs made slow circles. *Mine,* Beast purred. "Mmm," I echoed the sentiment. The full moon was soon, very soon, and while skinwalkers aren't moon-called, we are closer to our beast-selves at full moon. Beast was often hard to control then. Okay, impossible. I was usually along for the ride, not the other way around. Full moon? Beast was alpha.

I dropped my spoon and slid my hands up Rick's arms, over the scar tissue of werewolf bites, toward his shoulders. And jerked away. Leaped back. Hard. "What?"

Rick said, eyes wide. I looked at my palm. Two spots were red, not blistered, but close. Through his shirt the eyes of the cat-tats on his arm and shoulder were glowing golden. I held out my other hand, fingers close to the four glowing spots, two for the mountain lion, two for the bobcat. Heat came off them. Not enough to scorch the shirt, but—

Rick rolled up his sleeve and said, "This isn't good."

"Why not?"

"We're ready," Evan said. Rick and I looked at him. Big Evan's eyes were on the tats too. "You have spelled tattoos?" Rick nodded. "We need to talk sometime. For now, we need Jane in the basement." To Rick he added, "We're going to call an angel to bind a demon."

Rick dropped his sleeve. "No good Catholic schoolboy would miss that."

We started down the stairs after Big Evan when my cell rang. It was Aggie One Feather. I gathered all the formality around me that I had. Softly, I said, "Aggie One Feather. Elder of the *Tsaligi*. Please tell me you are the cavalry coming to the rescue at the last minute." Evan stopped and turned to me.

With a wry tone, Aggie said, "The cavalry usually slaughtered The People, but yes, I know what your witch summoned." I put her on speakerphone, her soft tones whispering clearly in the stairwell. "I fear it may be one of the Sunnayi Edahi, the invisible night goers. The most fearsome of these evil beings is Kalona Ayeliski, the Raven Mocker."

The thing in the basement screamed and thrashed in its trap. Kalona Ayeliski. We had its name. That gave us power over it. Big Evan smiled at me, a real smile, maybe the first one I'd ever received. "According to most of the stories," Aggie said, "the Mocker was a male Cherokee . . . *witch* is the European term that matches most closely. He could take the shape of a raven and fly to the bedside of a dying person. If the patient wasn't guarded by holy men who could drive him away, the Mocker would magically remove the dying one's heart and fly off with it. The patient would die. The mocker would eat the heart and grow younger by however many days he had stolen from the patient. The theft would leave no scar, but if the dead man's chest cavity was opened, there would be no heart inside."

I remembered what the demon had said about killing Cherokee on the Trail of Tears, and gaining many years of life. "The evil-deed-doing, big-bad-ugly is a shape-shifter *and* a witch *and* a demon. That covers three of the supernatural angles all at once."

"Yes. It cannot be killed, only bound and banished, as I feared."

"Yeah," I said. "That part we got. Thank you, Aggie One Feather. I'll call later." I thumbed off the cell and went down into the basement, standing with Rick in the corner. Kemnebi, in human form, studied the demon from across the room, paying particular attention to the sole surviving werewolf. Lincoln Shaddock had disappeared earlier and reappeared now in a burst of vamp speed and displaced air. He looked pinker and more spry, clearly having fed well. I didn't ask who he snacked on. He brought Pickersgill with him, the vamp placed in a comfy chair upstairs to guard Evangelina while we worked.

The basement room had been rearranged. All the paintings had been removed from the walls and stacked in the other room. There were a lot of us, five witches, a were-cat and a were-cat in training, a vamp, and a skinwalker. In the witch's circle were a sleeping, spelled werewolf and parts of a dead werewolf. And the demon, of course. The guest of honor.

There were talismans at each place of the pentagram: Molly had a holly branch that was still green. She must have spent some time foraging down the street, because nothing alive was left in Evangelina's garden. Big Evan had a flute carved of pale wood. Cia had a huge moonstone, something a museum might display, bigger than two fists held together, like an oval crystal ball, its surface catching the light in rainbow hues. The toddler was wide awake, strapped into his car seat, kicking and saying disconnected words about bananas. Molly seemed to understand what he said, but most of it was gibberish to me. He had a feather and a holly leaf tucked under one of the straps. Dad was an air sorcerer, and Mama was an earth witch, so they were logical choices.

Angelina had a pile of stuff: a black rock, a withered leaf, a piece of bark, a wilting daisy, a silver earring, a hawk wing feather, and a doll. It was *Ka Nvsita*, a Cherokee doll I had given her. It had been in Molly's van. Nothing in the pile made sense, especially the doll. All witches have an affinity to magical energy in one area or another: moon, earth, water, stone, air, sometimes to fire. Some witches can use other energies, but they all have one area of particular strength. Angie Baby had metal, stone, the daisy for earth, two dead things, the feather, and a man-made doll. I looked at Molly, who was watching me. When she saw my puzzlement, she lifted a shoulder and went back to her conversation. Molly wasn't worried. Angie was a witch whiz kid; kids weren't supposed to have magic until puberty. No one knew what was about to happen with Angie's gift.

The demon—the Raven Mocker—was standing as far away from the stairs as possible, hissing, looking more real and solid than ever. And more like an anzu than I expected—bigger, blacker, more wicked, but similar. Maybe all supernats had their good and evil forms, the polar opposites of each other, like skinwalkers and liver-eaters, witches of the light and blood-witches, civilized vamps and rogue vamps. One group that helped humans, one that thought they were tasty when grilled with onions. Or raw.

I slid away from them, to the floor in the corner, my back to the wall. This wasn't my gig, and there was nothing I could do to help except give blood, but, like Rick, I wasn't gonna miss it. He joined me on the floor, his thigh against mine. His eyes widened when he felt the knife belted there. I let my smile grow. "Better safe than sorry."

He grinned back. "I got thirty-eight silver reasons to agree." Meaning that he had a .38 handgun loaded with silver strapped to his ankle or in a boot sheath. We made a good team.

We stayed out of the way while the witches discussed the ways and language they would use to call the angel and planned out the working they would use to bind the demon. The Raven Mocker got more agitated, emitting whistles and chirps and setting the red motes in the *hedge of thorns* flashing. Almost as if they reacted to his tension. Almost as if they were alive.

Outside, the moon rose, and Beast rose with it, flooding me with the urge to hunt, to mate, to roam the dark, free and powerful. To feel the air in our pelt, scenting and tasting and hearing the life of the world. Kem looked at me, sharing the moon-call, Rick was feeling it too, his heart rate a little fast, his sweat smelling of excitement. The reddish wolf in the circle felt it the most—panting in his sleep, paws running.

Big Evan came to me, holding a cut-crystal bowl and an athame, a ceremonial knife. I held out my hand and with no warning, he grabbed my thumb and stabbed downward. I couldn't help my hissing indrawn breath. My blood welled, scarlet. Evan whispered the name, "Kalona Ayeliski."

The witches all sat. The Raven Mocker screamed.

CHAPTER TWENTY-SEVEN

Threw Her Over the Railing

I jumped in my spot against the wall. Rick laughed under his breath. "Not funny," I muttered. Big Evan glared at me. "If you can't be quiet, we'll ask you to leave. We have enough problems with the baby talk and the demon shrieking."

"Sorry," I mumbled. Rick's chest moved fast, quivering, as if he were suppressing silent laughter. I wanted to punch him, but I figured that would get me expelled from the room.

"We gather," Evan said. My humor disappeared as if blown away by a hurricane. It was similar to the words uttered by vamps when they *gather* for some important event. The witches started talking in a foreign language, in unison, like recitation. Irish Gaelic, I thought, the language Molly and her sisters use when they do a major group working. It was a beautiful and barbaric language, flowing like a stream down a narrow cleft, full of tshhhushhs, and odd-sounding Fs, and long, sibilant Hs. I found myself leaning in, closer to the mesmeric sound.

There was no drum or flute, as there might have been in a Cherokee ceremony. There was nothing but the purity of the voices, Big Evan leading the phrases, the others repeating them. Evan Junior was silent, his mouth moving as if he wanted to join in, his pudgy hands gripping the straps of the car seat. I was reminded of the toddler climbing up into my lap at the café, demanding that I help his spelled family.

And then I heard the word Hayyel fall from Evan's mouth. And the others repeated it. "Hayyel. Hayyel. Hayyel . . ." Over and over again, the syllables falling like a drumbeat, or a heartbeat, rhythmical, musical, and lyrical, as if the flowing stream of their words bounced against boulders and fell in a long arc. My heartbeat found the rhythm of the words of the angel's name, and, silently, I joined in the calling, for it was a *calling*, a repeated prayer. "Hayyel. Hayyel. Hayyel . . ."

Evan leaned forward and took the flute in his hands. The others each took up their talismans, and held them, even the toddler, who was holding both the holly leaf and the feather, one in each fist, his arms pumping up and down in excitement. Molly picked up the bowl of blood, mine and Angie's mixed. Angie Baby's eyes were wide, her lips parted, face flushed. "Hayyel. Hayyel. Hayyel . . ." they all said. She was holding the doll, the other things forgotten. And . . . *The doll's eyes were glowing.* I shrank back against the wall. The doll's eyes were glowing golden, like mine when Beast is rising up in me. There was no way that the black glass eyes could— But this was magic. *Magic*, ancient and foreign . . .

Inside the *hedge of thorns*, the werewolf woke up, eyes wide and mouth open in horror. I was vaguely aware of Lincoln Shaddock as he left the room, moving fast, the air of his passing like a faint, dry wind. "Hayyel. Hayyel. Hayyel . . ."

As the others repeated the chant of the angel's name, and Evan played a haunting melody on his flute, Molly added words to the chant, like a descant sung in soft minor notes, "Kalona Ayeliski. Kalona Ayeliski."

The Raven Mocker stood in the center of his cage and screamed.

A flash of light hit the *hedge of thorns* like lightning, pure and brighter than the sun. I shrank back, covering my eyes with both forearms. The images burned through my arms, my bones, my lids, into my eyes, into my brain, into my soul. I saw a winged being attacking the demon. Light and darkness. The light of an exploding atom bomb, the light of the sun's core, the light of the center of the universe. And the darkness of a black hole, empty beyond all understanding, full of nothingness. The sound of bells, high winds, roaring waves. Echoes and echoes of a perfect, pure note sung for eternity. Screams of agony. Trapped for a long moment together, in combat.

In the glare, Molly stood and dipped her fingers into the blood in the crystal bowl and flung the mixture over the *hedge*. Above it all, I heard Molly start the binding words, "Hayyel, *bíodh sé daor, le m'ordú agus le*—" The light went out. The burn on my retinas leaving me blind. After a stutter, Molly finished the binding. "*Mo chumhacht*, Kalona Ayeliski."

But the light had disappeared. The fighting angel and demon were both gone. Just . . . gone. The dead body was gone. *Hedge of thorns* was gone. The blood was gone. The salt composing the circle was gone. The black paint on the floor was gone, leaving a circle of concrete, seared pure white. And silence. No one moved except to blink against the retinal burn.

A werewolf lay on the floor in wolf form, asleep or dead; not the wolf he had been, not reddish brown and wild, but a huge, pure white wolf, with only a hint of gray in his ruff. Kem was on the far side of the room, in cat form, blacker than night, none of his spots visible after the blast of light. Rick was holding my hand in his, crushed against me in the corner, his eyes unfocused and wide. He smelled of cat, wild and musky. If he knew how to shift, he'd be a black leopard right now, only his tats holding him to human form. Everyone two-natured was affected. Except me. I just felt curiously . . . empty. I reached for Beast . . . *Beast?*

Upstairs, a door slammed. *A door?* Dazed, I shook my head to clear it. "Crap," I said. I shoved away from the wall and raced up the stairs, stumbling over Evil Evie's skirt, blinking away the afterimage of holiness and evil.

In the living room, Pickersgill was skewered to the floor with a stake in his belly, bleeding like a stuck pig. Evangelina was no longer asleep on the floor. And Lincoln, who had torn out of the basement, was missing as well.

An engine raced. The sports car fishtailed out of the

drive. I landed on my knees and shoved the couch over to get my bike key and go after her. It landed with a heavy thump. There was nothing underneath the couch. My travel tote, torn jeans, and the pink blood-magic-diamond were all gone. I raced outside, but the night breeze off the French Broad River was already carrying the scent of her car away. I went back inside, standing in the corner, staring at the chaos.

Pickersgill was bleeding out, the witches were falling all over themselves, panicked, and Angie Baby was crying. Pickersgill, hissed between his fangs, furious and scared, "My own master staked me!"

"Yeah, but he staked you to keep you alive or he'd have aimed higher and to the left," I said. I bent at his side, one knee on the floor. "I'll pull out the stake. Try to bite me and I won't be so nice." I pulled the stake from his gut and he disappeared to feed. I figured he'd live, if the undead can be said to live. Wiping Pickersgill's blood from my fingers onto the rug, I took Angie in my arms and stood in the corner, hugging her to my chest, her legs wrapped around my waist. The reek of vamp blood and magic polluted the air.

Evangelina had the diamond. And Beast—*Beast?* The word echoed through me.

Big Evan asked, "Did the banishing work? Did we bind the Raven Mocker?"

"I don't think so," Molly said. "I think Evangelina disrupted the spell." Which was her right as coven master. Then she ran away. With the diamond.

I wasn't thinking right. Not thinking clearly. Not thinking much at all. Because the disrupted spell and the appearance of the angel Hayyel had stolen my Beast. I was alone inside my own head. "Beast?" I whispered. I rocked Angie, holding her close.

The weres left together, Rick, silent and acting like a twitchy cat, driving fast. Having a first encounter of the third kind with an angel had to be a major wakeup call for a lapsed, or at least lackadaisical, good Catholic boy. The white wolf and Kem, stuck in black leopard form, were both sleeping in the bed of the truck, in cages borrowed from Evangelina's back room. I didn't know what would happen to the wolf. I wasn't even sure what the wolf was now.

Cia drove off in her car, leaving her sister's car in the drive. She mumbled something about needing to see Liz and Carmen in the hospital. Big Evan packed his family into the van with unseemly haste and drove off as if demons were nipping at his heels, leaving his rattletrap in the drive. None of us talked. We didn't even make eye contact. I don't think we could.

Fortunately I had a spare key hidden in the bike. I was halfway home when my tears started. *Beast?* The place inside me where she stayed was empty. And cold. And silent. I didn't know what to do. I had no idea. It was only as I neared the Asheville city limits that I realized how badly I had messed up. Not only was Evangelina on the loose with a diamond capable of almost anything, there was a demon unaccounted for. And Lincoln Shaddock had disappeared. Had Evangelina called him to her? *Crap.* I had lost one of my primary subjects.

I went to the hotel for my cell phones, to strap on some weapons—including the M4—and to change out of Evangelina's stupid impossible-to-ride-a-Harley skirt. I didn't speak to anyone, and I didn't stop to check on my vamp charge and his blood-servants. I was in and out as fast and unobtrusively as possible, a velvet jacket over one shoulder. *Beast was gone.*

Fang and I tooled around the city of Asheville, halfway looking for a red sports car, mostly hiding from other people. I was afraid to be alone with my thoughts, using Fang's roar to block out the part of me that was screaming in fear. *Beast was gone.* My mind was my own for the first time in over a hundred years. And it was scaring the crap outta me. I rode, not thinking, searching for something to muffle the sound of my own fear, and to stop the afterimage flashing onto the back of my lids each time I blinked. An angel and a demon. In combat.

Had I seen an angel and a demon fighting? Or had it been a mass hallucination, something artificial shared by the mismatched group? Or maybe a spell crafted by Evangelina and lying in wait for the right moment. No. Too many variables in any scenario except the real one. I had seen an angel. A freaking, dang *angel*.

My angel, who came when my friends called him, to take away an evil who was never supposed to be on earth. Ever. *My angel*, shared with Angie Baby, who could see angels, but never said so, who thought everyone could see them. Hayyel. The angel stole my Beast.

Fear rode me, sucking on my soul like a tick burrowed into my skin.

Molly hadn't talked to me after. Molly hadn't talked to anyone. Her daughter had a personal relationship with an angel and her sister had one with a demon. Her life had totally changed. Again. At least this time it wasn't my fault. Except for Evangelina getting her grubby witchy hands on the pink blood-diamond again. That was my fault, totally.

Stupid to hide it under the couch, with only a vamp as guard. Only a vamp. Pickersgill would have been enough to guard the witch. But not against his master. *Stupid, freaking stupid.* I fisted my hands on the handlebar and bent into the speed. *Beast?* She didn't answer.

I stopped for gas at three a.m. and checked my cell. I had missed an e-mail from Reach. He had sent pictures of Shaddock's escaped vamp. I remembered Thomas Stevenson from the scion lair. He stood five feet ten, brown hair and eyes, with a nose that had been broken and was flattened across the bridge—a deformity that hadn't been fixed by his maker pre-turn. Corrective surgery was something many makers did for any less-than-perfect scions before they turned them. But Thomas' broken, unenhanced nose was my good fortune—something that would make the otherwise ordinary man stand out in a police lineup.

I sent the photos from my expensive, traceable cell to my laptop back at the hotel, and accessed all the files Reach had sent me on Thomas Stevenson. Getting into them on the small screen wasn't the easiest thing in the world, but it was handy. Miracles of modern tech.

The guy had money all over the place, from offshore accounts to banks down the street. He had accumulated a lot of real properties, both private and commercial. Several cars were in storage, homes in gaited communities. Rental property. Strip malls. Undeveloped property. His estate was scattered all over North Carolina and Tennessee. One thing stood out. The nasty vamp had a collector's appreciation of houseboats. He had three houseboats in storage or in dock at different lakes within a couple hundred miles, the farthest on Douglas Lake in Tennessee. I might be willing to bet that, after spending the last few years sane and locked up with crazy-assed rogues, fed cooling pig blood running in a trough, he might like waking up at sunset on the water, maybe with a well-drained corpse or two on the floor beside him.

But that was just a guess. I'd be searching through the properties for decades to find the guy. Except for the last little text Reach sent, a text that proved he was worth every one of the thousands of dollars he was charging Leo. Thomas had accessed a credit card. The rogue-vamp had removed a car from storage, hit an ATM for cash, bought gas, then clothes, and each purchase had been in a linear direction, due west. The Naturaleza, human-draining, needs-a-good-staking vamp was heading into Tennessee.

My heart got lighter and my smile meaner. So, I'd hunt me some Naturaleza vamp butt and burn off the anger flaring deep inside, a char of hot rage I couldn't name and didn't want to look at too closely. And maybe the rage, and killing something, would chase away the fear that Beast wasn't coming back. Ever.

A small voice whispered that my protective fighting leathers were in storage and I was short on silvered blades and stakes, but I didn't care. I had guns and a mind to shoot something. I gassed up, removed the silver tipped stakes from my minuscule saddlebags, and sent Reach a text to keep an eye on Evangelina Everhart Stone's finances for withdrawals or credit card usage. Satisfied, I turned Fang's key. With the bike's roar, I headed west on I-40, into Tennessee.

Long before dawn, I had spent a lot of cash as bribes. A fifty to a clerk at a storage facility Thomas Stevenson owned, to get the kid to call if he spotted anyone matching the vamp's description. I had left another fifty with the night guard of a gaited community where Thomas had a small, elegant home. And two more fifties with others who might reasonably be in a position to notice if a hungry vamp came by. I also paid off the security guard at a marina on Lake Junaluska, and had just put three bullet holes into the hull of the fancy party boat/houseboat Thomas owned. I could have used the M4 strapped to my back, but the shotgun was far more noisy than the .380 semiautomatic handgun. Beast was still a no-show, and killing the fancy boat was intensely satisfying, I was watching it sink in five feet of water when my cell chirped. It was Reach.

"I'm not paying for this call," I said.

"Consider it gratis. Part of belonging to the human race, doing my good deed of the day." When I snorted, he laughed. "Right. I was checking police reports and got a notice of a man killed in what looks like a vampire draining not too far off of I-40."

"Where specifically?"

"Just outside the national park campground on Cataloochee Creek." He gave me the address of the campground and sent me a map of the place, not that I really needed it. There was only one way in to the valley, and unless they had paved it, that meant a narrow, winding, gravel road with steep drop offs and no guard rails, not the sort of place I wanted to ride a partially chopped bike in the middle of the night.

"Since you're being so helpful," I said, "why don't you compare the files of properties the vamp owns to the roads around the creek and campground."

"Help comes with a price," Reach said instantly. Without waiting for me to respond, he went on, "Stevenson once owned stock in Blue Ridge Paper Products. His great-grandfather, grandfather, and father owned land in the Cataloochee Valley. And yes, he still has the old farm near the creek."

Bingo, I thought, hearing keys click.

"Your pleasure is my profit. I'm checking on upgrades to the property's security system, sending GPS, and Google pics of the address. Okay, yeah. The security system is pretty standard, but it's gonna be a bitch getting in via the drive.

He concentrated his external security there. Cameras and motion detectors."

I looked over the pics as he talked. "How about security on the creek side?"

"Minimal. You swimming in?"

"Something like that. If we can prove that he's—"

"You're in luck. The system just went inactive and was reactivated. He's gone to ground at pappy's place. And while I'm being helpful, a call just went out to the local law that a man was seen shooting a pistol into a houseboat on Lake Junaluska." The connection ended.

"Funny guy." I closed the phone, pulled the silly velvet jacket on against the chill, and fired up Fang. I can't kill vamps if I'm in jail for malicious mischief or felony vandalism. If there is such a charge. I wasn't in a mood to find out.

When I was safely away from the houseboat I'd killed, I stopped Fang, and speed-dialed my pals, the paddlers. Neither answered, but I left a message for each. "I'm going after a vamp. I need transportation down Cataloochee Creek at dawn. If you can meet me at the river before sunrise, call. I'll need to hit land here." I gave the GPS of the destination— Thomas' place.

I figured that Thomas hadn't picked his first night of freedom and daytime lair by a coin toss. Cataloochee Creek was home, an emotional attachment to the human world, as much as any place would be home to a vamp so far gone in bloodlust that he believed humans were nothing but dinner.

Before dawn, I turned off I-40 on to the road—loosely defined—and started down into the Cataloochee Valley. The roadbed was worse than I remembered, maybe because it was so dark, I was running on no sleep, two shape-changes, and hadn't taken in enough calories to fuel the shifts. I had finished off most of the leftovers in Evangelina's fridge, but after the spell in the basement, I hadn't thought to eat, which was weird, for me. Now, I was hungry and worried; Beast was still nowhere in my mind. She didn't appear, not even when I concentrated on the herd of elk in the park. She hadn't thought anything snarky at

me, or even milked my conscious mind with her claws since
the bright light and disrupted spell in the *hedge of thorns*.
Nothing. Nada. If she were still alive inside me, wouldn't
she make *some* kind of comment?

Cataloochee Creek's boat access in the national campground provided easy access to the waterway. I parked and
wandered through the dark, trying to imagine the land
back when it was farmland, rich crops on the valley floor, or
timberland, all the trees gone, the earth laid bare, back
when it was family land, more isolated in some ways, less
isolated in others. Beast had lived in these mountains back
then, but she still wasn't offering anything interesting, no
insights, no memories, no thoughts, not even when I heard
an owl hoot, lost and lonely in the distance.

I got back two affirmative texts from the paddlers.
They were on their way. Dave asked if I had proper
clothes. I was wearing more than undies, so I wrote back,
"Yes," but had a feeling I was missing something. Waiting
for dawn, I took shelter under a covered communal picnic
area. And it started to rain, tiny drops, stinging and sharp
as ice picks. In seconds it was a deluge. *Great. Just freaking
great.*

Trying to stay dry, I checked the security schematic of
Stevenson's house. Ran through some possible scenarios.
Zipped up my jacket against the chill. I accessed the Naturaleza's personal history to discover that the man held a
black belt in karate, aikido, and kendo, which meant that if
he had access to swords or long-blades, things could get
dicey. Good thing I was planning to shoot him before I got
close.

Mike arrived at the park first, cutting his engine and
coasting the final distance to park. Quiet hours were adver-
tised, which I had busted to heck and gone with Fang. When
he spotted me in the dark, he pulled a two man raft from
his truck and turned on an air compressor, inflating the raft
in minutes. Mike was wearing a wetsuit with a dry-top over
it and looked cozy. Even with my enhanced skinwalker metabolism, I was shivering. I figured that denim and velvet
weren't the "proper clothes" Dave had meant. And my
wet-weather-riding gear was in storage in the same place as
my fighting leathers. Dang it.

Dawn was still a glint in Mother Nature's eye when Dave arrived, coasting down as Mike had done. At least they had good camping manners. He grinned and shook his head when he saw my bedraggled state, tossed me a poncho, which I pulled over my head. He hefted his hard boat and an armload of gear and carried it to the creek bank. He and Mike discussed the water flow—which was rising fast in the rain—the rapids and flat-water sections, and moments later, I was being instructed on raft safety. "And don't poke a hole in the raft with the knives or the shotgun," Mike said, tossing me a flotation vest. I figured the vest might come in handy if I went over while wearing so much steel. I had never weighed my gear, but swimming with it all would be hard. Or impossible.

"Or the pointy boots," Dave added, with a sly smile. I looked down at my Luccheses.

"Damn, girl." Mike boomed in his version of a murmur. "You go over and those boots'll fill up and weigh you down till you drown. What're you planning to do, paddle or ride a bull?"

"Both," I said, thinking about the danger of going up against a vamp on his home turf.

Dave skirted up and slid into his small boat, secured himself into the craft and pushed off into the current, nimble as a duck. In contrast, I crawled into Mike's raft like a landlubber, sitting on the bolster and inflated side wall as instructed, tucked my five-inch-toed boots into the crack as ordered, and took a beginner's class in paddling as we drifted downstream in the dark.

"I'll scout," Dave said over the roar of rain. Both men looked tense, as if this little trip was dangerous or difficult. And maybe it was in the dark. In the flood. And sudden wind.

This gig wasn't looking so promising now, and I almost said to beach the boats and hike back. But my cell vibrated in my pocket with a text from Reach, I read, trying to protect the delicate electronics. "Couple missing from karaoke bar. Car in lot. LEOs found blood. Waiting for security footage." LEOs were law enforcement officers. The bar was just off the highway that Thomas Stevenson would have taken to get to his homeplace.

We took the first rapid, the boat tilted, and I slid my body into the raft bottom. "That's nothing, girl. We got big water ahead." I nodded to show I'd heard, but before I could speak, the heavens opened up, proving that the previous hard rain was nothing. Rain pounded down, on the raft, the men, raising a mist on the creek, overriding the sound of rapids. The M4 and blades made sitting impossible, and I half kneeled, hanging on to the ropes at the sidewalls. I held on for dear life as the water whipped and whirled and dunked the raft, and I got more soaked than if I'd actually swam to the site, and I tried to breathe without getting rain and river into my lungs. Twice I called out to Beast, but still she didn't answer.

As indicated by the GPS data, the address of Thomas' family farm was hard river right, up a hill, about a hundred yards from the creek, invisible in the storm. "There's nothing there," Mike called over the white-noise of drumming rain on land and on river. But I could smell vamp and human blood.

"It's there," I shouted back. "Let me out." With a gesture that sent the raft whirling and swirling to scrape on shore, the river guide beached the small craft. The smell of blood was carried on the chilled breeze, diluted by the pounding downpour. I crawled out of the small raft, my boots full of water, my jeans wet, my body filled with a fine tremor from adrenaline and the cold. I pulled off the poncho and tossed it into the boat bottom.

"Get to the other side of the river. Wait for me where you can see this bank. If I'm not back in hour, get out of here. It means I'm dead. If anyone else comes to shore, or if anyone comes back to shore with me, peel out and get downstream fast." I handed him my cell. "Even if I call out for help. Even if I'm bleeding. Don't come back here unless I'm alone and moving under my own power. If I don't come back, hit SEND to call Leo Pellissier's right-hand man, George Dumas. Tell him what happened. He'll handle it. Got it?"

Mike boomed out, "Paddlers don't leave people behind."

"If I'm not alone, it'll mean I failed and he rolled me. If the vamp is still alive, rolls me, or kills me, it becomes Leo's problem to take him out." I wasn't trusting Lincoln Shaddock for anything, even if I knew where to find him. Leo would have to figure it out.

Dave nodded and made a little skirling motion with his paddle, maneuvering his tiny boat back into the current, nimble as a duck. Mike sealed my cell into his waterproof dry-box and rotated his raft back into the current. I waited until both men had their boats secured on the far shore before melting into the trees, walking hunched over, making myself deer-sized, trusting in the ten-year-old security system to mistake me for the local fauna. Beast was still silent, but I have my own memories of the stop-and-go motion of deer, the slow stroll punctuated by quick dashes, to stop suddenly, unmoving.

Dawn, delayed by the heavy clouds, gave me just enough light to see my way, the trees and underbrush providing cover even as they dumped rain down my collar, my clothes hanging wet and heavy, the silver and titanium necklace icy on my skin. As I moved, I went over what I knew and what I could infer about the vamp I was here to take out, weighing my strengths against his, trying to stay mentally and physically loose and ready. Trying not to think about the empty place in my soul. *Beast?* She didn't answer.

According to Reach, the perimeter of the house itself had decent security: cameras, motion detectors, and laser lights queued into a wailing alarm. But old motion detectors might be fooled, especially with the movement of rain and wind. Branches were swaying, rain was falling so hard it obscured my footsteps, even to my own keen ears, and filled my faint tracks with water.

Vamps aren't dead to the world by sunlight. They had a hard time staying awake once the sun came up, especially the young ones, like a kid trying to stay up past bedtime and being pulled under by the lure of dreams, but unless injured they seldom fell over in an undead snooze.

Once I breached the house, any advantage gained by the water access would be lost. I had speed, unexpected attack, silver bullets, and silvered blades. And while Thomas was a soldier and a black belt in several kinds of martial arts, he hadn't practiced since he was turned. Another thing in my favor—Thomas Stevenson was no vamp master. There would be no master's speed, no master's mind tricks honed over decades or centuries of hunting and mesmerizing prey. He was a young vamp with a god-complex and no vamp-experience. But he was also a vamp and Beast was absent, which was putting me severely off balance.

Once I was at the house, I could only hope that surprise, my own down-and-dirty brand of fighting, the blades, stakes, guns, and daylight filtering through the trees would be enough.

The house came into view, sitting on a bluff high above the creek, high enough to be safe from even the worst flood-stage rains, an early 1900s post-and-beam farmhouse, built around the original log cabin, updated in the late nineties with a state-of-the-art metal roof, vinyl siding, new windows. The grounds still showed the signs of a landscaper's hand in the placement of trees and shrubs, but likely hadn't been touched since Thomas was chained in the basement to cure. The area around the house was overgrown with knee-high grass, weeds, oversized trees in need of pruning, all moving with wind and rain, which would stress the security system. It would chirp, moan, buzz, and whine through the storm, and there was a chance that, like any homeowner, he would simply turn the system off. I could hope.

I made my way up the small hillock and moved slowly around the house, studying the windows and doors, all heavily draped or solid wood. They were under a twelve-foot-wide covered porch that circled the house, a porch made of old wood that would likely squeak when I put my weight on it. It wasn't a fortress, but it was well built. The doors looked securely set into the frame, like the portcullis in a castle wall.

A car was parked in back, a 1987 Cadillac Allanté convertible, top up. I could hear the engine ping from the woods. I could also smell blood and see two lumps in the backseat. I dropped to my elbows and knees in the wet grass, crawling to the car as river and rainwater drained from my boots. Half-hidden from the house by the car, I squatted and duckwalked close. Raised up and looked inside.

Two people—or what was left of them—were sprawled there, heads together as if posed, a man and a woman, both in their twenties, mostly naked, missing throats, covered in blood that looked black in the poor light. The rain let up as I stared, growing softer and fainter. Water trickled down my face. My arms. My spine and thighs. My hair was plastered to me, my velvet jacket sodden and heavy as lead. Their wrists were gouged and slashed as were their inner elbows. The girl's femoral arteries and veins had been worked over. She had a barrette in her hair and a small tattoo of a blue butterfly on her hip. I felt oddly light-headed, and forced in a breath. Smelled semen. Thomas Stevenson was not squeamish about feeding and raping at the same spot.

I wanted him dead. Something at the core of me went hard and dark and cold. I breathed shallowly, fighting to control my anger. I dropped back to the earth, the faces of the couple the last thing I saw inside the car. The scene was made worse by the fact that they were smiling, as if they had died happy. Silent, I crawled back to the cover of trees and made my way to the front of the house. I was taking this guy out. From inside, I heard a soft sound. A whimper. The sound a young girl might make after her first kiss. Or a woman might make as she died. Rage thumped a gout of adrenaline into my bloodstream. *Beast!* I thought. *Talk to me.* My mind was silent, empty, as if her soul had never been part of me. But with the adrenaline spike, I was feeling strength and speed, keener hearing and sight, all Beast-traits that had become part of my own body. That was at least something.

Drawing on that strength and speed, I pried a rock out of the ground—bigger than a football, smaller than a Smart Car—and hefted it, testing its weight and balance, a pitted oval of forty pounds or so. My best bet for getting inside fast was the large window in the front room. I pulled the M4, tucking it under my arm, a finger in the trigger guard. I drew in a long slow breath. Let it out. Drew in another.

Beast? She didn't answer. I bent low, still imitating a deer, and sidled up to the house, feeling exposed out from under the trees. My breath was too fast, my heart raced. The smell of human blood grew stronger as I got closer. The moaning grew more frenzied.

When I was at the edge of the porch, I stood upright, tossed the rock gently into the air, still testing, like a player with a basketball at the foul line. On its third bound, I dropped my elbow and swiveled my body. I launched the ball, half Olympic shot put, half NBA. It flew through the gentle rain. Time slowed so that the rock seemed to float. The M4 was wet and cold in my palms. My vision narrowed, growing sharper. The toe of my boot landed on the porch as I launched myself after the rock.

It impacted the window. Shattered glass exploded inward, flying shards dirty in the morning light. The rock disappeared inside, bulging the drapery. Pulling it from the rod in a puff of blues and greens and dust. Into the darkened room. Dim daylight filled the room. The stench of blood and semen billowed out in a soft, stinking poof.

I rammed the stock of the M4 forward, smashing the window at top, bottom, and to both sides, clearing the glass still hanging or standing in the frame. It fell, prolonging the crash. The element of surprise was gone. I leaped through the opening. From Reach's files, the floor plan of the house was crystalline in my mind. The kitchen was to the left, living room to the right of the door, hallway straight through, dogtrot style. Thomas hadn't expected to be turned. He hadn't planned to be a vamp, so there was no lair here, buried underground. He would be in the master bedroom, top floor, windows heavily swathed. I landed in the dim room, balanced and ready, spinning the shotgun forward, bracing it against my side. Pulled a vamp-killer left-handed, blade back for close-in fighting, the elk horn comforting in my grip. And I thundered up the stairs.

At the top, on the landing, Thomas Stevenson appeared, burning with pink light, red and black motes zinging all over him. Somehow, he'd been spelled by Evangelina. Or maybe the vamp who had set him free had passed him an amulet. He was vamped out, inch-long fangs pale in the dusky light. One hand was down, out of sight, a girl in the crook of his other arm, supported by the railing. Blond hair hung around her face, over her shoulders. Tiny breasts. She was naked. Blood trailed from her groin. She was no more than fifteen. She took a breath. Thomas threw her over the railing.

CHAPTER TWENTY-EIGHT

I Was So Going to Hell

In an instant, I saw how she would land. Table and chairs, two wingback chairs facing the couch. She would miss them all unless—

I leapt. Springing back down, over the railing. Pushing off with all the strength in my thighs and back. Torquing my body. An impossible angle. I dropped the blade. It spun away. I caught the girl around the waist. Pulled her against me. Into my spiral. I fell toward the couch, twisting in mid-air. I fired the M4 where Thomas had stood, into the ceiling above. It exploded. The recoil slammed my shoulder. I hit the couch. The girl's body landed on mine. My breath whoofed out.

Elbow as fulcrum, I pushed her to the floor. Gun barrel leading. Finger on trigger. To my feet. Thomas was in front of me. Pupils blacker than the doorway to hell, open in bloodred sclera. Fangs out. A short sword in each hand.

He cut forward with both, a scissoring motion. I fired the shotgun again. Point blank range. I could have sworn I saw the silver fléchettes fly. I whipped up with the barrel, into the path of one sword. Threw my body after it. Felt the other blade slice into my side, even as I twisted out of its way. The blade followed my motion, the cut from side to belly, upward, away. I drew another vamp-killer as I fell, this one a long slender blade. Throwing as it left the sheath.

It hit him at an odd angle, lower left side, above the hip.

Missing anything internal that might kill him quickly. I wouldn't survive until silver poisoning did its work. Thomas gripped and yanked the blade out. Tossed it to the side. He had a hole in his belly from the shotgun, big enough for my fist. It was pouring blood, filled with the swarming red and black motes of the spell. The lower hole, where the knife had been, bled too, his blood saturated with the pink spell. His skin was scorching from the dim light, but he was so full of blood he was fighting off both the burn and silver poisoning. Only then did I realize he was naked. And aroused. Vamped out, fully.

I landed on the floor. Sprawled. A leg bent under me. With a sword, he batted away the shotgun, the sound clanging, the blow reverberating up my arm. He leaned toward me, cutting at my clothes. Buttons popped and flew. Cold steel cut me, a paper cut of pain. Air hit my bare skin. With almost balletic grace, incongruous against his bestial expression, he set the swords aside. He moved my shirt away, exposing breasts, wound, and blood from his cut. I drew another vamp-killer as he fell forward. Lips back, exposing killing teeth. Fixated on blood. I braced the knife on my belt. Angled up. And he fell onto me. Onto the blade.

I felt it push through his stomach and up, into his aorta. Blood fountained over me. Hot and fast. As if his heart beat. His eyes changed. Looking puzzled. Confused. The pink haze of spell coalesced on his chest, at the point where the knife entered. Red motes swarmed in his blood, stinging my hand where his blood gushed over me.

I put an arm around his waist. Drew him closer, his face against the silver rings of my defensive collar. His flesh sizzled, scorching. I angled the blade higher. Shoved. He tried to roll away. I hooked a leg around his and let him push us over. Until I was on top. My favorite vamp-killer was beside his head. The one with the elk-horn handle. I didn't remember losing it. I took it in my left hand and cut into his throat. Severing windpipe, veins, arteries, tendons. I had never seen so much blood spray from a dying vamp, blood drenched in the pink light of the blood-diamond spell. It was a fountain, blinding me even as he tried to heal from the wound. The Naturaleza had fed fully and the power that much blood gave him was unexpected, startling.

I kept cutting. Sawing. Knowing that to kill a vamp and not have him rise as a revenant, I had to take his head. The pink spell whirred and whirled, an angry buzzing, stinging my skin.

At some point, his embrace relaxed. His arms fell away from me. His blood slowed to a trickle, the pink light hazing to a dull glow. But it still was not enough. I cut until there was only spine left, the bony protuberances and ragged tissue and blood. Blood everywhere. I wiped my face. Stood and found his swords. They were nicely balanced, the edges a gray, swirling steel. Using one, I swept down and through the spine in a single cut that I barely felt. I kicked the head away and stood over him. Hearing only my breathing, the soughing of the wind through the broken window, the softer breath of the girl he had been killing. The pink light of the spell died.

I looked around the crime scene—yeah, crime scene: dead bodies outside, dying girl—not sure what to do next. Confused. Hurt. I looked down at my bloody gaping wound. Hurt bad. I needed to shift. *Beast? Beast!* Nothing. A hollow, echoing emptiness. The girl moaned. I needed to call her an ambulance. I felt for my cell, but the paddlers had it. I needed a phone.

I walked to the kitchen, opened drawers until I found one with dishcloths. I wiped my face and pressed a handful to my side. Took several clean cloths to the moaning girl, pressing them into her wounds, which were less deep than I had thought.

I rolled her until her own body would keep the cloths in place and covered her with a blanket from the couch. Unlike the drapes, it wasn't dusty, and as I stood, looking around the room, I could tell it had been cleaned in the last few weeks. Weird, the things you notice when you were nearly killed while killing and beheading a vampire, and now were trying to make logical decisions while bleeding to death.

I spotted a phone on a small table. It was an old one, but did at least have push buttons and not one of the weird rotors telephones used to have. I picked up the receiver and leaned against the wall, weaker than I should be. I almost dialed 911, but couldn't remember where I was. Did they need to know? Could they figure it out?

The room swirled about me. I was light-headed, dizzy. Shock spread through me, paralyzing. My hands felt cold, and the pain from my side cut deep, filling me like water fills a lake bed.

Surprised that I remembered it, I dialed Bruiser's private number. Bruiser answered with a curt, "George Dumas," sounding all British and uppity and snobby. "Hiya, Bruiser," I whispered. "I just killed Thomas Stevenson, and . . . I think I'm dying."

"Jane?" He sounded unsure, maybe just the unfamiliar number on his caller ID.

"Yeah. And there are two drained bodies in a car in the yard and a girl who doesn't look too good on the living room floor." I looked down. "I'm not doing so good myself." I was bleeding. Pretty badly. Really badly. I pressed an arm to my side, the hand to my belly. Blood-soaked cloths squished under my hand. I slid down the wall to the floor. The phone slipped from my hand. "Oops." My vision telescoped down, into tiny pinpricks. I was pretty sure I was passing out. "Beast?" I called, the word a pained whisper of breath. And then nothing.

I woke up with Dave and Mike lifting me. Carrying me to the couch. I was only half awake as they cut away my clothes, made makeshift pressure bandages out of kitchen rags, and attached them to me with duct tape. That was gonna hurt when it came off. They covered me with blankets that smelled of vamp and sex and blood, and disappeared from view. I knew they were working on stabilizing the girl. I could hear her breathing. Pain thrummed out through my skin with my heartbeat, too fast. My breath was shallow and rapid, like a dog panting.

Mike said, "I'll go pick out a landing spot for the chopper." He disappeared from view. Dave nodded and tucked the blankets tighter around me. Lifted my legs and shoved pillows beneath my knees. *Treatment for shock,* I thought. It had been a while since my emergency medicine course, but some things you don't forget. I looked up at Dave, tried to talk. Had to moisten my lips. "You were supposed to go on down the creek." It came out a whisper.

Dave's blue eyes held humor and worry. "Your boss made an offer we couldn't refuse."

"Yeah. He's good at that. I always turn him down, though."

Dave chuckled breathily. "I have a feeling he makes you different kinds of offers. Ours was to come up here and get you stabilized. He's sending a helicopter for you and an ambulance for the girl."

"How much?" I meant how much to help me.

"A thousand each. On top of what you're paying us each to deliver you here. Not bad for a day's work, and I get to paddle too. It's all good." His tone was deliberately light-hearted, not that I believed it. Not a bit. I'd have laughed if I hadn't passed out again.

The next memories were fractured. Men in uniforms. Stretchers. A siren sounding outside. One of the twins, his head turned so I couldn't see his mole, pale-faced and stern. Mike squeezing my hand. A stranger inserting an IV with no regard for my pain. Me saying something not very nice about him. My phone ringing, Dave answered. Bruiser's voice in my ear, telling me to hold on. An argument between the B-twin and the stranger. Money exchanging hands. A lot of money. Rain on my face, outside. Mike and Dave disappearing into the trees, Dave with a lifted hand of good-bye. And more blackness.

I woke when they pulled me from the helo, seeing the hotel in the background. Later, I woke in my hotel bed. So cold. Shivering. The gas fire burning bright, flames whispering and hissing. Not alone. Grégoire over me, his blond hair hanging forward. His mouth on my stomach. His breath heated across my skin. Young boy face and old lover eyes, experienced, watching me as his tongue laved my flesh from navel to sternum. His hands roamed me, featherlight. Demanding. Claiming. Healing.

Heat like a drumbeat though my veins. The sound of my moans. The smell of my blood, of human blood and the sight of Brandon's face as his master fed from his neck. Blackness.

Waking to pleasure. Grégoire's tongue on me, sliding up my body. Slowly. The faint scrape of long canines, teasing. My hands reaching for him. The feel of his hair, like warm silk. The smell of his body like flowers and spring rain and desire. My need growing. Strength filling me. Tracing his face with my fingertips. Firelight reflected in wide, black pupils. The taste of him.

"Drink from me." Whispered words.

"No. I won't belong to you."

Blackness.

The sound of drums. Echoing through a cave. The feel of stone at my back, my pelt and spine pressed into it. The ledge high up, above the families below, around the curve of the cave wall, their fire glowing on the damp stone. *Tsaligi*, hiding from *yunega*. Hiding in Beast's cave. Out of sight of cave opening. Hiding from *yunega aniyowisgi*, white soldiers who would make them go west, as the others had gone west in the cold moons.

Tsaligi had not seen Beast. Four days and four nights the family had hidden here. Soon they would go back out, into the light, leaving Beast her den. Until then, Beast hunted only late at night. Returned to den, to hiding place, away from white men and guns and long-distance death. Away from *Tsaligi* and human kits. Closed eyes, listening to drums. Blackness.

I woke at dusk, warm, pain free, an arm across my waist, a head pillowed on my shoulder. I stiffened. My heartbeat raced. I felt his mouth curve into a smile. "*Mon* Amazon. George said you would be angry to find me here, in your bed. Please say that you are delighted instead." I moved my hand. I was naked. So was he. *Oh crap. Crap in a bucket. Crapcrapcrap!*

He sighed. I felt his breath exhale across my breasts. My *naked* breasts. He slid from the covers with that boneless grace the really old ones have. I pulled the covers over me. What had I done? I slid a hand down my stomach. Healed.

Around my waist. Healed. Panties? No. *Crap.* He stood over me, patient. I wasn't going to look to him. Couldn't look at him.

Minutes passed. He was still standing there. He was hundreds of years old; time was different for old vamps; he could stand like that for hours, waiting, and not get tired. Heart not beating, not breathing, unmoving as a stone angel in a graveyard. I blew out a breath. "What?"

"You are healed." There was just a hint of irritation in his voice. A hint of steel.

After a moment I said, "Thank you?"

"I did not drink from you. You are not my Enforcer. And . . . we did *not* make love." His words were carefully precise. Relief washed through me so hot I broke out into a sweat. "According to your provincial American standards," he added.

And with a little pop of displaced air, he was gone. *According to your provincial American standards?* What did that mean? I remembered his hands all over me. His tongue . . . I pulled the covers over my head and burrowed into the pillows. *Oh crap.* I was so going to hell.

And Beast was still absent. No snarky comment. No pad of paws across my mind, or prick of claw on my conscience or sly, sated happiness. Just a welling emptiness. But there had been the dream. I remembered the dream of the cave. *Beast?* She didn't answer.

After I checked in with Molly about the whereabouts of Evangelina—still unknown—and about the health of her injured sisters—improving quickly—and with Derek about the security status of everything else, I stayed in bed the rest of the day, regaining strength, ordering room service, the TV on in the corner—mindless game shows, mindless talk shows, trying to stay mindless, so I didn't have to remember that Beast was gone, or buried so deeply I couldn't feel her. So I didn't have to remember Grégoire and his talented mouth. Difficult to do, as his scent was in my sheets and my body was hypersensitive, every nerve twanging like a violin string. If Beast had been with me, she would have been purring. But she wasn't. The need for Beast and the memory of desire flickered through me with every heartbeat, every nerve ending sparking, so sensitive it was like riding a blade edge between pain and pleasure. To keep from calling Grégoire, I ordered room service—every meat and seafood dish on the menu and several they prepared just for me, and four pots of tea. Each delivery was brought up by a happy Hispanic guy whom I tipped really well. He was making a week's tips today as I regained my strength. Nearly dying when I couldn't shift to heal was debilitating.

At seven p.m., the sun setting late in the early fall, my cell rang. It was Rick. Guilt zinged through me like lightning. I opened the cell, "Rick."

"Help," a voice panted, groaning. *Rick. In pain.*

I swung my legs to the floor. "What's happened?" I heard a voice in the background and the sound of the cell hitting something. I started to call his name, but over the open airwaves I heard Kemnebi's voice, smug and satisfied. "The moon is full. It calls to your beast-nature."

Tonight? No wonder I'd been so . . . whatever I'd been with Grégoire. The full moon and sex went together for Beast like— *Beast . . . ?* She didn't answer.

"You will continue trying to shift but will not succeed. You will not survive. Not without my assistance." Rick screamed. The phone went dead.

Beast had been right, that Kemnebi would not honor his submission, that he was a human in cat skin. Kem-cat wanted Rick dead. He'd be in the woods somewhere. Lotta help that was.

I threw on clothes, taking care with hiking shoes, backpack, weapons. Someone had retrieved and cleaned my gear—had polished the blood out of and off of my guns and silvered blades. I dialed as I dressed. Bruiser answered, warmth in his voice. "Jane! How are—"

"Fine," I interrupted. "Three things. One, there won't be a parley tonight. Shaddock is on the run with the witch who spelled him, so Grégoire can take the night off. Again. Two, I need GPS positioning on the number I'm sending you, assuming it's in Big Creek National Park above the Pigeon River. Three, I need Leo to order Grégoire to send me there in the helicopter."

"One moment." I heard keys tapping and he said, "Yes, the call originated from that mountain. Sending you a topo map of the area. You'll be there in half an hour. Meet the helo at the hotel's pad. Parley is canceled, and all participants notified."

I clicked the cell shut and burst through the door into the common area just as Brandon answered his cell. "She wants to go *where*?" he said. Pushing the B-Twins to speed, talking as we raced to the helo pad, I dialed Derek and put him in charge of security for the night.

Brandon powered up Grégoire's helo. Over the engine's high-pitched whine, I was informed that Brian and he were both qualified pilots, and their master, Grégoire, loved to fly. A vamp with a death wish. Go figure. Even the undead had to be crazy to fly in a flimsy glass, air (and maybe a half pound of steel) contraption with no wings and no glide power. If it broke, it would fall like a rock. Beast had refused to ride in the helo. My heart clenched. She wasn't fighting me.

According to the B-Twins, chattering while they powered up and completed a checklist, the helo was a refurbished Vietnam Era Bell Huey. It had four permanent seats and gear for more, with heavy armament and black-out windows suitable for vampire travel. Like I cared. All I was interested in was its jet engine, functional weaponry slung under the carriage, and infrared tracker and laser-detection signalers. In case I had to track Kem and shoot him with a missile. The engine whine grew and I gritted my teeth, nodding where appropriate and finishing my texts.

At the last moment, a shrouded form leaped into the helicopter and slid the side door shut. The helo's whine went up in volume as I stared at the dark shape, my phone forgotten, one hand on a weapon. I sniffed. Vamp-scent. Grégoire. Dressed in vamp traveling clothes—layers of robes, tightly woven, gloves and boots and a full-face toboggan with black glass sewn into the eyeholes. I nodded to him. He nodded back regally, or as regally as a vamp can in that getup. He set a wicker picnic basket on the floor. I let go my vamp-killer and went back to work, texting requests to everyone on my list. I sent Derek a terse note that Grégoire was with me.

My meat-lovers buffet rose in my throat as we lurched into the sunset. The rain had stopped, the clouds were

breaking up, glowing golden in the western sky, but the un-
seasonable cold had come back, and the air was frigid. I was
shivering in the thin, damp air, but at least my boots were
on the correct feet and I had plenty of ammo, more than
half silvershot, just in case Kemnebi tried to kill Rick and I
had to kill Kem.

The helo angled into the sky. Beast, who hated the flying
machines, said nothing.

We got to the campground in less than half an hour and set
down onto a brand-new helo pad used to evacuate hikers,
campers, and idiot paddlers who tried to take the Upper
Big Creek in especially dangerous weather. Without waiting for permission, I leaped from the helo, ducked under
the whirring blades, and raced down the mountain. Water fell in big, slow drops from the leaves of tall trees and
landed with a heavy, icy punch that slammed through my
clothes. From somewhere down the mountain and behind
me, a dog howled, the frenzied sound fading as I ran. The
helo powered up and lifted off, taking a path right over me,
the thrum of blades like the fast heartbeat of a giant bird.
Off to do another favor for me—to hopefully bring me the
help I'd need to keep Rick alive.

My GPS led me down and down, off the path into thick
brush and dusky light. I could see nothing, and was forced
to slow my mad rush. If Kem was planning to kill me and
making it look like an accident, this was the perfect way. I
could plummet over a sheer drop-off and smash at the bottom. But ahead, a campfire glowed through the trees. I
raced for it, bursting from a laurel thicket into an open
space, to find Rick lying in front of the flames on a silver
foil, heat-retention, rescue blanket, naked and sweating. I
skidded to a stop. His back was arched in agony, every muscle in stark definition, sweat puddling beneath him. His
face was pulled with fierce pain, human teeth bared, white
in the shifting light.

Kemnebi lounged in a camp chair, a beer dangling from
his fingers. Empties had been tossed behind him and scattered across the ground, an open cooler at his knee. He was
staring at Rick with a fixed smile. It never wavered as he
drained the beer and tossed the bottle over his shoulder. It

landed with a clink. "We are gathered here, on this auspicious night, to watch my enemy die," he said.

I wasn't aware I had moved until the drunken wereleader tumbled out of his chair. He landed with a pained whoof and I kicked him, his body muzzy in the red haze of my fury. "Rick LaFleur will not die tonight, because if he does, I'll kill you myself." I was suddenly holding one of the pretty red-gripped .380s and I fired point-blank into Kem's knee. He screamed. "That's just a taste of what I'll do to you if he dies."

"It is silver! You shot me with silver!" he screamed.

"Yeah." I threw down my backpack, dropped down to my knees, and slid a silver-plated handcuff around Kem's wrist. With a snap, I snaked out a length of line and secured it to the nearest tree. "Silver will keep you from changing shape to heal, even with the moonlight pushing at you when it rises. But if you help Rick, I'll think about cutting the round out of your knee joint so you can shift. Up to you."

He screamed at me, cuss words in his native tongue, I was sure. I holstered the weapon and went to Rick, kneeling beside him, moving to the side a pile of clothes I hadn't noticed before. I kept my body at an angle, knowing Kem would kill me in a heartbeat now, if he could, so I wasn't turning my back on him. "I'm here, Rick. I won't leave you. And he won't be killing you when you shift."

He groaned, but he gripped my hand. The motion exposed the tattoos on his shoulder, the scarred and ridged tats of cats and mountains, mauled by werewolves. The golden eyes of the bobcat and mountain lion gleamed on his olive skin, glowing in the firelight. They looked hot, burning; I touched one and jerked my hand back. Scalding. The spell built into his skin was smooth as a stone, the glowing orbs glossy, like pieces of gold, the maimed cats watching me.

Once again I was hit with the feeling of destiny, as if someone up there had planned for us to be together but something had gone horribly wrong. Rick screamed again, his hand twisting mine, the grip so hard my bones ground. I held on, ignoring the demands and eventual pleading of Kemnebi, but kept my body angled so I could see him.

There was no water, but Rick needed something to replace the slick, greasy sweat that runneled his skin. He was dehydrating. When his cramps eased, I brought him three of Kem's beers and opened one, holding it to his lips. I had no idea what alcohol would do to a were trying to shift, but it was all I had. He drank it gratefully. Another cramp hit him. He screamed and arched his back. It was like watching lightning thrust through him. The golden eyes of his cats glowed, even when he thrashed to his side, into shadow. Magic. The magic that held him in this form.

Each time the spasms eased, I fed him more beer. Once I scavenged for deadwood for the fire. Time passed. What felt like a long time. Hours. The moon rose in the sky, brilliant white overhead, almost perfectly round, marred only by scudding clouds. Kem had begun to gasp in pain as well. He was getting a taste of Rick's torture, unable to shift with the silver in his knee and clamped to his wrist. He cursed at me long and hard in English and French as well as the liquid syllables of his mother tongue.

I looked up when Brandon and Brian walked through the thicket, carrying an assortment of cases. I knew they could see the naked hope on my face. But Grégoire stepped alone from the laurel behind them, the ancient vampire no longer shrouded in traveling clothes. He wore ironed jeans, thousand dollar hiking boots, and a silk shirt under a heavy cotton work shirt. His blond hair was tied back in a little tail. He looked like a male model on set for an L.L. Bean catalogue shoot, a metrosexual playing at being an outdoor guy. And he wasn't who I needed tonight. The vamp knelt beside Rick, studying him like a doctor might, while my breathing went ragged and tears filled my eyes. *He refused to come*.

Long heartbeats later, Big Evan stepped from the laurel thicket.

CHAPTER TWENTY-NINE

Butchery Disguised as Surgery

Hope shot through me like buckshot, burning and hot. Big Evan looked at me, frowning. I had saved Molly's life, maybe the lives of the whole family and coven, but it wasn't enough to make him like me, not after losing the blood-diamond to Evil Evie. He was here because, otherwise, Molly would come. Evan would never again let his wife go into danger with me, which is why I'd sent my request to him, not his wife.

Rick screamed again, the sound ululating, his limbs twisting and stomach muscles rippling. He panted through it, repeating, "Please, please, please, please," begging for help, for surcease from pain. Big Evan's face softened and his lips tightened, as if he were fighting with himself, unwilling compassion against anger and flint-hard judgment. The witch pursed his lips and said something under his breath. But he went to work.

He took two cases from the twins and shouldered the men out of the way. He knelt at Rick's side and opened them on the ground, revealing wind instruments, which he studied carefully. Big Evan lifted a wooden flute out of one case, sat on the ground near Rick, and started to play. He was an air witch, his power traveling through air as sound. The mellow notes filled the clearing, magic in the melody. Instantly, Rick's spasms eased. He curled into a fetal position, gasping. Moments later, Rick relaxed into a limp mass.

One twin opened out a fleece blanket and covered Rick. Another twin placed more deadwood on the fire, which crackled and sent sparks high into the air. Evan played on.

At the melody, even Kemnebi relaxed, the were-cat staring at me, hatred on his face. I grinned at him, tapping my gun with a forefinger as a reminder.

The twins opened chairs for themselves and their master, and produced a picnic and several bottles of wine, as if they had come for a show. Not that I could complain. They had gotten me here, and then picked up Big Evan. Maybe even convinced him to come.

Grégoire passed me a glass of wine. Confused, I took it and followed his pointing finger to Rick. *Ah. Not for me.* I held the delicate, crystal wineglass to his lips. Rick drank, sighed again, and closed his eyes. The night passed slowly after that. I left Rick's side only to relieve myself deep in the woods and—because I was feeling guilty—to cut the round out of Kemnebi's knee. I had aimed just above the joint, and was able to palpate the flattened round easily. It had formed a pustule on the inner side of his thigh, which made the butchery disguised as surgery easy. I used steel instead of a silvered blade to cut him—I was feeling magnanimous. Kem screamed long and loud, drawing out the note, the sound half cat, half human, and if the sign of his pain gave me pleasure, I kept it off my face. For the first time in my life, I felt entirely inhuman. And yet Beast was gone. I was totally alone.

I tucked the bloody silver round in my pocket and removed the silver cuff. Under the force of the full moon, Kem shifted instantly, gray energies playing over his form as he sprouted black fur. His bones snapped like dry sticks and reformed as his body shifted, able to heal the silver poisoning now that the round was gone. I clicked the cuff around his back leg the moment he was fully cat and before he could gather himself to bound away. The were-cat was not getting out of my sight. He wasn't hunting either. He'd go hungry. I leaped away.

Golden-green eyes stared at me across the dark. Kem-cat growled, showing his teeth, promising my death. "Get in line," I said, turning away from him. I took Rick's hand again, his flesh hot, feverish.

Evan's large fingers were strangely delicate on the flute, moving with a syncopated, almost disorganized beat, but one that was organic and melting, with his lips relaxed on the mouthpiece. The music continued with only short breaks for Evan to drink and rest, the tones low and melting, limpid and crystalline and somber. After long hours, when dawn was near, I felt the magic of the notes change, smelled them shift into something tart and spicy. No longer a calming sound, the mournful melody altered and sped, and I realized that Big Evan was attempting something beyond simply stopping Rick's pain. His eyes were on the mound beneath the blanket, and Rick rolled over, focusing on Evan. The two men held gazes as if they were newly met combatants assessing one another's strengths and weaknesses.

Rick sat up, the blanket falling away to bunch in his lap. His chest and arm muscles were harshly defined in the shadows; his black hair had dried in the passing hours, standing stiff; his beard had grown out, rough and scruffy. And he was still the most beautiful man I had ever met. He pulled his hand from mine and my palm felt the chill, deprived of his heat.

The music stopped. Evan set the flute in his lap and said, "I think I've got a handle on the spell woven into your skin. I *may* have figured out how to craft a counter-spell melody for it. It won't stop the pain or the moon-call, but it might keep both to manageable levels. If it works, I can make a CD and you can load it in a player and keep it with you. You'll have to play it all night during full moons."

"And if it doesn't work?" Rick asked, his voice raspy from screaming.

"You might go insane tomorrow night."

Rick chuckled, the sound conveying anger and self-loathing and resignation. "Well, what's not to like in that scenario? Go for it," he said. I lifted a hand to stop him, but Big Evan put the flute to his lips and began to play. The notes were haunting and trilling, rising and falling through the scales, part gypsy, part western Indian—Hopi maybe— part tribal African, part Middle Eastern. Rick's eyes started to glow, a pale amber light. The notes warbled. Rick growled. A big-cat growl.

Chill bumps rose along my legs and arms. Rick looked at me and pulled his lips back, exposing human teeth, but the gesture was pure cat. His eyes glowed golden, the gold orbs on his shoulder grew bright. The music dropped low, and the growl tapered off, disappearing entirely. Rick's eyes returned to his Frenchy-black.

The magic of the song danced along my skin like the fingers of a lover, the touch featherlight, delicate as falling rose petals, but electric and full of power. Somewhere deep inside me, I felt movement, the faint click of claws on stone. An uneasy sound. I eased away from Rick. The song played on, but I didn't feel Beast again.

An hour later, the melody came to a close and Rick smiled at Big Evan. Both men looked exhausted and drowsy and oddly content. "Thank you," Rick breathed.

"Don't thank me," Evan said. "Thank your fanghead here. He offered me a year's wages if I found a counterspell for your tats. My kids now have a college fund."

I turned my head slowly and found Grégoire's eyes on me. His blue gaze held the memory of my healing. Memory of the time in bed with me. Memory of . . . His lips curled up, his boyish face transforming into something like pure joy. *Oh. Crap.* "I can't be bought," I said steadily, challenging.

"I did not think that you could, *mon coeur.*"

Rick looked back and forth between us. "Did I miss something?" I didn't answer.

"It is nearly sunrise," Grégoire said, his eyes on me still.

The twins started packing up their cases, Big Evan lumbered to his feet, all the grace in his melody and his fingers gone. Grégoire, lounging in his chair, still watched me, I could feel his gaze though I kept my eyes on Rick's catlike beauty. "I'll help you get dressed."

I walked Rick through the dark to the tent site in the campground, Kem at my side, stalking on the leash. The cat tried to scratch me once and to get away twice, but the leash and the rattling of his silver cuff was enough to ensure good behavior. He might be near the top of the food chain in Africa, but in a lot of ways, he was more human than I was. Tonight had proven that to both of us.

At the campsite, I spotted the white wolf in his cage. I'd

forgotten all about Fire Truck, and wondered if he had been the dog I'd heard howling. I jerked the lead on Kem-cat; the were turned slit eyes to me and hissed, I mimed shooting him and blew on the tip of my finger, to remind him who was in control. He sat down with a huff and started to groom his front paws. I hugged Rick to me, feeling the weariness in his body, a fine tremor thrumming though him. "Eat. Drink a lot of water." I gave him the gun loaded with silvershot. "Shoot Kem-cat if he tries to eat you." The cat ignored us both, which I thought was a good sign. "I'll check on you tonight."

"I'll record the spell-song and send it to you later this morning." I jerked around to see Big Evan standing in the moonlight behind me. I hadn't heard him follow us. Hadn't heard him at all. My surprise seemed to amuse him, or maybe he just wanted me to see his pearly whites. "Come on Yellowrock. The fanghead and his dinners are waiting for us."

Silent, I hugged Rick and followed Big Evan up and down the trail—mostly up—to the new landing site. We made the bone rattling, noisy ride to Big Evan's front yard where we touched down only long enough for him to jump free and lumber to his house. Molly and Angelina stood in the doorway, and I could make out Angie Baby's lips move in the porch light. "I wanna ride in the helicopter with Aunt Jane!" I waved as we lifted off, hand against the smoked glass. I made it to my bed, alone, after dawn, and fell asleep, fully clothed, so tired my bones ached.

I woke an hour after sunset to the buzzing of my phone. It had been going off for quite a while, if the number of messages was anything to go by. Molly had called, so had Bruiser, Rick, Derek, and others. Shaddock's blood-servant and lawyer Adelaide Mooney had left several messages and one succinct text: CALL ME.

Though business concerns were pending, I called Molly back first, asking about Evangelina.

"We've been trying to track her," Mol said, her voice sounding tired and wan. "She's got something hiding her, a spell or the blood-diamond. We don't know. But we're pulling out all the stops after the sun goes down. We'll set a circle under the full moon and try to track her that way."

"I'm sorry, Molly," I said.

"Not your fault, Big-Cat. Not your fault at all."

Uncomfortable, I floundered for a less painful topic and asked, "Did a check get delivered today?"

Mol chuckled, sounding relieved, "Yeah. A cashier's check by way of a messenger service. And Big Evan told me you were responsible for it. Thank you."

A half smile played over my mouth, and my mood lightened. "He gave me credit for something good? That's a first."

She laughed softly, "Yeah. It is. He's been in his man-cave over the new garage all day, working on a music spell for Rick, working out specific notes, recording it, while my sisters and I work on finding Evangelina. Hmm?" she said, drawing her mouth from the phone. "Gotta go, Jane. We might have something."

"Call me when you need me. I'll be there when you corner her."

"Thanks, Big-Cat. But this isn't your fight."

"Evangelina made it mine, Mol. Call."

"Okay. Later, then." The phone went dead.

Holding the cell, I called out in my mind, *Beast? Talk to me.* I had heard her claws, seen one of her memories, but for now there was only the echoing silence of caverns and darkness. Grief welled up in me, flowing out from the emptiness. I crushed it down. I had work to do.

I pulled up the dossier on Evangelina and started dialing every number associated with her, hoping to hit pay dirt: cell, home, café, herb shop. She never answered, but I left the same lying message at each. "Evangelina Everhart Stone. Leo is in Asheville tonight, for one night only, staying at the Regal Imperial Hotel. You want him, you come get him." I figured she would take a few hours to get in place and come after the head-fanghead bait, and when she did, I'd be ready. Leo was expected to be here in three nights anyway, via his private Learjet, to finalize the parley. Of course, it hadn't been negotiated yet, which, in Leo's eyes, would be my fault.

I bit the bullet and called Derek back next. Before he could get in an opening salvo, I said, "Meet me in the lobby in thirty. We need to talk." I ended the call. *Way to go Jane.* Rick was next on my list and I got his voice mail. Disappointment cascaded through me, but I left a message. "I'm up. Call, okay?" My next call was to Bruiser.

"Jane," he said, sounding far less warm than usual. "Leo understands that you allowed Grégoire to take a flight before sunset. That you allowed him to sit in the woods with no perimeter defense and only two bodyguards. And that he got back to the hotel after sunrise."

"Yep," I said. "He had a ball. And if Leo had wanted me to tackle Grégoire and tie him up in his hotel room, he should have phrased our contract accordingly. Anything else? No?" I ended the call, feeling satisfied and a lot snarky. I had just silenced the primo blood-servant of the alpha suckhead of the Southeastern U.S. Go me.

My phone rang again and Bruiser preempted me by saying, "We are in Asheville, in the Evening Light Penthouse Suite of the Regal Imperial Hotel. My master was deeply disturbed over your call last night and the fact that you and his scion disappeared on *personal business*. You will attend Leo at sunset." His call ended.

Leo was here? *Crap!* It would have been nice to know that before I used him as bait for Evangelina. Like sixty seconds ago. It was a little late to call Evil Evie back and tell her not to come. I rubbed my face. So much for my little game of one-upmanship. My *personal business* had sent Leo chasing me all the way from New Orleans, only to be put into danger by me.

I sent Derek a text about Leo and warned him to be on the lookout for Evangelina—extra guards out front, loaded with antiriot gear, in Alpha One position. He'd have a cow, unless he already knew about Leo being in town.

Lastly, I dialed Adelaide Mooney while I stripped out of my dirty, sweaty, mismatched, wrinkled clothes. Her dulcet tones identified herself and I said, "Jane Yellowrock here. Have you heard from Lincoln Shaddock yet?"

"Yes, Jane, we have. It seems he's with the witch."

The vamp had disappeared with Evangelina, who had the blood-diamond again. She had the power to make him jump to her demands. She also had access to the demon. And she would be after killing Leo. "Leo is in town."

"Here?" Her voice was filled with alarm. "But the agreements aren't fin—"

"They're screwed to heck and back, Adelaide. The best-case scenario is strictly salvage. If I can get Lincoln back safely, you can bargin for more time. Ask for an extra decade based on Lincoln's great record with his chained scions."

"And worst-case scenario?"

"I'll find Evangelina and have to stake your boss."

I heard a click and another voice came over the cell, spitting mad. "If you kill my master, I'll cut off your head and feed it to my dogs." It was Dacy, Adelaide's mother. The cell call went dead. I needed to find Lincoln Shaddock and Evangelina before dark.

Anger and adrenaline beating through me with every heartbeat, I threw myself into the shower, dressed, slid in a few knives, holstered the pretty handguns, and headed for the lobby, only ten minutes late. As I took the stairs down, I dialed Reach and told him what additional info I needed and all the people I needed it on. At this rate, Leo was gonna make him rich.

Derek was standing at parade rest in a shadowed alcove off the lobby. I drew even with him and stopped, my brows raised in question. He floundered a moment, and then asked, "You ever gonna tell me what you are, Injun Princess?"

"What difference does it make. My money spends as good as the fangheads."

"Maybe the suckheads are easier to work with because I know what they are. They aren't hiding anything."

"Yeah. They're so transparent. And easy to understand. And gentle. And peace-loving."

Derek snorted, ironic amusement flashing across his dark-skinned face, to vanish like a shadow. "Trust is a two-way street, Lego."

Not that I let it show, but warmth filtered through my veins. He hadn't called me by any of my nicknames recently, and he'd used two in the space of seconds. He wanted equality, did he? "I'll tell you all my dirty little secrets if you tell me all yours. Starting with what you did for Uncle Sam in Iraq and Afghanistan."

"I signed a nondisclosure statement upheld by Homeland Security."

"And I have honor."

Derek considered that. After a long moment, he held out a hand, as if asking for rapprochement. I took it and we shook, once, firmly. He chuckled softly, the sound purrlike. At the thought, hurt shot through me, a pain I squashed. Beast wasn't gone. She couldn't be. The remembered, faint sound of her claws on stone gave me hope.

"Honor, huh?" When I didn't reply, he straightened his shirt and started to speak, but looked instead over my shoulder. I stepped to his side so I could see. The elevator dinged. The scent of human and vamp cascaded into the lobby. The twins. Bruiser. Grégoire. And Leo.

I checked the position of the security crew, the night blacking the front windows, and asked, "The boys?"

"Assembling in riot gear and moving to Alpha One. We need another five minutes."

Which meant we needed a delaying tactic. I stepped to the elevator doors and said, "Leo."

He held out his hand to shake mine, and though I didn't want to tie up my right hand when I was on the job, it wasn't something I could get out of without being embarrassingly rude. I tapped the mike and said, "Derek, you're on."

"I have command," he said into my earpiece.

Ignoring the fact that there had been an uncomfortable space between the hand being offered and taken, I took Leo's. "It has been brought to my attention," he said, "that I needlessly contributed to your difficulties on this parley, my *Enforcer*."

Oh crap. Enforcer. *I had to deal with that, still.* "Ummm, hunh?" I asked. I could have kicked myself for that scintillating comeback.

"When I banished Evangelina from my city, I did not know she had spelled my primo, George, and perhaps even me." Having nothing to say to that, I glanced at Bruiser, the aforementioned primo. When I didn't reply, Leo's lips quirked and he released my hand. "That was an apology, Jane."

Realization dawned. "Oh! Yeah, sure. Um, thanks. No problem." I glanced at Bruiser again. He was laughing at me silently. Great. I'd acted the socially inept idiot I really was.

To my side, at the front of the hotel, pink light poured through the night-black windows. It was Evangelina, responding to my lure of Leo, who was not supposed to be here yet. "Crap! Weapons!" I shouted. Knowing Derek would get the vamps under cover, I raced to the front doors, throwing myself to the side and peering out. Evangelina stood in the circular drive in the open door of her sports car, the convertible top down, and behind the antivamp protestors. Over them a huge, misty, black bird flapped its wings. The protestors moved forward, a man out front, leading. They each held small pots and splashed something on the drive with every step.

In the backseat of her convertible sat Lincoln Shaddock and a slumped form I couldn't identify. I wasn't sure if either of them was alive.

"Freaking dang Murphy and his freaking dang laws," I muttered, possible scenarios racing through my mind. "Brandon! Brian!" I shouted. "We got a Delta seven! Wrassler! I need my Benelli!" I needed the firepower of the shotgun, back in my room. I drew my puny .380 and checked the load.

CHAPTER THIRTY

The Blood-Diamond

To the desk I shouted, "Lockdown. You are under attack."
When no one moved, I screamed, "Lockdown! You are under attack!"

The little uniformed girl found her head and raced to
the phone. *Civilians.* Can't live with them, can't let them get
slaughtered. A news van rolled to a stop and a cameraman
jumped out, already filming. Especially can't let them get
killed in front of TV cameras. "Son of a freaking goat," I
whispered.

Out front, a bellboy decided to be a hero and shouted
something to the protestors. The bird overhead beat its
wings and called, a sawing sound. It attacked. The bellboy
disappeared inside the winged black cloud. A primal
scream of pain echoed against the building, cut off as if
with a blade. When the shadow withdrew, the only thing left
was blood splatter and a lower leg.

The protestors stopped as if petrified, their eyes on the
leg and foot. It was still wearing a shoe. The leader's mouth
worked but no sound came out. Evangelina pointed at the
doors and shouted, "The vampires did it! They killed the
boy! Get them!"

The demon overhead called again, a softer rumbling
note with three soft *tocks* afterward, a satisfied chirp. The
leader of the humans swiveled back to the hotel. His face
contorted, full of fury. He charged, flinging blood before

him with stained fingers. His supporters followed. Just before they reached the entrance, Derek slammed the metal rod into place, securing the door with a metal bar and deadbolt. He turned a key in the deadbolt lock and the metal tongue *schnicked* into place just as the protestors fell against the door with a hollow thud. "How long?" I demanded.

Derek said, "Twenty-eight seconds until they're in place."

A window shattered. A rock bounced across the lobby, sparkling glass shards catching the pink glow from outside. "As soon as the protestors are down, have the men draw back. That black thing is a demon."

"What thing?"

"He cannot see it, *me sha*." I rotated my upper body at the familiar French tones. "He is fully human," Leo said. Outside, the demon cast no shadow. He wasn't fully here. *Yet.*

The master of the southeastern vamps, and arguably one of the most powerful vamps in the U.S., shrugged negligently. He was wearing a tuxedo with a black silk shirt, white cummerbund, and bowtie. He looked beautiful. And deadly. His black eyes sparkled as if he knew what I had thought, and he reached out to smooth my hair back from my face, along my shoulder and spine, in a sleek caress. Beside him stood Grégoire, a slight figure in midnight blue tux with a blue silk shirt the color of his eyes. The vamps looked gorgeous together.

I put my weapon on safety, holstered it, and pulled them back from the door. "Go back to your rooms." They looked at each other, turned to the windows, and smiled, fangs clicking down. It wasn't charming. More like two feral creatures staring at prey. I got a bad feeling.

"It has been many years since we have been to battle," Grégoire said. "Our servants are restrained."

I scanned behind me. Ignored the rock that exploded into the room only feet away. Bruiser and the twins were sitting on the couches in front of the fireplace. Staring at nothing. I raced over and saw my weapons on the floor at the twins' feet. Wrassler was asleep on the rug. "Let them go," I snarled, weaponing up, strapping on blades, checking the M4. "I need them." The shotgun was loaded for vamp with silver fléchette rounds. I was hoping silver worked on demons, and I was the only one with silver. Leo's decision. A dumb one. I could lay blame later, if I lived. I took Leo's arm. "Please. Let the servants go."

"No. The little witch is ours," Grégoire said. He vamped out fully, his pupils growing wide as quarters in blood red sclera. "You have done well, bringing her to me."

He had ordered me to bring him Evangelina so he could kill her. *Crap.*

"And we must liberate Shaddock." Leo freed his arm from my fingers with a small shake that jarred my bones, peering out the window into the growing dark and increasing reddish glare of Evangelina's magics. Lincoln's head was still silhouetted in the pink energies. "Shaddock's master, Dufresnee, is sworn to me, and I to him. I have drunk from him. Shaddock is *mine*."

"Shaddock is a barbarian, but he is *our* barbarian," Grégoire agreed, sounding eager.

"Shall we?" Leo asked him.

Grégoire drew a sword from a sheath I hadn't noted, hanging at his side. "Forgive me if I precede you, my master." With a firm pop of air, like a drumhead hit hard, he disappeared.

"He is always first on a battlefield," Leo said, aggrieved. He vamped out faster than I could process the change and disappeared with a puff of air that moved my hair with its passage. Both men reappeared outside. It looked magical, but the movement of air and falling glass indicated that they had gone out through the broken windows. They faced off against Evangelina.

I swore succinctly and gathered myself to follow. Derek caught my arm. "You're not wearing a vest, Legs," he said.

"They don't have guns," I replied. "Time?"

"They're in place. On my order, I've instructed the men to target the humans and the witch on first volley. Where is this demon?"

"Your two o'clock. About ten feet off the ground. I have silver ammo," I said. "It might work on the demon."

His eyes promised me retribution for not telling him about the silver. "Go," he said.

Time had done that slow-down thing, where every sight

is sharpened, each sound is clear, crisp, and slow. Outside I heard the sound of firing, a boom-boom-boom of overlapping shotgun fire. Humans fell fast, downed by fat, nonlethal, antiriot beanbags fired at point blank range by figures dressed in night-combat black. Then they were shot by tranquilizer darts, to keep them down. But nothing hit Evangelina. She stood tall in the red car, behind a red ward, a *hedge of thorns* so strong, the concrete blackened and cracked where it intersected the ground outside of the tires. The ward sizzled a smutty black, like charcoal and flames, her arms out to her sides as she gathered power. Her scarlet hair flew to the sides, a wind buffeting her slender form, molding to her body.

Blue strobes lit the scene as cops pulled up. They'd be in the way, but there was no help for that. Beside me, Derek counted off the time for the shooters to get back to safety. "Three-one-hundred, two-one-hundred, one-one-hundred. *Go!*"

I dove into the fray, the M4 in one hand, stabilized against my side, and the semiautomatic in the other. The smell of human blood, witch, and vamp blood hit me. Demon burned my nostrils, acrid as smoke. I had weapons, but I needed more. "Hayyel!" I shouted as I ran, hoping my angel was still hanging around, keeping an eye on the blood-diamond.

Derek followed me, firing rubber bullets up, not hurting the demon, but drawing his attention. Allowing me to get in under the winged evil. Time slowed further, a thick construct that parted around me, allowing me to move faster than any human.

"Hayyel," I breathed, stepping beneath the Raven Mocker, his wings wide above me. His beak open. Screaming. The tail that constrained him was attached to his leg like a shackle, dropping to the earth, snaking across the hotel's drive along a trail of blood thrown by the protestors. Evangelina's blood. Shaddock's blood. Drained into bowls and splashed by humans. Humans who were now inactive. No longer throwing blood. The tail thinned. I had a feeling that if the Raven Mocker got loose, it would be bad. Really bad. "Hayyel. Please come get the Kalona Ayeliski, the Raven Mocker." The demon screamed and beat his wings, looming above me. "I give him to you on a platter of silver fléchettes."

Darkness and emptiness drenched me, swarmed over me, filled me with a pressure that stole my breath. It felt like being smothered in my sleep, drowning in the knowledge of failure, utter and complete. Like dying in the darkness, drenched in the blood of my brothers and sisters and children. The Cherokee on the Trail of Tears had been lied to, cheated, defeated, beaten, and banished, for the greed of the white man. They had walked the long trail, dying in despair by the hundreds, their lives cut short feeding this demon.

Wings flapped down. I saw them drop, shutting, closing on me. I tried to fire my weapons. Tried to duck. But my fingers wouldn't squeeze the triggers. I couldn't even fall. *Hayyel didn't come.* The wings swept in, enveloping me.

It was like being struck by lightning. Stealing my sight, my hearing, my energy. I fell then, a dizzying descent. I heard the sound of weapons hitting the ground, tinks of sound, almost lost in the emptiness of the void. I landed hard on one knee—the pain the only thing that proved I was still on Earth and not in the emptiness of a demon's hell.

Then, even the wrenching of the fall was gone. I was deep in the absence of . . . everything. All sensation vanished. All hope fled. I would have sobbed had I been able to draw a breath.

Beast? Help!

But Beast was gone. It felt as if part of me had died in Evangelina's basement, just as The People had died on the Trail of Tears. Their memories and despair swamped me. Lying in the frozen mud, sick, as white soldiers walked past me. Pain in waves, overwhelming. Dying. I was dying. And maybe it was best. Maybe I should give up the fight. The pain. Maybe the time of The People was past.

Far, far away, I heard a sound. Slow, slow, slow—thump . . . thump. Again nothingness, an ageless passage of time in the darkness, the *aloneness*, of the demon's world. Until . . . The abyss was punctured by a sound, resonant, resounding. Thump . . . thump.

A heartbeat. My heart, slowing.

There was no up or down. No me or it. But if I still possessed a body, I would have weapons. And there would be a blade, heavily silvered, in a sheath. Near my right hand. Near . . . here. I had trained to reach and draw and cut outward and upward all in one sliding motion, a parry built into the draw. *Fast.* Trained so hard and thoroughly that I never had to think about drawing the weapon.

I reached up, my mind pushing through the motions, the expectation of action. And though I felt nothing, I slid into the memory of fight, my mind moving even if my hand didn't believe it, my fractured faith taking over where reality had failed. I drew, cut outward, upward, and finished with a thrust, whispering in my mind, *Hayyel. The Raven Mocker is yours. Send him back where he belongs.*

Light blasted against me. Light and air and warmth. A flare of moonlight. A vision of angel wings and demon claws. A concussion of sound buffeted me, the roar of every battle that had ever been. It rolled me across the concrete, banging elbows, knees, jaw, and cheek. The M4 was beneath my hand. I caught it up. Continued the roll. Saw the demon above me, feathered and blacker than the sky above it. No time to finesse a shot. *No collateral damage,* the soft thought warned. I braced the weapon on the concrete, away from the blinding light. Fired carefully into the dark. *Boom. Boom. Boom.* I rolled again. Braced. Fired. *Boom. Boom. Boom.* I was on my feet, pulling blades and stabbing into the demon-dark. The light was blinding against the shadow.

I jumped back. Saw the demon constrict. Tighten where I had stabbed. The light arrowed in after the silver of my shots. The darkness drew in and down, into a large black bird, four feet tall, wings flailing, fighting for freedom, bleeding black blood, even as it was pulled into the blood splattered on the drive. Over him, a massive golden eagle flapped his wings, screaming a challenge, throwing off light and lightning. The blood on the concrete rippled and bubbled, a clotting, drying mass, like a trap. A tar pit for evil.

The demon was caught. Sucked down, into the blood. Gone in an instant. Just gone. So was the golden eagle. *My angel? Hayyel?* I blinked away the image of heaven and hell in battle.

Blue lights strobed the night. Shots echoed as cops fired

into the *hedge*. I saw a cop fall, Sam Orson, screaming, falling into the dark. I didn't know how long the spilled blood would hold the Raven. I didn't know how long I had been trapped. I didn't know much of anything except that I needed the pink blood-diamond. The Raven had been summoned with the diamond and the blood. If they got together—

Gunfire erupted to my left. I pivoted on the balls of my feet. In front of the red car, Grégoire and Evangelina struggled, lit by flashes of light, obscured by a swirling darkness the color of old blood. He was *inside* the *hedge of thorns*. He had a blade, and he was stabbing at the witch. She was bleeding on arms and one shoulder, but not badly injured. She was deflecting the sword somehow, using her magic. Grégoire dashed and cut, seeming to parry some unseen enemy, some invisible blade. And Grégoire was burning.

Red-orange flames rippled across his arms and upper back. In a whoosh, his hair caught fire. Flames shot into the sky. Evangelina laughed. Grégoire screamed, that glass-shattering sound they make when vamps are dying. Leo attacked the *hedge* with his blade, but where it had parted for Grégoire, it resisted Leo.

Grégoire thrust and parried. Silver flashed against the *hedge. He's using a silvered sword.* A weapon designed to kill his own kind. Outlawed by the Vampira Carta. It let him penetrate the *hedge of thorns*. I pulled my last blade, my favorite vamp-killer, held it out in front of me. And raced in, leaping. The blade pressed in to the ward. Pierced through. *Hedge of thorns* shattered against me. Over me. Flaring bright, white, hot. It was like being flayed with melting obsidian blades. I screamed. I was still screaming when I landed inside. Stumbled with the momentum of my charge. Fell. Into Evangelina.

The blade slid into her. No resistance at all. Deep. All the way. Hilt deep. Eighteen inches of silver. Heated by the *hedge* as the ward died.

My eyes tracked the damage—*midcenter. Between her ribs. Direct hit. Slicing through her aorta*—even as I screamed. *"Nooo!"* And still I fell forward, the blade shoving her before me. Into the car. Blood gouted out, pumping over my hand. I rode her down. Onto the leather seat. My momentum wasn't yet spent. I rolled across her, into the passenger floor. Caught myself with one hand. My hair slung forward. I was holding myself up with the hand that was coated, painted, with her blood.

Jane is killer only. Jane even kills her friends.

Beast!

She didn't reply. I levered off the floor. Evangelina lay on the seat, one hand to her stomach, as if to hold in the blood that pumped. With the other, she grasped at her throat. Clutching, grabbing at air. Seizing the necklace around her neck. The blood-diamond dangled, bright with the pink hue of its magic, with the brilliance of flickering lights. The gem spinning, beautiful, deadly, and dangerous as the hell the demon came from.

The Raven will possess the witch in death, Beast thought. *His goal from the beginning.*

Evangelina ripped down on the delicate chain. Breaking it. I lunged toward her, pushing off with my toes, up through my arches, ankles, calves, knees, a whiplashing thrust into thighs, hips, spine. Too slow. She dropped the blood-diamond into her wound.

The earth screamed. Darkness rose and covered . . . everything. Everything, everywhere, was nothingness. But I had been here before, in this place of emptiness. It could be defeated. Blind, I finished my leap, reaching down. Into the void of the warm, wet, bloody wound.

I took the diamond into my hand.

The world blazed around me, bright. Her blood sizzled. Her blood boiled. My hand scorched and froze in chorus, a duality of agonies that raced up my arm. Into my chest. But I was still leaping. Airborne. Out of the car. To land and stand, poised on the pavement. The gem in my fist. It had no warmth, no cold, yet it contained the energies of the Raven Mocker, the blood sacrifice of countless witch children over centuries. It was powerful beyond anything I had ever touched. And if I destroyed it, I might release an evil beyond my own imagining. A trilling cry sounded behind me. Slowly, I turned.

The Raven Mocker stood on the back of the car, illuminated by the lights from a van. And this time he threw a shadow. He was real. He was here. He was *free*. Evangelina's blood had bought his freedom. His huge, clawed feet dented in the trunk lid with dull thumps. His wings gathered close. Beak to the sky. He was singing, a hooting, warbling, *tocking* sound, his head back. Throat exposed. Then he reached down with his beak toward Evangelina. And she reached up to him with blood-stained hands.

My blades were all gone. The last one was buried in the witch. Movement caught my eye. I saw Molly and Big Evan, racing toward me, appearing out of the bright lights. Big Evan wore a grimace. Carried a knife in his fist. It was a twin to mine, the silver brilliant as moonbeams on the blade. He flipped it. At me.

Time slowed again. Thick as clotted cream. The blade glittered, scattering the light. It tumbled in midair, gliding at me, hilt first. I lifted my right hand. The one with the necklace in it. The chain wrapped around and around my wrist as I raised it, caught in the force of my movement. The hilt smacked into my palm. Perfectly planted. Big Evan opened his mouth, started to speak the round, fluid syllables of the ancient witches. I pushed off hard, leaping. To the back seat of the car.

Holding the blood-diamond, my hand coated with Evangelina's blood, I stabbed upward. Into the belly of the demon. I shouted, "Hayyel!"

The magic was cold. It swarmed over me like a blizzard, burning and icy. The demon's blood gushed over my hand, mixing with Evangelina's. Coating the blood-diamond. It flashed red, then black, and red again. My wrist burned where the chain touched me. Binding itself to me. The gold chain around my neck branding into me. The hilt of the knife heating. Evan invoked the name, "*Hayyel, take* Kalona Ayeliski, the Raven Mocker." He spoke the Irish Gaelic of the binding, syllables I couldn't reproduce if I tried. *"Bíodh sé daor, le m'ordú agus le mo chumhacht."*

The explosion sent me back, over the witch dead on the front seat, over the windshield and hood. To the ground where I hit, slamming the breath out of me, a shocking pain. I rolled, bounced, scraped over the driveway, leaving layers of my flesh. Light flashed over the night, so bright I saw my own bones through my skin. Wings, light and golden, black and shadowed, beat at the world.

It was all over when I finally remembered to take a breath.

All except the screaming. The grief. Molly wailed, clutching her sister to her. A reporter raced up to thrust a microphone at my face. I growled. Leo smoothly stepped between us before I coldcocked her. I caught a glimpse of Grégoire being helped into the hotel, the stink of burned vamp on the air. Derek handed me my weapons and put an arm around me. Shielding me. Steered me inside. Something crashed, and the light, so bright it had been blinding, went out. In my right hand was an elk-horn hilt and a melted blade. The chain of the blood-diamond was seared into my flesh, still so hot my skin blistered around it.

"Light?" I croaked.

"From the news van. They got the whole damn thing and sent it out live." He pointed to a TV discreetly on the check-in desk. It was a close-up of Leo, looking urbane and elegant, even with the smear of blood on his cheek. And beside him was Lincoln Shaddock, looking shell-shocked and lost, staring at a body on the pavement. Chen. Naked. Dead. With runes cut into his flesh. I remembered the lump in the car next to Shaddock earlier. Evangelina had sacrificed him to the demon.

My back and Derek's were in the background, something dangling against my hand. I tucked the pink diamond gem—the blood-diamond—into my pocket. I knew what it was now. A portal into hell. Guarded by an angel.

CHAPTER THIRTY-ONE

A Marriage Ceremony with a Death Sentence at the End

Two days later, I stood beside the hospital bed, awkwardly patting Itty Bitty's hand. The tiny woman was being released, her werewolf wounds healing with no trace of were-taint found in her blood. Gertruda, the Mercy Blade sworn to the service of Charles Dufresnee, the Master of the Raleigh-Durham area, sat at her other side, looking far more comfortable in the medical surroundings than I felt.

Gertruda still wanted nothing to do with me. She hadn't looked at me once since she walked into the room to give the injured witch her final healing. Still silent, she left the room, managing to convey her disdain of me and everything I stood for without saying a word. I didn't know what I'd done to the woman, but I was good at ticking off supernats.

And cops. I was real good at ticking *them* off. And men in general, even better. Itty Bitty's boyfriend sat in the corner of the room and glowered at me as if the wolf attack had been my fault. Which it had been. Sorta. It's hard to dodge well-deserved blame, and harder still to ignore the stab of guilt when I think about all the people hurt because I hadn't thought about two werewolves in jail and how they might react when their pack was slaughtered. And hadn't thought about the magical amulet locked in my gun cabinet in New Orleans. And hadn't thought about Evangelina and how weird she had acted while visiting me in New Orleans. And just hadn't thought at all.

I patted Itty Bitty's hand again. "Like I said. The Party of African Weres will pick up any outstanding medical bills. The leader assured me personally."

"Thank you for coming," she said. "You didn't have to."

I managed a smile, but from the reaction on her face, not a good one. "Yeah. I did." *Okay. Enough social-small-talk.* I waggled my fingers at them and left the room, fighting the urge to run. I'd rather face a pack of wolves than try to comfort someone.

Rick lounged against a wall in the hallway, his legs crossed at the ankles, looking long and lean in black jeans and jacket, and not trying very hard to discourage the two young women who were hanging around. They were dressed in brightly patterned scrub suits and one had a chest that Rick clearly found imposing. Maybe mesmerizing was a better word. "Come on, Ricky Bo," I said, "before your eyeballs fall out."

He grinned at me, his too-long hair falling forward, curling into his collar. "Sandra is Sam Orson's nurse." He nodded to the busty one. "She says the deputy's going to be fine. He just took a ricochet off the magical ward into the meaty part of his thigh." I hadn't realized I carried the weight of the cop's injury until it fell away. "You can quit worrying," he added more gently.

I stuck my hands in my pockets and shrugged, not knowing how to respond.

Rick pushed off the wall and draped his arm around my shoulders, not an easy thing to do when there's no disparity in height. "Come on. We need to talk."

Oh crap. We need to talk as in, *I bought a house and want you to move in?* Or as in, *I want to see other people, like the busty Sandra?* Or as in—

"I had a call from Grizzard. And from PsyLed. I've got job offers from both."

I thought about that as we entered the elevator and Rick pushed the button for the lobby. As the doors closed, I asked, "They know about you?"

"Yeah. They do. I told them. I'd be a detective with the

sheriff's department, with full moons off so I can listen to the spell music Evan made for me. The job PsyLed outlined is a kind of roving special agent with a territory covering seven Southeastern states." When I didn't reply he said, "I'm thinking about taking the PsyLed offer."

The elevator doors opened and we walked out of the hospital into the fall sunlight. It was Indian Summer, temps in the high eighties and days long enough to pretend that winter and snow and ice would never come. But cold always follows heat, as night follows day, and sadness follows joy. Fang and Rick's red crotch-rocket were parked close by the door, taking up one space. "You're a good cop," I said. "It had to help when you told the sheriff about the body in Evangelina's house." I had told him about the body after the battle with Evangelina, Shaddock, the angel, and the demon.

"Yeah," he said, nodding, agreeing. "I'm a hero."

I play-socked his bicep and he play-screamed and ducked as if injured. "Any word on what killed her husband?" I asked, grinning.

"Blunt object head trauma. Maybe a frying pan." At my look he said, "What? She's a chef. Anyway, ten years or so ago Evangelina whacked him on the head, rolled him in a carpet, and hid him behind the couch. She told her sisters he left her. Her daughter disappeared at the same time."

I straddled Fang and helmeted up. "The twins are ready to deliver us and the steer to the grindy. You up for a helicopter ride?"

Rick waggled his eyebrows at me. "Baby, I'm always up."

I rolled my eyes and keyed on Fang. Together we roared out of the hospital parking lot.

I was pushing Beast, like baiting a lion in her den, but so far, nothing had drawn her out. Beast was silent even as I strapped in to the helo and the engine's whine rose in pitch. I hated the flimsy contraptions, but I had things to do in a limited amount of time and the helicopter would make it all possible. Brandon—or maybe it was Brian, it was hard to tell with the com-gear on—gave me a thumbs-up and the bird lifted off. Rick was having a ball, the two men up front, talking back and forth on the com-channel. I was sitting in back, beside the shrink-wrapped steer carcass that smelled of old cold blood and maybe brine, and had my com-gear turned off, wearing it only to mute the noise.

I stared out over the city of Asheville as the bird rose and careened toward the hills. Everything looked closer together up here, the folds of the earth that made travel so time-consuming becoming inconsequential. I could get used to this. I could *If* I was going to remain in Leo Pellissier's employ.

I had stuff to do. Decisions to make. Places to be. And still so many things unfinished, hanging over me like Death's sickle. A sense of dislocation hammered at me. I literally had no home now. No one to call family. Molly had talked to me once on the phone, but she was grieving for her sister, and her sister's killer was difficult to be around, especially with the funeral in the works, law enforcement combing through Evangelina's home, and so much media attention focused on the Everharts and the Truebloods. All because of me.

The fact that Evangelina was a murderer and a blood-witch, spelling her coven, and keeping horrible secrets that would have come to a dangerous and deadly climax with or without me didn't make Molly's grief any less real or any less intense. Grief isn't logical. I understood, but it hurt. Life hurt. Angie Baby and I talked on the phone every day, often about her angel, but I hadn't been allowed to see her. Big Evan had asked me, politely, to stay away.

My belongings were packed in the back of an SUV here in Asheville and in my freebie house in Louisiana. But I had no place to send them. And . . . Beast was still silent. Even with me in a helo again, the rotor noise like an animal's roar.

The twins had reconnoitered the GPS location we were going to and found a landing site in a field nearby, but we flew over the cleft in the hills first. It looked different from the sky, flatter, muddier. The dammed up pond was gone, the logs and debris scattered downstream. But I got a glimpse of the cave, and the pile of bones, crows and buzzards on the limbs of trees in far greater numbers than before. At the helo's noisy approach, the birds scattered, flying low. The B-twin hovered over the site and Rick unstrapped, joining me in the back. Together, we slid open the helo door and braced ourselves against the sides. Rick held up three fingers, lips saying, "On three." His head jerked down three times, counting, and on three, we pushed. The steer carcass slid across the helo in its plastic wrap and tumbled out. The helo wobbled with the weight distribution and updrafts, before it stabilized and we stuck our heads out the open door.

I felt, more than saw, Rick laugh when the carcass hit the ground and bounced, right in front of the grindy's lair. Rick pulled me back, shutting the door as the helo banked and soared away, to the clearing we intended to use as a landing site. After that it was a strenuous hike back, requiring a lot of sweat, some blood from scraped knuckles, a ton of mud, and way longer than a helo. The value of speed wasn't lost on me. But Beast didn't comment.

We stood between the pile of bones and the cave mouth, the reek of death suffocating in the heat of the September day. I had smelled some bad things in my time, but the charnel-house/abattoir stench was beyond awful. The bear was foul, slimy, maggoty, even though the bones had been stripped of most of the flesh. *Gack, eww, ick.*

The buzzards and crows had come back to their stinky feast quickly, and one brave buzzard hopped to the top of the pile and spread its wings, claiming it and warning us away. "Don't worry," I told the bird. "It's all yours."

Rick chuckled and took my hand, pulling me inside the cave. The dark and coolness of the grindy's lair was a welcome relief. It smelled better inside, an air current I hadn't noticed moving from deeper underground, from the back of the cave and out the mouth, as if the mountain breathed through the opening. The grindylow was awake, sitting on the ledge, her legs hanging down from her nest swinging, oddly like a child. She was wearing clothes, wrinkled and none-too-clean, but she was covered, the clothing making her look less like an animal. Peeking out from the leaves and limbs of the nest were four, little, green-furred faces—her children.

"Thank you," she said, "for the gift. Food is welcome."

My mouth dropped open and I shot a quick look at

Rick, but it was clear he hadn't known the grindy could speak either. She smiled, showing fangs in her green-skinned face. "Uh, you're welcome," I managed. "For your babies."

She dipped her head, the nod of acknowledgment odd-looking on her. She studied us, her heels kicking, tapping the stone softly like fingertips on a drum. "Jane-cat, you are not worn. You do not fall under my judgment."

"No. I'm not." Confused, I added, "And, okay."

"But you, little cat," she said to Rick, "you are mine to judge. Come." She gestured with her three-clawed hand at him. I instinctively shifted, hands at my blades. "He is in no danger, Jane-cat. He has not tried to infect you with his taint." She cocked her bald head, studying Rick as he neared. "You have not shifted, little one. You are cat, and not-cat. Your magic is . . ." She made a little chirping sound and Rick tensed as the baby grindys crawled out in a swarm of wriggling green fur, huge black eyes staring at Ricky Bo. A series of chirps came from them, high-pitched and raucous, and they jumped back and forth over their mother and one another, like circus animals in an act. Rick laughed and held out his arm. One of the grindy babies leaped to him and scampered up his shoulder to nuzzle at his face. He petted it, gently, smoothing its soft fur.

The grindy went on. "Your magic is in stasis, balanced on a claw-blade of choice. You may never shift, which may give you magic of another kind, greater power, as you grow in acceptance and control over your cat-self. Or full were-power, as you shift for the first time. The choice will be yours to make."

The tiny grindy raced over Rick's head and nuzzled his other side, sniffing at the area of his tattoos as if a morsel of treat awaited her there. She chirped and whistled a tune that sounded, oddly, both happy and inquisitive. "Pea says your magic melds with hers. She is the littlest of my get, and has chosen you. Do you accept her?"

"Grindy, I don't have a place in my life for a pet," Rick said, as the green ball of fluff stuck its nose into his ear. He laughed and caught the baby, shifting her to the crook of his arm.

"Pea is not a pet, little cat-who-is-not," the grindy said

gently. "She is your death." The cave went silent. My hands tightened on my blade handles, palms sweating. "You have no choice but to accept one of my young. Lolandes has proclaimed that even in the Americas, all weres will have keepers. Three of my young will go to the werewolf-clan hiding in the north and one will stay with you. I will go back to the terrible heat of the jungle with the leopards, there to deliver another litter. Then I may go home."

Lolandes was another name for the witch who created the first weres, and then condemned the werewolves to eternal insanity. She had been worshipped as a goddess by tribal peoples for centuries. That brought all sorts of questions to mind, like, where is home to a grindylow, and where is the werewolf clan in the north, and mostly, *What?*

Rick was having an easier time with it, clearly, as he didn't pull his gun and shoot them. He said, "My death if I try to infect anyone. I accept that. I'd deserve it." He looked at Pea, who raced back up his shoulder, but still spoke to mama-grindy. "Can she talk?"

"Not human language. Not until she loses her fur in two decades, when she may gain the ability to speak. Many of my young have done so, though it is rare among my kind. Do you accept the joining of Pea for the balance of your life, knowing that you will come to love her, and that she will kill you without remorse if you stray?"

"It sounds a little too much like a marriage ceremony with a death sentence at the end, but yeah. I do." Pea chirped and raced around Rick's shoulders, whistling delightedly.

"Your fate is not written in the stars. You will choose as you will, and your life and death will play out accordingly," the grindy said. "Go now. Feed Pea as Kemnebi has taught you. And again, my thanks for the meat."

Rick turned to go and I let him pass me, keeping an eye on the grindy as he left the cave. She ignored me, gathering her three remaining young close and snuggling down as if to take a nap. Out in the sunlight, Pea had leaped from Rick to the steer carcass and ripped off a piece of raw meat, eating it, moving like the three-way love child of a raccoon, a squirrel, and a cat. But green furred. I headed up the steep hill. "Come on, Magic-Boy, and bring your new pet.

We have a helicopter to catch." Rick caught up with me, Pea riding on his shoulder, a strip of raw meat in its hand as we climbed out of the gorge.

The grindy had said Rick's future was his choice. The thought sat on my soul like a weight, pulling me down into my failure and loss. Grief was like dust and ashes in my mouth, despite my success in other areas. Evangelina was dead at my hand. Molly had withdrawn from me. Beast had withdrawn so far from me that I couldn't even feel her. Big Evan was being Big Evan. And yet, despite all that, I had done everything I was supposed to do. I had done the job I was hired for. I had killed a murdering vamp preying on humans. I had killed a murdering witch. I had kept Grégoire safe. I had sent in my report. I had pleased my employer. And soon it would all be over. And it would be decision-making time.

CHAPTER THIRTY-TWO

Double-Dead Bodies

My last night as head of security, the last night of my contract, was spent in the reserved hotel dining room with fifty-five vamps, double that number human blood-servants, and not nearly enough security personnel, watching the final results of the parley fiasco. Everyone was in formal wear, including me, and for once I was wearing the clothes Leo had sent without making a scene. I was wearing sparkling, loose black silk pants, a low-necked, black silk shirt, gold and silver embroidered vest, and a jacket designed especially for me by Leo's pet designer, with pockets and straps for my weapons and com-gear.

My hair was up in complicated braids, and I'd had a massage, a facial, and a mani-pedi in the hotel's spa courtesy of Leo, a way of saying thank you for a job well done, but not yet complete. With the new duds and the new do, I was wearing the gold and silver mesh collars Leo had given me, the chocolate diamonds and citrines sparkling in the lights, and silver stakes stuck out from my braids, catching the light like a deadly fan. I looked fabulous, and I knew it because of the way the vamps in the room kept looking at me. Like I was dessert and a silver blade—sweet and deadly. Leo stood at the dais, looking like sex-on-a-stick in his tux. I touched my mouthpiece, alerting my boys. "Ready." If there was going to be a vamp-riot with throats torn and double-dead bodies, it would be now.

Leo said, "Grégoire, blood-master of Clan Arceneau, of the court of Charles the Wise, Fifth of his line, in the Valois Dynasty, have you reached a conclusion in the petition of Lincoln Shaddock, master of the Shaddock Blood Clan, for rights to claim Asheville, North Carolina, and surrounding territory as Master of the City? To be granted hunting land and cattle and the rights to rule as Blood Master of the City?"

Grégoire rose, looking delicate as a child in gold brocade formal wear. He even had gold brocade gloves over his burns and a gold beret to hide his burned hair. "Yes, my master. Lincoln Shaddock, turned by Charles Dufresnee after the Battle of Monocacy, currently sworn to Clan Dufresnee, and with his permission, petitioning the blood-master of the southeastern United States. Rise."

Lincoln stood, looking grave—my lips twitched at the play on words—and elegant in all black. Beside him were his scions, Dacy in cloth of gold and Constantine in U.S. military dress blues, a lot of lettuce on his chest—awards he'd won in the service of his country. At Shaddock's side was Amy Lynn Brown, the reason for this parley after sixty years. Their faces were drawn and worried. Worse were the expressions on his blood-servants' faces. Everyone in the room had some stake in the outcome of the proceedings, and everyone in the room had seen the battle in front of the hotel. Lincoln at the scene, doing nothing. Unmoving as a statue while humans died and Leo and Grégoire and Big Evan and I fought his battles for him. None of that was good, and added in with the general Fubar'ed mess of Evil Evie, things were not looking positive for him. The only thing I could think that might save him, was that Leo himself had been spelled by the witch once, and that might make the chief fanghead cut him some slack.

There had been layers upon layers of reasons for Leo's decisions and actions relating to this parley. And none of them involved me. My lips turned up slightly, self-mocking.

Adelaide looked at me, the question in her eyes. I tilted my head in a shrug. The debate and discussion had gone on behind closed doors for two nights, as judgment was reached. If someone knew the findings, it certainly wasn't me.

Hope and dread filled Lincoln's face, and he was breathing occasionally with tension, oddly human on the undead, as Grégoire said, "Lincoln Shaddock is hereby given provisional permission to begin three new clans." The room exploded in applause and a number of cheers. Dacy closed her eyes and seemed to be saying a prayer. Constantine barked for order and the place quieted. "Said clans are to be headed by his heir, his secundo scion, and one other of his choice. The Mithrans will be taken from among the remaining young rogues in his scion lair, assuming they come out of the devoeo within the guaranteed five years. As the human blood-servant Sarah did not die from the attack, and has been turned successfully, none will be staked or declared rogue." There were more cheers, cut off quickly, and followed by a brittle, breathless silence.

"The position as Master of the City is to be denied Lincoln Shaddock at this time. In no less than one decade, Leonard Eugène Zacharie Pellissier, turned by, and heir of, Amaury Pellissier, his human uncle and Mithran father, blood-master of the southeastern United States, possessor of all territories and keeper of the hunting license of every Mithran below the Mason-Dixon Line, from the eastern border of Texas at the Sabine River, east to the Atlantic and south to the Gulf, with the exception of Florida and Atlanta, will send another envoy to reconsider Lincoln Shaddock's blood-master status hopes. Until then, and for the duration, there will be the customary and agreed upon exchange of blood-servants and scions." Grégoire turned and bowed to Shaddock, then bowed, much lower, to Leo. "This parley is concluded. My thanks to all who provided for us, kept us safe, and so well entertained in the city of Asheville."

And that was that. I nodded to Adelaide, who clearly wanted to speak to me, but my job took me elsewhere. I busted my tail keeping the idiot vamps and the celebrating blood-servants safe the rest of the night. Drunk and rowdy but safe. No one died. No one got turned. No celebrating vamp met the sun by accident or intent. Everyone ate and drank and partied and I learned that even staid old vamps can act the fool on a dance floor.

I fell into my bed after dawn, knowing that by sundown,

when Leo and Grégoire headed back to Louisiana, I was done.

I slept until sunset, showered, dressed, called the bellhop and the valet, and was ready to check out by nine p.m.—regular checkout time for vamps. And I still didn't know what I was going to do next, except return Fang, pick up Ditsa, and sleep for a few days. Dressed in jeans, jacket, and a minimum of weapons, I followed my stuff down the elevator and to the front desk. I was standing in the check-out line when I smelled the blood-servant scent, close by, familiar, deadly. The blood-servant was sworn to the same maker as the blood-servant who had attacked me in my suite. The guy I had killed.

Casually, I swiveled on the heel of my well-oiled Luc-chese boot, and looked out over the hotel lobby. No one caught my eye. No one stood out. Where was he? Derek and Wrassler exited the elevator and I caught Derek's eye. I held up a hand as if gesturing hello, but swiveled my index finger, an order to be sharp and look around. Instantly, his demeanor changed, the alert stance of the soldier taking over. Wrassler caught on fast, his gaze finding me; he stopped near the fireplace while Derek swiveled back to-ward the elevators, ostensibly looking at something on his phone, but one hand having pulled a weapon.

I opened my lips, scenting as I scanned. Finally I saw her, standing near the fireplace. The petite woman must have just entered. I pointed Derek to her and slid out of line, one hand on my Walther at my spine. Wrassler was closest. He smiled and said something to the woman, a really bad pickup line, by the anger in her shoulders. She was tiny, but wiry, and I picked out two bulges on her—a gun at her back and maybe a blade at her hip. The elevator door opened. Leo and Grégoire stepped around the corner, Grégoire's arms and hands still swathed in bandages from the burning he'd taken. The twins were behind them.

Everything happened fastfastfast.

The girl took a half dozen steps away from Wrassler, pulling a handgun. Derek leaped in front of Leo. I screamed to the twins. Wrassler pulled his gun and jumped at the girl with a bellow. I raced in, Beast-fast. Draw. Un-safety. No time to aim. Seeing the room as a slow-moving video. Hearing the first shot. From the side. My hand and gun were one unit. Firing. One. Two. Three. Chest shots, midcenter on the girl. Racing in. Seeing Derek fall, blood on his throat. She was still standing. Wearing a Kevlar vest. I squeezed off a single shot, midcenter forehead. Carefully placed. *No collateral damage.* The girl went down.

More shots sounded. The three burst rat-a-tat of a submachine gun. Leo diving. Grégoire diving. Something stinging my arm.

I whirled, seeing the others. Two. Male. Dressed in bellboy uniforms. Each with small, ugly, compact weapons held with professional ease. Firing. The scent of human and vamp blood on the air. No one was behind the bellboys. I emptied my weapon into them, even as one turned toward me. They didn't go down. *Vests.* They all were wearing bullet-freaking-resistant vests!

I dropped the Walther. Bullets wouldn't stop them.

Claws. Jane throwing claws.

I dodged hard right. The first blade left my hand. Flashing in the overhead lights. Imbedded itself in the gunman's throat. I'd aimed lower but I wasn't complaining.

My second blade hit the second gunman under his left arm. But the kill shot was Wrassler's two-tap to the forehead. I landed hard. On my wounded arm. And it was over except for the blood and the screaming and the cops.

I directed the emergency medical personnel to the wounded humans, including Derek, who had taken two nonlethal rounds to the flesh of one shoulder and thigh, and two hotel guests, who had been caught in the crossfire. I sent the cops to the twins who answered the legal questions. And I sat, alone, on a hotel sofa, watching it all with a goofy smile on my face. This was my life. Vamps and guns and getting shot at. My life was crap. And I loved it, now that Beast was back. She wasn't talking yet, beyond her orders in the fight, but I could feel her claws scrape across my mind, hear her breath panting. She was back, fully and completely, even if she was pouting.

Of course, I'd killed more humans. I'd have to deal with

my own responsibility at some point, though these humans had been trying to kill me and the people I was sworn to protect. That helped. Maybe enough to disperse any possible guilt that might later attack. I was getting better at dealing with guilt all the time. But maybe that wasn't such a good thing. Time would tell.

At some point, the EMTs realized I was bleeding and they treated me, bandaging and haranguing me about needing to be seen at the hospital. A round had grazed the inside of my upper arm, taking a groove of flesh with it on the way past. Ruining my lightweight riding jacket. And my shirt. But not my mood. With Beast back, that was doing great.

Later, I saw Leo and Grégoire into their car and out of the parking lot. And I was done. The job was a success. Except for the lingering question—which blood-master had just declared war on the MOC of New Orleans and the greater Southwestern USA?

Love Jane Yellowrock? Then meet Thorn St. Croix.
Read on for the opening chapter of *Bloodring*,
the first novel in Faith Hunter's Rogue Mage series.
Available from Roc.

No one thought the apocalypse would be like this. The world didn't end. And the appearance of seraphs heralded three plagues and a devastating war between the forces of good and evil. Over a hundred years later, the earth has plunged into an ice age, and seraphs and demons fight a never-ending battle while religious strife rages among the surviving humans.

Thorn St. Croix is no ordinary neomage. All the others of her kind, mages who can twist leftover creation energy to their will, were gathered together into Enclaves long ago; and there they live in luxurious confinement, isolated from other humans and exploited for their magic. When her powers nearly drive her insane, she escapes—and now she lives as a fugitive, disguised as a human, channeling her gifts of stone-magery into jewelry making. But when Thaddeus Bartholomew, a dangerously attractive policeman, shows up on her doorstep and accuses her of kidnapping her ex-husband, she retrieves her weapons and risks revealing her identity to find him. And for Thorn, the punishment for revelation is death. . . .

I stared into the hills as my mount clomped below me, his massive hooves digging into snow and ice. Above us a fighter jet streaked across the sky, leaving a trail that glowed bright against the fiery sunset. A faint sense of alarm raced across my skin, and I gathered up the reins, tightening my knees against Homer's sides, pressing my walking stick against the huge horse.

A sonic boom exploded across the peaks, shaking through snow-laden trees. Ice and snow pitched down in heavy sheets and lumps. A dog yelped. The Friesian set his hooves, dropped his head, and kicked. "Stones and blood," I hissed as I rammed into the saddle horn. The boom echoed like rifle shot. Homer's back arched. If he bucked, I was a goner.

I concentrated on the bloodstone handle of my walking stick and pulled the horse to me, reins firm as I whispered soothing, seemingly nonsense words no one would interpret as a chant. The bloodstone pulsed as it projected a sense of calm into him, a use of stored power that didn't affect my own drained resources. The sonic boom came back from the nearby mountains, a ricochet of man-made thunder.

The mule in front of us hee-hawed and kicked out, white rimming his eyes, lips wide, and teeth showing as the boom reverberated through the farther peaks. Down the length of the mule train, other animals reacted as the fear spread, some bucking in a frenzy, throwing packs into drifts, squealing as lead ropes tangled, trumpeting fear.

Homer relaxed his back, sidestepped, and danced like a

young colt before planting his hooves again. He blew out a rib-racking sigh and shook himself, ears twitching as he settled. Deftly, I repositioned the supplies and packs he'd dislodged, rubbing a bruised thigh that had taken a wallop from a twenty-pound pack of stone.

Hoop Marks and his assistant guides swung down from their own mounts and steadied the more fractious stock. All along the short train, the startled horses and mules settled as riders worked to control them. Homer looked on, ears twitching.

Behind me, a big Clydesdale relaxed, shuddering with a ripple of muscle and thick winter coat, his rider following the wave of motion with practiced ease. Audric was a salvage miner, and he knew his horses. I nodded to my old friend, and he tipped his hat to me before repositioning his stock on Clyde's back.

A final echo rumbled from the mountains. Almost as one, we turned to the peaks above us, listening fearfully for the telltale roar of an avalanche.

Sonic booms were rare in the Appalachians these days, and I wondered what had caused the military overflight. I slid the walking stick into its leather loop. It was useful for balance while taking a stroll in snow, but its real purpose was as a weapon. Its concealed blade was deadly, as was its talisman hilt, hiding in plain sight. However, the bloodstone handle-hilt was now almost drained of power, and when we stopped for the night, I'd have to find a safe, secluded place to draw power for it and for the amulets I carried, or my neomage attributes would begin to display themselves.

I'm a neomage, a witchy-woman. Though contrary rumors persist, claiming mages still roam the world free, I'm the only one of my kind not a prisoner, the only one in the entire world of humans who is unregulated, unlicensed. The only one uncontrolled.

All the others of my race are restricted to Enclaves, protected in enforced captivity. Enclaves are gilded cages, prisons of privilege and power, but cages nonetheless. Neomages are allowed out only with seraph permission, and then we have to wear a sigil of office and bracelets with satellite GPS locator chips in them. We're followed by the humans, watched, and sent back fast when our services are no longer needed or when our visas expire. As if we're contagious. Or dangerous.

Enclave was both prison and haven for mages, keeping us safe from the politically powerful, conservative, religious orthodox humans who hated us, and giving us a place to live as our natures and gifts demanded. It was a great place for a mage-child to grow up, but when my gift blossomed at age fourteen, my mind opened in a unique way. The thoughts of all twelve hundred mages captive in the New Orleans Enclave opened to me at once. I nearly went mad. If I went back, I'd go quietly—or loudly screaming—insane.

In the woods around us, shadows lengthened and darkened. Mule handlers looked around, jittery. I sent out a quick mind-skim. There were no supernats present, no demons, no mages, no seraphs, no *others*. Well, except for me. But I couldn't exactly tell them that. I chuckled under my breath as Homer snorted and slapped me with his tail. That would be dandy. Survive for a decade in the human world only to be exposed by something so simple as a sonic boom and a case of trail exhaustion. I'd be tortured, slowly, over a period of days, tarred and feathered, chopped into pieces, and dumped in the snow to rot.

If the seraphs located me first, I'd be sent back to Enclave and I'd still die. I'm allergic to others of my kind—really allergic—fatally so. The Enclave death would be a little slower, a little less bloody than the human version. Humans kill with steel, a public beheading, but only after I was disemboweled, eviscerated, and flayed alive. And all that after I *entertained* the guards for a few days. As ways to go, the execution of an unlicensed witchy-woman rates up there with the top ten gruesome methods of capital punishment. With my energies nearly gone, a conjure to calm the horses could give me away.

"Light's goin'," Hoop called out. "We'll stop here for the night. Everyone takes care of his own mount before anything else. Then circle and gather deadwood. Last, we cook. Anyone who don't work, don't eat."

Behind me, a man grumbled beneath his breath about the unfairness of paying good money for a spot on the mule train and then having to work. I grinned at him and he shrugged when he realized he'd been heard. "Can't blame a man for griping. Besides, I haven't ridden a horse since I was a kid. I have blisters on my blisters."

I eased my right leg over Homer's back and slid the long distance to the ground. My knees protested, aching after the day in the saddle. "I have a few blisters this trip myself. Good boy," I said to the big horse, and dropped the reins, running a hand along his side. He stomped his satisfaction and I felt his deep sense of comfort at the end of the day's travel.

We could have stopped sooner, but Hoop had hoped to make the campsite where the trail rejoined the old Blue Ridge Parkway. Now we were forced to camp in a ring of trees instead of the easily fortified site ahead. If the denizens of Darkness came out to hunt, we'd be sitting ducks.

Unstrapping the heavy pack containing my most valuable finds from the Salvage and Mineral Swap Meet in Boone, I dropped it to the earth and covered it with the saddle. My luggage and pack went to the side. I removed all the tools I needed to groom the horse and clean his feet, and added the bag of oats and grain. A pale dusk closed in around us before I got the horse brushed down and draped in a blanket, a pile of food and a half bale of hay at his feet.

The professional guides were faster and had taken care of their own mounts and the pack animals and dug a firepit in the time it took the paying customers to get our mounts groomed. The equines were edgy, picking up anxiety from their humans, making the job slower for us amateurs. Hoop's dogs trotted back and forth among us, tails tight to their bodies, ruffs raised, sniffing for danger. As we worked, both clients and handlers glanced fearfully into the night. Demons and their spawn often hid in the dark, watching humans like predators watched tasty herd animals. So far as my weakened senses could detect, there was nothing out there. But there was a lot I couldn't say and still keep my head.

"Gather wood!" I didn't notice who called the command, but we all moved into the forest, me using my walking stick for balance. There was no talking. The sense of trepidation was palpable, though the night was friendly, the moon rising, no snow or ice in the forecast. Above, early stars twinkled, cold and bright at this altitude. I moved away from the others, deep into the tall trees: oak, hickory, fir, cedar. At a distance, I found a huge boulder rounded up from the snow.

Checking to see that I was alone, I lay flat on the boulder, my cheek against frozen granite, the walking stick between my torso and the rock. And I called up power. Not a raging roar of mage-might, but a slow, steady trickle. Without words, without a chant that might give me away, I channeled energy into the bloodstone handle between my breasts, into the amulets hidden beneath my clothes, and pulled a measure into my own flesh, needing the succor. It took long minutes, and I sighed with relief as my body soaked up strength.

Satisfied, as refreshed as if I had taken a nap, I stood, stretched, bent, and picked up deadwood, traipsing through the trees and boulders for firewood—wood that was a lot more abundant this far away from the trail. My night vision is better than most humans', and though I'm small for an adult and was the only female on the train, I gathered an armload in record time. Working far off the beaten path has its rewards.

I smelled it when the wind changed. Old blood. A lot of old blood. I dropped the firewood, drew the blade from the walking-stick sheath, and opened my mage-sight to survey the surrounding territory. The world of snow and ice glimmered with a sour-lemon glow, as if it were ailing, sickly.

Mage-sight is more than human sight in that it sees energy as well as matter. The retinas of human eyes pick up little energy, seeing light only after it's absorbed or reflected. But mages see the world of matter with an overlay of energy, picked up by the extra lenses that surround our retinas. We see power and life, the leftover workings of creation. When we use the sight, the energies are sometimes real, sometimes representational, experience teaching us to identify and translate the visions, sort of like picking out images from a three-dimensional pattern.

I'm a stone mage, a worker of rocks and gems, and the energy of creation; hence, only stone looks powerful and healthy to me when I'm using mage-sight. Rain, ice, sleet or snow, each of which is water that has passed through air, always looks unhealthy, as does moonlight, sunlight, the movement of the wind, or currents of surface water—anything except stone. This high in the mountains, snow lay thick and crusted everywhere, weak, pale, a part of nature that leached power from me—except for a dull gray area to the east, beyond the stone where I had recharged my energies.

Moving with the speed of my race, sword in one hand, walking-stick sheath, a weapon in itself, in the other, I rushed toward the site.

I tripped over a boot. It was sticking from the snow, bootlaces crusted with blood and ice. Human blood had been spilled here, a lot of it, and the snow was saturated. The earth reeked of fear and pain and horror, and to my mage-sight, it glowed with the blackened energy of death. I caught a whiff of Darkness.

Adrenaline coursed through my veins, and I stepped into the cat stance, blade and walking stick held low as I circled the site. Bones poked up from the ice, and I identified a femur, the fragile bones of a hand, tendons still holding fingers together. A jawbone thrust toward the sky. Placing my feet carefully, I eased in. Teeth marks, long and deep, scored an arm bone. Predator teeth, unlike any beast known to nature. Supernat teeth. The teeth of Darkness.

Devil-spawn travel in packs, drink blood and eat human flesh. While it's still alive. A really bad way to go. And spawn would know what I was in an instant if they were downwind of me. As a mage, I'd be worth more to a spawn than a fresh meal. I'd be prime breeding material for their masters.

I'd rather be eaten.

A skull stared at me from an outcropping of rock. A tree close by had been raked with talons, or with desperate human fingers trying to get away, trying to climb. As my sight adjusted to the falling light, a rock shelf protruding from the earth took on a glow displaying pick marks. A strip mine. Now that I knew what to look for, I saw a pick, the blackened metal pitted by ichor, a lantern, bags of supplies hanging from trees, other gear stacked near the rock with their ore. One tent pole still stood. On it was what I assumed to be a hat, until my eyes adjusted and it resolved into a second skull. Old death. Weeks, perhaps months, old.

A stench of sulfur reached me. Dropping the sight, I skimmed until I found the source: a tiny hole in the earth near the rock they had been working. I understood what had happened. The miners had been working a claim on the surface—because no one in his right mind went underground, not anymore—and they had accidentally broken through to a cavern or an old, abandoned underground mine. Darkness had scented them. Supper . . .

I moved to the hole in the earth. It was leaking only a hint of sulfur and brimstone, and the soil around was smooth, trackless. Spawn hadn't used this entrance in a long time. I glanced up at the sky. Still bright enough that the nocturnal devil-spawn were sleeping. If I could cover the entrance, they wouldn't smell us. Probably. Maybe.

Sheathing the blade, I went to the cases the miners had piled against the rocks, and pulled a likely one off the top. It hit the ground with a whump but was light enough for me to drag it over the snow, leaving a trail through the carnage. The bag fit over the entrance, and the reek of Darkness was instantly choked off. My life had been too peaceful. I'd gotten lazy. I should have smelled it the moment I entered the woods. Now it was gone.

Satisfied I had done all I could, I tramped to my pile of deadwood and back to camp, glad of the nearness of so many humans, horses, and dogs that trotted about. I dumped the wood beside the fire pit at the center of the small clearing. Hoop Marks and his second in command, Hoop Jr., tossed in broken limbs and lit the fire with a small can of kerosene and a pack of matches. Flames roared and danced, sending shadows capering into the surrounding forest. The presence of fire sent a welcome feeling of safety through the group, though only earthly predators would fear the flame. No supernat of Darkness would care about a little fire if it was hungry. Fire made them feel right at home.

I caught Hoop's eye and gestured to the edge of the woods. The taciturn man followed when I walked away, and listened with growing concern to my tale of the miners. I thought he might curse when I told him of the teeth marks on the bones, but he stopped himself in time. Cursing aloud near a hellhole was a sure way of inviting Darkness to you.

In other locales it might attract seraphic punishment or draw the ire of the church. Thoughtless language could result in death-by-dinner, seraphic vengeance, or priestly branding. Instead, he ground out, "I'll radio it in. You don't tell nobody, you hear? I got something that'll keep us safe." And without asking me why I had wandered so far from camp, alone, he walked away.

Smoke and supper cooking wafted through camp as I rolled out my sleeping bag and pumped up the air mattress. Even with the smell of old death still in my nostrils, my mouth watered. I wanted nothing more than to curl up, eat and sleep, but I needed to move through the horses and mules first. Trying to be inconspicuous, touching each one as surreptitiously as possible, I let the walking stick's amulet-handle brush each animal with calm.

It was a risk, if anyone recognized a mage-conjure, but there was no way I was letting the stock bolt and stampede away if startled in the night. I had no desire to walk miles through several feet of hard-packed snow to reach the nearest train tracks, then wait days in the cold, without a bath or adequate supplies, for a train that might get stranded in a blizzard and not come until snowmelt in spring. No way. Living in perpetual winter was bad enough, and though the ubiquitous *they* said it was only a *mini*–ice age, it was still pretty dang cold.

So I walked along the picket line and murmured soothing words, touching the stock one by one. I loved horses. I hated that they were the only dependable method of transport through the mountains ten months out of the year, but I loved the beasts themselves. They didn't care that I was an unlicensed neomage hiding among the humans. With them I could be myself, if only for a moment or two. I lay my cheek against the shoulder of a particularly worried mare. She exhaled as serenity seeped into her and turned liquid brown eyes to me in appreciation, blowing warm horse breath in my face. "You're welcome," I whispered.

Just before I got to the end of the string, Hoop sang out, "Charmed circle. Charmed circle for the night."

I looked up in surprise, my movements as frozen as the night air. Hoop Jr. was walking bent over, a fifty-pound bag of salt in his arms, his steps moving clockwise. Though human, he was making a conjure circle. Instinctively, I cast out with a mind-skim, though I knew I was the only mage here. But now I scented a charmed *something*. From a leather case, Hoop Sr. pulled out a branch that glowed softly to my mage-sight. Hoop's "something to keep us safe." The tag on the tip of the branch proclaimed it a legally purchased charm, unlike my unlicensed amulets. It would be empowered by the salt in the ring, offering us protection. I hurried down the line of horses and mules, trusting that my movements were hidden by the night, and made it to the circle before it was closed.

Stepping through the opening in the salt, I nodded again as I passed Audric. The big black man shouldered his packs and carried them toward the fire pit. He didn't talk much, but he and Thorn's Gems had done a lot of business since he discovered and claimed a previously untouched city site for salvage. Because he had a tendresse for one of my business partners, he brought his findings to us first and stayed with us while in town. The arrangement worked out well, and when his claim petered out, we all hoped he'd put down roots and stay, maybe buy in as the fourth partner.

"All's coming in, get in," Hoop Sr. sang out. "All's staying out'll be shot if trouble hits and you try to cross the salt ring." There was a cold finality to his tone. "Devil-spawn been spotted round here. I take no chances with my life or yours 'less you choose to act stupid and get yourself shot."

"Devil-spawn? Here?" The speaker was the man who had griped about the workload.

"Yeah. Drained a woman and three kids at a cabin up near Linville." He didn't mention the carnage within shooting distance of us. Smart man.

I spared a quick glance for my horse, who was already snoozing. A faint pop sizzled along my nerve endings as the circle closed and the energy of the spell from the mage-branch snapped in place. I wasn't an earth mage, but I appreciated the conjure's simple elegance. A strong shield-protection-invisibility incantation had been stored in the cells of the branch. The stock were in danger from passing predators, but the rest of us were effectively invisible to anyone, human or supernat.

Night enveloped us in its black mantle as we gathered for a supper of venison stew. Someone passed around a flask of moonshine. No one said anything against it. Most took a swallow or two against the cold. I drank water and ate only stewed vegetables. Meat disagrees with me. Liquor on a mule train at night just seems stupid.

Tired to the bone, I rolled into my heated, down-filled sleeping bag and looked up at the cold, clear sky. The moon was nearly full, its rays shining on seven inches of fresh snow. It was a good night for a moon mage, a water mage, even a weather mage, but not a night to induce a feeling of vitality or well-being in a bone-tired stone mage. The entire world glowed with moon power, brilliant and beautiful, but draining to my own strength. I rolled in my bedding and stopped, caught by a tint of color in the velvet black sky. A thick ring of bloody red circled the pure white orb, far out in the night. *A bloodring.* I almost swore under my breath but choked it back, a painful sound, close to a sob.

The last time there was a bloodring on the moon, my twin sister died. Rose had been a licensed mage, living in Atlanta, supposedly safe, yet she had vanished, leaving a wide, freezing pool of blood and signs of a struggle, within minutes after Lolo, the priestess of Enclave, phoned us both with warnings. The prophecy hadn't helped then and it wouldn't help now. Portents never helped. They offered only a single moment to catch a breath before I was trounced by whatever they foretold.

If Lolo had called with a warning tonight, it was on my answering machine. Even for me, the distance to Enclave was too great to hear the mind-voice of the priestess.

I shivered, looking up from my sleeping bag. A feasting site, now a bloodring. It was a hazy, frothing circle, swirling like the breath of the Dragon in the Revelation, holy words taught to every mage from the womb up. "And there appeared another wonder in heaven; and behold a great red dragon. . . . And his tail drew the third part of the stars of heaven, and did cast them to the earth: and the dragon stood before the woman. . . . And there was war in heaven: Michael and his seraphim fought against the dragon; and the dragon fought, and his seraphim." The tale of the Last War.

Shivering, I gripped the amulets tied around my waist and my walking stick, the blade loosed in the sheath, the prime amulet of its hilt tight in my palm. Much later, exhausted, I slept.

Lucas checked his watch as he slipped out of the office and moved into the alley, ice crunching beneath his boots, breath a half-seen fog in the night. He was still on schedule, though pushing the boundaries. Cold froze his ears and nose, numbed his fingers and feet, congealed his blood, seeped into his bones, even through the layers of clothes, down-filled vest, and hood. He slipped, barely catching himself before hitting the icy ground. He cursed beneath his breath as he steadied himself on the alley wall. *Seraph stones, it's cold.*

But he was almost done. The last of the amethyst would soon be in Thorn's hands, just as the Mistress Amethyst had demanded. In another hour he would be free of his burden. He'd be out of danger. He felt for the ring on his finger, turning it so the sharp edge was against his flesh. He hitched the heavy backpack higher, its nylon straps cutting into his palm and across his shoulder.

The dark above was absolute, moon and stars hidden by the tall buildings at his sides. Ahead, there was only the distant security light at the intersection of the alley, where it joined the larger delivery lane and emptied into the street. Into safety.

A rustle startled him. A flash of movement. A dog burst from the burned-out hulk of an old Volkswagen and bolted back the way he had come. A second followed. Two small pups huddled in the warm nest they deserted, yellow coats barely visible. Lucas blew out a gust of irritation and worthless fear and hoped the larger mutts made it back to the makeshift den before the weather took them all down. It was so cold, the puppies wouldn't survive long. Even the smells of dog, urine, old beer, and garbage were frozen.

He moved into the deeper dark, toward the distant light, but slowed. The alley narrowed, the walls at his sides invisible in the night; his billowing breath vanished. He glanced up, his eyes drawn to the relative brightness of the sky. A chill that had nothing to do with the temperature chased down his spine. The rooftops were bare, the gutters and eaves festooned with icicles, moon and clouds beyond. One of the puppies mewled behind him.

Lucas stepped through the dark, his pace increasing as panic coiled itself around him. He was nearly running by the time he reached the pool of light marking the alleys' junction. Slowing, he passed two scooters and a tangle of bicycles leaning against a wall, all secured with steel chains, tires frozen in the ice. He stepped into the light and the safety it offered.

Above, there was a crackle, a sharp snap of metal. His head lifted, but his eyes were drawn ahead to a stack of boxes and firewood. To the man standing there. *Sweet Mother of God . . . not a man. A shadow.* "No!" Lucas tried to whirl, skidding on icy pavement before he could complete the move. Two others ran toward him, human movements, human slow.

"Get him!"

The first man collided with him, followed instantly by the other, their bodies twin blows. His boots gave on the slippery surface. He went to one knee, breath a pained grunt.

A fist pounded across the back of his neck. A leg reared back. Screaming, he covered his head with an arm. A rain of blows and kicks landed. The backpack was jerked away, opening and spilling.

As he fell, he tightened a fist around the ring, its sharp edge slicing into his flesh. He groaned out the words she had given him to use, but only in extremis. The sound of the syllables was lost beneath the rain of blows. "Zadkiel, hear me. Holy Amethyst—" A boot took him in the jaw, knocking back his head. He saw the wings unfurl on the roof above him. Darkness closed in. Teeth sank deep in his throat. Cold took him. The final words of the chant went unspoken.

ABOUT THE AUTHOR

Faith Hunter was born in Louisiana and raised all over the South. She writes full-time and works full-time in a hospital lab (for the benefits), tries to keep house, and is a workaholic with a passion for travel, jewelry making, orchids, skulls, Class III white-water kayaking, and writing.

Many of the orchid pics on her facebook fan page show skulls juxtaposed with orchid blooms; the bones are from roadkill prepared by taxidermists or a pal named Mud. In her collection is a fox skull, a cat skull, a dog skull, a goat skull (that is, unfortunately, falling apart), a cow skull, and the jawbone of an ass. She would love to have the thigh bone and skull of an African lion (one that died of old age, of course) and a mountain lion skull (ditto on the old-age death) and is looking for a wild boar skull, complete with tusks.

She and her husband own thirteen kayaks at last count, and love to RV, traveling with their dogs to white-water rivers all over the Southeast.

For more, see www.faithhunter.net. To ask questions and chat with Faith, see her facebook fan page at www.facebook.com/official.faith.hunter.

ALSO AVAILABLE IN THE
JANE YELLOWROCK SERIES

FROM

Faith Hunter

SKINWALKER

A Jane Yellowrock Novel

Jane Yellowrock is the last of her kind—a
skinwalker of Cherokee descent who can turn
into any creature she desires and hunts vampires
for a living. But now she's been hired by
Katherine Fontaneau, one of the oldest vampires
in New Orleans and the madam of Katie's
Ladies, to hunt a powerful rogue vampire who's
killing other vamps...

Available wherever books are sold or at
penguin.com

R0059

ALSO AVAILABLE IN THE
JANE YELLOWROCK SERIES

FROM

Faith Hunter

BLOOD CROSS
A Jane Yellowrock Novel

The vampire council has hired skinwalker
Jane Yellowrock to hunt and kill one of their
own who has broken sacred ancient rules—but
Jane quickly realizes that in a community that is
thousands of years old, loyalties run deep...

**Available wherever books are sold or at
penguin.com**

ALSO AVAILABLE IN THE
JANE YELLOWROCK SERIES

FROM

Faith Hunter

MERCY BLADE
A Jane Yellowrock Novel

Jane, a shapeshifting vampire-hunter-for-hire,
crosses paths with a stranger who has arrived in
New Orleans, enlisted to hunt vampires who
have gone insane—or so he says...

**Available wherever books are sold or at
penguin.com**